Daddy's Girl

BEN BURGESS JR.

http://www.benburgessjr.com/

Daddy's Girl: By Ben Burgess Jr.

Copyright © 2016 Ben Burgess Jr.

First Printing – June 2016
ISBN: 978-0-9883745-7-7 (paperback)
ISBN: 978-0-9883745-8-4 (ebook)
Library of Congress Control Number: 2016908414
Edited by: Autumn Conley
Cover Design by www.aleahdesign.com

This book is a work of fiction. Names, characters, businesses, organizations, places, events and incidents are the product of the author's imagination or are used fictionally. Any resemblance to actual persons, living or dead, events, or locales is entirely coincidental.

Printed in the U.S.A.

Dedicated to my daughter Jaelynn, the original "Ladybug."

Everything I do in life, I do to make you proud. I've always wanted my work to unite races and not divide them. You are proof that love can create beautiful things in a dark, ugly world. Continue to shine and improve the world.

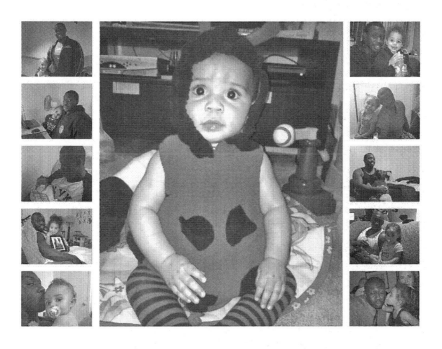

"A Father's tears and fears are unseen, his love is unexpressed, but his care and protection remains as a pillar of strength throughout our lives."

—Ama H. Vanniarachchy

MY DAUGHTER
BY BEN BURGESS JR.

I never had anything perfect in my life, but as soon as I heard of your conception, I knew you would be that exception. Your birth was like my resurrection because everything you do in life or endeavor, I know a part of me will live on forever.

When you were in your mother's stomach, I would hug it and rub it. I was eager to be a father and knew that I'd love it.

When the doctor announced that you were a girl, you became the center of my world. I counted all your fingers and toes, to make sure you had all of those. I thanked God for listening to my prayer to help me, and to make sure that you were born healthy.

I was amazed how fast you learned to walk. I was proud when you started to talk. The greatest feeling that I've ever had was the first moment you called me Dad. Every day you're growing and learning, and that's nice to see. I enjoy watching you look like a female version of me. More and more I feel like you were heaven sent. You are my greatest accomplishment.

ACKNOWLEDGMENTS

As always, I'd like to thank a lot of people who motivated me, inspired me, and supported me with making this book. For my family, I don't want to leave anyone out, so I'll just say thank you to my family that has supported me. (Yes JaWanda Burgess and Aunt Barbara Burgess-Parker, that means you too.)

★ To all my friends: *If I left anyone out, it doesn't mean I don't appreciate you. I couldn't add hundreds of names on here, but if I missed you, I will add yours in the next one.*

A big thanks and appreciation go to my friends: I wouldn't have fulfilled this goal if it weren't for you guys.

Lauren Burgess	Tyra Narvaez	Nina Gagnon-Wade
Tamara Teeger	Dianne Bylo	Jennifer Ray
Terry Small	Tamar Carlins	Nicole Blakley
Alvin Cameron II	Kelly Hirsig	Christina Cutolo
Joanna Ozuna	Philip Banks III	Denise Marie Johnson
Michelle Fecker	Candice Chester	Nybia Cooper
Marieta Shi	Charles Mack	Catherine Shim
Crystal Barbosa	Valleck Simmons	Vickie Jo Giles
Jay Fikes	Sharon Meade	Bonnie Toder
Jen Lindsey	Latoya Burton	Carmen Blalock
Valerie Sanzone	Leah Frieday	Rachel Korenstein
Marjorie Frazier	Jennifer Scarabin	Heather Blackmon
Liz Dinolfo	Kim Radan	Jasmine Harvin
Stacy Campbell	Kiera J. Northington	Laura D'Mello
Sequeoia Acacia	Sharon Clarke	Patricia Morris
Alisha M Simko	Sheri Thomson	Jennifer Jordan
Tiffany Tyler	Nia Merced	Jocelyn Boffman Green
Lisa Muhammad	LaTesha Wagstaff	Antonia Cato
Judy Mattone	Qiana Drennen	Vaneka Miles
Jeff Gatsby	Brenda T. Lang	Shatika Turner
Connie Zeda	CM Wright	Joey Pinkney
Kelly Sanchez	Kristin Campbell	Orsayor Simmons

*Another big shout out goes to all the members of my favorite Book Clubs:

- EYECU Reading and Social Network
- Don't Read me, Read a Book
- Real Divas Read
- IdefineDiva Milwaukee Sisterhood
- SoulSistahs BookClub
- Brownstone BookClub
- African-Americans on the Move Book Club (AAMBC)
- Only One keyStroke Away (O.O.S.A.)

FIRST QUARTER

In the Beginning...

CHAPTER 1

GAME CHANGER

Nick, April 16, 1989

It was two in the morning. The loud ringing of the phone on my nightstand amplified the pounding throb of my hangover. I felt like shit. I yawned, stretched, and knocked the phone off the receiver. I fumbled with it in the dark before I groggily answered, "Hello?"

"Nick? Nick!" Vickie yelled.

"What?"

"Wake up and get to Central General...now! I'm about to have this baby!" she wailed.

That woke me up.

I stuttered, "Wh-What? It's a month early."

"I'm aware of that, Nick. I need you to get your ass here now."

"I'm on my way."

"Did you hear me? You need to get here *right fucking* now."

I rubbed my hand over my face.

"Calm down. I said I'm coming."

"I'm not kidding, Nick. Uniondale is twenty minutes away. If you're not here within the hour, as soon as I have this baby, I'm signing it over to the state."

"Don't do that. I'll be there. I already told you I'll take care of us—*all* of us. I'm leaving now."

She hung up.

I stretched and yawned again, trying to thaw out and prepare myself for an eventful day. I wobbled when I stood, still a little tipsy, then stumbled over the empty beer cans scattered on the floor on my way to the bathroom.

I gargled, took a long piss, and washed my face. I looked in the mirror. Dark stubble lined my chiseled face. I looked rugged, but I didn't have time to pretty myself up.

My clothes were sprawled on the floor. I put on my jeans and sniffed my shirt; it was a little ripe but wearable, so I pulled it over my head and attempted to smooth out the wrinkles as I sprinted to my '86 Chevy Blazer and headed to the hospital.

★ ★ ★

I parked, ran into the ER, and spoke to a nurse at the counter: "Excuse me. I'm looking for Victoria De Luca. She's in labor right now."

"And you are?"

"Nick Johnson, the baby's father."

The woman gave me a once-over. Clearly unimpressed by a disheveled brother claiming to be the father of a married Italian woman's child. I peered down at my clothes and winced. *Damn. I should've dressed better,* I thought.

"She's in Room 204, with Dr. Turner," the nurse said.

She spoke briefly to a couple of women around her before turning back to face me again.

"Follow me," she said.

We walked past the waiting room, through the hallway, and into the delivery room. I stepped inside and immediately caught sight of Vickie holding the bed rails in a death-grip, panting. Her hair was plastered to her sweaty, flushed face. She looked as if she was in the middle of an intense contraction. She sat up quickly, nearly screaming her head off.

"I'm here, honey," I said, reaching for her hand.

Vickie grimaced in pain, pulled away, and snarled.

"Vickie, I need you to push harder, okay?" Dr. Turner said.

One of the nurses motioned for me to sit down on the chair next to Vickie's bed, then handed me a damp washcloth.

"Wipe her forehead now and then. It will make her a little more comfortable," she said.

Sweat dripped down Vickie's face, and I dabbed at it with the moistened towel. Vickie screamed, gritted her teeth, and clenched the sheets. She tried to follow the doctor's instructions and continued to writhe in pain.

"I-I can't do this!" she cried.

"You can, Vickie. I need you to stay focused and keep pushing," Dr. Turner encouraged.

Vickie took short, quick breaths, exhaling them between her chapped lips. Another set of sharp contractions rolled through her, evidenced by the pained expression on her face.

I grabbed the cup of ice chips by her bed, thinking it would help to moisten her dry mouth, but she slapped the cup out of my hand and left me standing there looking stupid, with no idea of what I should do.

"This is all your fault," Vickie said through clenched teeth, her eyes bloodshot.

I pulled my chair closer to her and rubbed her hand.

"You're scared, but everything's going to be all right," I tried to console her.

Another set of contractions struck her. Vickie pulled my fingers back so far I was sure she was going to break my hand.

★ ★ ★

Two hours and a lot of screaming later, Vickie shrieked and pushed with all her might.

"Here she is! Congratulations," Dr. Turner announced.

I was in shock. I'd never witnessed childbirth before, and at that moment, reality hit me: *I'm a fucking father.*

The nurses and staff wiped the baby off, cut the umbilical cord, and wrapped her in a blanket.

"She's tiny, just four pounds, nine ounces," a nurse said, smiling down at my daughter.

"She is, but listen to her cry. You've got yourselves a strong one here," Dr. Turner said.

The nurse attempted to hand the baby to Vickie, but she turned her head and refused to look at our child. Instead, Vickie stared at the fluorescent lights in the ceiling and pushed the baby away.

I wiped Vickie's moist face. I couldn't tell if it was wet from sweat or tears. I looked at the nurse and asked, "Can I hold her?"

After a nod of approval from Dr. Turner, the nurse handed the baby to me, wearing a look of uncertainty on her face.

I reached over to take my daughter, nestled her lovingly in the crook of my arm, and looked down at her for the first time. I rocked her back and forth to quiet her, and at that moment, I immediately fell in love. Her eyes were open, staring up at me. She was small but so beautiful that it nearly took my breath away. She had silky, black hair and beautiful gray eyes like her mother's. I couldn't help but smile as I looked at her. Vickie looked at me with a blank expression on her face.

"What are you going to name her?" the nurse asked.

I faced Vickie. "What about Lynn, after my mother?" I asked.

"Call her whatever you want."

"Can you at least *act* like you give a shit?"

The nurses and the doctor exchanged glances as I stood next to Vickie with our child.

"Isn't she beautiful?" I asked Vickie, but she turned her eyes to the ceiling and placed her arm over her forehead as if even seeing our child pained her.

Dr. Turner signaled for me to hand over the baby.

"We have to run some tests on Lynn to make sure she doesn't have any birth defects. Vickie, you'll be able to go home by the middle of the week, but Lynn won't be released until the weekend."

Vickie continued to look away and didn't even bother to answer him.

"What the hell is wrong with you?" I demanded, staring at her in disbelief.

"Nick, I'm a little emotional right now, okay?"

"I suppose that's our cue to leave," the doctor said. "We'll give you two some privacy so you can, uh…talk. We'll take the little one and get started on those tests."

The nurses nodded and followed the doctor out of the room, pushing the baby on a cart in front of her.

"Why are you acting like you're at a funeral instead of celebrating the birth of our child?" I asked as soon as they stepped out.

"Because I'm not doing this Nick. I'm not going to look at that baby when I know I can't be a mother to it. I'm not leaving Frank. This was a mistake. We were a mistake. Our fling was a mistake."

"What!? Don't give me that shit," I said, struggling to keep the volume down. "You can't back out now. This all stems from you. You came to me. You told me you hate the feeling of condoms. You begged me to fuck you raw, remember? You said you couldn't get pregnant."

"I may have said it, but you did it, so who's really at fault, Nick? You! My doctor told me it'd be damn near impossible. Frank and I tried for years, but nothing came of it. How was I supposed to know this would happen?"

"Well, obviously your doctor was wrong."

Vickie buried her face in her hands.

"I shouldn't have told you about the pregnancy. I should've just kept you in the dark like everyone else and given the baby up for adoption."

"I'll take care of us, Vickie. You gotta have faith in me," I said. Even though having a baby wasn't in my plans, there was no way I'd allow my flesh and blood to suffer in the system.

She laughed. "Nick, you can't even take care of yourself! Listen, you're fun to be with, but you can't seriously think we can be together."

"I've changed during your pregnancy, Vickie."

"Oh? You've changed? That's odd because I can still smell the alcohol on your breath from last night. You work bullshit home improvement jobs, don't have your own place, and don't even have insurance. As for the pregnancy, I've had to rely on my husband's health coverage for all of it. Thank God Frank never pays attention to this shit and leaves the mail to me. Now I have to intercept it, so he doesn't find out about this."

"Fuck it. Who cares if he finds out? You're gonna be with me anyway."

"Nick, I—"

"Look, I promise we can make this work, and that little girl's gonna change me for the better. You'll see."

Vickie laughed to herself.

"You know, he thinks I'm mad at him because he teased me about having a potbelly. We had a fight last night. Francine is going to tell him I'm still angry, and I don't want to talk to him. As an excuse, she's going to tell him I'm hanging out in the Hamptons for the week, to cover for this hospital stay." Suddenly, the smile left her face as she continued, "He's *connected*, Nick," she said, practically in a whisper. "He'll kill us both if he finds out I'm laid up in the hospital, giving birth to your baby."

I put my hand under her chin and gently turned her head toward me, then kissed her lightly. "Stop worrying."

For a brief second, her face softened, and it seemed as if she was beginning to calm down, but she pushed me away. "I'm drained. I need to rest...and think," she said.

"All right. Get some sleep. I'll be around. I'm gonna call my brother and tell him the good news."

She lay there, looking depressed, as I walked out and pulled the door shut behind me.

★ ★ ★

Out in the hall, I found a phone booth and gave Joe a call.

"Hello?" he answered groggily.

"You 'sleep?"

"Fool, what do you think?"

I hated that old childhood nickname. Dad gave us all nicknames. He called me Fool because he said I was born foolish and hardheaded, and my stubbornness made it impossible for me to make things easy for myself. "You're always gonna struggle in life and have to learn things the hard way," he warned.

Growing up, being addressed as Fool had made me feel stupid. Dad's nickname for Joe was Scout since he was a Boy Scout as a kid, the golden child of the family and the firstborn. I was in the middle, and our brother Jimmy, aka Chance, was the youngest. We were all nine months apart.

Chance was the fuck-up of the family. True to his moniker, even as a kid, he could never do anything right and always wanted another chance. As an adult, he hung out with his loser friends from high school, and they ended up putting him on to heroin. He's never been able to shake the habit and was in and out of rehab and our lives for years. At the moment, neither of us knew where he was or if he was still alive.

"Today's my only day off, and your dumb ass is waking me up early. You're lucky Rhea didn't wake up," Joe fussed.

"Can you stop cussing me and listen? Vickie had the baby this morning—a little girl, man! I named her Lynn, after Mom. I'm a father!"

There was silence for a moment.

"Hello?"

"I'm here, Fool. Wasn't the baby due next month?"

"Yeah, but she came early."

"Hmm... I bet she did."

"This is the part where you congratulate me," I said.

Joe sighed.

"Well, seeing as she's married, I don't think a celebration is in order. You're not thinking, Fool. Her husband's hooked up with those Mafioso types. I warned you about this. You knew you were playing with fire when you slept with her."

"I'm not worried about him."

"You should be...and you're putting me in a bad spot with Mr. Davis too. That old man runs a tight ship, and all those home improvement jobs you do come from him. An old friend of our late father's or not, he'll take this shit personally. He already warned you not to embarrass him or his business. He's gonna cut you off, man."

I rolled my eyes at his lecture but didn't bother arguing with him.

"How do you know the kid's even yours?"

"The baby's mine, man."

"But how do you know? She hid your affair and pregnancy from her husband. What makes you think she's telling you the truth? Maybe she had another brother up under her, playing handyman."

He was pissing me off, but as much as I hated what he was saying, I knew he was right, even if I'd never admit it to him.

Vickie had always been good at hiding things, and I'd be naïve if I believed I was the only guy she was sleeping with besides her husband.

"You know you're disrespecting the mother of my child, right?"

"Pssh. The mother of your child! Fool, I'm not worried about that married bitch or your feelings. You need to get a damn paternity test before you claim a kid who isn't yours."

"I *know* she's mine."

"Don't be stupid, Fool. Promise me you'll get a paternity test."

"I will."

"Promise me!"

"All right, man. Damn! I promise."

"Good. Now, genius, how are the three of you gonna live in your small, barely two-bedroom apartment in my house?"

"We'll get by. It'll only be temporary until I find a steadier job."

"Please don't give me that we'll-survive-on-love bullshit you were spewing the last time I saw you. Love doesn't pay the bills. You know that lazy heifer isn't going to work. How do you expect to keep up her lifestyle, and take care of yourself and a baby?"

"I'll be sacrificing a lot. She'll have to make some sacrifices too."

"Brother, you're delusional if you think that woman's gonna let go of her cushy life to be with you and a half-breed child."

With every word Scout spoke, I realized more and more how unprepared I was.

"I've got another question for you since you think everything's gonna be so happily-ever-after, do you even have a crib? A car seat? Anything?"

I sighed. "No."

"So where's the kid gonna sleep, Fool?"

"Well, I was hoping I could use all the stuff you and Rhea bought when she was pregnant."

There was a long pause before he answered, "That's asking a lot, man. It was hard enough convincing Rhea to let you stay upstairs. I don't know if she'll be cool with you using those things."

"She'll be all right. Tell her it'll be therapeutic to see everything being put to good use."

Scout ignored my response and asked another question: "Is Vickie going to breastfeed, or is she doing formula?"

"I don't know."

"You know that woman isn't going to do anything that'll make her tits sag, and formula and diapers aren't cheap."

"We'll handle it."

"Oh yeah? What are you going to do when her husband tells Mr. Davis, and he cuts you off from working? How are you going to pay for anything then?"

"Maybe he won't."

"You gotta be real about this shit, brother."

"I don't know."

"That's the problem. You never think before you act, and I always end up having to clean up your shit. It's nice that you brought another member into our family, but it isn't good that you have no way to take care of your baby."

"I know, Scout. I'm sorry. I didn't plan for this to happen."

"Well, I hope this child forces you to grow up."

"She will."

"All right. Keep me posted on that paternity test."

"I'll let you know when the results prove the baby's mine."

"You do that. I'll talk to you later."

After we hung up, I walked to the nursery and looked through the window.

"Excuse me. Mr. Johnson?" Dr. Turner said, tapping me on the shoulder.

"Oh, hey, Doctor."

"Is everything all right?"

"Yeah. I'm just looking at my daughter."

"Well, I don't blame you. She's beautiful," he said, then turned to walk off.

"Hey, Dr. Turner…"

"Yes?"

"While you're running those tests, can you add a paternity one to the list?"

"I figured that might come up. Yes, we'll add it to the rest of the tests."

I leaned in close and whispered, "Do you mind not bringing this up in front of Vickie?"

With a sympathetic smile, he assured me, "Don't worry. We never had this conversation."

He shook my hand and went on his way.

I watched my daughter sleeping, her face so angelic and innocent, and one thought crossed my mind: *Am I ready for this journey?*

CHAPTER 2

FORBIDDEN FRUIT

Nick, 1989

I tiptoed into Vickie's room, doing my best not to wake her. I quietly moved a chair close to her bed, sat down, and nodded off. My dreams reflected back on the months and events that had led to that very moment...

"Start with the kitchen," Frank instructed.

I nodded.

"Don't cut any fucking corners. I want this place mint. You got that?"

I nodded again.

"Follow me," he said with a snap of his fingers.

"Yes, sir," I said.

I gave him the finger as soon as his back was turned.

He was a real Guido. He had an olive color complexion and wore a partially buttoned polo shirt that displayed his gold chains and chest hair. He was a cocky asshole that always talked with his hands. He was in decent shape, and some of the other workers told me he had mafia connections, but I wasn't intimidated.

We walked around his huge house in Garden City. I hated rich assholes like him, who spoke to me like I wasn't shit. Frank felt he was God because the six successful businesses he owned throughout Brooklyn and Long Island made him wealthy.

"In my bedroom, I want that wall knocked down and the

bathroom retiled. I want the hardwood floors sanded and waxed," he instructed as he pushed open the door.

A woman nervously jumped, caught in the middle of changing her clothes. She was topless, and I won't lie, I stared at her tits.

"Hey! Turn your fucking head. My wife isn't decent."

I rolled my eyes but did as he asked. He was a dick, but I knew the job would take a while, and that meant good money for me.

"I've got the fucking help here, and you're walking around like you're on a Playboy shoot. Put something on, Vickie!"

"All right! Calm down already. I had no idea you were coming in here," she snapped.

Frank snapped his fingers.

"You! What's your name again?"

I kept my head turned and answered, "Nick."

"Nick, turn back around and look at what I'm fucking showing you."

The guy was testing my patience, especially with all that finger-snapping. I was about to lose it when Mr. Davis walked in with his son Chris and my co-worker, Vince.

"Gentlemen, is everything all right?" Mr. Davis asked.

"I hope so. Your guy seems to have an attitude problem that needs some adjusting. You think your boys can handle what I'm asking for, Davis?"

"My men are capable and willing. I wouldn't allow anyone to work on your house if I didn't think he was competent enough to do the job right."

"All right. I trust you, Davis. Your guys did some nice custom work on a house for a friend of mine, so I'm counting on the word-of-mouth and trusting they'll do the same here," Frank said.

"You have my word. I'll personally check over everything, and I'll be here to assist and supervise with the jobs on weekends."

"Perfect."

"Mr. De Luca, can you go over all the particulars again with Vincent and my son?"

"Sure thing."

Mr. Davis turned toward me, with a scowl on his face.

"Nick, I need to talk to you in the hallway…now," he said.

I nodded. "Yes, sir."

As soon as we stepped out in the hallway, Mr. Davis moved close to my face and said, "Nick, this job is bringing in good money to my business. I'm expecting you to act like a responsible gentleman, be here on time, follow instructions, and be respectful to this man and his wife."

"I'm trying my best, but he—"

"I don't need you to try, Nick. I need you to do. That includes not showing up to work drunk. You understand me, son?"

I gritted my teeth, struggling to keep my attitude in check. I knew if Mr. Davis felt I was sassing or showing him the slightest bit of disrespect, he'd pull me from the job, and I'd fall even farther behind on my bills.

"Your father, God rest his soul, wouldn't have needed a pep talk like this."

I fucking hated when he insinuated that I was a disappointment, that I somehow dishonored my father or was a disgrace to his memory, but I knew I couldn't complain about that either.

"Trust me, son. I know Frank's an ass, but his mindset toward Blacks is deeply rooted. You can either reinforce it and lose out on making money or show him, through hard work that you're better than what he thinks of you."

I stayed quiet. I wanted to fight and argue my case, but there's not much you can say when you're broke. I wanted to tell Mr. Davis that this man's money wasn't worth being disrespected, and losing my pride over, but I was desperate. Honestly, I needed this job. I barely had money to eat, and I couldn't keep asking my brother to help me out. It was bad enough I rarely paid him rent.

Mr. Davis went back to talk to Frank, leaving me to wonder if the money was worth the hassle. In the end, I decided that it was.

★ ★ ★

By Friday afternoon, Vince and I were exhausted. We spent the entire week making all sorts of improvements on the house, yet we still hadn't made a dent in Frank's long to-do list. Considering the amount of money he was pouring into so many upgrades, I thought he would be better off buying a new house.

Vince and I were putting up the crown molding in the living room when I heard Frank and his wife arguing in their bedroom. I walked over to the stairwell to get a better earful.

"What are you doing?" Vince asked.

"I want to know what they're fighting about."

"You're crazy, man! If they catch you eavesdropping, it'll be your ass."

I waved him off and crept up the steps, near the door.

"Fuck you!" Vickie screamed.

"Calm down. She's nothing to me, all right?"

"Nothing to you? You've been fucking the bitch for God knows how long, knocked her up, and she's nothing?"

"Settle down, Victoria. I told you I'll take care of it."

"I don't want to hear that, Frank. I want to hear that you'll stop fucking cheating on me. I'm here for you every night, to fuck you and suck your dick. You won't touch me, but you're always fucking these whores. Am I not good enough for you? What do they give you that I don't? Is this because we don't have kids?"

"Cut the fucking pity party. I said I'll take care of it."

Vickie was crying, and the bickering got loud to the point where I couldn't understand them. The yelling turned to screams and sounds of physical fighting. I heard loud slaps and a thud hit the floor, then more of Vickie's sobs.

The door flew open. I rushed down the stairs and pretended to work as if I never heard their scuffle.

Frank stormed into the living room, snatched his keys off the coffee table, and headed for the door, but he noticed me staring at him.

"What the fuck are you looking at? Mind your business and get back to work. I don't pay you to drag your feet," he said.

I turned my head and measured the next piece of molding as Frank stomped out and slammed the door behind him. As soon as he was gone, I turned to walk back up the steps.

"Nick, c'mon, man. Leave her be. Let's just get this shit done and stay outta these White folks' business," Vince pleaded.

"I'm just checking on her. I'll be right back."

When I got upstairs, the bedroom door was partially open. I peeked in and saw Vickie lying on the floor, sobbing uncontrollably.

"Mrs. De Luca?" I said as I gently knocked on the door.

"What do you want?"

"I just wanted to make sure you were all right." I slowly pushed the door open and helped her off the floor.

"I'll be okay. Thanks."

I nodded and headed out the door.

"Wait. Stay a minute," she said.

I tilted my head to the side.

"You sure?"

"Yeah. You're the only person who seems to give a shit about my feelings today. The least we can do is have a drink and talk a little."

Our conversation started with the usual bullshit generic questions, but one drink led to finishing three bottles of wine and talking for nearly four hours. On his way out the door, Vince shook his head as he stared at the Vickie and me drinking and laughing.

"Frank hasn't touched me in over a year," Vickie said, opening up to me about practically everything.

I shook my head, took another sip of wine, looked her up and down, and said, "That's crazy."

"Most of the time, he doesn't even come home, and when he does, he claims he's too tired because he works so hard to build an empire for the two of us. I'm not stupid. I know he's fucking other women. They call the house all the time, and he fucks so many that he doesn't have the energy for me. I was with him before he had money, you know."

"He doesn't appreciate what he has. If you were my woman, I'd be home every night."

"Thanks," Vickie said, blushing. "That's sweet of you to say."

I instantly regretted flirting with her, but I couldn't help it. She was sexy, five-nine, with a gorgeous face, gray eyes, and those huge tits I'd already seen in all their naked glory. She was shapely, with an ass and hips that rivaled those of sistahs. I was sure other brothers' tongues were wagging whenever they saw her on the street, and I honestly couldn't imagine Frank finding anything better than what he had at home. I guess behind every beautiful woman is a man who's tired of her shit, I reasoned.

"He never takes me places, and we never do anything together. I get so lonely in this house all by myself. I don't go out. I mean, I have friends, like Francine and Rosalie, and I hang out with them from time to time. They try to keep me company, but they mostly spend time with their husbands and families. I've got no one, Nick. I have this big, fancy house, and I'm all alone in it."

"Well, you have me now."

"Thanks. You're easy to talk to."

"It's no problem. Look, it's Friday night, and we're both young. Let's go out tonight."

I figured she would shut me down and put me in my place, but she surprised me when she said, "Okay. Where are we headed?"

★ ★ ★

We drove into Manhattan, and I took her to Copacabana. I had money in my pocket since Mr. Davis had just paid me. I still hadn't put a cent toward my bills, but I decided, fuck it! I'll worry about that stuff later. Tonight, I'm going to enjoy myself.

We walked into the club, and all eyes were immediately on us. Some of the White couples and even the Black ones glared at us and shook their heads. I heard their jeers and snide comments, and I was sure Vickie heard them, too, but I still proudly held her hand and walked her to the dance floor.

We had a good time dancing and drinking. Vickie was skeptical at first, worried that we stood out too much. She also feared she'd bump into someone she knew, but after she had a few more drinks in her system, she lost all inhibitions.

When it was all over, I drove her home. As she had mentioned earlier, Frank still wasn't there.

"Thank you so much for tonight, Nick. I really needed that."

"It was my pleasure."

I couldn't recall who initiated what, but before I knew it, we were kissing and groping one another in my car.

"Yes…" Vickie said, moaning.

I rubbed my fingers against her opening and slid a finger inside her.

Vickie's eyes fluttered closed, and she threw her head back against the headrest as my finger curled and massaged her G-spot.

"Oh, God! Keep going," she begged.

I rubbed the head of her clit with my thumb, teasing her until it was swollen and throbbing. Vickie squirmed in her seat, clutching the fabric. Her breathing quickened into short, hard gasps. I saw the flush rise in her cheeks; her body trembled and twitched as she came.

"Holy shit," Vickie whispered, with longing in her eyes, her loneliness on display, and I could tell she hadn't experienced passion like that in a long time.

When she rubbed her hands down my jeans, I finally came to my senses and stopped her. I looked around to make sure her neighbors hadn't seen us.

"We have to stop before we go too far."

Vickie sighed. "I know."

"I had fun tonight. We should hang out again soon."

"You promise?" she asked.

Her face told me she was serious about the question.

"I promise."

She smiled, we said our goodbyes, and she walked into the house.

I wanted to smack myself for letting my dick overrun my logic. She was the forbidden fruit I knew I shouldn't partake of, but as usual, I was foolish, thinking with the wrong head.

★ ★ ★

The sweltering summer sun beat down on me while I cut the kitchen tiles outside, in the driveway. I switched off the circular saw and dropped my work gloves to the ground, then rubbed my hand across my face to wipe the beads of sweat off my forehead before they dripped into my eyes. Frank wanted marble floors and countertops in his kitchen, the best of everything in his house, and it took a lot of hard work to give it to him.

As I dried my damp hands on my blue jeans, Vickie stepped out onto the balcony. Her robe was open, revealing her sexy lingerie. She stared down at me, took a drag on her cigarette, and smiled.

"Hey, Nick," she said, throwing me a flirty little wave.

I returned the wave and smile.

"When you're done for the day, come see me before you leave. I want to talk to you about something."

"Cool."

I went back to work, thinking about the last couple days. Vickie and I had been spending a lot of time together, and every time we did, I had to fight the temptation of fucking her brains out. We mainly partied in Manhattan, because she felt there was less of a chance of getting caught there by people she knew.

Eventually, Vickie told her friends, Francine and Rosalie, about our hangouts. They were huge bitches, and they didn't care for me, but the feeling was mutual. They were always making snobbish, condescending comments: "Vickie's always been the adventurous one in our group. Personally, I wouldn't be caught dead spending time with the help." They tagged along with us when we went dancing, but in a way, that was good, because it prevented us from going any further. One thing was for certain: Vickie and I were sexually attracted to each other, and it was getting very difficult to avoid acting on it.

Frank rarely came home or cared about Vickie's whereabouts, so we went to bars and clubs regularly. When we weren't drinking or dancing, we'd relax at her house, talk and vent to each other. It felt good to feel like someone understood me.

Since Vickie was comfortable with me being around her close friends, I introduced her to the people closest to me.

"Scout, Rhea, I'd like you to meet my friend Vickie. She's gonna hang out and watch the Knicks game with us tonight."

My brother looked at me, then back at Vickie.

"It's nice to meet you, Vickie. Nick, can I talk to you for a sec'?"

Rhea, catching the awkward vibe, chimed in, "Hey, Vickie. It's good to have another woman around for a change."

"I know nothing about sports," Vickie said.

"Me neither. I just like seeing muscular, handsome men running around," Rhea added, and the two shared a laugh.

"Tell me you're not stupid enough to bring the wife of the guy whose house you're working on, to your apartment," Scout said, as soon as we stepped into the kitchen, out of earshot of the women.

"Relax, Scout. I'm not fucking her."

"You better not be, but it doesn't matter. The fact you're even kicking it with her is wrong. You're playing with fire."

"I'm a grown man, and I know what I'm doing."

Scout shook his head. "You really are a damn fool."

"She's cool, man, and Frank is never gonna know."

"You're sloppy. You never heard about not shitting where you eat? How long have you been dealing with this chick?"

"Relax, brother. We just go dancing and drinking here and there."

"Why? What's the point, if you know nothing's gonna come of it?"

I shrugged.

Scout glared at me with disappointment, that same tough-looking, no-nonsense expression that seemed to be permanently etched on his dark-skinned, bearded face.

"C'mon. We don't want to be rude to your guest."

We hung out in my living room, and while Scout and Rhea tried their best to be polite, I knew Vickie's behavior irritated them. She wasn't used to being around people who'd come from humble beginnings, and it showed. She nitpicked at everything the entire time.

"Have a seat," I said to Vickie.

"I would if there was room for me."

I quickly moved the clothes and tools to create an empty spot on the couch.

As she sat down, her eyes went to the mountain of bills on my coffee table.

"Looks like I'm gonna have to find a lot more work for you to do around my house. You've got a lot of final notices there."

Rhea cleared her throat and looked as if she might say something, but I cut in, "I've been spending all my money having fun with you. I'll get to them…eventually," I said with a laugh, hoping Vickie would let it slide.

She didn't; instead, she turned up her nose and looked repulsed by my comment.

Not too long after that, Vickie grew bored with the game and started asking us to change the channel. When Rhea offered her bottled water, she turned it down, stating, "I'm sorry, but I only drink Evian."

Scout made steaks, but Vickie made sure to tell us, "I don't eat red meat." Then she went on to give us the whole spiel as to why we shouldn't either. She even complained that my place was messy and that my furniture was out of date and uncomfortable.

By the time the game ended, Rhea and Scout couldn't wait to say goodnight and get away from her. I excused myself from Vickie and walked them downstairs, to their part of the house.

"I hope you don't bring that bitch around here often. Once was enough for me in this lifetime," Rhea said.

"If you decide to continue with whatever it is you're doing with her, keep her upstairs with you. Don't involve us anymore," Scout ordered.

I sighed. "Fine. Goodnight. I gotta get back up there," I said, then rushed back upstairs to Vickie.

★ ★ ★

I packed up my tools since Vince and I were done working for the day.

"Cyrus and some of the guys are planning to meet at the bar. You wanna roll with us?" Vince asked.

"Nah, I promised my brother I'd help him with some shit around the house. I can't today," I lied.

"C'mon, man! You can help him with that shit another day."

"Sorry, but I can't keep blowing him off. I'll catch up with you guys another time.

"All right, man. Well, I'm out of here."

"Yeah, I'm just gonna sweep up, and then I'm heading out too. I'll see you tomorrow."

I watched out the window and waited for Vince to pull away before I ran upstairs. I found Vickie standing at the top, still in her robe.

"Took you long enough," she said.

"Sorry. He wanted me to hang out with him and some of our co-workers."

Vickie motioned for me to follow her into her bedroom, then closed the door behind us. As soon as we stepped inside, she began grinding her hips against me and pushed me down on a chair.

"I know you wanna fuck me, Nick. I've seen the way you look at me," she said, then opened her robe and straddled me.

22

I savored the soft, silky feel of her lips as she slid her hands down my shoulders, gently tracing my back and chest with her slender fingers. She wrestled with my belt for a moment, then shoved my pants down and pulled my t-shirt over my head.

"Vickie, we can't do this. I don't want to risk losing my—"

She grabbed the back of my head and kissed me to shut me up. She then moved her hands around in my briefs, stroking my dick. I immediately felt my restraint slipping, especially when Vickie licked her lips.

I found the clasp of her bra and released her huge tits. My hands roved over her curves, then slid down her back to grab her ass.

My head began to spin. I knew I needed to stop before we reached the point of no return. Vickie let herself fall back on the bed, then spread her thighs wide. While on top of her, I kicked off my shoes and held myself up with my arms. Vickie slid her arms around my neck and pulled me in. I slid her panties down her legs, letting them fall to the floor.

"Hold up. I'll get a condom," I said.

She held me and moaned. "Don't worry about a fucking condom. You can cum inside me. I can't have kids. It's fine."

As much as I loved the feeling of going bareback, the voice in my head told me it wasn't wise.

"I-I should put something on, just to be safe," I argued.

"Mmm… Don't fuck this up, Nick. I'm clean. Are you?"

"Yeah."

"Good. Then we have nothing to worry about. I hate condoms. It's like fucking with a plastic bag. I want to feel every vein on your thick cock."

I lowered myself between her spread legs and grinned as the tip of my manhood passed her pussy lips and entered her slowly, inch by inch. Her eyes fluttered, and she inhaled as I slid deeper inside her. I watched her grip the sheets with both hands.

"Oh my God," she said, then let out another moan.

I rammed the full length of my dick inside her, hammering her into bliss. Vickie wrapped her legs around my back and drew me closer as I pounded her. I stroked her with a steady rhythm, and her legs quivered.

"Oh fuck…"

I gradually picked up my pace.

"Shit! Yes!" she squealed.

Vickie's fingers dug into my back, and she bucked and shuddered under me, twisting her head on the pillow as she came.

I pulled out of her, grabbed her hips, and flipped her over in one swift motion. I spread her thighs and slid inside her.

"Ah..." she moaned.

I glided my left hand down her hair and pulled it tightly. With my right, I slapped her ass. Vickie moaned, overcome by a mixture of pain and excitement.

I looked at our reflection in the mirror as I buried myself in her, balls deep, from behind. I loved seeing her like that, completely at my mercy, and I smiled to myself. Frank thought of me as nothing, a nobody. He felt I was inferior to him and could never have all the things he had in life. That was why I savored fucking Vickie. Men like Frank usually ran the world and had control, but there, in that bedroom, his wife was under my control. For the first time in a very long time, I felt powerful.

"Ah, you feel so fucking good," Vickie said, her mouth open and her eyes closed. "Shit! I'm cumming again!" she screamed.

Vickie buried her face in the pillow as another powerful orgasm ran through her. I was turned on by her response, and a couple of strokes later, I groaned, jerked, and came inside her.

We collapsed on the bed next to each other.

"I'm gonna keep you around forever," Vickie said with a giggle.

I nodded in agreement and held her. Little did I know that our intimate moment would forever change my life.

★ ★ ★

Over the next few weeks, Vickie and I slept together regularly. Some nights, she slept over at my place. Scout cursed me out whenever he saw her car in the driveway overnight. It was obvious that we had feelings for each other, but we were both getting a bit too comfortable. Vickie openly bragged about our sex sessions to her friends, and they often warned her to be careful. Whenever Frank asked where she'd been, she snapped, "You never give me a straight answer when I ask you, so don't expect one from me. I've been out!"

She played the game well, though. Neither Frank, Vince, nor Mr. Davis knew that anything was going on between us. When they were around, she was a snob and treated me like I was less than a man and beneath her. She was so good at the role that if I weren't fucking her, I would have sworn she truly felt that way.

Things went smoothly until one eventful day when everything spiraled down.

I was tightening the faucet in Frank's kitchen when I felt hands grab my ass, and dainty fingers caress my dick through my jeans.

"Hey, sexy. I see you're packing a big tool," Vickie whispered in my ear.

I couldn't help but smile.

Vickie smirked, then dropped to her knees, unzipped my fly, and unbuckled my pants.

"Are you crazy? Not here in the open! We'll get caught."

"C'mon, Nick. I wanna suck it."

"Later. Not now," I whispered.

"I want you in my mouth…now," Vickie said, ignoring me. She slid my jeans down to my ankles, and when my dick sprang free and dangled in front of her face, she instantly palmed my manhood.

Once the tip passed her lips and she took me deeper into her mouth, I didn't put up much of a fight.

"Fuck," I mumbled.

Vickie's breasts bounced, and her head bobbed up and down on my shaft as she filled her mouth to capacity. The movement of her cheeks and the way her tongue curled around the head, slathering all over the sides of my dick, turned me on.

"Shit! I'm so close," I said, trying to keep my moans quiet.

Seeing her pretty gray eyes gazing up at me as I held the top of her head sent me over the edge. I tensed up and rocked my hips forward, then gasped and moaned loudly as I exploded down her throat.

"You all right in there, Nick? I got those screws we needed for—" Vince started, but he stopped in his tracks when he saw what Vickie was doing.

Vickie pushed off me, wiped the corners of her mouth, and sprang to her feet. "Oh my God!" she said and quickly ran away.

I was still leaning against the sink, panting and trying to adjust myself.

Vince smiled and slapped me on my back.

"Yo, I didn't know you've been fucking the paisano's wife!"

"I don't know what you're talking about."

"Oh, don't play dumb with me. You gotta be fucking her. No woman would suck you off out in the open like that, in the middle of the day if you weren't fucking her, especially with all these people working on her house. Anyway, I'm glad you're giving it to this douchebag's wife."

"Look, you can't tell anybody what you saw, Vince. Davis will fucking kill me if he finds out."

"Your secret's safe with me, brother man! Just keep tapping that ass!"

Of course, I knew my secret wasn't safe with him. Within two days, everyone who had ever worked for Mr. Davis knew about Vickie and me. Mr. Davis called me down to his office.

"You wanted to see me, sir?" I said, poking my head in the doorway.

Mr. Davis gestured to a chair across from him. "Have a seat."

I did as he asked and sat down, then began fidgeting in the chair.

"I've heard rumors that you've been sleeping with Frank Deluca's wife. Are they true?"

My eyes dropped to the floor.

"No," I said meekly.

Mr. Davis slipped off his reading glasses.

"Look me in the eyes when you answer me, son. I want to hear you tell me again. Are you sleeping with that man's wife? Think carefully before you answer. If you can look me in the eyes and lie, it means you don't respect me. It means you lack integrity and don't deserve to work for or be associated with me."

I looked up at him; my heart was pounding hard in my chest.

"No, sir, I haven't slept with his wife. We've talked a few times, and she's vented to me, but that's it."

Mr. Davis rubbed his chin and stared at me.

"You're telling me nothing else has happened between you two?"

"No, sir."

Mr. Davis leaned back in his chair.

"If that's your answer, we're done with this conversation. That's three times you've told me no."

I exhaled and rubbed my forehead.

"For your sake, I hope you're telling me the truth. I hate liars, and I especially despise men who sleep with married women. If I find out you just sat here in my office, looked me in the eyes, and lied three times to my face, you'll be dead to me. Your father and I were good friends. He always had my back when we fought together in the Marines. I promised him I'd always look out for you and your brothers, but even that friendship won't be enough for me to forgive you for lying to me. Do you understand, son?"

"Yes, sir."

"You can go," Mr. Davis said, waving me off.

I nodded and went on my way, knowing I needed to tread very, lightly when it came to my relationship with Vickie.

★ ★ ★

The work at Frank's house was finally finished, and I used those last two weeks to begin distancing myself from Vickie. I went back to spending most nights partying and getting drunk with Vincent, Cyrus, and the rest of our friends. Sex with Vickie was great, so I continued that, but we didn't go out as much anymore. I had no idea how much things were going to change the next time Vickie and I met.

The phone rang, and since my head was spinning, I debated over answering it. Finally, I willed myself off the couch and staggered toward the phone. "What?" I slurred.

"Nick, it's Vickie. I need to see you. It's important."

"Damn, woman; you can't get enough, huh?" I chuckled.

"This isn't funny. Both of our lives could be ruined."

"All right, all right. Calm down. Look, I'm in no shape to drive, so you'd better come to my place."

"I don't..." She sighed. "Fine. I'm on my way."

Twenty minutes later, she was on my couch, crying and holding her face in her hands, with a positive pregnancy test in her lap. "I can't believe this is fucking happening," She said.

My buzz was gone. I rubbed the bridge of my nose, stood, and began to pace.

"You said you couldn't get pregnant. How do you know this isn't a mistake?"

Vickie calmed herself down, faced me, and said, "I took six tests, and I got the same result every time."

I shook my head in disbelief.

"I went to a pharmacy far away from my house so no one would recognize me. Then I took the tests with Rosalie and Francine. After those came back positive, I had my doctor give me one. I'm pregnant, Nick."

I rubbed the stress lines on my forehead, stopped pacing, and stared at Vickie.

"How do you know the baby isn't Frank's?"

"Are you kidding? He hasn't fucked me since God knows when, and I haven't slept with anyone else but you. I can't believe you'd asked me that."

"I'm sorry. It's just… This is hard for me to take in. What did Francine and Rosalie have to say about it?"

"They said there's no way I can have this baby. They want me to get rid of it, but I can't. I'm Catholic, and I've already done enough to piss God off. I can't even fathom having an abortion. I guess this is my punishment for cheating on Frank."

I sat next to Vickie and held her in my arms while she bawled. "Relax, Vickie. Everything's gonna be fine," I said, not sure if I was trying to convince her or me. "You weren't happy with him anyway, right?"

"No, but—"

"He's cheating on you, too, and you don't love him anymore, do you?"

"Those things are true, but I—"

"You have fun with me. We enjoy one another's company and, to be honest, I have feelings for you. I know you feel the same way."

"Nick…" she said, then trailed off.

"Everything happens for a reason. This is fate's way of giving you a way out from Frank. Think about it."

I thought about the situation. I knew our lives would change once the baby was born, but even though I was scared shitless, I was sure things wouldn't be that bad.

"I'm gonna do everything in my power to hide this pregnancy. Once the baby's born, I'll give it up for adoption."

I knew my father would spin in his grave if a child I created were given up for adoption. I was far from ready to be a father, but I couldn't let her give my baby away.

"No, don't do that," I said. "We can raise the baby together."

"Nick, I'm not ready to be a mother. Unless you plan on raising the baby by yourself, I have to give it up."

"You're worried you're not gonna be a good parent. I'm scared, too, but nobody's ever ready for that. We'll be all right."

"Nick, you're not listening to me. I'm not going to be a mother to this baby."

"Everything will work out. You'll see."

★ ★ ★

Before I knew it, Vickie was dealing with morning sickness and gaining weight. I watched her fine body gradually change during the pregnancy. Her breasts grew larger and fuller, and her belly began to swell.

Vickie hid it well, though, ignoring her doctor's orders and working out at the gym like a maniac. She insisted on doing an hour of cardio twice a day, early in the morning and later in the afternoon. At night, she went through at least one or two aerobic videotapes before bed.

She ate healthy, mostly salad, fruit, and vegetables. She took prenatal vitamins but disguised them by putting them in her regular vitamin bottles. She tried to do everything in her power not to gain a lot of weight, fearing it would blow her cover. When she went out, she wore loose, flowy clothing and hid her growing belly by keeping it covered with her huge Mulberry purse.

Her mood swings and all those hormones had her acting like a raging bitch. We fought all the time. The further along she got in her pregnancy, the less fun she was.

As always, Scout freaked out and accused me of being stupid when I broke the news to him and mentioned that Vickie and I planned to keep the baby.

"You're making a huge fucking mistake!" he yelled.

Rhea nodded in agreement.

"Oh, stop worrying," I said.

"That's your problem, Fool. You never worry about shit. You go through life clueless, without a fucking plan. Then, when things fall apart, you blame them on bad luck."

I shrugged, not wanting to hear it. "So what do you suggest I do, oh wise brother?"

"Do what Vickie suggested and give the baby up for adoption."

"Listen to what you're saying. Dad would punch you right in the mouth if he heard you say that."

"Dad would've hit you for shitting where you eat and being a dumbass for sleeping with the rich bitch to begin with."

"You do know you're setting this child up to fail before it's even born," Rhea said, making sure to get her two cents in.

"How so?" I asked.

"What race will the child be? What will you say to your baby when it asks that question? No matter how light the complexion, we all know the one-drop rule. The world will see the child as Black."

I nodded. "So?"

"You're not taking this seriously," Scout said.

"Yeah, I am. I even bought Vickie this," I said, then reached into my pocket and pulled out the necklace I'd purchased from the pawnshop, a heart-shaped medallion with a lock and key.

Rhea snickered. "And what? You think that cheap piece of shit is gonna make Vickie stay with you? She gets jewelry from her husband, and it's worth fifty of those little trinkets. It won't make things any better, Nick. What does she think about y'all starting a family?"

I looked at the necklace. I had faith that once she saw it, she'd see that I was willing to change for her. *I'll be responsible,* I vowed. *We'll raise our baby together and be happy.*

"She doesn't talk about it," I finally answered. "Right now, she just wants to get the pregnancy over with. She's scared, but she'll come around. She's a woman. Once she sees the baby, emotions will take over, and we'll get through this together."

"Fool, that woman has never had a hard day in her life. She's not a survivor. She doesn't know the struggle. You'd better start being more involved with her and this pregnancy. Go to her doctor appointments and start working out a plan as to how you can provide for your so-called family financially."

"You think it's all about finances, but it's not just about the money. Our bond is bigger than that. I give her something Frank never could."

"Good dick doesn't pay the bills," Rhea snapped.

"It's more than that. She said I make her feel alive."

"She's really got you trippin'. All that woman wanted was Black dick, and you were there to satisfy her curiosity. Trust me, little brother. Once that uppity bitch has that baby, she'll give it up for adoption and drop you like a bad habit," Scout said.

"Whatever, man," I said, pissed. "You'll see."

"For your sake, I hope you're right. You'd better hope your little necklace and you showing more interest will be enough to motivate her to stick around after the kid is born."

★ ★ ★

I followed Scout's advice and started going to Vickie's appointments. Well most of them. Sometimes I'd hang out with the guys after work and lose track of time.

"Hey," I said as I entered the ultrasound room.

Vickie sighed. "You're late again Nick."

"Yeah, sorry. I got caught up in some shit."

She shook her head.

I sat next to her and held her hand. "I'm here now. That's all that matters."

Dr. Turner and the ultrasound technician exchanged glances.

Vickie shivered when the technician squirted the cold gel on her belly. She nervously squeezed my hand. I was excited to see and hear our baby's heartbeat on the screen, but I could tell by Vickie's face that she was terrified.

"Everything looks okay, but, Mrs. De Luca, you're not gaining much weight. We don't want the baby to suffer from malnutrition and come prematurely. Those things can lead to birth defects, and early birth is already likely due to your endometriosis. You need to eat more so your child will be healthy," Dr. Turner said. "Do you understand?"

Vickie nodded.

"I know you're worried about losing your figure, but you seem pretty disciplined. I doubt you'll let yourself go too much."

After the doctor had excused himself back to his office, I rubbed Vickie's belly and smiled.

The technician turned her nose up at me. "When will the baby's father come, so we can share the good news with him instead of your friend here," she asked.

Vickie curled her lips and bounced her foot.

I patted her hand, faced the tech, and said, "We're not waiting for anyone else. I'm the father."

She looked at Vickie's red, shamed face for confirmation, and Vickie gave her a slight nod.

"Oh," she said with a sigh, not bothering to hide the cynicism from her tone, "then you must be very, um...proud."

"We are," I said, proudly.

I'd be damned if I was going to let that woman look down on me. I was scared about the pregnancy, and I knew for damn sure that Vickie was terrified, but I had to show her that no matter what adversities we faced, we'd be okay.

The tech cleaned the gel off Vickie's stomach. Vickie stood, stretched, and pressed her hands against her lower back.

"C'mon, Nick," she said. "I have to ask Dr. Turner some more questions."

She discussed a few things with the doctor, and we left the office. Vickie stormed out the exit.

"What's wrong with you?" I asked.

"That whole situation back there was so humiliating," she spat, shaking her head at me. "I can't do this. I shouldn't have kept this baby."

"Don't talk like that. What's done is done. We'll make it through this together." I tried to pull her into my arms, but she clearly wanted no part of my affection.

"I have something for you," I said, "something that'll help you keep your faith in me." I then proudly pulled the necklace from my pocket and placed it around her neck.

She looked down at the pendant and held it up in front of her face for a moment, then let it drop to her collar.

"Nick, is this supposed to magically fix everything? How will a cheap necklace help my embarrassment or help you financially, huh?" She roughly pushed away from my embrace and put distance between us.

"You're not thinking realistically. You're acting like a kid," she said, sounding like my brother.

"It's to show you that I'm fully vested in this, in us. I can't make everything perfect for you, but I'll do my best, and I'm trying to be here for you. I'm making an effort to make you happy."

Vickie wouldn't look at me. She held her face in her hands. I tried to hold her again, but she pushed my hands away.

"You need to grow up, Nick."

"Where was all this talk before this pregnancy shit happened? You didn't think I needed to grow up then."

"I needed to grow up too. The reality of this shit is forcing me to. Thanks for the necklace, but I gotta go."

With that, she walked off, got in her car and drove away, leaving me standing there.

She wasn't the only one who wanted the nightmare to be over. I couldn't wait for her to have the baby, and I hoped she'd go back to being herself instead of the cold bitch she had become.

★ ★ ★

I woke up and opened my eyes to the sight of Vickie, Francine, and Rosalie, a trio of angry faces staring at me. I wished it was all a horrible nightmare, one I could wake up from, but I knew I wasn't that lucky.

CHAPTER 3

HARD TRUTH

Nick, 1989

The past two days had been hell. Vickie and I argued every day. She still wouldn't hold our baby, and she barely looked at her when the nurses brought her to the room. She blamed me for everything that happened, and it was hard to convince her and myself that things would eventually be good, and we'd have a happy life together. Every time I felt like I had mended things with Vickie, Francine and Rosalie visited and riled her up again. The only positive news I got was the confirmation that I was Lynn's biological father. Of course, I had to throw that in my brother's face, so I called him as soon as I got the news.

"What do you want, Fool?"

"I'm just calling to tell you that the paternity test proved what I already told you. Lynn's mine."

Scout sighed. "Congratulations…I guess. It was nice of you to name her after Mom. I've meant to stop by the hospital, but things have been busy at the shop. Plus, Rhea wanted to wait to see if… well, you know. When can you bring my niece home?"

It brought a smile to my face to hear him acknowledge my daughter as part of the family.

"Doc says by the end of the week, hopefully Friday," I said.

"How are things with you and your baby's mother?"

"Fucked up, but I'll make it work."

"The most important thing is that the baby's yours. Try to fix things with Vickie before she moves in here. I'm not gonna be stressed out in my own house."

"Once she's away from her bougie friends, she'll be fine."

"All right. Well, I gotta get back to work. I'll talk to you later."

After we hung up, I spent the rest of the day trying to convince Vickie that the next day would be the start of a great life together, but by the way she kept rolling her eyes at me, I was sure she didn't believe it.

★ ★ ★

Dr. Turner gave Vickie the okay to be released from the hospital. When I walked into her room, Francine and Rosalie were already there, talking her ear off.

"It's kind of early for the two of you to be here, isn't it?" I asked.

Francine waved me off. "I didn't know we needed the help's permission to see our friend," she snapped.

"I'm more than the help. If you really cared about your friend, you'd respect the man she's with."

"When we see a *man* worth respecting, we'll do that," Rosalie said.

"Enough!" Vickie yelled. "I have a fucking migraine, and I want this nightmare to end. I just wanna go home in peace, without all this damn bickering. Everyone, please shut up!"

"I couldn't agree with you more, honey. I'll pull the car up so I can get you out of here." I left the room, pulled the car around the front of the hospital, then hurried back inside.

"Don't worry about anything. I'm going to take care of us," I said to Vickie as we strolled to my car.

Francine and Rosalie walked next to us while I held Vickie's bags.

Vickie rubbed her face. She was very quiet. I knew she was worried about what the future held for us, but I was confident we'd make it through everything together.

"Comfy?" I asked as I helped Vickie into the back seat.

Vickie looked lost in thought and said nothing; she faced me and nodded.

"Nick, I left one of Vickie's bags in the room. Can you get it while we say goodbye? Francine and I have to get going," Rosalie asked.

"Yeah, I got it," I said, then looked back at Vickie. "You sure you're comfortable, babe?"

"Don't worry. We'll take care of her while you're gone," Francine assured me.

I ran into Vickie's room and searched everywhere for the bag. After ten minutes, I went back to my car, with no bag in hand, hoping Rosalie could tell me exactly where she saw it last.

To my shock, Vickie, and her friends were gone, and there was a note pinned to my windshield with the wiper. When I opened it, the necklace I'd given Vickie dropped to the ground. I snatched it up, and my hands shook as I read the note:

Nick,

I'm not leaving my husband for you. I begged Francine and Rosalie to help me. They contacted Frank and told him everything. Of course, he was angry, but we spoke on the phone while I was staying in the hospital, and we're going to try to work things out. Frank paid off the woman he knocked up and made her have an abortion. He promised me all will be forgotten if I forgave him for his cheating, and never mentioned you or your baby ever. I'm going back to Frank. What you and I had was fun, but it was a mistake and meant nothing to me. I tried to explain all of this to you nicely, but you didn't get the message. I guess the only way you'll understand, is if I'm brutally honest, so here it goes… I'm not giving up my well-kept life to live in poverty with you. The only "bond" we had was sex, nothing more, nothing less. I don't love you. I was lonely and vulnerable at the time, and I shouldn't have been involved with you in the first place. I kept my promise. I didn't give the baby over to Child Services, now I need you to promise you'll raise her on your own and leave me out of it. You wanted her, so you take care of her. Don't involve me in anything. I can't and don't want to be in the child's life or yours. Don't contact me and don't come to my house. My husband is a very powerful man. You're a nice guy, and I don't want to see you get hurt. Do yourself a favor and forget that you knew me.

Vickie

Tears trickled down my face and onto the paper. I squeezed her necklace in my left hand and brushed my tears away. "Fuck!" I yelled as I crumpled up the note with my other hand and shoved it in my pocket.

I never expected her to desert me like that, and I had no clue how to raise a child, now I had to go at it alone.

★ ★ ★

"Serves you right for sleeping with the enemy," Rhea said.

"Don't start with that bullshit. We're all Black when the lights are out."

"Yeah? Well, how's that working for you?"

I was sitting in Scout's kitchen with him and Rhea, trying to figure out what the hell I was going to do, now that Vickie wasn't going to be in the picture. Scout was as stunned about the note as I was, and Rhea couldn't stop saying, "I told you so."

"Now that you have a little girl, who's gonna do her hair and stuff like that?" Rhea asked.

I shrugged.

"Who's gonna teach her about her period and sex? Most importantly, how to be a woman?"

"If it's just the two of us, I'll have to do it," I answered with a shrug.

Rhea laughed. "A man can't raise a girl to be a woman."

"But a woman can raise a boy to be a man?"

"Yup."

"Oh please! That's a dumb-ass double-standard."

"It's not a diss, its fact. The difference of importance between a mother and father is like the human body. Livers can fail, and so can kidneys. Shit, you can be brain dead and still technically live, but if your heart stops, you're dead. Mothers are the heart and soul of raising children. Without us, it can't be done, and there's no way you can teach this baby everything she needs to know in life, especially about being a woman."

I rolled my eyes at her comment.

"The only positive from this cluster-fuck is that the baby's yours. You can't hide it, though," Scout said. "Sooner or later, you're gonna have to come clean with Mr. Davis, and that man's gonna cut you off without a second thought."

"I'll be all right."

"How do you figure that? How can you be so sure?"

I shrugged.

"That's just it. You won't. You never plan for the worst. You blindly get into things and think shit will magically fix itself."

"C'mon, Scout. I got enough stress. Cut me some slack."

"Well, when he cuts you off, I can use your help in the shop. That'll at least put some money in your pocket."

"That shop work isn't for me. That was always yours and Dad's thing."

Scout was a machinist, just like our father, the trade my dad learned in the military and tried to teach all three of us. He was always handy and figured he could save money if he fixed things on his own. He always said, "If you have the skills to repair and build things, you'll never go broke," and he taught us everything from home repair to masonry and construction.

Dad worked his ass off providing for us. He managed to go to trade school and did odd jobs here and there to save up money so he could open his own machinist company. He was big on education and pushed all of us boys to do well in school. As always, Scout excelled in academics; I was decent, but my grades couldn't compete with his. I was the athlete of the family. Our brother Chance wasn't good at sports or school, but since he was the baby, he got away with everything.

I worked with Scout a few times at Dad's shop, but it always made me feel like less of a man. It was bad enough that I didn't feel as significant as Scout, and working for him would only amplify that feeling.

"Well, Fool, what are you gonna do for money in the meantime then, while you're looking for work?"

"I'll think of something."

Scout sighed. "As usual, you have to do things your way, which is always the hard way. I'm going to put you down as an employee in my company. I'll pay, so at least you and the baby will have benefits. Hopefully, you'll come to your senses sooner rather than later and accept a guaranteed job working with me."

"Thanks."

"Don't thank me yet. Who's going to watch the kid while you work? Don't assume that just because you knocked someone up, we're going to give up our time and lives to cater to you. If you're man enough to make a child, you've got to be man enough to take care of it."

I turned to Rhea. "I was hoping you could watch her while I work."

"Oh? So you assume I'll take care of *your* baby while you hang out?"

"No, just while I work."

"We'll see."

★ ★ ★

Scout went with me to pick Lynn up from the hospital. We researched whether or not it was wise to ask Vickie to give up her parental rights, but we concluded that it was better to leave the courts out of it. Since I didn't have a steady job or income, I didn't want to open up a can of worms and risk my daughter being legally taken away from me.

The nurses handed Lynn to Scout.

"Wow! She's gorgeous," he said, looking up at me.

"I know. Let's take her home," I said.

Rhea and Scout had been trying to have kids for a while. Rhea had gotten pregnant twice, but as fate would have it, things didn't work out. The first time, she suffered a miscarriage during her thirteenth week. The second time around, Scout and Rhea were scared to even tell people they were expecting. During Rhea's second trimester, things seemed to be on track. They were excited and put the horrible experience of the lost pregnancy behind them.

Back then, Scout, Chance, and I were working on the expansion of the house. It was already a duplex, and before my parents passed,

Scout and Rhea used to live in the upstairs apartment, while my parents lived downstairs. Scout, Chance, and I expanded the bedrooms for the baby and their future children, and Rhea and Scout were eager to finally become parents, something they'd been planning for since they were first married.

Unfortunately, the umbilical cord wrapped around the baby's neck during childbirth, leaving their son stillborn. It was one thing to lose a child, but losing two and having to give birth to a deceased baby traumatized Rhea. She insisted on seeing her son, despite the fact that he passed. She and Scout named him Joseph Johnson Jr. and promised they'd never forget him. Since then, they'd had no luck getting pregnant again.

"Rhea!" Scout shouted as soon as we walked into the house with Lynn.

The door that separated my apartment from his part of the house was open. She yelled down, "I'm up here, Joe…in the nursery!"

Rhea was one of the toughest women I knew, but it had to be hard for her to see the nursery again, filled with the items intended for her deceased children. She had a hard enough time with me living up there, so knowing another baby was going to sleep in the room meant for hers had to be torture.

"Oh my God! Let me see her," Rhea said excitedly.

Scout handed Lynn to her.

There were tears in Rhea's eyes as she cupped the baby's head, adjusted the receiving blanket swaddled tightly around her, and tucked Lynn into the crook of her arm.

"Hello, beautiful," Rhea said, grinning.

Lynn made a soft, cooing sound and clenched her tiny fist as Rhea gently stroked her palm.

"She's precious, Nick. She's absolutely perfect."

All the negativity she and Scout said before was instantly gone. I knew nothing could ever replace the children they'd lost, but I hoped having my baby around would help ease the pain of those losses.

"I'm glad you feel that way because I'm going to seriously need your help."

CHAPTER 4

THE NEW GIRL

Nick, Five Months Later

Babies were born every day in this world, and I had one that was colic. The first five months of Fatherhood kicked my ass. I was sleep deprived and even worse, broke. Lynn cried all the time, and always wanted attention. Formula and diapers cost a grip. I was still drowning in debt, and I couldn't ask Scout for shit because I was staying in his house rent free.

Scout was right about Mr. Davis. As soon as I showed the guys from work my baby, word got back to our boss, and he fired me on the spot. That meeting in his office was brutal.

"Hey, Mr. Davis," I said, trying to sound casual.

"Sit down, Nick. We're not going talk to each other like gentlemen. It's clear that you don't respect me."

"That's not true, sir."

"You lied to my face three times. I have no place in my company for men without integrity. Your services are no longer required."

"But I—"

"I warned you, gave you an opportunity to come clean and be honest. You knew the consequences, and you chose to lie anyway. As I told you, I despise men who cheat with married women."

"But, sir, I—"

"No excuses, Nick. See your way out," Mr. Davis said firmly, pointing to the door.

My pride wouldn't let me fight with him, so I stormed out of his office, trying to convince myself that I didn't need him anyway. *I'll find my own home improvement gigs, make it without his help,* I told myself, even though the truth was I was barely making it at all. Rhea was right: I was clueless about raising a child and had no idea how I was going to do it alone.

It was two a.m., and I had to get up for work in four hours. Lynn was screaming her little head off inside her crib. I leaned on the railing and stared down at her kicking legs. Her face was as red as the ladybugs on her onesie.

"What's wrong, Ladybug? Are you hungry, wet, or just don't want Daddy to sleep?" I asked.

I lifted her from the crib and pulled at the elastic on her diaper. The stench hit me right away. She continued to scream while I carried her to the changing table to put her in a fresh diaper. Even that didn't calm her down, though.

"Are you hungry or something? God, I can't wait until you can talk, so I know what the hell you need."

I was in a daze, half-asleep, with the baby screaming in my ear. I went through the motions, making her formula. I grabbed the bottle from the simmering pot on the stove and tested it on the inside of my arm.

"Shit!" I yelled.

The damn formula was too hot and burned me.

Lynn screamed at the top of her lungs while I waited a few minutes for it to cool down before feeding her. She barely took any formula and still wailed.

I held Lynn in my arms, rocking her, but she wouldn't stop crying. I wasn't used to that shit, and the depression from struggling to find work, being sleep deprived, and frustrated because I was incompetent when it came to being a father had me worn out.

"Please stop crying," I begged.

I felt like I was getting sick, but I couldn't afford to be sick. I needed money. Lately, all I did was work. I didn't party with my friends, go on dates, or do anything recreational. My every waking moment was dedicated to taking care of Lynn. I've gotten used to operating on four, sometimes three hours of sleep.

At night, Scout and Rhea locked the door that connected our spaces. That way, none of us would walk in on another when we needed privacy. I called their phone downstairs. Rhea answered groggily.

"Hello?"

I felt helpless and pathetic.

"I'm sorry to wake you up, but I can't get Lynn to stop crying. I don't know what to do."

"I'll be up in a minute."

When Rhea arrived, she held Lynn and felt her forehead.

"She's a little warm. It could be a number of things. She could be teething, have a cold, or both," she said.

"What do I do?" I said, in a full-blown panic.

"The first thing you do is calm your ass down."

"Sorry."

"It's okay," she said with a smirk. "Her nose is stuffy, and she's tugging at her ears a lot. She could have an ear infection."

"What do we do for that?"

"Not much we can do at her age. Most of the time, they clear up on their own. If her temperature gets worse, we'll take her to the pediatrician for some antibiotics. Right now, we'll give her a fresh bath, get her some Tylenol to lower her fever, and if you have some Pedialyte, that'll help keep her hydrated."

Rhea helped me do all the things she suggested, and we talked while Lynn happily splashed in the sink.

"You like playing in the tub, Ladybug?"

"Aw. Is that her nickname?" Rhea asked.

"Yeah. When she's irritated, her face gets as red as the ladybugs on the onesie I always put her in."

"I like it. It's cute."

"Thanks for coming up here to our rescue," I said.

"It's no problem," Rhea said, then yawned.

"How do you know all this stuff about babies?"

"Well, I'm fourteen years older than my sisters. When Dad got sick, and my Mom had to work, I had to help raise them. I hoped that experience would come in handy with my own children. At least I'm keeping my skills up by helping you with Lynn."

"I appreciate it."

"You'd better!"

★ ★ ★

I walked into the house, depressed and angry. I worked my ass off, and I had no real money to show for it.

Rhea was sitting in the kitchen, feeding Lynn in her high chair.

"Hey," I said.

"Hey. How was work?"

"Shitty."

"Aw, that sucks. Well, you can always work with Joe. He won't say it, but I know he'd love for you to work alongside him," she said as she wiped Lynn's face and cleaned off the feeding tray.

I picked Lynn up. "Did you miss Daddy?" I asked as I held her.

Lynn jerked away from me, whimpered, and reached for Rhea. I felt a twinge of jealousy as I handed her back.

"Aw, don't be like that, Lynn. Daddy misses you," Rhea said.

My phone rang, and I quickly answered it: "Hello?"

"Nick!"

"What's up, Vince?"

"You gotta come out with us tonight, man. Cyrus's friend is a bouncer at this new club, and he can get us in! There'll be bitches galore in there, man."

I glanced over at Rhea, who was playing peek-a-boo with Lynn in her lap.

"You know I'd be there if I could, but I gotta watch my daughter," I said.

"You're always watching your kid, man. You never hang with us anymore. I swear, being a dad sounds more like a jail sentence than a blessing."

The remark irritated me; I was already in a bad mood, and it only added fuel to the fire. "Yeah, look, I gotta go. I'll catch up with you guys next time," I said, then hung up on him.

"Nick…" Rhea said.

"Yeah?"

"Go out tonight and hang out with your friends. You haven't

been taking advantage, and I know you've been working hard. You can use a little break. I'll watch the baby tonight."

"What will Scout say?"

"He's working late tonight. He got a new contract to make parts for the government, so he's putting a lot of time and energy into that. I'd rather keep busy and play with the baby than be bored and lonely downstairs. Go on and have fun."

I kissed her forehead.

"Thanks, Rhea! You're the best!" I said.

I hurriedly called Vince back.

"I'm coming out tonight!"

★ ★ ★

The line to get into the club wrapped around the block. The women standing in line wore dresses that left nothing to the imagination, and every guy there was mapping out who they were going to talk to first. Cyrus walked up to one of the bouncers, talked to him for a bit, and shook hands with him. As promised, his friend let us into the club.

"You've been outta the game for a while. You think you still got it in you to pull a PYT tonight?" Cyrus asked. "That's a pretty young thing, in case you've forgotten," he teased.

"The costumes and names might've changed, but the game's still the same. Talking to women is like riding a bike."

"That's what I'm talkin' about, Nick! You're back, baby," Vince said.

The place was packed. I did my thing and talked to some women, but I bought only a select few of them drinks; I was low on cash and needed to spend it on women who were really worth it.

While I was dancing with a homely sistah who dragged me onto the dance floor, I saw a fine, dark-skinned woman in a skintight, black mini-dress, with flawless makeup. The song ended, and I excused myself from the plain chick. She looked disappointed, but I wasn't interested in her anyway. I walked to the bar and motioned the bartender over.

"What are you having?"

I pointed. "See that fine woman standing over there, the one in the black dress?"

He nodded.

"Whatever she's drinking, give her another, on me."

"No problem."

The bartender made another mojito and placed it in front of her. I watched her mouth to him that she didn't order it, and when he pointed to me, I raised my glass in the air. She winked and did the same.

I walked up to her, smiling, slid next to her, and introduced myself. "How are you doing tonight? My name's Nick. What's your name, pretty lady?"

She giggled. "I'm Jasmine," she said.

"It's a pleasure to meet you," I said, shaking her hand.

Her friend standing next to her winked. "Mmm… He's cute," she said. "I'm gonna flaunt my ass around here. Hopefully, I can find a hot guy to buy me a drink too."

Jasmine and I shared a laugh.

As her friend walked off, I check Jasmine out. She was about five-five, with nice, full lips, long eyelashes, and dark brown eyes that matched her smooth, dark complexion.

I sipped the drink I was nursing and asked, "So…are you here with anyone?"

"Nah, just having a ladies' night with my girls,"

"You got a man at home?"

"Nope. I'm single and looking. You tryin' to be that man?"

I looked her up and down. "As fine as you are, I'll be anything you want me to be."

She laughed and pulled me onto the dance floor. "Let's see how you move here first, and that'll let me know if you're a worthy candidate to be my man."

We danced, laughed, and drank for hours, partying hard until the club closed. I passed my budget for the night, so I tapped into the credit card I'd just paid off, trying to impress the lady. *Oh well. Easy come, easy go.*

Since Jasmine and I were hitting it off and our friends weren't having much success, we introduced them to each other. Vince and Cyrus ended up leaving with Jasmine's friends, which worked out perfectly because it meant I had her all to myself.

Jasmine and I took our partying to her place. We sat on the couch in her living room, and my hands crept up her thighs. We kissed hungrily. We were moving fast, but I hadn't gotten any action since Lynn was born; I was horny and didn't give a shit. I needed a night where I felt free and uninhibited.

Jasmine unbuckled my pants and pulled my briefs down to my ankles. My dick sprang up, and her eyebrows perked up. Her eyes grew wide, approving my manhood. Jasmine licked her lips and dropped to her knees. I gasped as her tongue snaked around my shaft. I bit my bottom lip and watched her head bob up and down as she took my whole length down her throat. I came in her mouth, and she swallowed my pleasure. I quickly undressed her, sat her down on the couch, dropped to my knees, and returned the favor.

I lowered my mouth to her mound and sucked on the head of her clit, using my fingers to penetrate her. I enjoyed hearing her moan as I licked and slurped all her nectar. She squealed, twisted, and grunted in passion, closing her eyes tightly while I licked her all over. She was close, and I felt her twitching and clamping down on my fingers. She drew me deeper inside her, held the back of my head with both hands, and exploded on my face.

"Mmm…" she moaned, then leaned in and whispered seductively in my ear, "If you've got condoms, enough with the appetizer. I want the main course!"

I lifted Jasmine off the couch, carried her to the bedroom, and gently laid her on the bed, on her stomach. I slowly ran my tongue down the nape of her neck, down to her lower back, and ate her out again from behind.

"Goddamn," she said, then released another moan.

I stopped. "Stay right there. Don't you move," I instructed.

She writhed on the bed while I quickly grabbed my clothes from the living room and put on a condom. I hurried back in and jumped on the bed, then slid into her treasure while she lay on her stomach. In no time, I'd stroked her into bliss.

I inhaled the sweet coconut scent of her hair and kissed the nape of her neck. I gave her small, shallow thrusts and savored the feeling of the muscles in her treasure clenching around me. A smile crept across my face when I heard her begging me not to stop. Jasmine shuddered and clawed, screaming my name.

When our intense session was over, Jasmine lay on my chest, and we enjoyed a little pillow talk. Things went smoothly until I mentioned I had a daughter at home.

"Wait a minute. You have a kid?"

"Yeah."

"Fucking great."

I sighed when I saw the disappointment on her face.

"Are you married? Just my luck. I always manage to find the fucking married ones. I'm not trying to be anyone's mistress."

"No, I'm single. My baby's mother isn't around."

"Look, I gotta be honest. You're handsome, funny, a great fuck, and you seem like a decent guy, but I'm not interested in men with kids. Drama always comes with that, and—"

"Her mother's married to another man and wants nothing to do with her or me," I explained.

At first, she looked taken aback, but her expression soon changed to one of disbelief. "Mm-hmm. And what happens when she changes her mind and wants to be involved?"

"She hid the pregnancy from her rich husband and chose not to give up her wealthy lifestyle for me. Trust me. She's not coming back."

I knew I had her; if she were really turned off, she would have cut the entire conversation short and moved on, but she didn't. I could see in Jasmine's eyes that she was very attracted to me and curious to know more about my story.

"When I'm dating a guy, I want him to focus on me and only me. I can never be number one with you. Your child will always come first. That's how it should be, but I wanna be the only star in my man's life. I know it sounds selfish, but that thing most women have, that biological clock... Well, I don't feel any need to have kids. In fact, I don't even like children. I don't need them, and I never want to have them," she admitted matter-of-factly.

"I'm not asking you to change who you are as a person. All I want from you is a chance. Let me try to make you happy, Jasmine."

"I've dated guys with kids before, and it didn't work out, so—"

I kissed her midsentence. "I'm not those guys. Just give me a chance. You're not dating my daughter *and* me. You're only dating me. My child won't interfere in my relationship with you," I said, rubbing the top of her clit with my fingertips to entice her again. "I promise you that everything will work out."

★ ★ ★

"Shit!" I said, glancing down at my watch. "My sister-in-law's gonna kill me. I didn't realize how late it is."

"I didn't know you had a curfew," Jasmine said.

"I don't. She's watching my daughter, and I have to at least give her a call."

"C'mon, man. You don't gotta call Rhea. She won't say it in front of Joe, but she probably loves taking care of the baby all the time. It gives her a purpose or something. Y'all know women are better equipped for handling children," Vince said, then paused and looked at Jasmine. "No offense,"

"None taken. I'm not the typical woman," she said, then turned to face me. "This is *our* time together, Nick. You know I like you, but if you constantly have to check in, this relationship isn't going to work."

"Fuck it! Let's keep the party going," I said.

"That's the spirit!" Cyrus said.

Vince and Cyrus only cared about my relationship with Jasmine because they were fucking her friends; if things faded away with Jasmine and me, it would put an end to their romps as well.

The past four months had been great. I felt alive with Jasmine. I was still in debt, though, because as soon as I got paid, I spent all my money hanging out with her. I knew it was stupid, but when I was with her, I didn't worry about my responsibilities.

Jasmine was a secretary for a real estate office in Hempstead. She was content with her life and had no desire to better it or herself. I loved that because I felt similarly. Jasmine liked me for me, and I never felt like a loser around her. We partied at clubs every weekend and hung out at bars nearly every day. Of course, Rhea wasn't too thrilled about that, and she let me know it.

"You're missing all the little milestones that come with being a parent because you're out hanging out every night with your loser friends," Rhea said. "When I told you that you could use a break, I didn't mean a never-ending one!"

I sighed. "Lynn is just a baby, Rhea. What can I possibly be missing?"

"Well, you missed her first words, and she's walking now. She calls me 'Momma' and Joe 'Daddy.' Is that what you want? These are all experiences that you should want to be a part of."

"I do want to be a part of them, but—"

"Then keep your ass home for a change."

I told Jasmine about my family and past, and she didn't look down on me for it. I told Scout and Rhea about Jasmine, but they didn't seem too impressed, especially since I was coming in late, leaving them to watch Lynn all the time.

"How sweet. You found a woman who's just as stagnant in life as you are," Scout said

"While you're so busy worrying about the future, you forget that you have to live in the present. Is it bad to wanna enjoy my life while I'm young?" I asked.

"It's not, but you forget that you're the one with a kid, not me. You spend all your money as soon as you get it, hanging out with Jasmine, and you aren't paying any bills or even buying diapers and food for your own child."

"All right! I'll work on those things, but I want you and Rhea to meet Jasmine. Once you meet her, you'll see why I'm crazy about her."

"I already know you're out of your mind. You told me the woman doesn't want children. That, in itself, is a recipe for disaster in a relationship, especially when you're already a father."

"Give her a chance. Get to know her before you judge her."

"Yeah? Well, maybe she should get to know Lynn before she goes around saying she doesn't want kids," Rhea snapped, rolling her eyes.

★ ★ ★

"Here she comes!" I said.

It was a sunny Saturday morning, and Jasmine was about to meet Rhea and Scout for the first time. I was excited when she pulled up in the driveway and cut her engine, sure that they were going to love her.

"Do me a favor. Don't call me Fool in front of this one," I asked Scout.

"All right. I'm sure she already knows you're stupid, without me calling you by your nickname," Scout said.

I frowned at him, but Rhea chuckled at our brotherly quarrel.

"Rhea, can you hold Lynn for a second?"

"Sure."

I handed the baby to her, then walked to Jasmine and gave her a soft, loving kiss.

"Now *that's* how a woman should be greeted," she said.

"You know I aim to please."

Jasmine gave me a warm smile, and I stepped back to get a better look at her outfit, a nice, form-fitting Lycra skirt that hugged her curves perfectly. I even caught Scout sneaking peeks at her.

I walked Jasmine to the porch and introduced her to everyone. "This is my brother, Joe, and his wife, Rhea."

Rhea handed Lynn back to me, and she and Scout shook Jasmine's hand.

"And this little lady here is my daughter, Lynn."

The smile on her face faded when she saw my baby.

Sensing the tension, Rhea stepped in to break it. "Hey, girl, it's nice to finally meet you. Nick says so many good things about you that I feel like I know you already."

"Aw, thank you! Your house looks beautiful."

"Come in and check it out. We'll leave the baby with the men while I give you the grand tour and get to know you better."

Jasmine smiled. "Sounds good."

I mouthed my thanks to Rhea when Jasmine wasn't looking, grateful that she was being so friendly. She could be a real bitch to the women I dated, but she had her moments when she could be nice and sweet.

Rhea gave her a tour of the house while Scout and I went upstairs to my place. I put Lynn in her playpen, and the two of us cleaned up a bit before the ladies came up.

"This is the chick who doesn't want kids, right?" Scout asked.

"Yeah, she says that but I'm hoping once she's around Lynn, she'll change her mind."

"You still haven't learned your damn lesson, even after your fucked-up experience with Vickie. When a woman tells you how she feels about something, believe her."

"Jasmine is different."

"Yeah, well, at least you brought a sistah home this time."

I gave him the finger just as Rhea and Jasmine came upstairs, laughing and continuing with their girl talk.

Lynn was fussy while I prepared her food, but her little legs kicked with excitement when I placed her in her high chair.

Jasmine watched me happily talking to Lynn while I fed her. I kissed Lynn's soft, warm cheeks while her small hands gripped my fingers, and I noticed a slight smile on Jasmine's face.

"You wanna hold her?" I asked.

"No thanks. I'm good."

"C'mon! I want to see the two most important women in my life together."

She smiled broadly but frowned when I handed Lynn over to her. Lynn must have sensed her tension because she immediately began to cry.

"Did she shit herself?" Jasmine asked rudely, scrunching up her nose. She lifted Lynn up and sniffed her, then turned her head and held Lynn away from her. "Ugh! She did. Take her back."

Before I could reach for her, Lynn threw up all over Jasmine's legs and outfit.

"Fuckin' gross! This is why I fucking hate kids," she yelled.

Rhea looked irritated by her statement but kept her cool. "We're about the same size. Let me see if I can find something else for you to put on."

"I'm sorry. Let me clean that up," I said. I cleaned Lynn's face, put her in the playpen, then rushed to the hallway closet and wet some hand towels. I frantically wiped her legs and said, "I'll pay for you to get your clothes dry-cleaned, and I'll buy you a new outfit,"

Scout remained silent but stared at me, seething mad.

Jasmine scrunched her face and irritably tapped her foot. She was skeeved out by the vomit, but I needed to convince her that having a baby wasn't so bad.

"Enough with wiping *her* legs, Foo…er, Nick," Scout said, catching himself. "Your daughter is crying. You should tend to her first."

Jasmine cut her eyes at him, and he responded with a look that showed he didn't give a shit.

I picked Lynn up and rubbed her back to calm her down.

Rhea came back and handed Jasmine a striped tank-top and some black leggings.

"This is cute! Thanks, Rhea. I'll wash it and bring it back the next time I see Nick."

"No worries."

After Jasmine had gone to the bathroom to change, I asked, "Well? What do y'all think of her?"

"She doesn't care for your daughter, and it doesn't look like that's gonna change. I don't know if I like that or her right now," Scout confessed.

"She's nice, but I have mixed feelings about her too," Rhea said.

"Damn!" I said, staring Jasmine up and down when she stepped out of the bathroom. "You look good in everything,"

"Thanks," she said, winking at me.

"So, Jasmine, do you have any brothers or sisters?" Scout asked.

"Nah, I'm an only child."

Scout slowly nodded, assuming she was a spoiled, selfish princess. "And what do you think about Nick having a baby?" he probed.

"I'll admit that I'm not thrilled about it, but Nick and I have an agreement. I'm not dating him *and* his daughter. I'm only dating him. He promised me that his baby won't interfere with our relationship."

"Do you see yourself having your own kids in the future?" Scout asked.

"Hell no! I have no desire to give up my freedom. That mothering instinct most women have… I guess I don't have it. I don't find babies cute, and I don't ever wanna change diapers or get thrown up on. I guess I need to reemphasize that last one with Nick. You don't have any children?"

Scout was about to answer, but Rhea interrupted him.

"We did, but we lost them due to miscarriage."

"I'm sorry you feel that way about children," Scout said.

"I'm not," Jasmine said.

"Well, you need to understand that Nick can't waste time and money with you every day. He has responsibilities to take care of first, before worrying about your feelings," Scout blurted.

The rest of that day was spent with me going back and forth, trying to defuse small tiffs between Jasmine and Scout. Unfortunately, I didn't learn my lesson from everything that was said that day.

★ ★ ★

Rhea was asleep in my recliner when I entered my apartment. Completely shit-faced and stumbling all over the place, I dropped my keys and knocked the remote off my coffee table, which woke Rhea up.

She immediately looked at her watch.

"Nick, it's four in the morning. You're late again, and Joe's pissed. He planned a surprise date night in the city for me. We had dinner reservations, and he bought expensive tickets to see that Broadway show, *Cats*, but we didn't go because you were nowhere to be found, and we couldn't leave the baby."

Scout stomped up the stairs, and Rhea took Lynn to her room and placed her in the crib. "You're an inconsiderate dickhead. Do you know that?"

I sucked my teeth and threw my coat on the couch.

Scout grabbed my arm and spun me around to face him.

I wobbled, still tipsy from earlier.

"You're out there getting plastered every night, leaving your daughter with Rhea and me. The shit stops now."

I was way too drunk to fight with him, so I just stood there, struggling to stay conscious.

"Despite what you might think, the world doesn't revolve around you, Fool. I work all the damn time. I finally set up something nice for my lady and me, and I can't go through with it because I have to take care of your shit. I love my niece, but she's your daughter, your responsibility."

"I'm sorry, Scout. I—"

"I'm tired of your lame-ass apologies! Are you gonna give me my money back for last night?"

"You know I don't have it."

"I didn't think so. Rhea doesn't deserve this shit, and neither do I. You and your latest conquest better start taking the car seat on dates, because we're going to cut back on the babysitting significantly."

My head was spinning, and Scout was making it worse. "I don't need this shit. I already apologized," I said.

"Yeah, well I don't accept your bullshit apologies anymore!"

I threw my hands up.

"I can't wait to get my own place so I don't have to listen to your bitching all the time." I regretted the words as soon as they slipped out, but the liquor had loosened my lips.

Scout stepped right up to my face. "Is that right? Then find a fucking place already! Hell, I'll even pay the deposit and first month."

"Joe," Rhea started, but he waved her off.

"Nah, babe. He's a big boy, aren't you, Fool?"

"Yup, a grown man, and I can take care of myself."

"Good! Like I said, find a place, and I'll pay the deposit and first month's rent. If it means getting you outta my house and not supporting your ass anymore, I'm all for it."

"Joe, I know you're upset, but let's be realistic," Rhea said.

This time, I stopped her. "It's fine, Rhea. I don't need anyone. I can take care of everything myself."

She nodded slowly but looked offended. "If you say so. Good luck finding childcare."

I didn't mean to hurt her feelings, but I needed them to know I could stand on my own two feet, whether it was true or not.

★ ★ ★

I hurriedly placed Lynn in her car seat. It probably wasn't a good idea to stay up late last night drinking with Vince and Cyrus in my Livingroom, but I needed to relax. Life's bullshit had me stressed, but drinking last night caused me to oversleep, and I was running late to my much-needed job interview. I was drowning in debt, so finding a job was essential. When I fought with Scout and Rhea, I didn't factor in how expensive daycare was. Now, the center that watched Lynn was threatening to kick her out daily for nonpayment. I flirted with the owner every chance I got, but my charm was starting to wear off. My car payment was four months past due, and every day, I prayed the repo men wouldn't take my only vehicle in the middle of the night. I ducked my landlord daily as well; I was two months behind on my rent, and all my credit cards were maxed out. The only bill I paid somewhat regularly was my phone bill so I could get job offers, but even that was late and in danger of being cut off. I had to take any type of handyman work I could get, and some of those areas had no places to park, so on top of my regular bills, I'd also accumulated plenty of parking tickets. Being a procrastinator didn't help either. I was constantly late for shit, which led to me getting a good amount of speeding tickets too.

Scout and Rhea stayed true to their word. After our fallout, they didn't help me with anything. I regretted everything I said and really did need help, but I didn't want to beg Scout and Rhea for it. Life seemed bleak, but I was hoping all of that would change with the job interview.

I'd been talking with the Garden City Hotel for two weeks, about a possible maintenance man position. Luckily, one of my new customers recommended me to the hotel for the job, after I did good work in updating his bathroom, so the interview was really just a formality. As far as I knew, the job was pretty much mine.

I sped to the daycare center to drop Lynn off.

"No, Nick, we're not watching Lynn today," Irene said, holding her hand up to stop me from walking through the door.

"C'mon, Irene! Today is important."

"You haven't paid me in over five months. Being able to pay my employees is important too."

"I know, I know. I'm a little down on my luck. I'll have your money soon. I promise. I have an interview today. Please help me out."

Irene's eyes roved over me. She saw me dressed for success in my suit, licked her lips, and smiled.

"Well, you do look handsome today. Just promise me you'll use your first check to pay me and take me out on a date, and I'll do it."

"You have my word, pretty lady!"

She was far from pretty. In fact, Irene was skinny, borderline anorexic, with thinning hair and missing almost all her front teeth. I had no desire to take her out, but I was willing to do that and then some if it meant she'd cut me some slack and watch Lynn.

I ran out of the daycare and reached for my car keys when I realized I didn't have my damn wallet. I rushed home, grabbed it off the dresser, and sped past a stop sign. I looked in my rearview mirror, only to see a fucking cop flashing his lights and blaring his sirens behind me, ordering me to pull over.

"Fuck!" I yelled, slapping the steering wheel. I had ten minutes to make it to my interview, and it was a fifteen-minute drive to get there. I turned on my blinker and pulled over to the curb.

The heavyset white cop strolled to my car, with his hand gripping his gun, looking through my back window.

I kept my hands on the steering wheel and rapidly tapped my foot, wishing he'd hurry up and get the ordeal over with.

"License and registration," the officer said.

I hesitantly handed him the cards.

"Do you know why I'm stopping you, sir?"

There was no way in hell I was going to admit that I'd done anything wrong, so I answered, "No, sir."

"You breezed through that stop sign back there."

"I apologize, Officer," I said, my finger tapping hastily against the steering wheel.

"You look anxious. Are you in a rush to be somewhere? Why do you look so nervous?"

"I'm sorry. I'm late for a job interview, and I really need the job."

The cop looked inside my truck and stared at my suit.

"All right. I'm going to check your license. If everything's legit and your record's clean, I'll let you go with a warning. Be honest with me. Do you have any outstanding tickets or warrants? Tell me now. If you lie to me, and I find something when I check, I can't help you."

I had a bunch of tickets, but I didn't know if he was being nice or setting me up to bust me, so I answered, "I don't have any tickets or warrants, sir."

"All right. Sit tight. I'll be back."

I watched him walk back to his squad car and talk into his radio.

Three minutes passed, and the cop's door finally flew open. He slammed it closed, stormed up to my car, and yelled, "Step out of the car!"

"What? What did I do?"

"Get out of the car now, sir!"

My hands shakily opened my truck door, and as soon as my feet touched the ground, the cop spun me around and handcuffed me.

"What am I being arrested for?" I asked.

The cop turned me to face him. "I gave you a chance to be honest. If you would've told me the truth before I radioed it in, I would have let you slide and drive to your interview. Instead, you chose to lie about the warrants for your outstanding tickets. Once I go over the radio with your info, I have no choice but to take you in."

"Fuck! I'm two blocks away from my house. Please, uh…" I looked at his name badge. "Officer McNerny, I can't miss this interview. I need this job. I've got a little girl at home, man. I need the money."

"I tried to help you, but you refused to help yourself."

"Come on, man. I need this job to take care of my daughter. I'm all she has."

Officer McNerny sighed as he placed me in the back seat of his car. He didn't seem like the typical asshole cop, which was somewhat of a relief.

"Look, I'm supposed to have your car towed also, but I'll cut you some slack and leave it parked on the street. At least you won't have to pay to get it back once you're released. When we get to the station, I'll let you call to reschedule your interview."

"Thanks," I said, lifting my head to look at him.

"You're having a bad day, kid. Learn from this so you have a better tomorrow."

★ ★ ★

"Mr. Johnson, we need you to sign here and here," the precinct desk sergeant said, pointing at the form.

I placed my signature on the dotted lines, while Scout paid my bail and my tickets. I rubbed my wrists as we walked out, still feeling the pain from those tight handcuffs. Even though I'd been quickly released, I felt defeated as we climbed into Scout's car.

As promised, when I got to the station, Officer McNerney allowed me to make a call to the interviewer. When I explained that I needed to reschedule because of an incident beyond my control, I was told I'd be marked as a no-show. Because of that, they chose another applicant to fill the position, and I was right back to square one.

"Thanks for coming," I said to Scout.

He didn't answer me, and since I knew he was furious, I didn't push it.

"Can you drive me to pick up my car? It's two blocks from my house."

He nodded but still said nothing.

Unfortunately, when he pulled up to the block, there was no sign of my car there. There was no glass on the ground, nor were there any indications that the car had been stolen, so I could only assume Officer McNerny had gone back on his promise that it wouldn't be towed.

"Come on! What more can go wrong today?" I fumed.

Scout and I drove back to the precinct to see if my car was there, but the female officer at the desk assured us it hadn't been towed by the police. As she was filing a stolen vehicle report, she discovered that the repo men had taken it.

"Scout, I can't survive without that truck, man. I can't go to work, search for work, or pick Lynn up without it. I know you've already done a lot for me, gone outta your way today, but is there any way you can help me get my truck?"

"C'mon, Fool," he said, his nostrils flaring. "I'll have to go to the bank to take out more money for your stupid ass."

We drove in silence to the bank and tow yard, and he paid to have my truck released, then followed me back to my place.

I handed him a beer while we sat on the couch.

"Thanks for everything. I know you're tired of carrying me, but when I get on my feet, I'm gonna pay you back."

He shook his head.

"Right. You and Chance have been sayin' the same shit since we were kids. When will that be, huh?"

"I had a job interview today. That's why I'm all dressed up. I'm legit trying, Scout. I'm just having bad luck."

"This doesn't have shit to do with luck. You can't get out of your own way, and I'm not sure if you'll ever be able to."

I sucked my teeth. "I have to pick Lynn up, so—"

"So that's it? I lay some truth on you, and you just dismiss me? Am I no use to you now that I've served my purpose? You don't care about me, so I guess I'm the real fool because I enable you. Pop always said family should take care of each other, but I can't keep putting myself in debt because of you and Chance."

I was angry at myself, mad about my shitty day, and I felt guilty for the stress I was putting my brother through, but my pride caused me to take my frustrations out on him.

"Look, I appreciate your help," I said, rubbing my hand over my face, "but you don't always have to throw it back in my face and treat me like I'm a fucking loser."

"There's the asshole I know and love! I offered you a steady job, working with me, and you turned me down. Despite your snub, I put you down as an employee so you and your daughter have benefits, but you still can't get it through your hard head that *I'm* not the one holding you back. Your dumb-ass decision-making is."

I was tired of him acting more like my father than my brother. He never acknowledged the shit I did right, and I was sick of him criticizing my mistakes and flaws.

"You need to stop talking to me like I'm a kid. I'm a grown man."

"Is that right? Well, maybe when you start acting like the big man you claim to be, I'll treat you like one. I spent over four grand today on your dumb ass."

"Like I said, I'm grown, and I don't need you for shit. I had a little setback today, but when I get back on my feet—which I will—I'll pay you your damn money. Don't worry. If I need help again, I'll remind myself not to call you."

He laughed. "I'll let myself out. I guess I'll see you again the next time you need something from me."

"Whatever, man."

Scout stomped out of the house and slammed the door behind him.

I had enough shit to be angry about, and I certainly didn't need extra from him.

★ ★ ★

After being cursed out by Irene at Lynn's daycare, I was relieved that Lynn fell asleep on the car ride home. I told Irene the truth about not getting the job, and she called me a bum and told me to never come back. "I'm tired of your bullshit lies, just trying to get me to watch Lynn for free," she said.

Jasmine stopped by after work, and I explained my shitty day to her. We attempted to squeeze in a quickie while Lynn was napping; I needed some loving to relieve me of this stress-filled day.

"Yes, Nick! Yes! Give it to me!"

Jasmine moaned as I spread her legs wide. I pressed her knees to her chest and rhythmically stroked her. My hands pressed down on her hamstrings. She held the back of my neck with one hand and a fistful of sheets in her other.

Suddenly, I thought I heard Lynn crying and calling me. I slowed my strokes and listened to confirm what I heard, with Jasmine still writhing and moaning beneath me.

"No, Nick. Don't you dare stop. I'm so fucking close. Don't do this to me. This is *my* time," Jasmine said with a whimper, pulling my face back to hers.

"Hold on, baby. I think I heard something." I raised up again when the crying became steady. "I have to check on Lynn,"

"She'll live. She ain't going nowhere."

"I'll be right back."

I slid out of her, and she reached up, grabbed my erection, and pulled me back inside her warmth.

Lynn continued to wail.

"Honey, I gotta check on her."

"Get off me then!" Jasmine yelled, pushing me.

"I'm sorry, babe. I'll be right back."

"Don't bother. Way to kill the fucking mood."

I slipped into my underwear and pulled on some sweatpants. I walked in to pick Lynn up from her crib, bounced her up and down, and carried her back to my room.

Jasmine sucked her teeth and grabbed her clothes off the floor when she saw Lynn in my arms.

"She's not the only one who feels like crying," she snapped. "How would you like it if I stopped right before you were about to cum, huh?"

"I had to check on her."

"She could have waited a few damn minutes. You should've finished with me first. You never put me first, and I'm getting tired of it."

"Not today, Jasmine. I have enough stress."

"Well, you need to do yourself a favor and beg Rhea to start watching Lynn again. While you're at it, beg Joe to get your old job back. From what you've told me, you were making consistent money back then, compared to the pennies you're bringing in now."

"I'll think about it."

"Think about it? The way I see it, you don't have much of a choice. You're broke, and I'm already breaking two of my rules by being with you. I don't date poor men...or men with kids," she said, then grabbed my crotch. "You're lucky you have me sprung on this. If your dick wasn't so good, I would've been gone a long time ago."

I smirked, then walked away, with my daughter in my arms.

I managed to rock Lynn back to sleep and placed her gently back in her crib. I returned to my room, stripped Jasmine naked, and finished what we started. I needed to keep her happy.

★ ★ ★

Jasmine was right, so a week later, I decided to set aside my pride and have a heart-to-heart talk with Scout and Rhea.

I woefully carried Lynn up the porch steps of Scout's house. Lynn was sleeping peacefully in my arms while I rang the doorbell.

Scout opened the door, shook his head, and glared at me like I was the last person he wanted to see.

"What do you want?" he asked.

"Who is it, Joe?" Rhea shouted in the background.

"Nobody important," Scout answered. He tried to close the door, but I blocked it with my foot.

"Can I come in?"

"Nope. Now move your foot before I move it for you."

"C'mon…"

Rhea hurried to the door and touched his shoulder. "Baby, he's family," she said.

"Bullshit! He thinks he's slick, bringing the baby with him to guilt-trip me. I don't know why he's here. The last time I saw him, he told me he's a grown man who doesn't need shit from me."

"I didn't mean it. You know that."

"What do you want from me this time, Fool? The only time you give a shit about Rhea or me is when you need something, so let's get this over with."

I felt guilty; in a way, he was right. Still, I needed their help, so I had to swallow my pride and ask for it.

"Rhea, can you please watch Lynn for me during the week, while I go to work?"

She looked at Scout.

"I know you miss her, Rhea. If it's what you want, do it," Scout said.

Rhea gave him a quick peck on the cheek.

"Besides, I know I can't stop you anyway,"

"Damn right," she said jokingly.

Once I had that covered, it was time for the hard part.

"Scout, can you ask Mr. Davis if I can come to his office for a man-to-man talk? I need steady work. He won't answer my calls, and he doesn't let me step foot in his office when I try to stop by. I need work, man. My bills are piling up. You already know I didn't get the job with the hotel. The side work I've been doing is starting to dry up, and I haven't heard anything back from the other jobs I've applied for. I'm dead broke and desperate."

Scout folded his arms and shook his head.

"Sounds like a personal problem if you ask me," he said.

"I barely have money to feed Lynn. I really need your help on this."

"Joe, I know you're mad at your brother, but if you can't do it for him, do it for you niece," Rhea urged. She looked past me and asked, "Hey, isn't that Jimmy walking this way?"

"Well, ain't this a bitch?" Scout said as he caught sight of our brother.

"Joe, calm down. Don't do anything crazy."

"I'm not trying to disrespect you, honey, but whatever happens next, stay out of it. This is a brother thing. I haven't seen that bastard since he stole my TV and your jewelry, and now he thinks he can waltz up here, and all will be forgiven?"

"At least he had the decency to leave my wedding set," Rhea said.

"Rhea, don't try to downplay his fuck-ups."

All the noise woke Lynn up. Rhea picked her up and rocked her, trying to calm her down again.

Scout pushed past me and headed toward our brother.

"Baby, don't do anything stupid," Rhea pleaded.

Scout grimaced and waved her off, then ran toward Chance like a freight train.

Chance looked bad. He was rail thin, and his clothes were dirty and tattered. As soon as Scout approached, he extended his arms to hug him. "I'm sorr—".

Before Chance could finish apologizing, Scout punched him square on the chin, and he collapsed, face first, on the ground.

"Joe!" Rhea screamed. She handed Lynn to me, then ran to Chance's aid.

Scout walked past me and into the house while Rhea frantically checked to see if Chance was okay.

"I guess he's still mad, huh?" Chance asked, rubbing his jaw. "Damn, was I gone that long? When did he have another baby?" he asked, looking at me.

"She's not Scout's. She's mine."

"Shit! He must've hit me harder than I thought. I could swear you just said that baby's yours, Fool."

"Little brother, you've got a lot to catch up on."

★ ★ ★

We finished eating dinner at the table.

"Well, you've still got a mean right hook," Chance joked, holding a towel full of ice on his jaw.

"Shut up. You're lucky I allowed your ass back in my house after the shit you pulled last time."

"I told you I'm sorry," Chance said.

"I don't wanna hear that bullshit," Scout said, shaking his head. "You and Fool are always saying you're sorry, but you don't really mean it, or you'd change."

"I know you're still mad, but I'm clean now. I wasn't in my right mind. You know I never stole anything from family before."

"You should never steal from anyone, period. And you may be clean now, but for how long this time? A week? A month?"

Rhea patted Scout's arm, to calm him down. Scout gave her a reassuring nod.

"I'm for real this time. Sitting' in jail the last couple months, I had a lot of time to think. I'm done with heroin," Chance said confidently.

"You may be done with it, but is it done with you? How's that junkie girlfriend of yours doing?"

"I needed to do this on my own. I knew I'd never get clean if I stayed around Crystal," Chance answered sincerely.

"Well, how do I know that the moment shit gets bad for you, you won't relapse and go right back to shooting up and right back to her?"

"I don't want that life anymore."

"Yeah? I've heard that shit before."

Chance rolled his eyes. "Look, I was just wondering if I could stay with you for a while, till I get on my feet."

"What!? Have you lost your damn mind? You robbed my house while my wife was in the shower. Not only did you steal her jewelry, but you also took our deceased mothers. Hell no, you can't stay in my house."

"Come on, man. I can just stay with Fool upstairs, like last time. I promise I won't even come down here."

"Ah, so you don't know. Big man over there moved out. Maybe Fool's stupid enough to let you stay with him, but it ain't happening here."

Chance turned to me. "Well? How about it, Fool. Can I stay with you?"

"I'm barely making ends meet my damn self. I don't have enough money to take care of me, my daughter, and you."

"You don't have to worry about me, man. I'm a survivor. I just need a place to crash, and I'll figure out a way to eat. While I was locked up, I learned how to cut hair. I can do that around the neighborhood and help you out around the house," Chance offered.

"He'll help you out around the house all right. One day, you'll come home, and it'll be cleaned out after he's stolen all your shit," Scout teased.

I glared at Scout as I said to Chance, "You're family. Of course, you can stay with me. You've made some mistakes, but family forgives and helps you, no matter what."

"Keep talking that shit, and you can forget about me asking Mr. Davis to take your silly ass back," Scout chimed in.

I had no comeback for that, so I simply shut my mouth.

"Thanks, bro," Chance said. "I promise you won't even know I'm there," he assured me, and I hoped I could take him at his word.

★ ★ ★

"Babe, I wanna introduce you to my other brother, Jimmy," I said to Jasmine as I sat on the floor, playing with Lynn and her dolls.

He extended his hand. "My family and friends call me Chance. It's nice to meet you."

Jasmine looked at him skeptically and meekly shook his hand; he was so thin that it was obvious to her that he was a junkie.

"Nick didn't tell me you were so gorgeous," Chance said.

"Thank you," Jasmine said, unaffected by his flirting.

"Chance is gonna stay with me for a while."

He signaled for me to hand Lynn to him, and I was surprised when she seemed so calm in her uncle's arms.

"Yeah, I'm gonna help out around the house to earn my keep. I'll even watch the baby for you two so you can have date nights."

Jasmine's eyes perked up when she heard that. "I love him already," she said.

"I've got some more good news for us, babe. Scout called Mr. Davis, and we have a meeting tomorrow. He might give me my old job back."

"Great. It sounds like you had a good day," she said, giving me a small peck on the lips.

"It'll be even better when I get you in that bedroom tonight."

"Ooh! I like when you get fresh with me."

Chance cleared his throat.

"Oh, sorry about that," I said, having forgotten he was standing there. "I'll clear out the room where I keep my tools, and you can stay there. It's not that big, but at least you'll have your own space."

"No problem, man. I'm just glad to be off the street."

★ ★ ★

The next day, Scout and I went to see Mr. Davis.

"I'm a busy man, Joe. I'll give you five minutes to state your case," he said, pointing at me. "Frankly, you're lucky I'm allowing you to step foot in my office."

I remained quiet, as I didn't want to risk saying anything that might ruin the discussion before it even started.

"Thank you, Mr. Davis," Scout said.

The man only nodded, then looked at me sternly again.

"My brother shouldn't have lied to you," Scout continued. "He tried to apologize, though. I know you're a man who sticks to your word, but I'm asking you to please reconsider and allow Nick to work for you."

"Joe, you're a good man. You're honest and respectful, and you're doing what a good man should do, trying to stick up for your family. What example would I be setting for my son and my workers if I allow a man to openly lie to me and still reward him with work?"

"I think Nick should answer that, sir."

Mr. Davis faced me. "He's right. State your business, young man."

"I was stupid, sir," I began. "I wasn't thinking with the right head. I'm not asking. I'm begging you for help. Joe goes above and beyond to help me out because I'm barely working. I'm not only asking for me, though. I've got a little girl at home. She's the result of my stupid mistake, but now I gotta take care of her. If you'll just give me another chance, I swear on everything that I love that I'll never lie to you again. I need this work."

Mr. Davis let out a long breath.

"I'm getting too damn soft. I'll start you off with small jobs until you earn my trust back."

"Thank you, sir!"

"Don't thank me. If it weren't for your Daddy, your brother, and your child, I wouldn't even be talking to you right now. You can thank them."

"Yes, sir. When can I start?"

★ ★ ★

The next month went smoothly, and Chance was actually a big help. He kept the house clean and watched Lynn when I wanted to be alone with Jasmine. I called and checked on him regularly when he did; I knew I had to be cautious with him around my daughter.

Scout bought Chance some hair clippers and spread the word around the neighborhood that his brother could cut hair. That kept Chance busy, and it also put a little money in his pocket.

I was on edge the first couple days because I wasn't sure if I could have faith in him. Every day, I tested him. I usually kept my bill money in a manila envelope in one of the kitchen drawers. I watched carefully to see if he'd take it, but when I checked again, it was all still there, even though he was aware of where I stashed it. Little by little, Chance began to gain my trust.

Financially, I was also getting back on my feet. The steady money from the gigs Mr. Davis landed for me made life more comfortable, but I was still spending too much money taking Jasmine out all the time. I knew I had to think of some way to pacify her with fun, cheap dates.

★ ★ ★

"Hello, Jasmine. May I take your coat?" Chance asked.

She handed it to him.

"What is all this?" she asked, confused as she looked around at all the candles illuminating my living room, kitchen, and dining room.

"Nick wants this night to be perfect for you," Chance said with a shrug.

"That's right. I wanna treat you like the queen you are," I said, then pulled out her chair at the dinner table.

Jasmine nodded in approval.

"Not bad. In fact, this is all really nice!"

I dimmed the lights while soft music played in the background. I had wine chilling in a bucket of ice on the table.

"I have everything planned," I said, beaming with pride.

"What about your daughter?"

"Luckily, I talked Scout into letting Chance watch Lynn at his place, so we have the whole night to ourselves."

"Ooh! I love the sound of that!"

I heard a car horn and looked out the window.

"There's your ride, Chance," I said, giving Scout a wave.

"All right, I'm almost done," Chance said as he hurriedly packed an overnight bag for Lynn.

I gave him some pocket money. I had promised to give him more to buy dinner for him and Lynn, but I only had five dollars left on me, so I walked to the drawer in the kitchen where I kept my bill money and handed him another twenty.

"Bye, Ladybug. I'll see you tomorrow."

Lynn fussed, cranky and irritable.

"Don't worry. I got her. You two enjoy your night," Chance said, then walked out and closed the door behind him.

I smiled as I reached over and refilled Jasmine's wine glass.

I spent the night spoiling her. I hand-fed her chocolate-covered strawberries while I bathed her. After drying her off, I lathered her up with lotion and gave her a full-body massage. That led to us making love, the way she wanted and deserved.

★ ★ ★

Two months went by, and I tried many variations of that romantic, homemade date, but it didn't seem to cut it anymore. Jasmine wanted to party and travel. She appreciated our time together, but she was getting bored, and I had to think of something quick if I was going to keep her satisfied.

Chance had been doing well, but something felt different about him. I hoped he wasn't thinking about getting high again.

"You don't look so hot," I said to my brother.

"He's fine. You heard him. He said he'll watch her," Jasmine chimed in.

I had promised Jasmine I'd take her on a well-deserved weekend trip to Atlantic City. We were going to have dinner close to home, go clubbing, then drive to Atlantic City around three a.m., while traffic was light.

I had a bad feeling about leaving Lynn with Chance. He hadn't been his regular self lately. He was always fidgety, itchy, and sweating profusely.

"I don't know. I've never left Lynn alone with you for so long," I said. "You sure you can handle this, Chance? You gotta be straight with me, man. Are you using again?"

Chance wrung his hands repeatedly. "Nah, I'm good, man. I'm clean. Y-You still got that fifty bucks for me, right?" he stuttered.

"C'mon, Nick. Just pay him so we can fucking go already," Jasmine bitched.

I reached into my wallet and pulled out the money.

A huge smile spread across Chance's face as he greedily snatched the money from my hands.

"Thanks, brother man. And, hey, if you wanna give me a little extra as a bonus, that's cool too. You don't gotta be a Rockefeller to help a fella! You know what I mean?" Chance said, playfully nudging me.

"Don't push it. Look, I'm trusting you with my daughter, man. This is serious. You can't fuck it up."

"I got this. Relax, brother."

★ ★ ★

On our drive to the restaurant, I had to fight the urge to turn back and cancel our plans, but I managed to get us there on time.

"Hi, I'm Nick Johnson. I have a reservation for two."

"Yes, Mr. Johnson. If you would please follow me..." the hostess said. She then grabbed our menus and led us to a quaint, candlelit table. The dim, intimate lighting gave the restaurant a classy yet comfortable feel.

We had small conversations throughout our meal, but my mind was on Chance and Lynn.

"Nick? Earth to Nick," Jasmine said, snapping her fingers and kicking me under the table.

"Oh, sorry."

"You promised you'd focus on me tonight, and you're a million miles away. I'm about to leave your ass here with your thoughts."

"No, baby, I'm here with you. I've just got this nervous feeling that I should check on Chance." I stood. "I'm gonna call the house, so I'll have a little peace of mind. I'll be right back."

"This is getting real old, Nick."

"I'll be quick."

"Not quick enough," she muttered under her breath as I walked away.

I walked to the phone booths near the bathrooms and dialed. The phone rang, but there was no answer, and that wasn't a good sign. I hung up and dialed again, but still, no one picked up.

"Well? They're good, right?" Jasmine asked when I walked back to the table.

"I'm not sure. Chance didn't pick up the phone, and it's not as if he has a car. Where is he, and why isn't he answering?"

Jasmine groaned. "Don't be so paranoid. He probably fell asleep. Everything is fine, Nick. Tonight's supposed to be about us. Don't you trust your own brother?"

I wanted to answer that I absolutely did, but Chance had a history of being an unreliable fuck-up, and I couldn't put too much faith in him. I had this gnawing feeling that something wasn't right.

"I know tonight's about us, baby, but before we go ahead with it, I gotta stop and check on things. Once I have that peace of mind, I'll be all yours, uninhibited and freaky," I promised, bouncing my eyebrows and flicking my tongue at her.

She reluctantly smiled. "All right. Just make it quick."

★ ★ ★

I pulled up to the house and immediately knew something was wrong. The lights were off, and my door was slightly open. I parked in the driveway and shook my head. "See? Something not right here," I said again.

Jasmine sighed. "He's probably keeping the house dark so the baby will go to sleep quicker."

"But why's my door open?"

"Have you ever smelled your place? It's not the freshest, Nick. Maybe he's airing it out."

"That's too many maybes for my taste. I need to see my daughter."

I crept cautiously to the door and poked my head inside. I heard a faint cry in the distance. "Shit!" I yelled, then ran inside in a panic. "Chance?" I hollered.

There was no answer, and I didn't hear any noise except for the cries of my baby. I was scared that Lynn and Chance were hurt or in danger. *What if one of the drug dealers he deals with found out where he lived and tried to kill him?* I thought, only one of several horrible scenarios that whirled around in my head.

"Chance!" I screamed at the top of my lungs.

The silvery moonlight filtering through the shades gave me a glimpse of my tossed living room. My dinner and coffee tables were overturned, the carpet was scattered with shards of glass, and all the kitchen drawers were open. The envelope I kept my bill money and rent in was empty and tossed to the floor. My stereo and TV were gone, and my furniture was all torn up and ripped open.

I ran from room to room, frantically turning on lights and calling for my brother, with the sound of my baby crying getting even louder as I moved through the house. Jasmine trailed behind me as I bolted into the nursery.

I found Lynn sitting on the floor beside her crib, scared and bawling her head off. I crouched down and took my daughter in my arms, and she instantly calmed down enough for me to check her for any signs of injuries.

"Oh my God! Is she all right?" Jasmine asked.

"She's wet, but she looks okay…just scared."

It was then that the grim reality hit me: *My brother robbed me and left my daughter to fend for herself.* I was angry, hurt, and disappointed. I trusted Chance, and he'd gone and fucked me over. When we were kids, Dad taught us never to steal from family. *I guess heroin erased that lesson from his memory.*

"So I guess our trip is canceled," Jasmine said with a sigh.

"Yeah, I'm gonna have to take a raincheck on that."

"I'm sick of this shit, Nick!" she said, then sucked her teeth like she always did when I made her angry. "Something's gotta give. I know your daughter's a big responsibility, but you're the one who's supposed to be tied down with that, not me. I'm still going out tonight."

"Where?"

"I don't know. I guess I'll call my girls and go to the club like I planned to do with you. I'm gonna enjoy the rest of my weekend. I'll call you later."

I carried Lynn in my arms while I walked Jasmine to the door.

"Nick, I care about you, but if things don't change soon, we're going to have to break this off. I'm not going to waste my time investing any more feelings in a dead-end relationship."

"Things will be better. I promise."

"I hope so," she said, then gave me a quick kiss, "because I really like you. I'll call you tomorrow."

I closed the door behind her and looked down at Lynn, who was smiling up at me, with her little hand in her mouth. I leaned my forehead against hers. "It looks like it's just the two of us, kid."

CHAPTER 5

A SHOCKING ULTIMATUM

Nick

When I couldn't come up with my rent money, it was the straw that broke the camel's back—or at least the landlord's. "I've had enough!" he yelled. "You're always paying me late, making excuses, and I'm sick of it. Get out immediately."

That left me with no choice but to crawl back to Scout again and beg him to help me.

"See? This is exactly why I didn't let him stay with me. You wanted to play the hero and now look at you. He fucked you too."

I covered Lynn's ears at his vulgarity as I bounced her on my lap.

"What do you want from me? More money, I'm guessing."

"I do need money," I said

He threw his hands in the air.

"But it's not like that, Scout," I quickly said. "I was doing a lot better until Chance robbed me."

"I tried to tell you he's no good. He's not our brother when he's shooting up that shit. As for you, you must think I'm made of money. I got bills and shit to take care of too."

Again, I covered Lynn's ears and glared at him.

"Sorry," he said.

"I found another house to rent in Roosevelt. It's smack dab in the roughest part of the 'hood', not the best of areas, but it's cheaper than the place I was staying in. I need to borrow $3,500 to get in it."

"What do you mean, borrow? You and Chance are bottomless pits when it comes to money, and I know I'll never get a cent of it back. Who are you trying to fool with that borrowing stuff?"

I didn't want to be put in the same category as Chance, but I had to bite my tongue. Scout was my only hope. If I had asked him, he probably would've let us move back into my old apartment in his house, but I needed to be on my own. I didn't feel independent when I stayed with him.

"Thanks again for getting my job back with Mr. Davis. I'm working more so I can make a legitimate effort to stop depending on you as much. I really am trying to do better, Scout. You could at least admit that." I said.

"I'm not your get-out-of-jail-free card, Fool. I can't keep bailing you out every time you're in a bind. Who helps me when I need it, huh?"

"I know, and I'm working on it."

"All right, fine. I'll lend you the damn money, but I'm not helping you move."

★ ★ ★

On a rainy Friday, two weeks after I spoke to Scout, I'd spent the bulk of the money he'd given me, to move into my new place. Now, I was sitting on the floor playing blocks with Lynn, feeding her bits of chopped-up hot dogs.

Jasmine looked hot in her short leather jacket and a clingy black skirt, dressed for clubbing. She looked bored and frustrated as she paced next to the window.

"Ugh. Can't you call Rhea and ask her to watch the kid? I wanna go out tonight," she whined. "I'm tired of being cooped up in the house every weekend."

Jasmine fussed with me a lot, but she was a good woman. Sadly, I was extremely low on cash and running out of creative, inexpensive ideas to pacify her.

I stood and wrapped my arms around Jasmine while Lynn walked around on the carpet, playing with her empty plate and fork.

"Baby, I'll ask, but I'm sure Scout will tell her not to help us. I still owe him money. If he knows we're going out, he'll say, 'If you've got money to hang out, you've got money to pay me back.' I'll take you somewhere nice next week. I promise."

The lights flickered, and Lynn let out a shriek, still hanging on to the fork she'd stuck into the wall outlet. Fearing what the electric jolt would do to my little girl, I knew I had to act fast. I grabbed the wooden broom from behind the refrigerator and knocked her away from the wall.

"Oh my God!" Jasmine yelled.

I held Lynn in my arms and stuck my finger under her nose. I was horrified to discover that Lynn wasn't breathing. I checked her pulse and listened for a heartbeat but heard nothing.

"Oh no! She's… Hurry! Call 911!" I yelled to Jasmine in a panic, terrified that I might lose my daughter due to my own irresponsibility. "C'mon, baby. Breathe for Daddy," I begged.

I hurriedly thought back to the classes I'd taken with Vickie before Lynn was born. I wasn't sure if I remembered how to perform CPR on a child, but I had to try. I took a deep breath and gave her mouth-to-mouth, then five chest compressions with my palm over her heart. I frantically repeated the process again and again, praying I'd get a response.

"Babe, EMS is here," Jasmine said, then hurried over to open the door.

The EMTs rushed into the house and pulled out an AED. They placed the pads on her little chest and started the process. It was torturous for me to watch her body jolt with the shocks, but when she fluttered and wailed, alive once again, I let out a sigh of relief.

"Sir, there are burns on her hands that need to be treated, and she could have some internal damage," one of the paramedics said. "We need to take her to the hospital to check for damage to the brain or other organs."

"Yeah, that's fine. Do whatever you need to do. I just need to know she's okay."

"We'll do our best, sir."

Hysterical, I called Scout and Rhea to tell them what had happened. They were just as worried as I was and said they'd meet us at the hospital.

"I'll follow you in my car," Jasmine said.

I nodded and stepped into the ambulance. Seeing my daughter in pain, I realized I was a horrible father. When I saw my little girl hooked up to all those machines and monitors, constantly being pricked with needles and syringes, I felt like I had failed her. I was selfish, always thinking only about myself. At that moment, I made a promise to Lynn and God that I would be a better parent, the father she deserved.

I watched Lynn crying on the gurney and thanked God for not taking my daughter from me.

★ ★ ★

Jasmine, Rhea, Scout, and I spent the rest of the night sitting in the hospital waiting area.

Finally, the doctor stepped into the waiting room.

"How is she?" I asked, quickly rising to my feet.

"Your daughter is going to be okay, Mr. Johnson. She hasn't suffered any permanent damage, but I want to keep her under observation for at least twenty-four hours before we release her."

"Thank God," I said, breathing a heavy sigh of relief.

"She's very lucky to have suffered only minor burns to her hands. They can be treated, but she's going to be in pain. I'll prescribe some acetaminophen for her."

"Thank you, Doctor."

He smiled and walked away.

Scout and Rhea sat down in front of Jasmine and me.

"Fool, you—"

I cut Scout off with a harsh glare, and my aggravated expression signaled to him that I didn't appreciate being called by my nickname in front of my lady.

"Sorry. Nick, let's be real. You're not cut out to be a father. You're more of a...free spirit, someone who wants to party and hang out. You're not the fatherly type, a man who can be responsible and care for a child."

I didn't respond. He and Rhea looked at me as if I was a disappointment, and deep down, I felt like one. I knew part of what he was saying was true, but I thought it best to remain silent and see where he went with it.

He exhaled. "I'm offering you an out. Once again, I'm trying to clean up your bullshit. I already talked to Vickie, and she's ready to sign anything she's gotta sign to forget the whole pregnancy even happened. All that's left is for you to sign your parental rights over to Rhea and me, and we'll raise and take responsibility for Lynn."

"Wait. You contacted Vickie?" I asked angrily.

Scott's tone matched the aggression in mine. "Man, I've bailed you out, paid to get your car out of the repo, got your job back, put you on my company's health insurance, paid for you to move into your first and second places, and... Damn, am I forgetting anything? I've been saving your ass left and right. I figured it would only be a matter of time until you begged me to take Lynn off your hands anyway, so yes, I contacted her mother. She thinks Rhea and I will be better parents too."

"I don't care what that bitch thinks. What does she know about being a parent? You had no right to contact her!" I yelled.

"Gentlemen, please lower your voices, or I'll have to ask you to step outside to finish your conversation," warned the nurse at the desk.

We apologized and lowered our voices, but it wasn't easy.

Honestly, his offer made sense. I knew Scout would probably be a better father than I ever could and that he could at least provide Lynn with a good, stable life. Still, while all that was true, there was no way I would ever give her up. Lynn was my daughter, my flesh and blood, and I had fought for her to be born. I'd also sworn to take care of her, instead of handing her over to the state, and just as I fought for her then, I insisted on fighting for her now.

"Nick, I'm asking this with Lynn's best interests in mind. I'm doing this for both of you," Scout said.

"Really? You sure it not just for you and Rhea? Don't play the good guy with me. I know how bad you two want a baby. No one deserves a child more than you, and you'd be great parents, but that don't give you any right to take mine!"

"You need to watch your mouth before you say something you'll regret. Stop acting like I'm attacking your pride and do what you know is right."

"Bet! Nick, they're right. You should—" Jasmine started.

I raised my hand to stop her mid sentence, then continued talking to my brother. "Scout, what you're saying might be true, but—"

This time, it was Rhea's turn to interrupt me. "Might be true? It's fact! You're too selfish to be a father," she said.

That hurt. I knew she didn't mean it maliciously, but the fact that she believed it showed how little faith she had in me and my character.

"Nick, you need to jump on this," Jasmine said, huffing mad.

"Baby, please," I said, holding my hand up to stop her again. "I got something else I need to say." I then turned to my brother. "Look, Scout, there's no doubt in my mind that you'd be able to give Lynn a better life than me, but—"

"Nick—" Jasmine cut in.

I shushed her and continued, "But Lynn is my daughter. I'm gonna be a man and raise her."

Scout sat back in his chair as Rhea shook her head and chuckled.

"Look where we are, Nick," Rhea said. "You got lucky this time, but what about the next time? Besides, who do you think will pay this bill for her hospital stay? You? No way! As always, Joe will be left to pick up the pieces and fix your problems."

I couldn't argue with that. I didn't have money for Lynn's prescriptions or any other expenses, but I still wasn't going to give up my daughter.

"Just sign the fucking kid over, and let's move on with our lives. You can always visit her," Jasmine blurted, coldly rolling her eyes.

"C'mon, baby. This is an important family decision."

"Well, you need to make the *right* decision."

"You're making this harder than it already is."

"Do you feel we have a future together, Nick?" she asked, arching an eyebrow at me.

"Of course, I do, but this isn't about us."

"It is too! In fact, this has everything to do with us. Do my feelings ever even cross your mind?"

The decision to keep and raise my child had nothing to do with Jasmine, but I had to let her vent. No matter what, she always found a way to get her two cents in, and then some.

"When we first met, I told you I don't like children, that I don't want any and don't usually date men who have any. You begged me to give you a chance, and you promised your kid wouldn't affect or interfere with our relationship, yet here we are." She looked me in the eyes and said, "Think what you'll gain by signing her over. You'll get back that freedom you lost when she was born. No more checking in and no more waking up in the middle of the night to take care of her." She took my hand in hers, and her expression softened. "Not only that, but it'll be just us, baby, just me and you."

"You don't understand the magnitude of what you're asking of me," I said. "This isn't a stuffed animal or a pet. This is my kid we're talking about."

Jasmine frowned. "I never thought it would come to this, but you've left me no choice. What's it gonna be, Nick? A life of happiness with me or a life of misery raising your daughter?"

"That's not fair! After everything that's happened recently and tonight, how can you even ask me to make a decision like that?"

"Because you're in a losing battle, and you're dragging me along with you. Let me make this really simple for you. You either agree to sign your child over to them, or I'm gone. It's your child or me."

"Don't say that. Don't put me in that position with an ultimatum like that."

"I already said it, and you're already in it. Now, what's it gonna be, Nick?"

"Jasmine, you know I care for you, but if it really comes down to you or my daughter… It's gonna be her. I won't abandon her like her mother did."

"Well, in that case, I guess we're done here," Jasmine said. Tears streamed down her face as she stood and jogged to the exit.

I caught up with her and reached for her arm, but she pulled away from me. I sprinted in front of her, cutting her off.

"Wait! Can you please talk to me? Don't leave like this, baby."

Jasmine pushed past me, continued toward the exit, and walked to her car.

"Baby, please talk to me!" I cried from behind her.

Jasmine stopped, leaned against the car, shook her head, and said, "How did we get here, Nick?"

I shrugged. I had no idea what the right words were for such a predicament, but I knew I had to say something.

"Stay. We don't have to end our relationship tonight."

"If you let Joe take care of Lynn, I'll stay."

"I can't do that."

Jasmine frowned, shoved me, and turned to open her car door. "Take care of your daughter. I've wasted damn near two years of my life fucking with you. I should have trusted my gut, and stuck with my intuition. Goodbye, Nick. Don't ever call me or contact me again. I want nothing to do with you."

With that, she slammed her door and sped off, leaving me standing there in the hospital parking lot.

I slowly walked back inside, feeling defeated.

Scout was waiting for me at the door and patted me on the back, then led me back to where Rhea was seated.

"Despite everything that just happened, you did the right thing. As a man, I think you're fucking nuts," Scout said, "but as your big brother, I couldn't be prouder of you. You made the choice to be a father to your daughter, so now you have to live up to it."

I sucked my teeth. "Couldn't be prouder of me? This is your fucking fault. If you wouldn't have spewed that bullshit about me signing Lynn over to you, Jasmine and I wouldn't have broken up."

Rhea held Scout's arm to keep him from attacking me.

"What!?" Scout said, not bothering to lower his voice this time. "You're gonna try to pin this shit on me when I've been taking care of all your responsibilities? Don't worry, you ungrateful motherfucker. After today, you'll be on your own. We're not helping you with shit from here on out." He then turned to Rhea, seeking her approval. "Right, honey?"

"Joe, we can't spite Lynn because of Nick's silliness. Let's all calm down, and then we can talk about this," she said, glancing over at the nurse, who appeared to be frustrated with the volume again.

"No, Rhea. I need you in my corner on this. Fool is a thankless piece of shit, and we're not gonna help him out anymore, period."

Rhea reluctantly nodded.

"That's fine with me," I said.

Scout shook his head and looked at me as if I was pathetic. He turned to Rhea and said, "Let's go, babe. We're done with him."

She nodded and got up to follow him, and they left me sitting there.

Damn. I need this shit to stop, I thought as I sat there alone. Why does everything have to fall down around me all the damn time?

CHAPTER 6

WOMEN

Nick, Five Years Later

"Oh my God," Debbie said, moaning.

I met her at a party a month earlier, when I went out with Vince and Cyrus. We'd been out on a few dates since, and we had just recently begun having sex regularly.

"Right there, baby. Don't stop!" she begged.

Debbie's strong orgasm caused her head to sway from side to side, and she dug her fingernails deep into my back. I kept pumping, and I felt the pressure of my own orgasm building.

"Daddy! Daddy!"

I tried to ignore Lynn's continuous call and continued trying to get my rocks off before I went to see what she wanted.

Suddenly, Lynn opened my door and rubbed her eyes. "Daddy?"

Debbie and I both jumped and covered our naked bodies with the blankets and sheets.

"Ladybug, you need to knock before you open Daddy's door," I scolded.

"I'm sorry, Daddy, but I'm scared. I had a nightmare, and there are monsters under my bed," she said, crying.

"It's okay," I said with a sigh, "and there are no such things as monsters under the bed, baby."

"Uh-huh! Can I sleep in your bed with you and your friend?"

"No, uh…gimme a minute, okay? Go sit on the couch, and I'll

be right there,"

She continued to rub her eyes, yawned, then finally did as I said.

"I guess that's my cue to leave," Debbie said.

"No, baby, please don't. I didn't even get to... Stay," I pleaded.

It was too late, though, because she'd already stepped into my bathroom to shower.

I sulked, rolled the condom off my unsatisfied erection, then threw it in the trash next to my bed. I lay there, frustrated that I didn't get to finish.

The water stopped, and I glanced through the open door of the bathroom and saw Debbie in her panties, putting her bra on and slathering her body with lotion.

"Tonight was fun until we got distracted," she said. "You've got my number, we can meet up sometime next week. Hopefully, there won't be any interruptions next time."

I shook my head and half-heartedly laughed. Once she finished dressing, I walked her to the door.

"Don't look so sad. I'll see you next week. Look at it this way. At least you know I was pleased!"

"Lucky me," I said jokingly.

We shared a laugh, and I gave her a kiss goodbye.

After Debbie left, I stepped into the living room and saw Lynn sound asleep on the couch. I smiled, lifted her gently, and carried her to her room.

I wasn't too mad about the Debbie situation. I knew nothing was going to come out of our fling anyway. She was just like Jasmine and wasn't ready to be tied down with children. Clearly, I hadn't learned my lesson about dating women like them.

For the last five years, half a damn decade, I had wasted time and money buying drinks and going on dates with women who wouldn't give me the time of day or take me seriously because I had a daughter at home. In the past, I never dealt with women who had kids. I always figured there'd be too much baby-daddy drama, and I didn't want to fight with their kids, so I steered clear of Mommas in general. Now, the tables were turned, and I was the one constantly being dropped because I had a child.

It didn't take long for me to realize that raising a daughter was fucking hard. Over the years, there were many times when I had to set my pride aside and admit that I needed help. There were just some things I couldn't do on my own, and I had to rely on women to teach me.

Scout and I talked sporadically, but luckily, Rhea was glad to give me help whenever I needed it. Scout knew she was helping me out, but it was a don't-ask/don't-tell situation: As long as Rhea didn't tell him she was coming over to help me, he didn't question her whereabouts. Rhea taught me how to do Lynn's hair and how to properly bathe her. Not only that, but she was the tough one whenever Lynn needed to be disciplined.

As Lynn physically matured, I could easily see traces of me in her face, but she mostly looked like Vickie. I loved Lynn, but she was also a constant reminder of my stupidity.

Over time, I realized I had to stop dating childless, carefree women. Of course, I slipped every now and then, as I had with Debbie, but I knew I needed a woman who was in the same boat as I was, one who could understand where I was coming from.

One thing I did promise myself was that I wouldn't settle for an ugly soccer mom. I had to find someone sexy and strong, a woman who would be a good role model for Lynn.

★ ★ ★

I hadn't slept since Vince, Cyrus, and I decided to stay up all night drinking and playing poker in my living room. I was somewhat sobered up, but I made coffee to make sure I was good to drive Lynn to school for her first day of first grade.

"Wake up, Ladybug. You got to get ready for school," I said, nudging her gently.

She continued to sleep peacefully.

I pulled the covers off her and gently shook her. "Ladybug, c'mon now. You have to get up."

Lynn's eyes slowly fluttered open. "Daddy, I'm tired," she said in her sleepy voice.

"I'm tired, too, but you got to get ready. You don't want to be late, do you?"

"No."

I picked Lynn up and carried her to the bathroom, then ran some water in the tub to give her a bath. That was never a quick process with her, so I thanked God I'd woken her up early enough to get her ready, and I was glad that splashing around in the water seemed to liven her up a bit.

Ring!

"That should be Aunt Rhea," I said when I heard the doorbell. "Lotion up and get dressed, Lynn."

"Okay, Daddy."

I opened the door, and Rhea kissed me on the cheek as she walked in.

"Good morning. How's it going?" she asked.

"Pretty good. Can you help me fix her hair? I still haven't mastered that yet."

"I noticed. She looked like a hot mess the other day. Don't worry. I got it."

I shamelessly poured some schnapps into my coffee while I made Lynn's cereal.

"It's kind of early to be drinking, isn't it?" Rhea asked.

I winked. "It's never too early. You want some?"

"I'll pass."

"Morning, Aunt Rhea," Lynn chirped as she walked into the kitchen.

"Good morning, baby girl. Come here and let me do your hair."

Lynn sat in the chair while Rhea stood behind her with a comb and some grease.

"Ow! Dang, Aunt Rhea. That hurts."

"Oh hush, child. Your hair is too straight for you to be so tender-headed." Rhea quickly braided Lynn's hair into two ponytails, then headed back home to make breakfast for Scout before he left for work.

"All right. Hurry and eat. You got ten minutes," I said, then turned on the small TV in the kitchen so she could watch her cartoons before school.

Thoroughly engrossed in her show and not paying attention, Lynn accidentally spilled her cereal all over her clothes.

"Shit!" I yelled.

"Ooh! Daddy said a bad word."

I sighed. "I know. I'm sorry for cussing, but we don't have time for this. Hurry and change…and brush your teeth, Ladybug," I yelled as she rushed out of the kitchen.

I cleaned up the mess while she changed and brushed, and we made a mad dash to my truck. I fastened her into the booster seat and threw her book bag on the front passenger seat.

Worried, I quizzed her during the entire ride to school. After all, my little girl was about to start first grade, and it was a milestone for us both. She was no longer in preschool or kindergarten; she was growing up.

"You know our phone number and address, right?"

"Yes, Dad."

"If a stranger comes up to you, what should you do?"

"Scream and look for a cop or teacher. Daddy, I know what to do."

Lynn held my hand and stayed close to my side as I walked her into the building.

"Aunt Rhea is going to pick you up, but as soon as I get home, I want to know everything about your first day, okay?"

"Yes, Daddy."

We hugged, and she ran into her class. I smiled as I watched her interact with the other kids.

"They grow up fast, don't they?" a man asked from behind me.

I turned around and saw an Asian guy, looking into my daughter's class.

"Yeah, it's weird," I answered. "I mean, I'm excited but worried about her at the same time."

"I know the feeling. I'm Peter Yee. My son James is in your daughter's class."

I looked around, but I didn't see any Asian kids in the classroom.

He noticed the questioning look on my face and explained,

"James is, uh…mixed. My wife's Hispanic," he said, pointing at a Latino-looking boy in the crowd of kids.

"Oh, that's cool, man. It's good to see I'm not the only father here who's a little uncomfortable on the first day."

"Yeah, man. Our kids are extensions of ourselves. We'll never stop worrying about them."

Peter and I chitchatted about sports a bit before we went our separate ways, and I went to work a little less worried about Lynn after talking to him.

★ ★ ★

As soon as I walked through the door, Lynn ran to me excitedly. "Daddy!" she screamed.

I picked her up and spun her around. Worked sucked, and my life was pretty shitty in general, but Lynn was so happy to see me when I came home at the end of the day, and that gave me the strength and faith to believe things would get better.

Lynn pulled me by the hand, leading me into the living room. "C'mon, Daddy! You said you'd play Ninja Turtles with me."

I laughed. "Gimme a minute, Ladybug. I just got here," I said, then turned to give Rhea an appreciative hug. "And how was *your* day?"

"Meh, I can't complain. Do you still need me to watch Lynn later?"

"Yeah, if you don't mind. I'm going out with Vince and Cyrus tonight, but it shouldn't be an all-night affair."

"Mm-hmm. Well, I'll tell Joe I'm going to stay until you get back."

"I won't be home too late."

"Yeah, I've heard that one before."

"He'll be mad, huh?"

"Your brother is used to you by now, Nick."

"Love ya, Rhea."

"Pssh. You just love my babysitting. Hurry now. Your daughter is waiting for you to play with her," she said, smiling at me.

When I finally walked into the living room, I found Lynn impatiently tapping her little foot and staring at me, with her arms crossed. "C'mon, Dad," she said.

Rhea laughed when she saw her.

"When your daughter says, 'Let's play,' I guess you gotta play," I said with a shrug.

"I'll get started on dinner," Rhea volunteered.

"You're not going home to eat with Scout?"

"No. He's been under a lot of stress lately, trying to build his business up and working long days and nights to get things organized. He's got a lot of new government contracts now. It brings in steady work, but most nights, I don't even get to have dinner with him. Tonight's going to be one of those nights."

I nodded, then turned to play with Lynn. I helped her with her homework while Rhea made dinner, and after we had eaten, I got ready to go out with my boys while Rhea got Lynn ready for bed.

"Aunt Rhea, can you read to me before I go to sleep?" Lynn asked politely.

"What do you say, sweetheart?"

"Please?"

"C'mon," Rhea said, picking up a storybook.

Lynn sat on Rhea's lap, rested her head on her shoulder, and pointed at the pictures. Truly, I envied their relationship. Lynn and I were close, but I felt like she cared more about Rhea than she cared about me.

The doorbell rang, and I greeted Vince and Cyrus at the door, both of them looking quite dapper. Vince's pinstriped suit seemed to swallow his thin frame, and Cyrus was sporting a navy-blue suit that looked like it was painted on him. He was in good shape and liked to flaunt his physique to the ladies.

"Cyrus, you need to buy your suits in your size, man," I chided.

"You don't know what you're talking about. This suit looks fly. Can you hurry and get ready so we can go?"

"In a minute." I pointed to Vince. "As for you, take that damn toothpick outta your mouth, man. You ever wonder why you've been striking out with women lately? No woman wants to see that shit."

Rhea walked in the living room and said, "He's right. No respectable woman wants to see a man twirling a toothpick around like some type of pimp."

"I'm not looking for the *respectable* ones," Vince casually admitted, with a smirk on his face. "I'm looking for the slutty ones!"

"You ain't shit, Vince," Rhea said with a laugh, shaking her head at him.

"You're lookin' good tonight, Rhea," Cyrus said.

"Hey! Stop hitting on my sister-in-law," I said, smacking Cyrus upside his head.

"I can't help it. She's hot."

"And *respectable*," Rhea said, raising her hand and wiggling her occupied ring finger. "I'm flattered, Cyrus, but I'm happily married."

"Damn," Cyrus said, snapping his fingers.

She laughed again, then turned to me. "Nick, I'm gonna take Lynn home with me. Joe's on his way home, and I haven't seen him all day. I packed a bag for her, and she's already in her pajamas. I'm sure once I get her in the car, she'll be conked out before I reach the house."

"Thanks again. I'll pick her up in the morning."

"Bye, guys. I know it's going to be hard, but don't do anything stupid tonight."

"We can't promise that," Vince joked.

I thanked Rhea again, kissed sleepy Lynn goodbye, and got ready for my night out.

★ ★ ★

At The Tunnel on 12ᵗʰ Avenue in Manhattan, Vince and Cyrus leaned up against the wall, sipping Hennessey and firing off pick-up lines to every woman who passed them. I joined them in the fun, staring at women's asses and scanning the room, trying to decide who I would approach next.

"Looky here, looky here! Those two over there got it goin' on!" Vince said, nodding his head in their direction.

I looked at the ladies he was talking about, and he was right. They were both tall and shared the same caramel complexion, thick thighs, and huge tits. In fact, there was such a resemblance between them that I was sure they had to be related.

"Vince, you ready to show Nick, here, how to take home the baddest women in the club?" Cyrus asked.

"Let's do this!" Vince answered.

Cyrus approached the thicker of the two women and asked, "What's up, ladies? Y'all wanna dance?"

The women laughed in their faces and turned away from them.

"Fuck these stuck-up bitches!" Vince shouted.

Every guy in the place tried to run their Mack-daddy lines on the women, but they weren't having it. The ladies basked in the flattery but dismissed nearly every guy immediately.

They were intimidating, but I didn't let that stop me from trying. I loved a challenge! I weaved through the crowd and approached the woman Cyrus had hit on earlier. We made eye contact, but the smile on her face immediately waned. Not one to be easily defeated, I sipped my beer and strolled around her.

"Excuse me. Is this seat taken?"

"It's a free country."

There was some apprehension in her voice, rejection even, but I was up for the challenge.

I laughed and introduced myself, "I'm Nick Johnson."

"*Dick* Johnson?" she asked, annoyed.

"No, Nick, *Nick* Johnson. What's your name?" I asked, smiling and extending my hand.

She looked me up and down, inspected me from my hair to my clothes and shoes, then turned her head and took a drag on her cigarette. "Hazel...and I'm not interested," she said.

She was definitely the hottest woman in the club, but she wasn't the only attractive one here. I thought about moving on to a less bitchy woman but figured if I was persistent, I could at least get her number and end the otherwise unproductive night on a positive note.

"Can I buy you another drink?"

"You can, but I still won't be interested."

"Can I ask you for a favor?"

"Depends," she snapped with a shrug. "What's the favor?"

"Can we sit here, enjoy some drinks, and get to know each other? After you get to know me, if you're still not interested, I promise I'll leave you alone to enjoy your night. Can you do that?"

She sighed, took another long drag on her cigarette, and let the smoke slowly waft out of her mouth. "I guess."

"And who's this pretty lady next to you?"

The woman next to Hazel laughed at me as if I was pathetic.

"This is my sister, Dominique. Look, why don't you just state your business so we don't waste any more of each other's time?"

I pulled my chair closer to her.

"Before we even start, do you have a job?" she asked.

"Yes, I work."

"What do you do?"

"I specialize in home repair and construction."

"So basically, you're just a handyman," she said, darting her eyes around at the other men in the club, as if I wasn't the least bit important and didn't deserve her attention.

I didn't appreciate her talking down about my profession, so I asked bluntly, "Would you prefer me to sell drugs or some other illegal shit? Look, I may not be rich, but I'm not poor either. I make honest money, and I work hard for it."

Hazel sipped her drink and eyed me over the rim of her glass. The slight grin on her face showed that she liked my aggression. "I respect that," she said. "You still have my attention, so go on. Tell me more about yourself."

I spoke over the noise and told her the truth about where I was in life, and I also mentioned that I had a daughter at home. I didn't feel like hiding shit from her and wasting time. If she accepted my truth, we could move forward; if not, I would keep it moving and find some other woman. Instead of being turned off by the fact that I had a daughter, it seemed to capture her interest, and that only made her more interesting to me.

The loud thumping of the blaring music made it difficult for us to hear each other, so we stopped trying to have a conversation. In the few minutes of small talk we did manage to make, I learned that Hazel had two kids, a son, and a daughter. They both had different daddies, but neither man was in their lives.

"You wanna dance?" I asked.

"Sure, if you think you can keep up."

"I know I can."

"Prove it!"

On the dance floor, Hazel grinded on me and rubbed her ass against my crotch. I showed her what I was working with, leaning against her closely so she could feel my erection. All the while, Vince and Cyrus were by the bar, flirting with Dominique and rooting for me.

Hazel and I danced to a few songs, even a slow one, but as soon as the last one was over, she brushed me off, just as she had all the other men who'd approached her that night.

I wrote down my number on a coaster from the bar, but I didn't bother to ask her for hers.

"I hope I hear from you. If not, it was good talking with you tonight," I said as I handed it to her. I felt like a chump when she grabbed it and waved me off, but I said, "I like feisty women who keep me on my toes."

"That's good to know. I intimidate most brothas."

"Strong women only intimidate *boys*, not men."

"I guess we'll see. Goodnight, Nick."

★ ★ ★

A week had passed. It was early Saturday morning, and Lynn was throwing punches at my palm.

"Nick, stop teaching that child how to fight. She's a girl, not a boy," Rhea said.

"Even little girls should know how to defend themselves."

"I guess."

My phone rang, and I quickly answered it: "Hello?"

"Hi. This is Hazel. We met at The Tunnel last week."

"Oh, hi! It's good to hear from you."

"I found the coaster you wrote your number on in my car. Out of all the so-called players who've approached me lately, you're the only one who seems like a decent man."

"Thanks."

"I usually don't call guys who give me their numbers at clubs, but I guess everything happens for a reason. There has to be a purpose to why I found your number today."

I can't wait to brag to Vince and Cyrus about this, I thought with a smile on my face.

"I agree. What's your schedule like? Maybe we can have dinner one night this week."

"What are you doing right now? My sister is watching my kids."

"Well, I'm home with my daughter right now, and—"

"That's good. What's your address? I'll stop by, and you can take me to breakfast."

"Right now?"

"Who is that?" Rhea mouthed to me.

I covered the receiver and answered, "A woman I met at the club."

Rhea shook her head. "Oh, God. Not another one," she murmured.

"Yeah, now. Why? You got something to hide?" Hazel asked.

"No. It's just... Well, I didn't think you'd be ready to meet my daughter on a first date."

"This isn't a date, Nick. It's an interview, to see if you're worth my time."

"Wow. You're really direct," I said with a laugh.

"I say what I mean and mean what I say."

"And I dig that."

"So what's your address?"

I told her where I lived, and within the hour, she was pulling up in her fully loaded Landrover.

"It's good to see you again," I said, then kissed her on the cheek.

Rhea stepped out of the house. "All right, Nick. Joe made plans for the two of us today, so I need to head out," she announced.

Hazel glanced back and forth between Rhea and me. "Whoa now! Who's this?" she asked, looking at Rhea suspiciously.

Just as I was about to explain, Rhea beat me to it. "Hi. I'm Nick's sister-in-law, Rhea," she said, extending her hand.

Hazel stared her up and down.

Rhea pulled her hand back and returned the attitude.

"Hazel, this is my daughter's *aunt*."

"You sure it's not more than that?"

Pissed, I retorted, "Look, this is my brother's wife, and I don't appreciate you even insinuating that there's more to it than that."

Hazel backed down, and her face relaxed a bit as she turned to face Rhea.

"Sorry about that. I've dated so many dogs that it has me tripping. Plus, after dealing with my children's fathers, I have trust issues with men."

Rhea's eyes were still tight. "I'm sorry to hear that, but you sure aren't making a good first impression," she said, then turned to me. "Good luck with this one, Nick." With that, she walked away.

I walked Hazel into the living room and introduced her to Lynn. "Ladybug, this is Daddy's friend, Ms. Hazel. Hazel, this is my daughter, Lynn."

"Hi," Lynn said timidly.

Hazel grunted. "She looks awfully white. Is her mother Spanish or something?"

Lynn looked down at the floor as if she'd been insulted.

"Italian," I said.

"Interesting. You don't look like the type of brotha who'd be a sellout," Hazel said.

I laughed at her frankness. She was a bitch, but she was sexy, especially in her blue blouse with skintight leather pants. Hazel was tall for a woman, about five-eight, but her heels made her legs look even fuller and longer. She was thick in all the right places.

She bent down and asked Lynn, "How old are you, little girl?"

"I'm 7," Lynn said.

"Hmm. My kids are older. My daughter Carmella is 10, and my son, LJ, is 9. Maybe one day, I'll bring them here so y'all can play."

I liked the sound of that since Lynn wasn't really around kids except at school. I was sure a playdate would be good for her.

"Where do you want to have breakfast?" I asked.

"The South Bay Diner would be nice," Hazel responded.

"Where's that?"

"Lindenhurst."

"Daddy, can I have pancakes?" Lynn asked.

"Sure, Ladybug. Let's go."

As we walked to my truck, Hazel scrunched up her face in disapproval.

"Uh-uh," she said. "Let's take my car, but you can drive." She tossed me the keys.

At the diner, we enjoyed scrambled eggs, bacon, pancakes, and coffee. The waitress thought Lynn was adorable and gave her some coloring books and crayons to entertain her while Hazel and I talked.

Hazel told me more about her children's fathers and her dream of becoming the next Whitney Houston.

"Damn. Beauty *and* talent? Let me hear something, girl."

Hazel nodded, cleared her throat, and began singing loudly, right there in the diner. She was decent, but she was no star. Still, I was sure she would land a record deal on her beauty and tenacity alone. She told me about all the places where she'd performed and the industry stars she'd met. I was impressed. Whenever she talked about music, the sparkle in her eyes made it clear that singing was her passion.

Back at my place, Lynn ran around the house and played with her toys all day while Hazel and I continued chatting. As we sat on the couch, she told me all about her goals and fears, as well as a little more about her baby-daddies.

"My story's a lot like most single women's. I'm an independent woman, raising two kids on my own," she said proudly.

I nodded.

"I'm always working for that big record deal, performing at clubs, talking to music executives, and saving for studio time for my demo tape. The window to become a star in the industry is small, so if I'm gonna do this, I gotta do it now."

"Juggling all that stuff and being a mother must be time-consuming."

"It is, but my sister helps out a lot. I'm always on the go. I know I don't have time to waste, so that's why I'm so picky and come across as a bitch when I'm out. I do it to weed out all the men who aren't worth my time. I'm sorry I acted like that with you. You're a good brotha, Nick."

"Don't worry. I didn't take it personally," I said. "Besides, I like a woman with a little…attitude."

"Good. I'm only like this because my kids' fathers are losers and set me back."

"What are they like?"

"My oldest is Carmella, and her father's name is Cameron. We had a lot in common. He was trying to break into the music industry too. He owns a small recording studio in Hempstead. Stupid me! I mixed business with pleasure and ended up going into debt and eventually bankruptcy trying to help his dumb ass with his business.

On top of that, I ended up pregnant. Everything changed between us after that. He wanted me to have an abortion, and I refused. Now, we can't stand each other. He hates me and holds some sort of foolish grudge because he feels like I trapped him, but as long as he pays his child support; I don't give a shit if he wants nothing to do with our daughter."

"Damn. I'm sorry."

"I don't need pity. I'm doing fine," Hazel said defensively.

"It's not pity, baby. I admire your strength."

"Thanks."

"Tell me about your son's dad."

"There's really not much to say about him. I'll be honest. When I met him, I was in my bad-boy phase. Lamar is the typical drug dealer. He dresses nice and always has money, but he's not the marrying type. We're cordial, and he sends money every month, but he wants nothing to do with his son. I want a man who'll be a good father figure to my kids, and I don't think that's too much to ask."

"I'm looking for the same for Lynn, a good Momma."

"I want to have another child in the future too."

"Hmm. I haven't put much thought into that, but I guess I wouldn't be opposed to it down the road," I said, considering it for the first time.

I went on to tell her about my experience with Vickie and the struggles I'd faced raising Lynn without a mother.

"I love that you take care of your daughter. Real men do that. You're cute, too, so you get extra points."

We laughed.

"Boy, you weren't kidding about this being an interview, huh?"

"Nope," she said emphatically, shaking her head. "I'm feeling you so far, Nick. Who knows? Maybe we've both found what we've been looking for."

CHAPTER 7

PLAYDATES

Nick

"Give it back!" Lynn screamed.

"Relax. Nobody wants your ugly doll anyway," Carmella said.

LJ laughed as his sister and Lynn squabbled.

"Humph," Lynn grunted, then ran over to me. "I don't like them, Daddy," she tattled.

"Maybe they don't like you either," Hazel said.

"Babe, please. That's not helping."

"I don't care. You're daughter's a spoiled little brat," Hazel said.

"All of you need to knock it off," I said to the kids.

"I'm not doing anything to them. They're bothering me. Yell at them or do something. You never stick up for me, Dad," Lynn whined.

"Carmella, LJ, Lynn is younger than you two. Please be nicer to her," I said.

"Wow. You sure told them, Daddy," Lynn said sarcastically.

Lynn sulked and watched the trees whiz by as I drove. The past few times we'd brought the kids together, they'd been at each other's throats. Hazel's kids constantly ganged up on Lynn, but part of me wanted to toughen my daughter up, so I let it slide. Streetwise, I felt she was equivalent to a housecat, while Hazel's kids were more like tough alley cats. I wanted Lynn to be able to handle herself in the real world, so for the most part I didn't interfere. Hazel wasn't a fan of me disciplining her kids, but while we clashed on that often, we always made up later.

"All right, Nick, I think the kids have had enough fun for today," Hazel said when we got back to my place. "We're gonna head home. Walk me to my car so I don't get mugged or shot," she joked.

"My neighborhood isn't that bad," I said.

"Oh yeah? Then why are the cops on your block every other minute?"

I had no answer for that, so I just turned to talk to my daughter. "Lynn, come with me to say goodbye to everyone."

"Do I have to?"

"Yes, you have to."

Lynn sulked and stomped toward the door. "I can say goodbye from here," she grumbled.

"Come on, Ladybug. Don't be like that."

When we walked outside, one of my childhood acquaintances, Zeke drove down the block. He was a big-time drug dealer, and I knew he used to sell to Chance and probably still did. I wasn't a fan of his, but I preferred to keep things cool, rather than making a dangerous enemy. Zeke gave me a cordial wave, and I returned it with a nod.

Hazel was right about the area. There were junkies two houses down, leaning against the fence and nodding off. The corner was home to young brothas who were always fighting. Before that fight turned into a shootout, I quickly kissed Hazel and sent her on her way.

"Let's go inside and get ready for bed, Lynn."

"Is Aunt Rhea coming to tuck me in?"

"Not tonight."

Lynn sucked her teeth. "Aw, man. Why not?"

"She's spending time with Uncle Scout."

"Well, I hope she reads *him* a good bedtime story then," she said rolling her pretty eyes.

★ ★ ★

Lynn took a bath, brushed her teeth and changed into her pajamas before I tucked her into bed.

"Daddy?"

"Yes, Ladybug?"

"How come you never stick up for me when LJ and Carmella fight with me?"

"I do."

"It doesn't feel like it. They're always making fun of me, and I hate it."

"You'll be all right. You're tough."

Lynn looked disappointed. After thinking for a moment, she asked, "Daddy?"

"Yes, Ladybug?"

"Am I Black?"

"Why are you asking that, baby?"

"Carmella, LJ, and the kids at school say that even though I walk, talk, and act white, I'm really Black."

"Okay. Um…where are we going with this?"

"Well, am I?" she asked with tears in her eyes. "I need to know what I am, Daddy."

I was confused as to why she was so upset, but I wanted to answer her the best I could. "You're half-Black, but most people in the world would consider you just Black, so I'd say yes, you're Black, honey."

"But I don't wanna be!" she shouted.

Taken aback by her emotional response, I frowned and shifted in my chair. "What!? Why the hell not?" I yelled.

Lynn looked up at me. "Because black people are bad, Daddy."

"Who the hell told you that bullsh…" I took a deep breath and willed myself to calm down. "Why do you think that, Lynn?"

"Because every day when we come home, I see the guys on the corner either selling drugs or taking them, and they're all Black."

"So?"

"Dad, I see Black guys around our neighborhood getting arrested every day. When Aunt Rhea and I go to the corner store, she always says we have to walk on the other side of the street because those same Black guys are out there fighting, smoking, drinking, and rolling dice. That's all they do every day, except when the policemen take them to jail."

I shook my head, struggling to find an answer for her.

Lynn continued, "On TV and in the movies, lots of the bad guys are Black. They kill, steal, and hurt people."

I closed my eyes, took another deep breath, and exhaled slowly. I didn't want to lash out and further tarnish her view of our people, but I needed to make a point.

"I'm Black. Am *I* bad?"

She shook her head slowly and said, "No."

"Your Uncle Scout and Aunt Rhea are Black. Are they bad?"

"No," she said again.

"Have you ever seen me, your uncle, or your aunt do any of those things you mentioned?"

"No, but you guys are different 'cause—"

"We're not different," I said, interrupting her. "The color of a person's skin doesn't make them bad or good. A person's actions determine that. There are good and bad people in every race."

"I know, but—"

"But what? Your mother is White, and I'm Black. Both of us are a part of you, and hearing you say you don't want to be Black makes me feel like you wish I weren't your Daddy."

Lynn reached up to hug me. "I didn't mean it like that, Dad. I'm sorry."

"As you get older, you're going to hear people say a whole lot of mean things about Black people, Ladybug. Always remember that you have both Black and White blood in you, and that makes you who you are. Never hate anyone based on their race, whether they are Black or White or any other race."

"Ok, Daddy, can you tell me more about mommy now?"

"Maybe another night, baby."

★ ★ ★

The next day, I introduced Hazel and her kids to Scout and Rhea. While Scout entertained the young folks, I pulled Rhea into the kitchen.

"Rhea, can you set aside that first meeting and try to like her?"

"I'll try, but I can't make any promises," she said.

"Okay. Can you talk to Lynn later too? Last night, she asked me if she's Black."

"I knew that was coming. What did you tell her?"

"I told her the truth. I told her she's mixed, but most people will view her as just Black."

"How did she take that?"

"She cried. I told her not to judge people by their race or color, but individually, by their actions."

"Aw. Okay. I'll talk to her about it tonight."

"She asked about Vickie too."

"Did you tell her anything about her?"

"Nah, I'll save that for another time."

"Don't put it off too long, Nick. You're gonna have to face that sooner rather than later."

"One step at a time, Rhea. Right now I'm trying to get things right with Hazel."

"Ugh. You're such a sucker for a pretty face and a fat ass."

I winked.

When we walked back into the living room, Hazel was singing for Scout.

"Wow. That was...something," Scout said.

Hazel sucked her teeth. "What? You don't think I can sing? Whatever. What do you know about music anyway?"

"You have skills. It's just, uh... At some points, it felt like you were trying too hard."

"I know I'm good at what I do," she snapped, "and I don't care what you think."

"If you can't accept criticism from me, how are you going to handle it from a music executive?"

"I haven't heard any complaints yet."

"You're not signed to a record deal yet either."

I knew that hit a sore spot with her, so I had to step in. "Hey, Joe, I need your help with something in the kitchen."

"Yeah, talk to your brother and teach him some fucking tact," Hazel said.

"Maybe by the time I come back, you'll have picked up some talent," he lashed back.

"C'mon, man," I said, pulling Scout away from her before any more hostile words were exchanged.

"What do you see in that bitch?" he asked as we walked into the kitchen.

"She's tough and feisty like Mom used to be. She acts tough, but she's a good woman. She takes care of her kids, and I think she'd be a positive mother figure for Lynn."

"Well, I'm not feeling her," Scout admitted as Rhea walked in to join us.

"I knew I wasn't the only one," Rhea agreed.

"Y'all are just gonna have to get used to her. I'm trying to keep this one around."

★ ★ ★

The kids were in school, and I took the day off to spend time with Hazel. I surprised her with a trip to Sabella Studios in Roslyn Heights, where I paid for studio time so she could record her demo tape.

"Oh my God! Thank you so much! No one has ever done anything this nice for me," she squealed, looking like she was close to tears.

"You deserve it. You're special to me."

"Nick, seriously, thank you."

Hazel sang five songs for her recording, a variety of styles to show off her range. The producers all politely told her to tone it down a little so her voice sounded more natural instead of forced, the same wise advice Scout had given her.

When we left the studio, she was ecstatic, excitedly clutching her demo tape and CD. I took her to Mapo BBQ to enjoy some Korean barbecue for lunch.

"This is the best date I've ever been on, Nick. Thank you."

"I'm glad I made you happy."

"My kids are going to my sister's after school, so you'll have me all to yourself," she said seductively, licking her lips.

I grinned to myself.

Hazel finally invited me to her place in Hempstead. We pulled up to her raggedy apartment building, and I noticed that the front walls and door were covered with graffiti. The lock was broken, and empty crack vials littered the lobby. The elevator was out of service, so we had to walk up six flights of stairs.

"My place is at the end of the hallway," she said.

I nodded and followed her. The hallway was dark; most of the lights were dead, and only one flickering light remained.

When I stepped into Hazel's cramped studio apartment, I noticed that she didn't have much furniture. There was a futon that served as a couch and a bed, sitting right in the middle of the room, and her children's bunk beds were against the wall. To maximize the small space, she'd filled several storage bins with their clothes, and the bins were neatly stacked around the room.

"This is how I live, Nick. I'm always praying for a record deal or a man to save me from this hell. I don't deserve this, and, more importantly, my kids deserve more out of life."

I nodded. My mind was all over the place. On one hand, I had my own problems and responsibilities, but on the other, I felt like together, we could help each other out. She seemed like a good woman who would be a good influence on Lynn, and I knew I was a good man and would be a good father figure to Hazel's kids—far better than their real daddies were. Of course, my financial situation wasn't much better than hers. I had debt and barely made ends meet my damn self, but at least I had Scout and Rhea. All Hazel had was her sister Dominique.

"I'm old school," she continued. "In my eyes, the man should be the breadwinner. The woman is supposed to complement the missing part of her man's personality. Unfortunately, I haven't been dealing with real men. The little child support I get from my kids' fathers doesn't help enough."

I nodded.

"I'm really struggling, Nick, but you gave me hope today by helping me with my demo." She kissed me, tugged on my belt, and jiggled my zipper.

"I'm falling for you, you know," she said, then stuck her hand down my pants.

I hardened instantly.

Hazel looked me in the eyes and said sincerely, "I love your relationship with your daughter. You work hard to take care of her, and I respect that. I'm looking for a man who'll do that for my kids and me."

She dropped down to her knees and gripped me tightly at the base of my shaft. She worked her mouth around my manhood, and I let out a gasp as she pumped her hand up and down my length.

"I can be that man for you." I said.

She took her mouth off me and stared up at me.

"That's what I'm hoping for, Nick. I'm very particular when it comes to who I share myself with. If we're gonna take things there, I need to know you're the man I've been looking for."

"I am. I can see us having a life together—you, me, Lynn, and your kids."

"Good." She then took me back in her mouth and deep throated, causing me to tremble, close to cumming.

"Slow down, baby. I wanna feel you inside me before you blow your load," she said.

Hearing her say that almost made me cum right there. Hazel stripped down, and her body was on point, without an ounce of fat. Her thick, smooth thighs and full breasts looked amazing. She lay down on the futon bed and spread her legs wide for me.

I rolled a condom onto my length, dropped down, and placed my mouth directly on her treasure. I licked and sucked on the head of her clit. I did all the tricks that drove most women wild, but when I looked up, I saw that Hazel was drifting off, staring mindlessly at her fingernails. I raised my mouth off her and asked, "Does it feel good, babe?"

"Oh yeah, baby. It's so good,"

I felt like I wasn't pleasing her, and she confirmed my suspicion when she rode me. Her face was emotionless. She swiveled her hips, hooped and hollered, moaned, and went through all the motions, but her body language told a different story.

I wanted her to enjoy our first time, so I said, "Talk to me, baby. How do you want it?" I asked, trying my best to sound more sexy than pathetic.

"Let's try doggie."

"Cool."

I knelt behind her, and Hazel reached back, grasped my cock, and, in one swift motion, shoved me inside her. I felt her fingertips graze against my shaft as she rubbed her clit. I pounded her from behind, and her hips met me, thrust for thrust. I watched her enormous breasts bouncing wildly in the mirror.

"Shit, that's it, baby. Yes!"

Hazel spasmed and clenched tightly around my cock. Watching her writhe and moan brought me to cum too. After that, I panted, caught my breath, and walked to her toilet to flush the condom.

"You could've thrown it in the trash," she said.

"True."

"Well, why didn't you?"

"I don't know. I didn't really think about it. A force of habit, I guess."

"Mm-hmm," she said. "Well, just so you know, now that you're my man, if I ever get pregnant by accident, I'm keeping it."

I was surprised to hear that shit, and no woman had ever said such a thing to me after sex before. It had me wondering what other surprises were in store for our relationship.

CHAPTER 8

BLACK AND WHITE

Nick

After a lot of begging on my part, Rhea agreed to watch all the kids while Hazel, Dominique, Cyrus, Vince, and I went out dancing at Village Underground in Manhattan.

Hazel and Dominique were dressed to kill. One thing I really loved about Hazel was that she was a show-stopper. Men, women, and everyone turned their heads in amazement when she walked in the room. Even better, every second I was away from her, she was turning men down and pointing to me.

"Damn, your girl is fine. I've had a couple eights in my life, but—" Vince started before Cyrus cut him off.

"What!? You ain't never had no eight. You might have had a couple of good fours, though."

We all shared a laugh at Cyrus's expense.

Dominique kept most men at bay by hanging around Cyrus and Vince all night, so she never had a second alone to be hit on.

It was late, and Hazel, Cyrus, and Vince went to the bathroom before we headed out.

"My sister really likes you, Nick," Dominique said.

"I feel the same way about her."

"Do you see yourself marrying her anytime soon?"

"Whoa! It's way too early for that put-a-ring-on-it talk. We just started dating."

"Well, you should still think about it. The clock is ticking. Neither of you is getting any younger. I know for a fact she'd like another baby."

"In time, we'll see about all those things. Right now, we're still learning each other."

"Don't waste her time if you don't want those things. She's been really good about turning down guys tonight, but she gets approached all the time by men. If you fuck up, you can be easily replaced."

I gave her a fake smile. "Good to know. Nice talk."

I knew I had to take Dominique's words seriously. Hazel and her sister were very close. If she wasn't spending time with me, she was almost always with Dominique, so I knew she was telling me the truth.

★ ★ ★

I took the kids over to Scout's house, as I had a nice, romantic night planned at the house for Hazel and me. All the expensive dates and trips with the kids were taking a toll on my wallet, so I figured a night in would be good for a change.

"Why are we back here?" Hazel asked as I pulled up to my place.

"I thought we could enjoy a nice time together here tonight."

"No, Nick. I'm not a McDonald's or going Dutch kinda chick. You can't cut corners and think cooking a cheap meal is going to appease me. If you're gonna disrespect me by being cheap on our date night, you can go back and get the kids and take us home right now."

"No, no, we'll go somewhere else," I said, a bit pissed.

I thought after sex, I'd have Hazel wrapped around my finger, but it backfired. The woman had me sprung, and in no time, I found myself falling right back into debt, spending nearly every penny to try to impress her with extravagant gifts: jewelry, designer bags, and even clothes for her and her kids. On top of our dates, she also wanted me to take the kids on fun playdates as well, and those never came cheap. I knew I needed to cut down on my spending, but I didn't know how to do that and keep her happy.

To keep up with Hazel's expensive tastes and my growing bills, I had to work more. On top of my usual jobs with Mr. Davis, I took on any other handyman projects I could find. I missed spending time with Lynn, but I was working to provide for her and possibly find her a decent mother in Hazel.

On days when I worked late or was called in for a project, Rhea picked up my slack with Lynn. I thought things were going smoothly until she chewed me out one night.

"We need to talk, Nick."

"About?"

"About you being a shitty father. You're working all the time, and you're neglecting your child."

"Can you please get off my fucking back? Damn, Rhea, I get this shit enough from Joe."

"You don't get it, do you? I've been putting your daughter to bed almost every night, and I'm tired of answering the tough questions. She asks, 'How come Daddy didn't come to parent/teacher night? Why didn't Daddy come to my school play? Why doesn't he play with me anymore? Why doesn't Daddy tuck me in at bedtime?' And lately, she's even been asking, 'Where's my mom?' That shit breaks my heart, Nick. It isn't right that I'm left to deal with it."

"I'm tired, Rhea. It's not like I'm out there partying like I used to. I've been busting my ass every damn day. All I've done since Lynn was born is sacrifice. Everything I do is for her, and when I finally do get to come home, I wish everyone would cut me some fucking slack!"

"You're *supposed* to make sacrifices for your child. If you can't do that without complaining, you don't deserve to have one. I'd love to have a baby of my own, but that doesn't seem to be in the cards for me. Being a parent is a gift, and you take it for granted."

I shook my head. "I don't—"

"From now on," she said, rudely cutting me off, "you're gonna put your own daughter to bed every night. I'm done bailing you out when it comes to the parenting. If the school calls, I'm directing them to you."

I rolled my eyes. "Fine. So we're done here?"

"Yup. Go be with your daughter…like a father should."

★ ★ ★

"Move over," LJ said.

"You move over! I'm on my side," Lynn snapped.

"Now you're squishing me," Carmella yelled at LJ.

The bickering continued as we made our way to the Bronx Zoo. As much of a pain in the ass as it was sometimes, I knew those family trips were important if I wanted my relationship with Hazel to work. I needed Lynn, Carmella, and LJ to learn to get along so we could eventually be one big, happy family.

"Stop fighting back there, you three," I yelled. "We're almost there."

I looked in the rearview mirror and saw Lynn sulking and pushing them back. She was having a hard time getting along with Hazel's kids, and it was getting on everyone's nerves.

After a torturously long ride, we finally arrived at the zoo. I bought our tickets and handed one to everyone.

LJ and Carmella heckled Lynn everywhere we walked, and I began to lose my patience. At the albino monkey exhibit, their teasing became relentless.

"Look, Lynn. That monkey looks like you," LJ said.

"That one looks like her mom," Carmella added.

Instead of putting a stop to the cruel insults, Hazel chuckled.

I tried to hold my tongue and maintain my composure, but when I saw both of them pushing Lynn, I lost my temper and leaned down to get right in LJ's face.

"You and your sister have been teasing Lynn all day, and I'm sick of it. Knock it off."

"Don't yell at my children," Hazel hollered, putting her hand on her hip and staring at me.

"Well, someone has to, because you sure aren't disciplining them. They've been calling my daughter names all day, and you've done nothing to correct them. I'm not gonna—"

WHACK!

Hazel slapped me so hard my head snapped back. My eyes opened in shock, and I felt a rush of embarrassment. A crowd of onlookers stopped to watch us and whispered amongst each other. Hazel quickly kissed me, laughed it off, and stroked my face, but I moved her hands off me.

"What the fuck, Hazel?"

"I'm sorry, baby. I guess my temper gets the best of me some-times, especially when you get...cheeky."

"Dad?" Lynn said, stunned.

"I'll make it up to you tonight. I promise," Hazel whispered.

I took a deep breath and calmed myself. "It's okay, Ladybug, Hazel was just, uh...playing rough."

Lynn shook her head and looked disappointed. "It didn't look like she was playing, Dad."

I ignored her and tried to avoid looking at the smirks on the faces of Hazel's kids. When everyone saw that there was no more drama to stare at, they finally went on their way.

"You heard your father," Hazel said. "I was only playing." She faced her kids and said, "We're spending the night at Nick's house again."

"Ugh. So now we're stuck hanging out with Light Bright all day *and* all night?" Carmella complained. "Can't you drop us off at Aunt Dominique's place?"

"Nope. She has a date tonight."

"Dad, Carmella called me a name again."

Hazel turned to me. "I got this," she said, then grabbed her kids' faces. "Both of you listen to me now. I don't wanna hear you calling Lynn by anything other than her name, or there's gonna be hell to pay. Y'all understand?"

"Yes, ma'am," they said in unison, sulking and giving Lynn hard stares.

★ ★ ★

That night, I put Lynn to bed first.

"Daddy, I don't like Hazel,"

"Why, Ladybug?" I asked, though it came as no surprise to me.

"She isn't nice to me, and she's not nice to you either. She yells at you, and she hit you today. You always tell me hitting isn't right."

"Hazel wasn't really yelling at me. She just has a loud voice. Plus, she was only playing when she hit me."

"She wasn't playing, Dad. She's mean."

"Enough, Lynn. You need to give her a chance. She might be your mother one day, you know."

"What!? She'll never be that, Dad." She sighed, obviously frustrated with me. "You never listen to me, Daddy. I just want to go to sleep now," she said, then rolled over to face away from me.

My little girl was emotional, and I knew nothing I said would help, so I did as she asked and left her alone. "Goodnight, Ladybug," I said softly as I walked out of the room.

"Goodnight!" she snapped angrily.

After Hazel had put her kids to bed, we lay down together.

"Nick, I'm sorry I hit you today," she apologized. "In fact, I want to show you how sorry I am."

She stroked my erection and dragged her tongue over the tip of my dick. Hazel toyed with me, stopping every once in a while and looked up at me, my cue to watch my cock graze across her lips. I fumbled to grab a condom from my nightstand, and Hazel sucked and fucked me until I was begging for mercy.

★ ★ ★

I was sure she would never hit me again, but I was wrong. A couple weeks later, it happened again.

"Happy Father's Day, Mom," LJ and Carmella said to Hazel as they rushed into my bedroom to surprise us with cards.

"Thank you for remembering, babies," Hazel said, smiling at the cards her children handed to her. She faced Lynn.

"Did you make a card for me too?"

"No. Why would I?" Lynn asked, handing a card to me instead. "You're not a man...and you're not my father."

"Whatever, little girl," Hazel said.

"LJ and Carmella didn't make a card for my dad either. Anyway, why would I make a card for a woman on a man's holiday?"

I laughed, trying to ease the tension. "Do you really expect cards on Father's Day, Hazel?" I asked.

"Damn right I do! I take care of them by myself and play the role of both parents. I deserve a card on both days."

"I get what you're saying, but if that's the case, I should get Mother's Day cards too, right? I know how it feels to play both roles, but I don't see the point in claiming both days as—"

WHACK!

Just like that, Hazel smacked me in front of our kids again. It wasn't a playful tap; it was a full-fledged slap.

My hands shook as I tried my hardest to restrain myself from retaliating. Her kids snickered as I glared at Hazel and sternly warned, "That's Strike 2, the second time you hit me. Don't ever raise a hand to me again.

"Then don't give me a reason to, Nick. You were talking all that shit about me getting a card, thinking you're special because you're one of those rare brothas that actually takes care of his child. That doesn't make you special. You're doing the same shit women have been doing since the beginning of time."

I gritted my teeth. "I don't care how upset you get from what I say, Hazel. Don't ever hit me again."

Hazel and her kids laughed at me as if I was pathetic. "Or what?" she said. "You'll hit me back? The day you put so much as a finger on me is the day your ass will land in jail. Now dry your tears and let's move on with the rest of our day."

Lynn watched and heard it all. She gave me that embarrassed, ashamed, disappointed look I'd grown to hate. I felt the same way she did, but I wanted to set a good example. I didn't want Lynn to grow up thinking it was all right for a man to beat on her, but Hazel was pushing it, deliberately disrespecting me in front of my daughter and her own kids.

The entire day, I was distant with Hazel. I paid for lunch, dinner, and the movies. Not once did she reach into her damn wallet, not even on Father's Day, and that, on top of everything else, annoyed me greatly.

She and her kids spent the night again, so as soon as she put her kids to bed, I let her have it.

"What's up with you today?" she asked, noticing my attitude. "You still hung up on that little love tap from this morning?"

"There should be no love taps like that, Hazel. Look, I care about you, but I'm tellin' you don't ever hit me again."

"Oh, calm down, Nick. It was nothing."

"No, *you* calm down. Today's *Father's* Day, Hazel. Relationships are supposed to be about give and take, but lately, you've been doing nothing but taking. You could've at least showed your appreciation by treating me a little today, but instead, all I got was a slap in front of my daughter and a whole lot of money out of my damn pocket! You did nothing to celebrate me being a father, and you know damn well I've been fulfilling that role for my daughter and your kids lately."

"But you're not—"

I held up a hand to stop her. "Don't even say I'm not your kids' father. Who bought them those fancy Easter clothes, huh? Who feeds them and treats them his own? Me!"

"I'm sorry, baby," she said, her voice and expression softening. "I've been going through a lot lately. I haven't landed any new singing gigs, even after giving out dozens of demos, and it's depressing that I haven't heard from any labels. Not only that but lately all my home girls are either having babies or getting married. I want those things too, and since I'm not getting any younger, I'm scared I'm going to miss out. I know I've been taking my frustrations out on you, Nick, and I'm really sorry."

Hazel was usually all about tough talk, but I liked her the most when she was honest and real with me. I knew her bitchy attitude was just her defense mechanism, to protect her from getting hurt and prevent people from messing with her. Deep down, she was sensitive. She rarely showed that side in public, but when we were alone, it was her sweet side that made me love her.

"Do you forgive me?" she asked, kissing the side of my face.

I didn't want to give in. I wanted to stay mad, but once she climbed on top of me, that anger dissipated quickly.

She whispered in my ear as she straddled me, "I'm really sorry. You can put it in any hole you want tonight! Happy Father's Day!"

CHAPTER 9

THE BIG 180

Nick

"Just like that, baby," I said, smacking Hazel's ass as we made love at her house. Dominique helped us out by taking the kids to Chuck E. Cheese's.

She glanced over her shoulder at me as she slid up and down my length, riding me reverse cowgirl. She smiled and leaned forward; her ass spread wide, and she quickened her pace when she heard me moaning. My breathing intensified. Watching her ass bounce up and down on me, I held onto her hips for dear life, shuddering as I spurted so hard my toes curled.

Hazel hopped off me and took out a cigarette. Her eyes tightened when she watched me flush my condom down the toilet.

"Did you cum, too, babe?" I asked.

"No, I have a lot on my mind," she said flatly.

For the last four months, we'd been fucking like rabbits, but she never seemed sated. I felt like I'd failed to satisfy her, and it made me self-conscious.

"You want me to go down on you?" I offered, flicking my tongue. She looked at me in disgust. "No."

"What's on your mind?" I asked.

"First of all, what is that shit?"

"What shit?"

"Always flushing the condoms after you cum. Don't you trust

me? Do you think I'd try to trap you?"

"It's not like that, Hazel."

She shook her head. "What are we doing, Nick?" she asked.

Dumbfounded, I replied, "What do you mean?"

"I'm not about wasting time, Nick. I want to get married and have another baby with a man I love. I want that with *you*, but if we're not working toward that, maybe we need to end this."

"Hazel, I want those things, too, but—"

"Then what's stopping us? Let's go to City Hall and get married right now."

"Hazel, we've only dated for a few months, and—"

"And what?" she said, interrupting me. "If you can fuck me and tell me you're making love to me, you know whether I'm marriage material or not."

"It's way too early to think about marriage or having children."

"Not for me, it isn't," she argued. "God, Nick, look at this shithole of an apartment I live in. My kids' fathers aren't in their lives, and I'm struggling to make it in the music industry. I need a man who'll take care of me and treat me like the queen I am. If that isn't you, if you can't see those things with me, we're wasting each other's time."

"Look, Hazel, I'm not ready for all that," I explained honestly.

Hazel folded her arms and sucked her teeth.

"I do want you and your kids to move in with me, though," I suggested.

Her eyes lit up. "What? You really mean that?"

"Of course, I mean it. Before we even think about marriage, we need to see how all of us handle living together. Once we build and strengthen our relationship, we'll get married."

Hazel looked at me with a sultry look in her eyes.

"That's the kind of talk that gets me hot. You ready for Round 2? I know we can squeeze in another quickie before the kids get home."

"Sounds like a plan to me," I said with a grin on my face and another erection quickly growing down below.

★ ★ ★

I walked through the door, exhausted and depressed, feeling as if my life was moving backward instead of progressing. I was disappointed that I was back to square one, living in my old apart in Scout's house.

Lynn was sitting with her back pressed snugly against the windowsill, with her forehead touching her knees, rocking and staring out the window. I wasn't sure why, but she'd been doing that a lot lately.

"What are you doing, Ladybug?"

"Looking for Mommy. Carmella and LJ said she'll never come here, but maybe she will today. Then I can finally meet her."

I felt bad and sorry for her, but seeing her waiting for Vickie also irked the shit out of me. I'd been avoiding the talk about her mother for years, yet she still loved and longed for her. *How can she miss someone she's never known?* I wondered.

Too tired, frustrated, grouchy and hungry to entertain that subject, I plopped down on the couch as Hazel walked out of the kitchen.

"Hmm," she said loudly, standing over me. "I don't see anything in your hands. What are we supposed to eat for dinner?"

"Hazel, I'm not in the mood for this shit right now. You were home all day. Couldn't you have made something?"

"Do I look like your personal fucking chef? No, Nick, I didn't make anything."

I looked around at our dirty place. Frankly, I was getting tired of it; nothing was ever done around there unless I did it myself.

"A real man would've called home to ask what I wanted him to bring for dinner," Hazel said.

I ground my teeth together and sighed at her comment. "A real man, huh? Well, you're a real woman, aren't you? What the hell did you do all day? Here you are giving me the third degree as if you aren't capable of cooking. I swear, Hazel, every time anything needs to be fixed or cleaned, you throw all those responsibilities on me, while you sit around doing nothing all day."

Of course, that remark didn't go over well, even if it was the truth. She quickly spat, "You son-of-a-bitch! For your information, after I went to the gym, Dominique and I were busy handing out demos…"

Then, she went on for the next half-hour to chastise and belittle me, right in front of Lynn and her kids.

Life with Hazel had quickly done a 180. As soon as I moved her and her kids in with me, she became a different person, as if all the feelings she had for me suddenly died. Emotionally, physically, and financially, our relationship had gone to shit. Thanks to the added stress, I spent most nights drinking my anger away on the couch.

When I first met Hazel, she was ambitious. She tried to get singing gigs wherever she could, but now, she did little more than stay home all day, sitting around and watching TV. Every time I called her out on it, there was a fight, and she always stormed out and went straight over to Dominique's.

I couldn't stand that Hazel demanded more of me than she did of herself. She wanted the best of everything, but she refused to look for work; in her eyes, any job other than singing for a living was beneath her. She expected designer everything for her and her children, and since I was the only one working, I had to bust my ass to provide for the five of us. Whenever I asked her to help out, to contribute even a little, she insisted on emasculating me right in front of the kids, telling them I was "a sorry excuse for a man."

Things got so hard on me financially that I had to move us out of my house, swallow my pride, and beg Scout to move back into my old apartment. He wasn't thrilled about all of us living in his house, and he only agreed to it when I swore to pay him rent on time and in full every month. Hazel hated that we had to move, and she cursed me out religiously over it, but I promised her it was only a temporary arrangement until I could get a handle on things.

Lynn's strong dislike for LJ and Carmella quickly turned to hatred. The three of them had to share an even smaller room than before, and that was hellish for all of them, but I explained that they would have to make it work until I had enough money to move us into a bigger place. I hoped the experience would force them to get along.

Hazel's only income was the child support from her kids' fathers. She dogged those men regularly, right in front of her children, and I began to notice a pattern in that. On the rare occasions when we were civil, her top priorities were marriage and having more children. She didn't care about her career anymore, and her only goal was to get pregnant. That made me question her feelings for me: *Are they real, or is she just lookin' for another sucker to knock her up, so she'll have another source of income?*

The worst part of it all was Hazel refused to fuck me. We had barely touched each other since she moved in, and it had been months. In the few times when she did take pity on me and gave me some, I had to initiate things. We always argued about using protection, because I wanted to and she didn't, and that would ruin the mood and left me wondering if I'd made a mistake in inviting her to shack up with me so quickly. Most nights, I pathetically tapped her on the shoulder, begging her to show me some sort of intimacy or love; she almost always pushed me off, spurning my advances and disregarded my need for affection.

On top of the mental and emotional fatigue of it all, I was exhausted and sore from doing side jobs all day. I had tucked in Lynn earlier in the evening, and now Hazel was putting her kids to bed. I quickly showered, in the hopes of getting a little loving before she went to sleep.

Certain that she'd had plenty of time to cool off, I walked into the bedroom, stark naked. I slid into bed behind her and kissed the back of her shoulder.

Hazel didn't respond at all; she kept her back to me while I stared at the ceiling, disappointed and sexually frustrated.

I decided to try again and rubbed my hands down her thighs.

"Stop!" she said, slapping my hands away, clearly agitated. "I'm not in the mood tonight, Nick."

"When are you ever?"

She huffed and turned to face me. "Maybe I'd be in the mood more often if you weren't such a pussy."

"What!? What the fuck are you talking about?"

"Every time I mention marriage or us having a baby, you act like it would be some sort of death sentence."

I exhaled and rubbed the stress lines on my forehead.

"Look at us, Hazel. We live in a two-bedroom apartment in my brother's house. I can't even afford to take care of the five of us. How the hell would having a baby better our situation?"

"If you were a real man, you'd figure it out. We live like fucking paupers because you won't man up and get a better job."

"My job puts food on our table and clothes on your back and your kids. You know I'm doing the best I can. I barely get to see you and the kids because all I do is work."

"That's another problem."

"What?"

"You've been...neglecting me."

I turned and faced her, staring at her as if she was out of her damn mind.

"What?"

"You should *own* your own business, not work as some glorified slave for Mr. Davis. He's living like a king while feeding you scraps."

I shook my head and had no words.

"You don't have time for me," she continued. "You come home expecting some ass but wanna wear a stupid condom because you're scared that putting a baby in me will hurt your pockets. Don't you see how pathetic that is? A strong Black *man* wouldn't do that!"

"Things would be easier if you'd help me out financially."

"A woman should never have to open her pocketbook for a man. Until you get that straight in your damn head, you're not getting any of this pussy," she said, then coldly rolled over and went to sleep, leaving me with only the warmth of my hand to satisfy me.

CHAPTER 10

SIBLING RIVALS

Nick

I walked up the steps to Northern Parkway Elementary for the fifth time in two weeks. Once again, Lynn had gotten into another fight. I knew I couldn't keep leaving work early to tend to stuff like that because Mr. Davis would have my head if I didn't get all my work done by the deadlines he set, but no one else was there to deal with Lynn's problems.

I'd been at the school so much that the security guards knew me and didn't even bother asking me for I.D. I walked right into the main office and saw my daughter sitting on a bench, pouting, with her arms crossed. Beside her were two other girls, who looked like they'd gotten their asses kicked. Lynn's clothes were slightly wrinkled, but the other girls were bruised, with busted lips. I wasn't surprised that Lynn had the lesser of the injuries; she was taller than every kid in her grade, and I'd taught her how to defend herself.

"Hello, Mr. Johnson. Can I talk to you in my office please?" Principal Meade said.

I nodded.

"Lynn, honey, you can come too," she said.

Lynn grabbed her book bag and stormed into the principal's office, just as she'd had to so many times before.

"I'm sorry we had to disturb you at work," the principal said as I took a seat across from her. "We called your house and spoke with your girlfriend, but she explained she was busy and gave us the number to contact where you were working."

Busy? With what? I thought, shaking my head.

Lynn plopped down in the chair, slouching and pouting.

I glared at her. "Sit up," I said sternly, then turned my attention back to the principal.

Mrs. Meade was fine. She had a deep, dark chocolate complexion and a firm, fit body. In every way, she was far more attractive than the principals and teachers I had growing up.

"Mr. Johnson, you saw the other children on the bench when you walked in. It seems Lynn has gotten into yet another altercation with her classmates."

Lynn tapped her foot against the chair.

I smiled sheepishly. "Kids will be kids," I said.

Mrs. Meade didn't return my smile but instead continued with a serious look on her face, "Mr. Johnson, fighting is not acceptable behavior for a young lady or any students in this school."

Lynn continued to tap her foot against the chair.

"If not for the fact that I personally saw the others initiate the attack, Lynn would be placed on suspension. In this case, it was self-defense, but I would suggest that you have a heart-to-heart with her about choosing other means of defense, something other than physical violence."

"Thank you, Mrs. Meade. Lynn, what do we say?"

Lynn's face was beet red. She continued tapping her foot and refused to say a word.

"Stop with the foot, Lynn," I scolded.

She stopped but continued to pout.

"Now, what do you say to Mrs. Meade for not suspending you?"

"Thanks," Lynn mumbled.

"You're welcome. I think the two of you should talk at home, Mr. Johnson. Lynn has to learn how to handle situations like these without fighting. As of now, I'm suspending the other two for bullying. I won't tolerate that type of behavior in my school, especially when we're…teasing our own people if you understand what I'm saying."

"Can I ask what they said to her?" I chimed in.

"That's something you two need to discuss in private."

"All right. Well, thank you again, Mrs. Meade. I'll talk to Lynn, and we'll make sure this doesn't happen again."

"Let's try to at least make it less frequent," the principal said, finally allowing her face to break into a smile.

I stood and shook her hand, then turned to Lynn. "You ready, Ladybug?"

"I hate it when you call me that."

"Since when?"

Lynn rolled her eyes, stood and grabbed her book bag.

I sighed. "Are you ready? You need anything from your desk or locker or—"

"No, Dad," she said, sighing back at me. "Can we please just go? I hate school."

Mrs. Meade looked at me with a concerned expression on her face when she noticed Lynn's sassy tone.

"I'll talk to her," I assured her, then followed my daughter as she power-walked out of the school and to the car.

"Slow down! What's your problem?"

"Nothing," she said, then quickly got in the car and slammed the door.

"What did those girls say to you?" I asked as I pulled away.

"I don't want to talk about it."

I pulled over. "Well, I want to talk about it. Tell me what they said."

"Nothing. Can we please go? Is Aunt Rhea home?"

I put the car in drive, irritated that my daughter would rather talk to her aunt about her problems. She was as stubborn as I was, so I knew I wasn't going to change her mind right now. I decided it was best to let her be.

I laughed to myself. "You really put a whoopin' on those girls, huh, Ladybug?"

A slight smirk flashed on her face but faded quickly, and she said nothing.

"You know you can talk to me about anything, right?"

"Sure, Daddy."

"What made you so mad at school today?"

"I'll talk to Aunt Rhea about it later."

The rest of the drive home was spent in silence. When I pulled into the driveway, Lynn was quick to hop out of the car and run inside, to Scout and Rhea's side of the house.

I walked upstairs to my apartment and found Hazel sitting on the couch, watching TV again, with a cigarette in hand.

"Um...hello," I said as I set my tool bag down.

She didn't even bother to acknowledge me or look away from the TV.

"Would you mind not smoking that inside? Scout fights with me about it smelling like smoke in here, and I don't want to hear it."

"Fuck him. As long as we're paying rent, we'll smoke whatever the hell we want in here."

"We?" I wanted to say since I was the only one paying for anything, but I knew there were more important issues to address.

"I had to leave work early to pick Lynn up from school. They said they spoke to you."

"Yeah. So what?"

"So why couldn't *you* pick her up?"

"She's not my fucking kid. She's your problem."

"The school said you told them you were busy."

"I am," she said, chuckling to herself as she changed the TV channel.

"You're laughing now, but if I miss too much time at work, Mr. Davis will cut me off from any other projects, and we'll be broke."

"Uh, correction. *You'll* be broke, Nick. A real man of the house wouldn't have to worry about another nigga giving him scraps. You need to find a steady job, one where you can make real money."

I was furious; once again, she was attacking my manhood.

"And what are you supposed to be doing as the woman of the house?"

"My mother never had to work a day in her life. My father, God rest his soul, was a true gentleman. He provided and made sure we never wanted for anything, which is more than I can say for your sorry ass."

I sucked my teeth and was about to say something when Lynn came through the door.

My little girl seemed calmer than before, but she still looked miserable. Lynn sat down near the window, pulled her knees up and hugged them to her chest. She stared aimlessly out the bay window of our living room.

The door was open, but Rhea still knocked before entering. Hazel didn't bother to acknowledge her and kept staring at the television.

"Nick, can I talk to you in the kitchen for a minute?" Rhea asked.

"Sure," I said, then followed her and took a seat across from her at my small table.

"You need to talk to your daughter," Rhea said. 'Most importantly, though, you need to do something about your girlfriend's bad-ass kids."

I rubbed my temples. I'd just gotten home after a hellish day. I was already stressed out and in no mood for more of it. I released a heavy sigh and asked, "What do I need to talk to Lynn about? And what are Hazel's kids doing now?"

"She being teased and bullied at school about not having a mother and being mixed. When she comes home, Hazel's kids terrorize her and tease her about the same shit, and it's making her miserable."

"As far as school goes, kids will be kids. When I was little, kids used to call me Blacky. It's part of life, and it'll toughen her up."

"Nick, she doesn't need to be toughened up. She needs her father to comfort her. She's just a little girl, and she can't even find peace at home because these little terrors start picking on her as soon as she steps through the door."

I knew Lynn wasn't too fond of Hazel's kids, but I figured in time, we'd all be one big, happy family, and they'd learn to love each other.

"Did you know she sits there every day, staring out the window like that, hoping her mother will come for her?"

I had noticed that but hadn't thought much of it. I busted my ass every day to provide for Lynn, yet all she thought about was her fucking mother. For once, I wanted to feel appreciated, especially since I was the one who wanted her and took care of her.

I rubbed my hand over my face and asked, "What do you want me to do?"

"Try acting like you give a shit. You need to do something because your daughter needs you right now. You're her father, and you need to act like it."

I nodded, as LJ and Carmella skipped into the kitchen.

"Can you give us a minute? We're talking about something important," Rhea said.

"You're on our side of the house. We don't have to listen to you," Carmella sassed while, reaching into the fridge to grab sodas for her and her brother.

"Well, you have to listen to *me*, so step out of the kitchen so we can talk. Go now!" I yelled.

They sucked their teeth, took their sodas, and left.

Rhea shook her head and patted my hand. "Please, Nick," she said with concern on her face. "Joe and I try our best to calm and console her every day, but she needs more than us. The only person who can help her is you."

"I'll talk to her tonight."

"That's a start, but talking to her once will only put a Band-Aid on a huge wound. She needs you to be more involved in her life."

"I'm doing my best."

"Well, your best isn't cutting it, Nick."

I stood up, "I'll take care of it."

When Rhea and I walked out of the kitchen, we found Lynn with her hands and forehead pressed against the window, still staring hopefully outside. "Is that lady over there Mommy?" she asked.

LJ and Carmella snickered. "Is that Mommy?" they mimicked, mocking her.

"Knock it off, you two!" I yelled.

"Is Mommy coming home soon, Daddy?"

"I'll talk to you about that later, Ladybug."

The time had come, just as I always knew it would, and finally, it was time to tell her the truth about Vickie.

Like most nights, I read to her from her favorite *book, The Giving Tree.* LJ and Camilla went to bed an hour later, so that gave me time to talk to Lynn in private. I was still contemplating how I'd ease into explaining Vickie to her as I put the book back on the shelf. *Maybe I'll do it another day.*

"Daddy?"

"Yes, Ladybug?"

"Can you tell me about Mommy now?"

I tucked her in, sat down on the edge of her bed, and brushed her jet-black hair away from her face; its silky texture was just like her mother's.

"What do you want to know?" I asked hesitantly.

"What's her name?"

"Vickie."

"How come you always tell me to make Mother's Day cards for Aunt Rhea and not her?"

"Because Aunt Rhea has been more of a mother to you than Vickie has ever been. The cards are a good way to thank your aunt for all she does for you."

"Where is she? Did she die?"

"No! Don't talk like that. Why would you ask that?"

"Well, why doesn't she live with us? Why doesn't she ever come to see me?" Lynn asked, her lips quivering.

"How come she doesn't love me?"

I pulled my troubled daughter into a hug as I thought about what to say next. The last thing I wanted to do was give my daughter a complex, and I knew I needed to choose my words wisely. Even though it was safe to say I hated Vickie for putting me in the predicament, I didn't want our daughter to hate her, so I placed the blame solely on myself and answered, "Your mom loves you very much. It's me she doesn't love."

"Oh."

"Your Mom doesn't think she's good enough to be the parent you deserve, so she left you with me. She knows I'll always take care of you, no matter what."

Lynn stared at the floor, speechless.

I gave her a kiss on the forehead and prayed my answers were good enough. "Hold on, I have something for you," I said.

I got up, ran to my room. I frantically dug through my sock drawer to find the letter and necklace I'd kept hidden for all those years in some subconscious attempt to hold on to what Vickie and I once had. I had promised myself I would never show them to Lynn, but now I hoped it would bring some comfort to her.

"What is it, Daddy?" she asked when I walked back in the room.

"It's a necklace. It belonged to your mom, and I know she'd want you to have it."

Lynn beamed with joy as I put the necklace on her.

"You have to take care of it and promise not to lose it."

"I'm never gonna take it off," she said, staring down at the pendant I'd bought for Vickie so long ago. She hugged herself, excited to have that slight connection with her mother. "What was Mom like?"

"A lot like you actually—beautiful, smart, funny... She loves to dance, and..." I stopped myself for a moment. Remembering little things about Vickie had me caught in my feelings, and it took a moment before I could continue. I cleared my throat and said, "Your mom is a determined woman. When she sets her mind on something, she does it."

"Do you think Mom will come back someday?"

"I don't know. Maybe she'll change her mind someday, but even if she doesn't, I love you, and I'll always take care of you."

"I love you, too, Daddy."

"Does she live close?"

"No. She lives far away with her husband."

"Where? And her husband, Daddy? Why didn't she marry you?"

I sighed, not sure how to answer the questions. "Um, I think she's in...California," I said randomly. "Your mom liked me enough to help me make you, but she didn't love me enough to marry me."

"I don't understand."

I scrambled for a quick way to explain it, then asked, "Do you love LJ?"

"Ew! Heck no. I hate him."

"Don't say that, Ladybug. You don't love him, but you still share a room with him, right?"

"Not by choice."

I had to laugh at that. "Well, your mother felt the same way about me. She thought I was okay enough to be her friend and help make you, but she didn't love me."

"How did you guys make me?"

I laughed nervously and answered, "That's a discussion for another time, Ladybug. In fact, I might need your aunt to help me explain that when the time comes. In the meantime, get some sleep. You've got school in the morning."

She nodded. "Okay. Goodnight, Daddy," she said, holding the pendant tight, like a cherished treasure.

I kissed her hair. "Goodnight, baby."

I closed the door, feeling like a weight had been lifted off my shoulders, and for the first time in a long time, I actually felt a little better.

★ ★ ★

Two weeks passed, and every night before bed, Lynn asked me lots of questions about her mother. She wanted to know everything about Vickie. She touched the necklace every chance she got, admired it in the mirror, and proudly showed it to everyone and anyone who would give it a look. Unfortunately, while my talks with Lynn were helping, the abuse she suffered at home from LJ and Carmella still hurt Lynn's confidence.

Wanting to see it for myself, I came home early, so I'd be there when Lynn got home from school. I kept the garage door closed and worked on the lawnmower since Scout had told me it was acting up. I heard voices in the driveway, and I looked out the window just in time to see Carmella pushing Lynn down on the ground.

"Stop it!" Lynn yelled, quickly getting to her feet.

"Where do you think you're runnin' off to, Mellow Yellow?"

"Leave me alone, or I'm gonna to tell your mom."

"Snitches get stitches," Carmella threatened.

"Are you stupid?" LJ asked. "Our mom won't be mad at us for teasing an annoying little half-breed."

"She's too dumb to understand," Carmella said to LJ. "Maybe if she had a mom, she would."

"Do you know why your mother left?" LJ asked.

"My dad told me it was because—"

"Who cares what your dad told you? She really left because you're so ugly and stupid," LJ said, interrupting her.

"Shut up!" Lynn screamed.

Rhea had told me they'd been teasing Lynn about her mother, but I couldn't believe they were so brutal. Before I interfered, I wanted to see her act tough and stand up to them.

LJ and his sister circled Lynn.

"Look at you! You're a fucking albino," LJ teased.

At that point, Lynn's light complexion turned red. "I am not!" she yelled.

"I am not!" Carmella mocked. "You gonna cry, Light Bright? You look like a zebra."

"Yeah, that's it! She's an ugly zebra baby."

LJ and Carmella continued circling Lynn, tormenting her with cruel chants: "Zebra baby, zebra baby... Little albino zebra baby!"

"Shut up, shut up, shut up!" Lynn cried, using both hands to cover her ears.

While Lynn's hands were on her ears, Carmella walked up to her and looked condescendingly at her. "I'm sick of you wearing this stupid, cheap piece of shit around your neck," she said before she tore the chain right off of her.

Lynn's chest heaved, and she balled up her fists. Tears filled her eyes as she lunged forward to grab the necklace as Carmella dangled it just inches away from her.

"Give it back!" Lynn cried.

LJ and Carmella laughed at her for crying, then tossed the necklace back and forth to each other, playing keep-away with it.

"Give it to me! It's mine!" Lynn said, kicking Carmella in the shins.

"Ow! You stupid bitch," Carmella screamed, then knocked Lynn to the ground again.

Finally, I'd heard and seen enough. I stomped out of the garage.

"You two knock that shit off right now. What the hell is wrong with you?" I yelled.

"Who you cussin' at? You ain't my daddy," LJ said.

"Boy, don't you ever challenge me in my fucking house. Just wait until your mother comes home."

"Whatever. Momma ain't gonna do nothing, especially when we tell her you were cussing at us," Carmella said.

I looked over at Lynn and had never felt so bad in my life. As her father, it was my job to protect her and help her when she was in need, but I'd stood by for too long and allowed them to hurt my daughter.

I dusted Lynn off, stood her up, and dropped down to her level to face her. She buried her face in my chest and wept while I pulled her into my arms, kissed and hugged her tightly.

"Lynn, I'll take care of this," I said, holding her by the shoulders and looking directly into her eyes. "I promise, okay? I won't let them tease you anymore."

"How can you stop them, Dad? You're always at work," Lynn said, then sniffed and wiped her nose with the back of her hand.

I brushed the remaining tears from her face, cupped her head in my hands, and kissed her forehead.

"Don't worry about that. I'll be here for you."

★ ★ ★

Hazel came home while I was setting the table. When I asked her where she'd been and what she'd done all day, she didn't answer, so I didn't bother to press the issue. I knew she wasn't going to cook, so to avoid another argument, I ordered dinner from Boston Market.

As soon as LJ and Carmella realized she was home, they ran to her and tattled, telling their mother that I'd yelled at them.

"Nick, bring your black ass here."

I stormed into the living room to face her.

"Have you lost your mind? Don't curse at me like that in front of the kids," I said sternly.

"Have you lost yours? Who do you think you are, talking to my children like you did in the driveway?"

"Despite what you think, Hazel, your kids aren't angels. They torment Lynn every day, and I had to set them straight." I turned to face Carmella and LJ and said, "I'm telling both of you again, in front of your mother this time… Don't ever challenge me in my house again. Also, the picking on Lynn ends today. You hear me?"

They both sucked their teeth.

"Your house? This ain't your house. It's your brother's," Hazel said, standing face to face with me.

Instantly, all eyes were on us, staring at us from the dinner table. I knew if I let Hazel get away with punking me yet again, her kids would never respect me, and Lynn would continue to be bullied.

135

I'd let Hazel get away with disrespecting me for far too long, and I wasn't going to let it go on any longer.

"Don't yell at my kids again," Hazel said. "If your daughter is too prissy to fend for herself, then she deserves to get picked on. Unless I say otherwise, my kids will do whatever the fuck they want!"

I stood up straight, towering over her and stared her down.

"No, they won't! You are not going to stand here and overrule what I just said. Everything your kids are wearing, the food they're eating, and the place where they're living is because of me. I'm not taking that shit from you, and I'm damn sure not taking it from them."

Hazel's nostrils flared. "Who the fuck do you think you're talking to?"

"To you, damn it!" I said, refusing to back down. "You've disrespected me in front of the kids for the last time."

"Oh, so you're trying to show off now? You wanna act tough? Keep talking, and I'll—" Hazel started before I cut her off abruptly.

"You'll what? Stop contributing financially? I'm not worried about that. You don't do anything anyway. You'll what? Stop showing me affection? Physically, you treat me more like your brother than your man. What will you do, Hazel? Leave? Right now, the only thing you leaving would do is save me some damn money! Now, like I said, your kids *are* going to listen to me, and you *are* going to stop disrespecting me. If any of you have a problem with that, y'all can move the fuck out!" I said, then pointed at the door.

Hazel scowled and quickly swung at me, but I was ready this time and grabbed her by her wrists.

"The hitting shit ends today too. Keep your fucking hands to yourself. I let you slide the last couple times, but it's not happening again. You understand me?" I asked, then swiftly dropped her hands.

Hazel looked stunned by my outburst, but that shit had been festering in me for a while, and I couldn't put up with it any longer. She didn't defy me openly, but she mumbled something under her breath.

"Is there a problem? You got something to say?" I said, holding my hand to my ear.

She stopped muttering and froze where she stood.

That night, Hazel and her kids ate in silence. Lynn smiled at me, and, for the first time in a long time, I felt as if I'd finally made my little girl proud.

CHAPTER 11

CLEANING HOUSE

Nick

I gave Lynn a firm nudge as she drove to the basketball hoop. She smirked and slapped my hand away.

"Is that all you got, Hybrid?" I taunted.

Lynn's eye tightened as she stopped and took an off-balance jump-shot; my heckling got her off her game.

"Hold up, Ladybug. You just let me get in your head and mess up your shot. You need to know those names people call you are just names. You're better than that, baby. Take all that pain and anger and use it for strength to do better," I said, placing my arm around her. "When I was your age, kids used to make fun of me for being dark."

"They did?"

"Yup. I used basketball as my release. Once all the kids saw how great I was, it helped me make friends, and kids stopped picking on me."

Lynn smiled and nodded, then sneakily drove past me and made a perfect jump-shot.

"Nice! Now do it again," I encouraged.

Lynn rolled her eyes and shot another, with perfect form.

"Good. Now give me fifty more, and that'll be it for today."

"Fifty! C'mon, Dad," she whined.

"You want to get better or not?"

Lynn sighed but did as she was told.

For the past six months, I've been going to work earlier and skipping lunch so I could pick Lynn up after school. Once her homework was done, I taught her how to play basketball. It was nice bonding with my daughter. On days the weather permitted, we practiced in the driveway. On days the weather was bad, we practiced inside Lynn's school. Going there all the time because of her fighting, I befriended the janitor. I told him what I was trying to do with her, and he had no problem letting us use the gym to practice. Every day, that was our time, and I made sure I was consistent and never missed a day.

When I was growing up, playing ball was my way of escaping everything that stressed me out. It also boosted my popularity. I felt that was something I could pass down to Lynn to build up her confidence and help us bond, and little by little, it seemed to be working. It wasn't an easy process, though. She needed to toughen up. Her self-esteem was already shitty because of the bullying she suffered from her classmates and Hazel's kids at home.

When we practiced, I was sometimes physical with her. I pushed her and purposely irritated her, even calling her names that made her angry. It wasn't easy for me to do, but I needed Lynn to understand that those actions and words couldn't stop her from succeeding unless she let them.

Rhea, of course, hated everything I was doing.

"Nick, you're not raising a son," she complained. "Lynn's a girl, your daughter. She should be playing with dolls, not shooting baskets and roughhousing with you. You play too rough with her, and you tease her with the same cruel names the kids call her in school."

"This is what I know, and this is what I'm going to teach her," I retorted. "I can't coddle her. She needs to be tough, or she's never going to survive. When I was a kid, I was picked on too. Basketball helped me overcome everything."

"You also had your brothers Joe and Jimmy, who helped you beat up those kids. Don't forget I went to school with you guys," she said with a laugh. "I know how y'all are."

"You know what I mean. Basketball was my stress relief. You tell me all the time that I need to do more with her, and that's what I'm doing. The best gift I can share with her is to teach her how to play sports. I tease her and play rough with her so she'll learn how to deal with it. You can help me with the nurturing part, but this is something I have to teach her as her father."

Rhea sighed. "Fine. Just don't make her too…boyish. She should still be feminine."

"I know, Rhea," I said with a laugh.

I enrolled Lynn into some youth basketball leagues, and she bonded with the other players and made some new friends. That really helped, since she felt as if she had no friends at school.

As I expected, she was a natural, better than all the girls and even some of the boys. After every game, we did our signature fist-bump. Win or lose, and I couldn't have been prouder of her.

While things with Lynn were good, unfortunately, life with Hazel hadn't gotten any better. We barely spoke after my outburst, and it began to feel like we were merely roommates; actually, since she didn't pay rent or any other bills, it was more like living with a squatter. She still wouldn't fuck me, work, or do anything constructive around the house, so instead of busting my ass trying to please her all the time, I substantially cut back on buying things for her and her kids.

Since I was spending so much time with Lynn, I wasn't working as much, and I really couldn't afford any extravagant dates and gifts anyway. Hazel was furious about that, but she still wouldn't show me any love or take care of my needs, so I really couldn't have cared less how she felt.

Earlier in our relationship, I was so caught up in Hazel's bullshit that I forgot what mattered to me most, and that was Lynn. To correct that and make amends, I poured all my time and energy into making sure my daughter was all right. I bought Lynn her first bike and taught her how to ride it, my sneaky way of keeping her active when she wasn't playing ball. I loved seeing her happy, and making her happy gave me joy. Sometimes she fell asleep on me while we watched Knicks games together. When I watched her sleeping peacefully, I realized that with all the hectic chaos in my life, she was the only thing that gave me happiness. My best times, my happiest times, were the moments I spent with Lynn, both on and off the basketball court.

★ ★ ★

Hazel put her kids to bed while Lynn and I were snuggled up on the couch, watching and studying the Knicks game.

"I'm going to sleep," Hazel said.

"All right. I'll be there soon. I'm just gonna finish watching this game with Lynn, then tuck her in," I said quietly.

Hazel nodded. She looked as if she had something on her mind but didn't say anything.

The game ended, and I tucked Lynn in for the night, showered, went to my room, and slid into bed, spooning Hazel from behind. I touched her shoulder and kissed her cheek, but I got no response. I knew she was up, so I nudged her.

"You seem stressed. You wanna relieve some of that?" I asked.

"Fuck off," she responded coldly.

I sighed and turned over on my side. "Whatever."

"You fucking somebody else?" Hazel suddenly blurted.

"No, but maybe I should ask you the same question. You're never in the mood, and I'm tired of begging you. You've been a nasty, cold bitch, to the point where I'm wondering why we're even together. Maybe I *should* start fucking around."

I didn't care how she felt about what I said because I meant every word of it.

Hazel was silent, her leg irritably bouncing on the bed. Before I knew it, she had opened her nightstand drawer, ripped open a condom, and was pushing me to my back on the mattress. She straddled me, stroked my manhood until it rose in her hand, and then rolled the condom on me. She spat on my dick and shoved it inside her dry treasure. She placed her palms on my chest and rode me. There was no affection, no warm embrace or kissing; she didn't even look at me. I've had jerk-off sessions that were more intimate.

She continued riding me in a daze, almost looking past me. Clearly, she was mercy-fucking me. I flipped her over, onto her back, and she just lay there, going through the motions, with her arm resting across her eyes. I finished my business and lifted myself off her, as callously as if I'd just fucked a prostitute. I got up and flushed the condom down the toilet, then walked back to the bed to find Hazel staring aimlessly at the ceiling, her eyes unblinking as she let out a long breath. I stared at the ceiling, too, trying to put my life in perspective. *This can't be love,* I decided.

★ ★ ★

The next morning, Hazel was gone before I woke up. Where she went that early in the morning had always baffled me, but I welcomed the time apart, the freedom from hearing the nastiness she spewed from her mouth all the damn time. Rhea helped me ready the kids for school and put them on the bus.

After taking care of my fatherly responsibilities, I went to my new job assignment at the Courtesy Hotel in West Hempstead, a real shithole. The Courtesy Hotel was always in the news, as countless crimes were committed there. The manager was trying to clean up the hotel's image, so he was willing to put money into upgrading the rooms. My usual crew, Vince, and Cyrus, were assigned to help me, and Mr. Davis and Chris were going to join us to help us get started. The rooms needed a lot of work, and management wanted us to do one at a time. Vince worked on the heating and cooling system, Cyrus worked on the bathroom, and Mr. Davis, Chris, and I worked on putting up the new sheetrock.

A couple had rented the room next to us, and we heard giggling and laughter on the other side of the wall. I put my ear against it and heard muffled talking and heavy breathing. Within a few minutes, the bed started creaking, and the headboard banged against the wall in a steady rhythm.

"Whose pussy is this?" the man asked.

"It's yours, Daddy," the woman replied.

Then, they began fucking like bunnies, sexing nonstop for at least forty minutes. One thing was for sure: The woman was definitely a moaner.

"Oh my God! It's so big," she screamed out.

When the headboard-banging, grunts, and moans finally stopped, I grinned.

"We gotta see the couple who put on a performance like that," I said.

Everyone except Mr. Davis laughed.

"All of you need to focus on your work and stop wasting time. I don't pay you guys to fool around," He said.

"Oh, c'mon, Mr. Davis. Happy employees are productive employees. As soon as we get our laughs, we'll get right back to work," I pleaded.

He waved me off and continued installing the insulation in the wall he was working on. Cyrus, Vince, and I leaned against the wall in the hallway, directly in front of the couple's room.

The door flew open, and I stood there, frozen in place, with my mouth hanging open.

There was Hazel, adjusting her short skirt and blouse back to decency. Her lipstick was smeared, and her bra straps hung limply on her shoulders.

Instantly, as soon as Vince and Cyrus saw her, they stopped snickering.

"Hazel?"

She jumped when she looked up and saw me standing in the hallway. I met her eyes, and we stared at one another for a long moment. Behind her, the man laughed and adjusted the huge, bulging erection that still protruded in his pants. When Hazel stepped to the side, it left the guy and me standing eye to eye.

"Damn, this is fucked up. I'm going back to work. Handle your business, Nick," Cyrus said.

"Yeah, this is crazy embarrassing. I'm headed back too." Vince said, then followed Cyrus to the worksite.

My jaw tightened, and I opened and closed my fists.

"You got a problem, nigga?" the man asked with a smirk.

"Who the fuck is that, Hazel?" I demanded.

"This is my son's father, Lamar."

When she said it, my fists closed and didn't open back up. I was so fucking embarrassed as the two of them laughed and walked past me, toward the elevator.

"Hazel!" I yelled after her, my bottom lip trembling.

She ignored me and kept walking.

"Hazel!" I repeated.

She stopped, huffed, and turned to face me. "What?" she snapped.

I lowered my head. "How could you play me like this?"

Hazel was clearly unmoved by my words or the pain in my voice.

"I needed a man to pay attention to me, to buy me nice things and take care of me sexually. You sure as hell weren't doing it."

"You said you wanted a man who'd treat you right and support your singing career. I did all that. You said you wanted someone to step up and be a father to your kids, and I've been doing that. I took care of you and those little bastards when he and your other baby-daddy barely paid you child support, and this is how you do me? After all the things I've done for you and your kids, all the money I've spent to treat you like a queen, this is what I get?"

"Boo fucking hoo! Grow a pair, Nick," she said, then turned to walk away.

I followed her and grabbed her by the arm.

"Get the fuck off me!" she yelled, pulling away from me.

Lamar stepped up as if he was about to take a swing at me. I said nothing. I just stared at Hazel with disdain, my gaze unwavering, and she wouldn't dare look me in the eyes. I bit my bottom lip and shook my head.

"How long has this shit been going on?" I yelled.

"None of your—"

"How fucking long?" I yelled again, cutting her off.

Mr. Davis grabbed my shoulder.

I shut my eyes tight and reopened them to find sympathy in his gaze.

"You have a daughter to take care of. Her mother isn't in her life. Don't do something you'll regret, something that will take her father from her too."

I nodded.

"Yeah, you'd better listen to the old man before you get your ass kicked, boy," Lamar said.

"Don't let him get to you. Take the rest of the day off," Mr. Davis said.

"Thank you," I said. I turned to Hazel. "I want you gone when I get home. Make arrangements to live somewhere else. Pack your shit...or, better yet, I'll do it for you."

"You're really gonna put me out on the street over this? Where are me and my kids supposed to go?"

"Not my problem. I don't give a fuck where you go, but you're not staying with me anymore. Why don't you stay with your sister or this chump?"

"You'd better mind your business and watch your mouth," Lamar said.

"Nick—" Mr. Davis started.

"I'm good, Mr. Davis," I interrupted. "I'm not going to act up on the job, but I'm serious. She's not living with me after this. I want her and her brats gone."

"Fine. I don't need you anyway!" Hazel said. She turned to face Lamar, batting her eyes at him and making a pouting face. "Can we stay with you for a while?"

He laughed.

"Bitch, you crazy? Hell no, you can't stay with me. Don't get it twisted. You know what this is. The only thing you'll get from me is a hard dick. Why do you think I never take you to my crib? We're just fuck-buddies, and you know it."

"Fuck both of you!" Hazel screamed, utterly humiliated.

"You'd better watch your tone, bitch. I drove us here, remember? Keep cursing at me, and your homeless ass will be walking to your sister's to get your car. Now come on."

Hazel obediently shut her mouth and woefully followed him.

"So you choose this guy who disrespects you? Typical," I said, shaking my head.

After that horrible scene was over, I took Mr. Davis's advice and left work early. I left the hotel, rushed to my car, picked Lynn up early from school, and drove home. I knew if Lynn were there, it would keep me from doing anything stupid that might get me arrested.

"What's wrong, Daddy? Why did you pick me up?" Lynn asked.

"Hazel and her kids are moving out."

When we pulled in front of the house, I saw Rhea outside gardening.

"You're home early," Rhea said.

"Yeah, I gotta pack Hazel's shit. She's out of here."

"What? What happened?"

"Lynn, go inside and start your homework, okay?"

Without another word, she nodded and did as she was told.

I gave Rhea a quick breakdown of everything that had happened.

"I knew she wasn't shit. I hope this doesn't get ugly," Rhea said.

"Me too, but I'm done with her," I said.

I ran upstairs to my bedroom. I jerked all her clothes off the hangers, grabbed her shoes, makeup, and other belongings, and threw them into garbage bags. I did the same with her kids' clothes and possessions. She had no furniture, and all her other shit was in storage or at her sister's house, so packing her stuff up was easy.

An hour passed. Rhea had called Scout to tell him what was going on. He left work early and sped home to ensure that I wouldn't do anything I'd regret.

I looked out the window and saw Hazel pulling up in the driveway with her kids. I opened the door and met her at the doorway.

Hazel turned to LJ and Carmella. "Babies, go wait in the car. I have to talk to Nick for a minute."

They rolled their eyes at me and stuck their tongues out.

"What is this shit, Nick? Are you seriously putting me out?" Hazel asked, staring at the bags on the doorstep as if she was surprised.

"I wasn't kidding, Hazel. It's over. You've been using me, and now you can find some other sucker to leech off of."

"You can't be serious. You're really gonna throw me out over today? We can get past this, Nick."

"I'm already past it. I'm over you."

"Baby," she said, her tone softening, "I've been under a lot of stress. No one's called be back about my demo, and I haven't been getting any new gigs. Plus, you're always working, and—"

"Save the bullshit. I meant nothing to you. You said it from the beginning, but I didn't get it. You told me you wanted a man to take care of you, but you never said anything about loving him. You wanted to marry me for security, not for love. You've never loved me."

"I was…getting there."

"Sure you were. Anyway, all your shit and your kids' things are in these bags. I was thorough, so there's no need for you to ever come back here again."

"Nick, where do you expect me to go?"

"You always liked to use the excuse of visiting your sister, right? Stay with her."

"So that's it? You're just gonna throw me out on the street with my two kids? What kind of man does that?"

"You did this to yourself."

Hazel huffed, grabbed a couple of her bags, and stormed to her car.

I closed the door and went inside.

Lynn was staring out the window, hugging her knees to her chest and rocking back and forth, as usual. Scout, Rhea and I stood next to her, watching Hazel load her Landrover with her bags.

"I'm sorry you had to find out like this, Fool. I'm glad you're finally kicking the heifer out, though," Scout said.

Hazel looked up and saw all of us staring at her through the window, and she rudely gave us the finger before she turned to her kids and yelled, "Come on. Fuck him! We don't need his punk ass."

After she sped off, Lynn hopped down from the windowsill.

"You giving up on waiting for your mom today?" Rhea asked.

"Yeah. I don't think I'm going to wait for her anymore."

"Why's that, Ladybug?" I asked.

"LJ and Carmella were right. She's never gonna come for me. I'm wasting my time. I wasn't waiting for her today, though. I just wanted to see them leave. I'm glad they're finally gone."

"Out of the mouth of babes," Scout said with a laugh.

SECOND QUARTER

Change is coming

CHAPTER 12

PERSISTENT

Nick

"Daddy, wake up!" Lynn yelled, nudging me.

"What is it, child?" I groaned, with my eyes still shut.

Lynn lifted one of my eyelids.

"We're gonna be late for my first practice with my new team."

I drifted back to sleep.

Lynn shook me vigorously.

"Dad! You have to get up!"

"I'm up, child."

"No, you're not, Daddy. C'mon."

I sat up, with my eyes still closed, and rubbed my temples. After putting Lynn to bed the previous night, my loneliness had led me to guzzle a pint of whiskey, and I had passed out on the couch.

After Hazel left, I spent the next three years dating women with the sole intention of getting into their panties. I had a vasectomy, so I didn't have to worry about ever getting a woman pregnant again. I didn't tell Scout or Rhea because it wasn't any of their business, and I didn't want them to talk me out of it. In any case, I had decided to give up on trying to find love. Part of me still wanted Lynn to have a mother, but it didn't look like that was going to happen.

I went to the bathroom, turned on the faucet, and splashed cold water on my face, trying to jolt myself out of my drunken stupor. I washed up, put on some sweatpants and a tank-top, and slipped on my sneakers.

Lynn rushed me to the car.

"Hurry up, Daddy."

"All right, all right. Why are you in such a rush?"

"That girl Erica is on the team, the one everyone says is as good as I am."

"Who says that?"

"Everyone, Daddy. Some of the coaches say she looks like me too, with the same gray eyes and everything. At first, some of them thought she was me, playing in other leagues. Her mom is the coach of this team."

"Hmm…" I said, rubbing my throbbing head.

I'd heard about another biracial girl who'd been scoring a lot in other leagues, but I hadn't given it much thought.

"Well, let's go."

Thanks to my hangover, my eyes were super sensitive to light, so I put on my shades when I walked Lynn into practice, wanting no part of the fluorescent lights in the gym.

We stepped on the court, and I got a glimpse of the coach, a gorgeous woman in a form-fitting, blue running suit that seriously showed off her figure. She had thick, full lips, painted with deep brown lipstick, but I could tell she was pretty on her own, without needing too much makeup, and that was a definite plus.

"Sorry we're late," I said.

"Please make sure Lynn is here on time from now on. I want to instill discipline in these girls, to keep them prepared for the court and life."

"I agree. I'm sorry about that, Mrs., uh…"

"Oh, it's Ms. Green, Jonna Green."

"Well, Ms. Jonna Green, you have my word that Lynn will never be late again."

"I appreciate it," she said with a beautiful smile.

There was something about Ms. Green that drew me in. I watched her run practice with the girls, and I was impressed. She spoke with diction and had an air about her that screamed strength and confidence. She was patient with the girls and didn't show any favoritism to her daughter, at least not any that I noticed. It was easy to see that Jonna was passionate about coaching.

After watching Lynn go through the drills, Jonna knew my baby was good. She didn't team her up with Erica; she put them on opposite teams to push each other. At first, I worried they'd end up butting heads and fighting, but by the time practice was over, they were complimenting each other's game.

"It looks like our daughters are getting along nicely," I said.

Jonna smiled. "Looks like it," she said, looking at her clipboard.

"Your practice is pretty intense. Did you play college ball?"

"Yup."

"This is your chance to brag. Tell me about yourself."

She put the clipboard down to her side and faced me.

"I played college ball for Sacred Heart. After that, I played two seasons in France. I missed my family, so I came back home, got my masters in physical education at Hofstra, and now I'm a gym teacher for Hempstead Schools."

"Impressive!"

"Thanks. I guess you played in college, too, huh?"

"Yeah, for Syracuse."

"Interesting. What have you been doing since?"

"I'm in the home improvement business. I renovate houses and do home repairs. If you ever need anything done in your house, let me know."

"I rent, so I can't do much to my place. Your house must be gorgeous, though."

"I rent too. It's my brother's house, so I try to keep it up to date."

"You live with your brother? Is he your roommate or something?"

"No, no… It's a two-family house. I rent the upstairs, completely separate."

"Ah. Well, I'm guessing the home improvement business isn't making you rich."

"It's enough to get by," I said with a shrug.

Feeling I wasn't doing a very good job of impressing her, I quickly changed the subject.

"Have you coached long? This looks like a lot of work."

"I've been doing it for about four years. I've been asking the league since year one for an assistant, but they haven't given me anyone yet. It's overwhelming sometimes, but that's okay. I make the best with what I have, and I love coaching these girls."

I nodded, hesitated for a moment, then asked, "So... Can I call you sometime?"

"Nope."

"Why not?"

"I don't date the parents of the girls I coach. It's a conflict of interests." She winked at me and said, "See you next practice though... and please remember to get Lynn here on time."

"We won't be late," I promised with a grin.

After practice, Lynn couldn't stop talking about how much she enjoyed playing against Erica.

"How would you feel if I helped Ms. Jonna coach the team?"

"That'd be cool, Daddy!" she said, excited.

"Yeah, I think so too."

The next day, I went to league headquarters and applied for the assistant manager position. I explained that I still held scoring records for all of Long Island and that I played college ball for Syracuse. Once the heads of the league heard my credentials, they practically handed me the job.

I thought being Jonna's assistant would bring us closer, but she wasn't thrilled about it.

"Hey! Guess who your new assistant coach is."

"I heard. Let me make this clear, so you understand. *I* run this team. If you think you're gonna come in here and take over, you're highly mistaken."

"I know you're in charge. I'm not trying to force you out or take over. I just want to get close to you, to get to know you better."

"What?"

"Well, since I'm no longer just a parent of a girl you coach; can I get your number?"

"You already have it. You're the new assistant coach. I'm sure the league gave it to you."

"They did, but they only want me to use it to discuss practices and games with you. I'm trying to get to know you so I can take you out. Can we go out sometime to get to know each other better?"

Jonna laughed and shook her head. "Nope. I don't shit where I eat."

★ ★ ★

Being Jonna's assistant helped me overall. I still did my work and over-time with Mr. Davis, and I took on side projects here and there, but Jonna influenced me to set a schedule for myself, so I was never late any-more. I started dressing better, kept my hair trimmed and on point, and shaved often, in an attempt to make myself more appealing for Jonna. On the court, we never clashed. I helped the girls with their condition-ing and moves, and Jonna was the mastermind behind strategic plays. Despite my improvements, though, Jonna remained distant with me.

"So? What's up with you?" I asked one day.

"What do you mean?"

"Why are you so bothered by me? You hardly give me the time of day. Do I scare you or something?"

"I'm not scared of anything."

"Hmm. Well, then you shouldn't be afraid to let me take you out sometime."

She smiled to herself. "Nick, you're a nice guy, but... Well, no offense, I just don't think it's a good idea."

"Why?"

"I don't want to sound like a bitch, but I'm looking for a man who's, uh...family and goal oriented, responsible and financially secure. I'm not getting those vibes from you."

"I've had a couple of setbacks in life, but I'm improving things steadily. I'm no slouch. Instead of trying to feel vibes, why don't you get to know me and see the real me for yourself?"

"You're persistent. I'll give you that."

"So can I call you to talk about things that aren't Basketball related?"

"Not today. One day...if you're lucky," she said with a wink.

I smiled at her, still determined to get her to go out on a date with me.

★ ★ ★

It took three weeks of flirting and heavy begging, but Jonna finally gave in and let me call her.

"Hey, Jonna, It's Nick."

"Hi. This is a first."

"Huh?"

"Well, on the rare occasions when I give men my number or in your case, the green light to call me, they usually wait days before calling me."

"I'm not like other guys. I'm interested in you and couldn't wait."

"Why? What makes me so special?"

"I like your style. You're beautiful, and smart…you're a great role model for little girls. Lynn thinks the world of you."

"Well, I like her too. If you don't mind me asking, though, where's her mother?"

I went on to tell her mine and Vickie's history, short as it was. Reliving the story hurt, but I was honest, and I knew Jonna appreciated that.

"Wow. What kind of woman does that, just abandons her daughter? Anyway, I think it's admirable that you're taking care of Lynn. Most men wouldn't."

"Like I told you, I'm not like most men."

"Yeah, I've heard that one before."

"Erica looks similar to Lynn," I noted. "Is she mixed too?"

"Yup."

It seemed like she wasn't comfortable delving into that topic yet, so I changed the subject.

"I didn't see a ring on your finger, but I have to ask. Are you still seeing her father?"

"Nope."

"Care to elaborate?"

"In time…if things go that far. Do you think I'm the type of woman who'd tell you to call her if I was still seeing him?"

"Uh, no. I didn't mean it like that," I said, tripping over my words.

"Good. Just so we're on the same page Nick, I'm not the type to bring men around my daughter. I have self-worth, and I don't share myself with a man unless I feel he's worthy. I don't mean to be blunt, but if you're looking for an easy fuck, I'm not the woman for you."

"And that's what draws me to you. That's what I want."

"What? A challenge?"

"No. I want a strong woman."

Jonna chuckled. "We'll see about that. Well, I gotta make dinner. It was good talking to you."

"Thanks for finally letting me talk to you as a friend instead of just your assistant. What made you give in?"

"I just wanted you to stop pestering me."

We shared a laugh.

"Well, I'm still intrigued by you, so I hope I'll get to talk with you again soon."

"You will. I'll be at practice tomorrow," she joked.

"All right. I'll see you then. Goodnight."

"Goodnight, Nick."

I talked to her on the phone regularly and made her laugh at practice. Every day, I grew more infatuated with her, but I began to feel as if we were moving at a snail's pace.

One day at practice, I decided to push it to the next level. "We keep winning," I said. "Maybe the two of us could...celebrate."

"Nick, I don't have time for a social life. It's just Erica and me. Between working full time, coaching, and helping my daughter with projects and homework, I don't have time to date."

"I'm going through the same things."

"I don't have money for a sitter, and—"

"You don't need one. Bring Erica with you, and I'll bring Lynn."

She hesitated for a moment, then agreed, "All right. I'm free Friday."

"Friday is perfect!" I said, thrilled. I knew I had to make the date count.

★ ★ ★

Lynn stood on top of my bed, helping me with my tie.

"Daddy, why are we getting so dressed up to see Ms. Jonna?" she asked.

"I want to make a good impression on her."

"Why do we have to wear our Easter clothes to do that?"

"I don't want Ms. Jonna to think I'm a bum. I want to look extra nice for her so she'll want to hang out with us more."

"Erica will, too, right?"

"Yup."

"Cool!" Lynn said, clearly excited about the idea.

Before we drove to Jonna's, I stopped by Oberle's Florist in East Meadow to pick up a gift for her. Lynn and I stood in front of Jonna's building, and Lynn pressed the button on the intercom while I held roses to surprise Jonna.

"Hey," Jonna said over the intercom.

"We're here."

"All right. Erica and I will be right down."

When Jonna came downstairs, she was stunning. Her black pencil skirt showed off her curves, and her heels made her already fabulous ass look even better. Her hair was neatly pinned up and professional-looking. When I greeted her with the six long-stemmed roses, she smiled.

"You look very handsome, Mr. Johnson." She turned to Lynn. "You look pretty, too, young lady."

"Thanks, Ms. Jonna. My dad got you flowers!"

"I see," she said, taking them from me. "Thank you. Six?"

"Yup! One for each win you've helped us get so far this season."

She gave me a slight grin, and by the time we walked to the car, the kids were already chatting and enjoying each other's company; it was a far cry different than the way Lynn had been with Hazel's monsters.

I swiftly jogged over to open Jonna's door for her when she got close, and she smiled at me again as she slid into the seat.

We went to Friendly's for dinner, and we laughed and talked as if we'd know each other all our lived.

When the waiter returned with the bill and placed it on the table between us, Jonna grabbed her purse and asked, "How much for Erica's and mine?"

The fact that she even asked, impressed me. When I dated Hazel, she never even considered paying for anything. I patted Jonna's hand and pulled the bill over to me.

"That's a nice gesture, and believe me when I say I appreciate it, but I got this. You're my date," I said, winking at her.

"Thanks," she said.

156

We quickly paid and walked back out to my car.

"The nights' still young, and it's not a school night. You wanna hang out some more?" I asked Jonna.

"Please, Mom? Please? I don't want to go home yet," Erica begged.

"Sure. What do you have in mind?"

"Hmm. The beach maybe?"

"At night?"

"Yup. It's free, and it's not crowded."

"Sounds like fun."

When we reached the beach, I grabbed an old blanket from the back of my truck, and the two of us walked barefoot in the sand, hand in hand.

The kids ran and played while Jonna and I laid the blanket down, made ourselves comfortable on it, and talked for what seemed like forever. We looked up at the stars and had one of the best conversations I'd ever had in life.

"Well, you now know everything about my history with Vickie, but you've never told me about your ex. What's his story?"

She sighed as if the memory still pained her.

"He left me two years ago."

"We can talk about something else if you want."

"No, it's fine. Talking about it is...therapeutic. It will help me avoid making the same mistakes."

Jonna cleared her throat before she continued, "He didn't want to be responsible anymore. He told me he loves Erica and me, but he loves himself more and isn't cut out to be a father and husband."

I rubbed her hand. "I'm sorry."

"Don't be. Christian leaving helped me."

"*Helped* you?"

"When he left, I was angry at first. I hated him, and I needed answers. I needed to understand how he could just up and leave me. He planned to stay with his parents until he found his own place, so I sped over there to curse him out." She swallowed, then continued, "I remember thinking he was pathetic for moving back with his parents. I laughed to myself when they called him to the door to talk to me. I thought he was a loser, a joke, but the joke was on me. He was brutally honest and told me I was never supportive of him, that I treated him like a child, picked fights and made the angry Black woman stereotype seem more like fact than fiction. He finished up by telling me I'll end up alone, like my mother."

"Damn. I'm sorry."

"Don't be! He was right. In the back of my mind, ending up like Mom has always been a fear of mine. I thought about what Christian said, and I looked back at my previous relationships. All my ex-boyfriends said similar things. Every relationship ended with me being dumped and heartbroken because of my attitude. The women in my family—my grandma, mom, and aunts—have treated men just like I did, and every one of them was left alone and single, to raise their kids on their own. It was a pattern I needed to break, not only for myself but also for Erica. I needed to set a good example for my daughter."

"So you're taking the blame for Christian leaving? I'm sorry, but I won't ever put all the blame on myself for Vickie abandoning Lynn and me."

"In your situation, I wouldn't expect you to take the entire blame, and I don't take all of it in my situation either, but I believe we have to own up to the mistakes we make. If we don't, we'll just keep making them."

I nodded, indicating that I understood.

"Christian's far from a saint, but once I stopped feeling like a victim and focused on improving myself, life got better. Unfortunately, he didn't wait to see my change. That was his loss. His parents said he got a job in North Carolina somewhere and didn't want to be reminded of our daughter or me. He feels child support and alimony are enough to satisfy his duty as a father. I can't change his feelings toward me, but I've learned from my mistakes, and he has to live with his. I'm ready to have a real, healthy relationship with the right man."

I nodded again.

"I want to find my soulmate, Nick, a man I can fall in love with, marry, have another child with, and grow old with."

When she mentioned the marriage and having another child, I thought about Hazel and remembered how she tried to manipulate me into the same things. I considered telling Jonna about my vasectomy, but our date was going so well, and I didn't want to ruin it.

"So? What's your story, Nick?"

"What do you mean? You already know about Vickie."

"What led you to where you are in your life right now?"

It was a hard question, something I was honestly afraid to delve into. I was already struggling to impress her, and I figured she already considered me a loser; I didn't want her to hear my story and view me as an even bigger failure.

"I guess the turning point for me was college," I said.

"What happened then?"

"Shit went downhill," I confessed. "I was playing college ball, on top of the world, and BOOM! I tore my ACL."

Jonna looked at me with sad eyes.

"I didn't have a back-up plan. I'd never asked myself what I'd do if I didn't make it. My dreams were to go pro, make tons of money, and be remembered as a playground and NBA legend. There was never a doubt in my mind that I'd make it." I paused and snapped my fingers. "Then, just like that, my dreams were taken from me. After I was injured, the college didn't give a shit about me. I wasn't anything special anymore. I lost my scholarship and had to return home. I started just existing, not living. I made some mistakes, but Lynn was the good thing that came out of all that. Being a father has made me feel alive again."

"You're a better guy than I gave you credit for, Nick."

"Really? Good enough for a second date?"

She smiled. "Yes."

"Good," I said, smiling back at her. I wanted that night to be the first of many dates for us.

CHAPTER 13

ONE-ON-ONE

Nick

We went on more dates, talked on the phone, and grew closer over time. As I got to know her, I realized that Jonna was different than any woman I'd ever met. She was perfect to me, but I wanted to know how Rhea and Scout would feel about her. For that reason, I invited Jonna and Erica to the house on a Sunday to meet them.

"Girl, you are too cool," Rhea said.

"I'm enjoying you too. Nick should've gotten us together a long time ago," Jonna said.

They stuck their tongues at me and laughed.

"They seem to be hitting it off," Scout said

"Yeah, that's a good sign. She never likes anyone I bring home."

"I haven't seen any alcohol in your hand in a couple of months," Scout noticed. "You're dressing better too. You must be really trying to impress this one."

"She's just…different than any woman I've ever dated."

"Here we go," he said, rolling his eyes. "You know, you say the same shit about every woman you date. I think it's interesting that you're trying to change for her, though."

"I know you think I'm bullshitting, but I'm serious. This one's different. She's educated and driven, and she makes me want to be those things too. She's worth changing for. Jonna's important to me."

"I've never heard you say any of *that* about a woman. I bet the sex is better than with Hazel."

"This has nothing to do with sex, Scout. Honestly, I haven't touched her. That's how I know what I feel is real."

"Really? Wow. I like this one already."

Rhea and Jonna made dinner while Lynn, Erica, Scout and I sat on the couch and watched the Lakers game. As we ate dinner, I realized that Jonna was quite comfortable with my family; I loved that because they were a big part of my life, and that was important to me.

We continued dating and often went on family outings like the circus, the zoo, the movies, and basketball games. Jonna and Rhea made plans to hang out regularly too. Rhea even agreed to watch the kids so Jonna, and I could go on dates alone, something she always hated doing for Hazel and me.

It was at a Knicks game where I realized how special Jonna was. "Hey, I got you a little something," I said.

"You didn't have to, Nick."

"I wanted to," I said, handing the brand new Coach bag to her.

"Nick, it's beautiful, but I can't accept this."

"Why not?"

"I know how much this retails for. I'm flattered, but it's just... not in your budget."

"It wasn't, but I like making you happy."

"I'm a simple woman, Nick. If you want to make me happy, return the bag and take me on more dates."

"You're the coolest woman I've ever met."

Jonna leaned in close, looked me in the eyes, and said, "I know."

After that, we couldn't help but laugh and enjoy the rest of our date together.

★ ★ ★

It was ten minutes before our game against the worst team in the league. So far in the season, the girls were undefeated.

Jonna's back was turned, and while she grabbed her clipboard, I brushed my mouth gently against her ear.

"You know there are twenty letters in the alphabet?"

162

A small smile grew across her face.

"I think you're missing a few."

I stroked my chin. "Nope. U–R–A–Q–T are just reserved for you," I said with a wink.

She giggled.

"Corny…but you're still missing one."

"Don't worry. If you play your cards right, I'll give you the D later."

She laughed and playfully pushed me.

"You're so fresh. Stop that before the kids see us."

When I looked over and saw Lynn and Erica grinning at us, I knew her warning was too late.

Jonna and I hadn't done anything sexual yet, but I wasn't mad about that. We flirted with each other all the time. The sexual tension was there, but Jonna told me she would only go that far when she knew she was in love. I respected that, and I wanted to be that man.

The game started, and while it should have been an easy win for us, the girls were slaughtered. Lynn and Erica were playing great, but the team wasn't holding their own. Still, I couldn't help hollering from the sidelines when I saw where improvements could be made.

"Lynn, what are you doing? Take her to the basket every time. She can't stop you!" I yelled.

Watching my daughter dominate on the court, with my number fifteen on her jersey, was a way of living vicariously through her. I wanted her to be a legendary ball player, to go to college and have all the opportunities I never had. I was hard on her, but it was just to push her to that next level.

We lost the game by twenty points, and the girls were devastated.

"Lynn," I said, walking up to my daughter, "next time we play those girls, you need to be more physical on defense. You were great offensively, but its defense that wins games."

"Yes, Daddy."

"Nick…" Jonna said, pulling me to the side.

"Yes, beloved?"

"I love it when you call me that. Anyway, don't you think you're being too hard on her? She did great tonight. It was the rest of the team who didn't come out to play."

"I'm not trying to put her down. I want her to learn so she'll get better and won't make the same mistakes next time."

"It wouldn't kill you to hug her when they lose, instead of just yelling at her. She needs to know you're proud of her, regardless of what the scoreboard says. She needs to think of playing ball as a release, not a chore."

"You're right," I said, then walked over to sit next to Lynn on the bench.

Erica was trying to cheer her up, but Lynn was super competitive like me and took the loss hard.

"Ladybug, you played a good game out there today," I said, pulling her into a hug as she continued to sulk. "I'm proud of you, baby, and I'm sorry for all the yelling. I'm just passionate when it comes to the game."

"I know, Daddy. Me too."

After the rest of the team and all the spectators were gone, Jonna prepared to lock up the gym.

"Hey, girls," she said, "you wanna watch me beat Nick in a game of one-on-one?" Jonna said.

"Yeah!" they yelled in unison.

"C'mon, Jonna," I said. "You sure you want to do this?"

"It'll cheer the girls up. Plus, I want to teach them something."

"All right."

I put on my knee brace and tied my sneakers. Jonna pulled her hair back in a tight ponytail.

"All right. We'll play to sixteen," Jonna said.

"I only play when something's at stake," I said, winking at her.

"A little bet, huh? What did you have in mind?"

I smirked.

Jonna laughed. "Don't be fresh, Nick."

"Okay, if I lose, I'll give you a kiss. If you lose, you'll give me one. Deal?"

She chuckled. "Deal! Let's do this!"

"You're gonna lose, Nick," Erica said.

"You're going down, Dad!" Lynn yelled.

"Thanks for the encouragement, Ladybug."

Jonna and I went at it. I soon learned that she was a lioness on the court—calculated, poised, and smooth yet aggressive. There was no doubt that she had played the same way in college and overseas. She knew I could physically overpower her, but it didn't stop her from going all out. She pushed me physically, and I couldn't slack off even a little. I had to play defense against her, and I would be damned if I was going to let her beat me.

Our kids watched and only cheered for Jonna, but that gave me added motivation to win. I loved the competition, and Jonna brought out the best in me—not just in the game but in overall life. She was supportive without nagging. Her competitiveness matched mine, and I loved that about her. I had to admit that I was falling in love with her.

Jonna hit me with a jab step, then caught me with a pump fake that had me in the air while she made her easy lay-up. The girls cheered loudly for her, clapping their hands. She was still down by five points, and I needed one to win the game. She knew I was weak on the left, due to my bad knee, so she drove to the basket on that side, but I was ready for her. I timed her move perfectly and swatted her lay-up against the backboard. I grabbed the rebound, cleared the ball, and shot a midrange jumper to end the game. I had to admire her for being smart enough to try to use my weakness to her advantage, even though it didn't work out as she hoped.

Our kids booed, but Jonna and I laughed.

"All right, Nick, are you ready for your reward?"

I nodded, stared at her, and drew her in for the kiss. It started off slow, then evolved to open-mouthed and hungry.

Jonna opened her eyes as I eased away from her.

"Damn," she said. "I haven't been kissed like that in a long time."

"My feelings were in that kiss."

"Mine too."

Our kids looked excited, but there was an awkward silence for a moment before Lynn asked, "Jonna, why did you play my dad one-on-one if you knew he was gonna win?"

"He might be bigger and stronger than me, but that doesn't mean he'll win every time. Look at him!"

"He looks tired," Lynn said, noticing that I was huffing and puffing, and my jersey was soaked with sweat.

"I went all out and pushed him to do the same," Jonna explained. "As a woman, you have to do your best in everything you do. Use whatever advantage you have to accomplish what you set out to do. You understand, girls?"

"Yes," they said, nodding.

Lynn looked at Jonna with admiration, and at that moment, I saw exactly what I was looking for in a positive mother figure for her.

CHAPTER 14

BITTERSWEET BEGINNINGS

Nick

Seven months later...

I'd known Jonna for about eighteen months, and we'd been dating for seven of them. In that time, we'd coached the girls to two LIYB basketball championships and had gone on numerous dates, but this was the first time I'd seen the inside of her apartment. Rhea and Scout took the girls to the Six Flags so we could enjoy a nice day to ourselves.

"Well, this is my place," she said, showing me around her nice, two-bedroom apartment. She had a large, tan leather sectional sofa and a huge big-screen TV in the living room. Her bookcase was filled with works by African-American authors like Richard Wright, Langston Hughes, and Ralph Ellison.

"This is nice."

"It isn't much, but it's the best I can do as a single mother," she said.

"Your place is fine. I rent from my brother. At least you're living on your own."

She nodded.

"You're the first man I've brought to my apartment in years."

"Don't I feel special?" I joked.

"You should. I don't bring men around my daughter or here, and now you've done both," she said, chuckling to herself. "You make me break all my rules."

"And you make me a better man. I love you, Jonna."

"I love you too…punk," she said, then playfully punched me.

We laughed; our version of *"I love you"* wasn't traditional, but it was us. We were different, but we balanced each other out.

Jonna held my hand and led me to her bedroom.

"I haven't shared myself with a man in a long time either," she said.

I slipped my arm around her waist and pulled her tightly against me.

"And I hope I'm the last man you ever share yourself with."

I undressed her slowly, taking my time to appreciate her, running my hands over all her curves. I breathed in the fresh scent of her hair, lifted her off the floor, then carried her over and laid her down on the bed. I climbed on the bed and lowered myself on top of her, then kissed her breast and licked all the way down, from her belly button to her treasure.

I licked the folds of her flower while she held my face between her thighs. I placed full attention on the head of her clit, licking and sucking on it.

Jonna's hips jerked helplessly, and she clawed and gripped her sheets.

"Shit!" she cried out.

Her eyes fluttered closed, and she trembled from the strength of her orgasm. I put on a condom, turned Jonna on her side, and entered her. She felt so wet and tight. Her fingertips lightly grazed my chest while her ass smacked loudly against my hips. I flipped her over on her stomach, held her hands, and stroked her. I sucked on her neck, cupped her breasts, and dipped in and out of her with long, deep strokes.

"Mmm…" she moaned.

I quickened my pace, and she began moaning uncontrollably. My own orgasm started building, and I grasped her hips and tightly rammed myself inside her with all my strength. Jonna buckled underneath me, and we came intensely together.

We lay there, panting, and when I finally caught my breath, I said, "I want to make things official."

"I want that, too, but if we do this, we have to promise to always be straight up and honest with each other. No bullshit, Nick," Jonna said.

"That's what I'm looking for, and I want it with you," I said, smiling.

As much as I meant those words, my conscience bothered me. I knew I should tell her about my vasectomy. It was the perfect time, but I didn't want to risk ruining the moment or our relationship. I knew women like Jonna only came once in a lifetime, if at all. *I'll worry about it when the time comes,* I finally decided and kept my secret to myself.

Things with Jonna were great. She knew how to push and motivate me, and it never felt manipulative or controlling. She helped me budget my money, so I was finally able to get myself out of debt and pay off all my credit cards.

With that weight off my shoulders, I wanted to help her too. To conserve money and see if we were truly up to the challenge of one day taking our relationship to the next level, I convinced Jonna to give up her apartment and move in with me. Scout and Rhea loved the idea. Scout felt Jonna was helping me become the man he always knew I could be, and Rhea viewed Jonna as her best friend and loved having her around all the time. The kids already referred to themselves as sisters, and I'd never seen Lynn so happy.

I was open and honest with every aspect of my life, all the positives, and all the negatives, except for the secret of my vasectomy. Life was good, and I was terrified of ruining it. I continued keeping that to myself, and I hoped it wouldn't blow things apart when it all came to light.

CHAPTER 15

SISTERS

Lynn

"Goodnight, girls," Jonna said, tucking us in and kissing us goodnight.

"Goodnight," we said in unison, giggling.

Jonna smiled and pulled the door closed behind her.

It was our first night sharing a room, and we talked for most of it.

"I don't know if this sounds weird, but I feel like we're really a family now that you're living here," I said.

"Nah, that's not weird. I feel the same way."

"I've always wanted a mom, and I feel like I finally got one, along with a sister."

"Thanks! I like your dad too."

"Can I ask you a question?"

"Go ahead."

"I never met my mom. I only have an idea of what she's like, from what Dad and Aunt Rhea told me. You lived with your dad. What was he like?"

"I don't know. I don't really remember," Erica said.

"You don't? It wasn't that long ago."

Erica huffed. "I hate him. I don't want to remember him."

"I'm sorry."

"It's not your fault. I'm mad that he selfishly left Mom and me and didn't even bother to call or write to see how we're doing. He just doesn't care."

I understood how she felt because I felt the same way about my mom. It was dark, but I saw Erica roll over on her side, trying to hide the fact that she was crying. I walked over and sat on the edge of her bed.

"Are you okay?" I asked.

"No, not really. You're lucky. Your dad loves you. Mine never cared about me. White people don't care about Black people."

"Don't say that!"

"Why? It's true. Your White mom left you, and my White dad left me. Don't you see the pattern there?"

"Just because they're stupid, that doesn't mean the whole race is. My dad said that even though people see me as Black, I'm really both, so hating either side would be like hating half of myself."

"I don't care."

"Well, both sides of me think you're great."

Erica laughed a little. "You're a cornball, but thanks."

"You love my positivity! Anyway, Dad says the color of a person's skin doesn't make them bad or good. A person's actions determine that. There are good and bad people in every race." I paused and scrunched up my nose. "Ew! Did I just quote my dad?"

"Yeah, you did," Erica said, laughing. "I guess he's right, but at least you have your dad to talk to you about stuff like that."

"You have your mom."

"Yeah, I know. I just wish I had both of them, and things were different."

Since Erica lived in my town now, she also transferred to my school. When the other kids picked on us, which they often did, we stood up for each other. It felt good to have someone my age around, someone like me, a person I could talk to because she really understood me.

On the basketball court, we dominated. We knew each other's game so well that we could beat almost any team by ourselves, no matter how bad the other girls on our team were. We were the perfect dynamic duo.

★ ★ ★

"What are you doing?" Erica asked when she caught me staring out the window again.

"A family is moving in across the street, a Black lady, and some White guy. It looks like they have a daughter our age," I said.

"Let me see!" Erica said.

"I hope their daughter doesn't get too comfortable. It'll only be a matter of time before her dad will get tired of them and split."

"Don't be like that, sis. Let's go say hi."

Erica sighed and rolled her eyes but agreed to go with me. We walked across the street and introduced ourselves.

"It's good to meet you, girls. I'm Gladys. My husband, the one over there putting up the basketball hoop, is Caleb, and that's our daughter. Jackie, come here and get to know our neighbors."

Jackie walked over to us. She was pretty but a little on the chunky side and taller than both of us. She had hazel eyes, and her complexion was as light as ours. Jackie's mom, Gladys, was pretty, with brown skin and so much makeup that she looked like she was about to step on the red carpet. Just by the way she talked with her hands and the way she dressed, I knew she was too prissy to be a ball player.

Caleb, on the other hand, was about my dad's height, six-three, with dirty blond hair. When he saw us, he waved and went back to working on the hoop.

"Hi," Jackie said shyly.

"I'm Lynn, and this is my sister, Erica. We live across the street. Do you play ball?"

"Yeah. I used to play for a team in my old neighborhood in Rockville Centre."

"That's cool. We play too," I said.

"Are you any good?" Erica added.

"Pretty good. I was the leading scorer in my league."

"Well, that won't mean anything here. I played against girls in that town, and they were soft."

"Erica!" I yelled, nudging her.

"It's okay. She's right. Those girls weren't much competition. Dad's setting up the hoop so I can work on my post game."

"You wanna come over and shoot with us until he's done?" I invited.

"Sure."

★ ★ ★

We were sitting in the lunchroom, and I saw Jackie standing there holding her tray, looking lost, lonely and confused about where she was going to sit.

"Hey, Jackie! Come sit with us!" I invited.

She smiled and walked toward our table.

"Ugh, I don't like her," Erica said.

"Why? Be nice, sis."

Erica rolled her eyes.

"We don't have to be friends with every mixed girl we meet, Lynn."

"Don't be like that. Jackie seems really nice. Plus, there's strength in numbers."

"She talks too damn much," Erica argued. "She's too bubbly and friendly, to the point where it's sickening. Not only that, but she's also a spoiled little preppy princess."

"Come on. She's not so bad. She's on our basketball team now, so having her around us is a good thing. You remember what your mom says. A close team is a strong team."

"Well, she should thank you. I'm only nice to her because of you. I'd never be friends with her if you didn't push her on me."

I playfully lifted Erica's cheeks into a smile, which made her laugh.

It was true about Jackie. She was spoiled and lived a sheltered life, but there was more to it than Erica was telling me. She would never admit it, but Erica was jealous of Jackie's close relationship with her dad. At games, whenever Jackie's parents cheered and hugged her, Erica always made faces and mumbled under her breath. Deep down, Erica was still mad that her father had abandoned her, and she took that anger out on Jackie.

Jackie sat down next to me. "Thanks. The other kids haven't been very nice to me."

"Well, we're teammates. You can hang out with us anytime."

"I appreciate it."

In time, Jackie grew on Erica. We were all close, but I was the glue that kept us all together. Having Jackie around was like having another sister.

CHAPTER 16

NOT FAIR

Scout

"Joe, it's okay," Rhea said, reassuring me.

I slipped my briefs back on and sat on the edge of the bed, feeling dejected and hanging my head. I held my face in my hands in embarrassment.

"It's not okay, Rhea. A man should be able to please his damn wife."

"You do please me, baby. I enjoyed you going down on me."

"But I ruined everything else by going limp-dick on you, right?"

"That isn't what I meant."

I punched the bed. "I don't know what the fuck is wrong with me."

"You're just stressed out. You barely sleep, you're always working, and you're constantly worrying about taking care of your brothers. You're burnt out. I'll plan a vacation for us. Getting away from everything will do you some good."

I slumped my shoulders. My lips and hands began to tremble. I felt pathetic. I was on the verge of crying, but the last thing I wanted to do was look like a bitch in front of my wife.

"Joe, maybe you should see a doctor," she said quietly.

"I don't need to waste my time and money on that. All I need is a vacation, and everything will go back to normal."

"I don't doubt that, baby, but you should see a doctor just to make sure it's nothing...internal. I love you, Joe, and I want you to be okay. Promise me you'll see someone."

I looked in Rhea's eyes and saw nothing but love and concern for me. We had married right out of high school, and she'd always been supportive, patient and loyal. She didn't deserve the shit I put her through, but she supported me anyway. I never wanted to take her for granted; I owed her the world because she was my world.

"All right. I'll go to the doctor, but I'm sure there's nothing physically wrong with me."

"It's better to be safe than sorry, Joe."

In spite of what she said, I was ashamed of myself. I knew a man should be able to satisfy his wife, yet I couldn't stay hard enough to even have sex with her. For the past year, it had been more and more difficult for me to keep an erection; the desire was there, but my body simply wouldn't respond. It got so bad that I started putting in more time at work to avoid sleeping with Rhea. Spacing our intimacy out worked for a while, but eventually, even that strategy stopped working. I had to come to terms with the fact that my dick was becoming dysfunctional. Rhea deserved more than that, so I agreed to go to the doctor to see if it could be fixed.

★ ★ ★

I went to the doctor and told him about my problems. After a couple of visits and several tests, he decided to give me a needle biopsy, just to be safe. The next visit changed my life forever.

"What's up, Dr. Donadio?"

"Hey, Joe. Have a seat. There are some things we need to discuss," he said, his face solemn.

"What's the problem?" I asked. "Do I need to stay away from sweets and get more sleep or something?"

"Joe, it's a bit more serious than that. The biopsy results came back. You have prostate cancer."

"What!?" I cried, standing up from my chair and staring at him in disbelief. "No! That can't be right."

"I know it sounds scary, but it isn't a death sentence. If we act quickly and aggressively, you have a very strong chance of survival, and—"

"No, Doctor! Your tests are wrong," I screamed, cutting him off. In a rage, I grabbed the chair and slammed it on the floor repeatedly.

"Joe, please stop. I know you're upset, but—"

"You don't know shit. You don't know what this feels like. What am I supposed to tell my wife, huh? Am I supposed to say, 'Oh, sorry, baby. I can't fuck you. I'm dying of cancer'?"

"Joe, I'm really sorry. I truly am, but I'm sure your wife cares more about your survival than sex. More than anything, she wants you to be healthy."

At that moment, after he gave me that horrible diagnosis, I felt like more of a failure than I'd ever felt like in my life. I'd never be able to give Rhea the children she and I always wanted, and now I was scared I would end up being a burden on her. I imagined her taking care of me while I withered and died. I'd never know fatherhood. I wouldn't have a chance to pass down the business to my child, the way my dad did for me.

I shook my head. "This isn't fair," I said.

"We have to act swiftly, Joe."

"Do I really have any chance of beating this thing?"

"Yes, as long as we get started on treatment."

"Will I ever be able to make love to my wife again?"

Dr. Donadio sighed. "Joe, the two bundles of nerves that control erections, have been significantly damaged by the cancer. Your prostate has to be removed. Erections might be possible with the help of a mechanical pump, and…" He paused to look at me while I stared at the carpet. "Are you okay?"

"Yeah, go on. What else?"

"Well, after surgical removal of the prostate, you won't be able to have sex for six to eight weeks. Then, even with the mechanical assistance of a pump, it's going to be difficult to achieve an erection, due to the mental barriers and personal frustrations that usually come with not being able to achieve erections on your own. In time, though, I believe you can accomplish it."

My anger melted into deep sadness as I sat back down in my chair and began to weep. "Just tell me what to do next."

Dr. Donadio and I set up appointments, but I was in such a daze that I didn't hear a word he said.

During my drive home, I thought about how to break the news to Rhea. I even questioned killing myself, but I couldn't do that to her.

When I walked into the house, Rhea was cooking dinner.

"Hey, baby," she said excitedly, then walked over to kiss me.

"Hey."

"How was your day?"

"Uh…eventful."

"Question. What do you think about Lynn coming with us on the vacation?"

"Fuck no! Fool can watch his own damn daughter. Ever since that child was born, we've spent more time with her than he has. You'd think his selfish ass would realize we might want to spend some time alone without babysitting his kid."

"Joe, I didn't think you'd be that upset about it. I'm sorry I asked. Did everything go okay with your doctor appointment?"

I knew there was no point in hiding it from Rhea, so I slowly told her everything. She wept for a while, then composed herself and held me.

"Rhea, I think we should get a divorce. You should leave me."

She slapped me. "Stop talking crazy!" she snapped.

"I can't give you a child, Rhea. I can't be a real husband to you anymore. Not only that, but I might not even make it."

"When I married you, I made a vow before God to love you in good times and bad, in sickness and health. Our marriage means everything to me. I love you, Joe, and I'm not going anywhere. We'll fight this together, and we'll make it work."

"Baby, I can't ask you to do that for me."

"You're not asking. You have no say in the matter. You took those vows, too, and now you're stuck with me."

All my life, I had done things by the book, everything I was supposed to. I was responsible. I rarely ever drank and never touched drugs.

The day Dad died, I promised Mom I'd take care of the business and the family. Now, I was facing the possibility that my days were numbered, and that reality was hard to take. As I thought about coming to my own end, I remembered my last day with my father…

★ ★ ★

"Scout," Momma called, barely audible.

I held her as we cried together in the hallway after the doctors explained to us that Dad had passed away from a stroke. Dad and I were in the shop when he collapsed, working on a machine.

Momma was a wreck. Rhea rubbed her back while we walked with her to the waiting area.

"Thanks for being here, baby," Momma said.

"Of course."

"Have you heard from your brothers yet?"

I shook my head.

"Oh," she said, disappointed.

"Stay with your mom. I'll call the house again to see if they're home," Rhea said.

I was sure Chance was somewhere getting high with Crystal and Fool was hanging out with Vince and Cyrus, chasing women. Neither of them was there in Dad's last moments, and neither had any clue that he'd passed away.

"Scout, you're daddy has always been proud of you. He knew you'd be the one to run the business someday," Momma said, choked up with emotion. "I miss him already," she said.

"I know. I miss him too."

"I love all you boys the same. You know that."

"I know, Momma."

"You're all special in your own unique ways, but you're the first-born and the most responsible. I need you to promise me a few things."

"Anything, Momma."

"Promise me you'll take care of your father's business. Don't sell it or give it to anyone outside of our family."

"I promise."

"Your daddy poured his heart and soul into that business. He worked too hard for too many years to have it all thrown away."

I nodded.

"He always wanted the three of you to work together and run it when he was gone, but I guess the Lord has different plans for your brothers."

I patted her hand.

"Your brothers aren't as strong as you. God blessed y'all with different talents, but he made you wiser than them. I need you to promise me that you'll always take care of your brothers. Promise me, baby."

"I promise, Momma."

I kept my word and did everything I was supposed to do. I went to college and got my bachelor's degree in business. I didn't go away for school like I wanted; out of a sense of responsibility, I went to St. John's University so I could stay close to home. While my dumb-ass brothers were always fucking up, I was learning the business and planning for the future.

When Dad died, my brothers were nowhere to be found. When it came to handling things for the funeral and bills for the house, I had to cover it all by myself. Our dad always handled the finances, so when he died, Momma was lost. A couple of years later, her diabetes got the best of her. She passed away from cardiovascular disease shortly after that, and I was left with the burden of handling everything alone, while my brothers coasted.

Money was tight. For the business to grow, I begged Rhea to let me put our life savings into it and take over the mortgage for my parents' house. I convinced her that we'd make the house our own and fill up my childhood home with lots of children.

Chance was a dope fiend, always in and out of jail. Fool was a lazy-ass dreamer who had done nothing with his life. Nevertheless, I was the one who ended up with fucking cancer. Both my kids were taken from me by miscarriage, but Fool had a beautiful child, after all the dumb-ass messing around he did. I was tired of being the punchline of God's cruel life joke. *It just isn't fucking fair!*

CHAPTER 17

TESTS

Nick

Rhea and Jonna were excited about making dinner for Easter Sunday, and Lynn and Erica helped out in the kitchen while Scout and I sat in the living room, channel-surfing.

"Joe, can you and Nick go to the store and pick up some more cheese for this macaroni?" Rhea asked.

"Sure, babe," he said.

I didn't know what his problem was, but Scout seemed crankier than usual. We drove to Pathmark in silence, until I spoke up and asked, "You all right, man?"

"Never better."

"You look pissed off about something."

"Leave me be."

Inside the grocery, I purposely bothered him, hoping it'd force him to start talking. I playfully pushed him and threw random shit in the shopping cart.

"Stop! You act like a fucking child sometimes."

"I'll stop when you tell me what's wrong."

"Just drop it."

On the way home, I turned the radio up and sang loudly in his ear as he drove.

"Enough!" Scout yelled, turning the radio off.

"What's up with you? You're moping around and snapping at

me for every little—"

"I've got cancer, Fool," Scout said, interrupting me.

"What!?"

"You heard me. I have cancer."

"Shit! Does Rhea know?"

"Yeah, she knows everything. She's not taking it well. She wanted me to tell you while she told Jonna and Lynn. That's what this whole food store trip is really about."

"How'd you find out?"

"Well, I've been trying to get Rhea pregnant for a while now."

"Yeah, I know."

"I've been having a hard time, uh...getting it up. At first, I thought it was my blood pressure since I've been stressed and tired a lot. Rhea has been patient with me, but I didn't want to push it. I needed to figure out what the hell was wrong."

I nodded.

"Anyway, I went to the doctor and had lots of tests, blood work, and a needle biopsy done. The results came back saying I have prostate cancer."

I had to be strong. I didn't want my fearful expression to depress him or make him feel as if he'd been handed a death sentence.

"You'll be all right. You're blessed, man. You'll pull through this," I said.

Scout pulled over to the side of the road. His hands were shaking on the steering wheel, and tears filled his eyes instantly.

"The two bundles of nerves that control erections got fucked up by the cancer. On top of that, my prostate has to be removed."

He looked at me sternly, with tears streaming down my face.

"The doctor says I won't be able to get erections anymore without a pump, and even that might not work. What kind of man am I now, huh? If Rhea stays with me, she'll never have a chance to be a mother. How can I be a husband to her when I can't even please her?" he shouted, then punched the steering wheel. "This isn't fair. She's doesn't deserve this," he said.

For the first time in my life, I witnessed my brother break down and cry. I held him while he sobbed. I felt his pain, but I didn't know what to say to make him feel better. I did the best I could.

"Rhea loves you, Scout. What you two have together is more than sex. She and I will help you get through this. You'll beat this."

"What if I don't?"

"You will!"

"There's no guarantee. This shit might kill me. How do you know I'm gonna beat it?"

"Because you will, man. Have faith. What did the doctor say?"

"He's sending me to an oncologist. He wants me to start getting radiation, chemo, and surgery ASAP."

"I got your back. Everything is going to be okay," I said, though I wasn't sure if I was trying to reassure him or myself more. I was terrified. We argued a lot, but I could never imagine living my life without him.

"I'm glad you said that because I need you to do something for me," Scout said.

"Anything. What's up?"

"Stop dicking around and work with me at the shop. Dad started that business, and I'll be damned if I have to close it or sell it before I die."

"Don't talk like that."

"Don't make me then. You'll make more money working with me than Mr. Davis pays you. I'll teach you everything. That way, if I do, pass, you'll be able to keep it going and run it when I'm gone."

"There's no way I could ever run that business without you."

"Dad built it for *us*. I need you to act like a man and do this with me. Now, are you in or not?"

I sighed, not quite sure if I could pull it off, but I felt I had no other choice.

"Okay. I'm in," I finally said.

We drove back to the house, and Scout continued telling me things about the business, but as we got closer to home, we became quiet, lost in our thoughts.

"Fuck no! Not today!" Scout yelled when we pulled up to the house. "What the hell is he doing here?" he said, looking in shock at Chance, our brother, sitting on the curb in a ragged t-shirt, smoking a cigarette. As soon as Scout parked the car, he got out and stormed over to him. Chance stood to look him in the face.

"Hey, Scout. It's been a long time."

Scout didn't say anything, but a deep crease formed on his forehead and his jaw tightened as he continued to stare down our little brother.

"When did you start smoking cigarettes?" I asked Chance.

"Just a stupid habit I picked up."

"Yeah, you're used to dumb habits," Scout grumbled.

"The last time I was around, I messed up big. I wasn't in my right mind, and I'm here to correct that. No more bullshit. I'm done with heroin…for good this time," Chance said, then reached to shake Scout's hand.

Scout's face was etched with anger. He lunged toward Chance and tackled him to the pavement. Chance was scrawny. Scout easily manhandled him, mounted, and pummeled him, landing punch after punch on his face. I ran over and dragged Scout off him. Scout jerked away from me and dusted himself off.

Chance stood, his legs still wobbly from the beat-down. "I deserve that and more," he said.

"Damn right you do," Scout barked. He then turned to me. "The last time you saw this junkie, he abandoned your daughter and trashed your place. Why the hell are you breaking up the fight, Fool? Hell, you should be stomping his ass with me."

"I've changed," Chance said.

"You sound like a broken record. Every time you pop back around, you say the same bullshit. You play the game, gain our trust, and then fuck us over, but guess what. It's not happening this time. You, Rhea, and no one else is gonna convince me to help you."

"Rhea feels the same way you do. She wouldn't let me in the house. She told me to keep my punk ass outside until you came home."

"There was no point in waiting for me. I'm done with you for good. You're a disgrace to our parents' name."

"Go ahead. Yell at me. Tell me I'm a piece of shit. Call me a disgrace. I know I'm a fuck-up, but I want to fix that now."

Scout shook his head and chuckled. "I promised Momma I'd always take care of the two of you, no matter what, but Chance, you've pushed me past the point of keeping that promise. You let Charles and Crystal bring you down, and—"

"Crystal is dead, Scout. She died in my arms, overdosed right in front of me. My girl and all my friends are either dead, in jail, or ruined because of heroin. I'm done. I have no one right now. Every time I relapsed, it was to get back to Crystal. I loved her, but her death has given me the strength to finally get this monkey off my back. I'm trying to pull my life together and make something of myself."

Scout clapped his hands.

"Bravo! You're misusing your talent. You should be a salesman, trying to sell me that crock of shit."

"I'm serious, Scout. Just gimme a chance."

"No."

"I have nowhere to go, Scout."

"Go back to whatever hole you crawled out of. You stole from your family like we were just suckers on the street. I'm sorry you lost your girl, but those who live by the sword, die by the sword. You chose this pathetic life for yourself."

Chance looked desperate, and I couldn't help feeling sympathy for him; even after what he did to me, he was still my brother.

"Scout, he's fucked me over, too, but he's our blood. Don't be like that," I pleaded.

Scout shook his head and walked to the house. "I swear, if this cancer doesn't kill me, you two will be the death of me. Bring your silly asses in the house, and let's eat dinner."

"Wait, what did he just say? Does Scout have cancer?" Chance asked.

"We'll explain everything in the house."

★ ★ ★

"Jonna, this is my baby brother, Jimmy. We all call him Chance."

"How are you?" he said, shaking her hand,

"I'm well. It's nice to meet you. This is my daughter, Erica."

He waved and quickly cast his eyes down at the floor, clearly embarrassed by the way he looked.

"Ladybug, you might not remember, but this is your Uncle Jimmy."

He smiled. "Wow! You got so big. I remember you when you were just a baby."

"Hi, Uncle Jimmy," Lynn said.

"Ugh. Don't call me that. Uncle Chance is fine."

Dinner was good but awkward. Everyone was aware of Scout's diagnosis, and no one knew what to say to Chance.

After dinner, Scout asked Chance and me to join him in his home office.

"Rhea and I are gonna give you one last shot, Chance," he said. "Tonight, the three of us will move my office stuff in the garage, and you can stay in here, in our old room."

"Thank you."

"Don't thank me. Just don't cross me."

"I won't."

★ ★ ★

"Pull over," Scout mumbled.

"What's wrong?" I asked.

"Just pull over!" he shouted.

I did as he asked.

Scout jumped out of the car, bent over, and threw up along the side of the road on the way home from his chemo and radiation session; they always made him sick as a dog.

Scout had the surgery to remove his prostate, and we were in the fourth month of a six-month chemotherapy cycle. It hurt his pride tremendously, but we were all just happy he was alive. He spent most of his time at the shop, teaching Chance and me the business.

Chance took in what Scout taught us, but he wasn't interested in working at the shop; he wanted to be his own man. He continued cutting hair around the neighborhood like he used to and went on job interviews often, but he was having a hard time finding work because of his record.

I took Chance with me when I went to break the news to Mr. Davis that I wouldn't be able to work with him consistently anymore.

"It's good to know Joe is doing well after the treatment. My wife Eleanor died of lung cancer, from second-hand smoke, so I know how hard cancer can be on the family. You're doing the right thing, working with your brother. Your daddy always wanted that anyway."

"I can still do smaller projects on the side, just nothing major."

"I'll keep that in mind," Mr. Davis said.

"Dad taught *all* of us how to work on houses," Chance chimed in. "Is there any way I can fill in for the bigger jobs, the ones Nick would have done? I need the work and the money. I'm trying to change my life and stay busy, but I'm not getting any job offers. Would you be willing to give me a shot, Mr. Davis?" Chance begged.

Mr. Davis stared intently at Chance. "I'll give you one, Jimmy, but don't waste it. I'm aware of your struggles with drugs, and I won't let anyone give my business a bad reputation."

"Mr. Davis, I've put all that behind me."

"Good. Keep it there, and we won't have any problems."

★ ★ ★

A year went by, and things were going well. The girls continued winning championships in all their leagues. Scout showed major improvement after his cancer treatments, and the doctor even said he was close to being in remission. Chance was surprising us all, working and turning his life around, and Jonna and I were happy together and still going strong. Life was testing all of us, but we were handling it well.

THIRD QUARTER
Truths

CHAPTER 18

GROWING UP

Nick

"Daddy!" Lynn screamed at the top of her lungs.

Jonna and Rhea were out running errands, Scout was resting after getting his treatment, and Chance and I were changing the oil in my truck when I heard her shriek from inside the house. We dropped our tools and ran inside, worried that Lynn or Erica had gotten hurt.

"Lynn?" I yelled. "Where is she?" I asked Erica.

She pointed down the hallway.

"I'm in the bathroom, Daddy."

I heard Lynn sobbing behind the door, but when I twisted the doorknob, I found that it was locked.

"Ladybug, what's going on in there? Are you all right?"

"When is Jonna or Aunt Rhea coming home?"

"I don't know. What's wrong?" I asked.

"You okay, kid?" Chance asked from behind me.

I twisted the doorknob again.

"I-I'll let you in, Daddy, but only you. Nobody else can come in here."

"All right," I said, exchanging a curious look with my oil-covered brother.

The door opened just enough for me to squeeze in. When I stepped inside, I saw Lynn wringing her hands together. She was wearing her bathrobe, and I noticed a wad of toilet tissue with blood on it.

"Did you cut yourself?" I asked.

"No," she said, her lips trembling. "My stomach was really hurting bad, and I was gonna take a bath, but I just...started bleeding from, uh...down there. This is so embarrassing."

My eyes widened when I realized what was going on. My baby was growing up and going through puberty. She was having her first period at 13. I stood there awkwardly for a few seconds, feeling uncomfortable in the situation but also a little happy that I was there to help her through the experience.

"It's nothing to be ashamed of, Ladybug. Do you know what's happening?"

"Sort of. Aunt Rhea told me a little about it, and some of the girls on the team have already gone through it. Am I having my period, Daddy?" she asked meekly.

"Yeah. It's normal for a girl your age. It means you're healthy, and you're growing up, so don't be shy about talking to me about it," I said, wrapping my arm around her.

She eased out of my embrace, still looking mortified.

"What do I do now?"

"Well, let's have a look around here to see if Rhea or Jonna have a pad you can use."

"Then what? What do we do? Do you know how to use them?"

"Not really, Ladybug."

Lynn groaned.

"We can read the instructions on the box and figure it out together."

Her face softened a bit.

I searched the cabinet under the bathroom sink and found a box of Always pads. I had no idea what I was doing, but I had to play it cool to keep Lynn from freaking out.

"It'll be okay," I said. "We can tough it out until Rhea and Jonna get home. When they get here, you can ask them all the questions you want."

Lynn drained the water, pulled the shower curtain closed, and took a shower while I squinted to read the tiny instructions printed on the box. When she was finished showering, she stood behind the shower curtain while I handed her a thick, terrycloth bath towel, her clothes, and the pad. I told her what she needed to do, and when it was all over, she seemed calm and relaxed.

"You all right, baby?" I asked.

"Yeah. Thanks, Daddy," she said, pulling me into a hug.

I smiled. "No problem, Ladybug."

"Don't tell Uncle Chance about this, okay? I don't wanna talk about it in front of him."

"We won't. I'll just say you weren't feeling good." I smiled at her. "Put your socks and shoes on."

"Why? Where are we going?"

"Out for ice cream. My little girl is turning into a woman, and we've gotta celebrate that. We'll grab some really quick before your Aunt Rhea gets home."

"I've never heard of anyone celebrating a period before, Daddy."

"Well, there's nothing wrong with starting a new tradition!"

★ ★ ★

When Rhea and Jonna came home, I told them what was up.

Chance went upstairs to watch TV, while I stayed behind, listening to them teach Erica and Lynn about women's hygiene and the birds and the bees. In all honesty, I learned a thing or two myself during that conversation.

"Remember, girls, anyone can have sex, but sex without love is meaningless," Aunt Rhea said.

"If you do decide to give yourself to a man, make sure he's deserving of your love. Whenever you are intimate with a guy, you're giving him part of yourself, part of your soul. You don't want to give something so precious to just anyone," Jonna added.

I was happy Lynn had two strong women to help her on the path to becoming one.

When the talks were over, and the girls were put to bed, Rhea, Jonna, and Chance told me about a trip they had planned.

"Last year, when Joe was diagnosed, I promised him we'd take a nice vacation together. I held off for a while because the chemo and radiation made him so sick, and I want him to enjoy the trip. He's improved a lot lately, so we're planning to go next month. Joe isn't into amusement parks and stuff like that, so I rented a huge cabin in the Poconos, big enough for all of us. I researched it, and there are a whole bunch of activities we can do there," Rhea said.

"That sounds good, but I don't know if I can go. I'm still learning the business. Besides, I'm sure Joe doesn't want any of us tagging along on your trip."

"He's the one who brought it up, believe it or not. He wants you all there."

I looked at Jonna questioningly.

"I'm all for it," she said.

Chance nodded. "It'd be good to get away for a while."

"All right. Cool. I'm down then," I said.

CHAPTER 19

MY DOWNFALL

Chance

"Babe, can you take a picture of the three of us brothers together?" Scout asked Rhea.

She nodded. "Sure."

"Come on, Chance," Fool said, waving me over.

After we had taken a few snapshots of the three of us and all the ladies, we reminisced about our late parents and laughed at the trouble we used to get in as kids. It felt good to be around my brothers, and I felt like I was a real part of the family again. We hadn't been together like that in years, and it felt nice.

I enjoyed the time with my brothers, but it also depressed me. Scout had a good woman in Rhea. He was recovering and getting stronger every day from his cancer. He'd made Dad's old business more successful than our father ever could've dreamt. Fool was doing well too, working with Scout and enjoying his relationship with a good woman of his own. I never thought he'd change, but having Lynn brought out the best in him. As always, I felt like everyone was doing well but me.

I had finally stopped doing dope, but it constantly called me. I felt it all the time, but whenever I fell into depression, the craving only got stronger.

It was a rainy day, and we decided to stay in and watch movies. While Scout channel-surfed, Jonna yelled out, "Wait! Go back."

"What's up?"

"*Why Do Fools Fall in Love?* is on. I love that movie."

Scout flipped back a few channels.

"Oh, good. It just started. Y'all don't mind if we watch this, right?" Jonna asked.

Everyone shook their heads.

"Hey, Fool, they made a movie about you and Jonna," Scout teased.

Fool shook his head. "Ha-ha," he said, rolling his eyes.

"I'm all for it, girl. That Lorenz Tate is so handsome," Rhea said.

"Hey now!" Scout said.

"Oh, baby, don't be jealous. He comes second to you, of course." Rhea said, then gave him a peck on the lips.

"Damn skippy."

Watching the movie and seeing Frankie Lymon's downward spiral only threw me into deeper sadness. I knew what it felt like to have that monkey on my back, to need that high to take me away from my shitty reality. My brothers never knew what it was like growing up in their shadows. Scout was good at everything, and Fool was legendary on the basketball court, but I had nothing to make myself or our parents proud. Our parents loved all of us, but I knew they didn't love me the same as they loved my brothers. Nothing I did ever pleased them, and I always felt like a failure.

I was the only one who didn't go to college. My brothers had career options, but I was limited. I knew I would never truly be my own man like I wanted to since the only decent job I could get was working with Mr. Davis or working with them. During the numerous times when I was sober and trying to clean up my act, I went to interview after interview, but they all ended with the same result. As soon as they asked if I'd ever been arrested and found out I'd done time, the interviews were over, and all opportunities flew out the window. It was hard not to relapse when my future looked so bleak. Once that needle was in my arm, I didn't think about the dreams I'd never fulfill or the people I had hurt and disappointed. I was numb to the pain. Heroin helped me to exist in a life that felt meaningless.

Like a lot of men in history, my downfall began with a woman. I wasn't always a fiend. I started out with the goal of wanting to be a dealer…

★ ★ ★

"Make sure y'all never get hooked on this shit," Charles warned.

My friend Zeke and I listened as he taught us all about drug dealing while Crystal tied up his flabby arm.

We'd known each other since we were kids, growing up on the same block. I never really liked Charles, but I stuck around for Crystal. They always fought, so I figured it would only be a matter of time before they'd break up and I could step in and take her for myself.

She flirted with me all the time and even gave me head once to get back at Charles for cheating on her. It was our little secret, but I wanted more. I wanted her. The only problem was that I was broke, and I had no future. Unlike my brothers, I didn't have any universities begging me to attend. Charles had money, and I didn't. I wanted everything he had, and so did Zeke.

"You ever chase the dragon?" Charles asked.

"Nah."

"What about you, Zeke?"

"Nope."

"Well, if y'all wanna make it in this game, you should try it at least once. Crystal, hook 'em up with a little taste," he said.

"I'm good," Zeke said.

"Suit yourself. Jimmy, you getting in on this?"

Crystal looked at me and smiled.

"Yeah, I'm down," I said.

Zeke shook his head. "It's called dope for a reason, Jimmy. Only dummies do it."

"Fuck off!" Crystal yelled.

Charles laughed. "It's all right to party once in a while, Jimmy. You're only a dope if you get hooked on the shit."

Zeke shrugged. "Well, I ain't tryin' to take that chance. I'm all for getting this money, though."

I didn't know it at the time, but that day would mark the beginning of my downfall; nothing in the world would ever replace the warmth I felt in my veins.

I watched both of them shoot up. They looked so free and happy like nothing could bring them down. I desperately wanted that feeling. My whole life had been down, and no matter what my intentions were, I always made the wrong decisions and fucked things up. *If heroin can help me escape that reality for even a small amount of time,* I reasoned, *I don't mind dabbling in the Land of H for a while...*

★ ★ ★

The greatest trick the devil ever pulled was convincing the world he didn't exist, and Zeke really was the devil. Charles, Crystal, and I should've seen it coming, but we thought he was our friend. I wasn't good at selling, and I often got caught by the cops and arrested. I couldn't tell Momma, of course, so Scout always had to bail me out.

"I can't keep doing this for you. What's wrong with you?" Scout said.

"Nothin', man. I just don't got it easy like you. You got a wife now, and you're successfully running Dad's business. Momma's proud of you. I got nothin'. I'm just trying to do some little side hustles to get by."

"Nothing is easy for me, Chance. My life is prosperous because I've worked my ass off to make it that way. Stop making excuses and do something with yourself. Momma is sick. If she knew how many times I dipped into my savings to bail you out, it would kill her."

"What? Sick? What's wrong with Momma?"

"Her heart's all messed up from the diabetes. She's been in and out of the hospital lately. You're into this heroin shit too deep. You need to cut this dealer shit out and work with me."

"That's not my style," I said, shaking my head. "I'll be all right."

"You're just as stubborn as Fool. You need to stay away from Charles, Crystal, and Zeke. They're bad news."

I knew Scout was right, but I wasn't ready to do anything about it.

Zeke was always popular, and he took Charles, Crystal, and me to parties all over the place. Whenever Charles and Crystal partied, they shot heroin; like an idiot, I did it too, but Zeke never indulged.

"Don't worry about it, Charles. Don't take from your stash. Take some of mine. You still got a lot to sell from yours," Zeke said.

"Thanks, bro."

"No problem."

"Jimmy, Crystal, I'll hook you guys up with some, too, on me."

We went to these parties feeling like he was showing us love, but slowly but surely, the three of us developed a habit.

Zeke convinced Charles to hook him up with his supplier, and once he had that info, his reputation, and his popularity only grew. Unfortunately, that was bad news for the three of us.

CHAPTER 20

CHANGE OF POWER

Chance

It wasn't long before Charles was doing more heroin than he was selling, and our habit was growing at a rapid pace, becoming an impossible addiction. While Charles's drug dealing was declining, Zeke's was rising, and it wasn't long before he became the man around the neighborhood. Soon enough, Zeke permed his hair and wore a big gold rope chain. He drove a money-green Lexus around town and did the majority of his dealing out of Centennial Park in Roosevelt.

Things were slowly crumbling the day Charles died. I was sitting in the living room with my brothers when the phone rang, and Fool picked it up.

"It's for you," Fool said. "It's Crystal, crying and rambling about something. I don't know what the hell she's blubbering about, man."

I snatched the phone from him. "What's up?" I asked.

"Jimmy, he's dead!" she said, sobbing.

"Who's dead?"

"Charles! Charles is dead. Zeke's friends killed him. They fuckin' killed him, Jimmy!"

As much as I hated Charles, I'd never wish death on anyone. Crystal told me Charles tried to rob some of Zeke's dealers with a BB gun. Unfortunately, they shot him in the face with a real one. Crystal was with Charles when it happened, and when she broke the news to his family, they blamed his death on her. They kicked her out over it. Her family had already disowned her for doing heroin and dating a known drug dealer, so she had nowhere to go.

"Can I stay with you?" Crystal asked.

"My momma would never go for that."

"I'm not staying in a shelter, Jimmy. They rob and rape women in those places."

I borrowed Scout's car and drove Crystal around, trying to find a place for her to stay. We settled on an abandoned school on Nassau Road in Roosevelt. It was still in good shape, and I brought an old mattress from my basement, blankets, and other supplies to make her comfortable. The school became our new hideout.

"This place isn't so bad. The rooms are still intact. It's empty, and at least it'll keep you out of the bad weather."

Crystal held herself, rocking back and forth and looking as if she was on the verge of crying. "I'm all alone now."

"You're not. You always have me," I said.

I kissed her and held her tightly.

"I won't let anything happen to you. We're in this together," I reassured her.

Crystal kissed me again. Before I could blink, she was straddling my naked lap, riding me. I had wanted her for so long. In my head, I'd made love to her thousands of times, but the real thing was heavenly.

I spent lots of nights with her so she wouldn't be alone. Sometimes, I snuck her into our house, on the nights when I had to go home.

"Hey, Scout, lend me some money," I said.

"I'm not giving you shit. You already owe me $200. You need to drop Crystal and clean yourself up before it's too late."

I wasn't trying to hear his lectures; I only wanted money. Since he wouldn't help me, I started stealing shit to support my habit. I promised that no matter how sick I got, I'd never steal from my family. It wasn't long before I was locked up again, for shoplifting at the mall. I was so high that instead of running from the security guards, I sat in the food court and nodded out. I called the house, looking for Scout, but Momma picked up the phone. Once she paid for my bail, she threw me out.

"Get out!" Momma demanded.

"C'mon, Momma. I just need—"

"Jimmy, I mean it. Get out of my house. I'm not going to support that nasty habit of yours, and I'm sure as hell not going to watch my baby slowly kill himself."

"But, Momma—"

"You heard me! Get out."

"Momma, please!"

Tears were in her eyes when she pushed me.

"No! Pack your shit and go." She covered her mouth with her hand. "If your father could see you now, he'd be so disappointed."

That remark broke me. I grabbed one of my dad's old military duffle bags and packed my shit.

"Don't worry about me, Momma. I'll go. I won't disappoint and embarrass you or Dad ever again. I'm gone."

"Hey!" Crystal said when I walked into the school.

"Looks like we're gonna be living together. Momma kicked me out."

"We'll be all right. We have each other."

Crystal and I swore that night that we would give up heroin, but deep down, I knew I couldn't fulfill that promise. Not only that, but I didn't really want to.

It was surprising how easily I lost track of time while I was on dope. Before I knew it, years had passed, and I was still going through the same daily cycle of struggling for money. We never had money beyond our next hit, and every cent went toward the next high. The apex of our day was feeling that warmth in our veins, and every other moment was spent worrying and trying to gather more money, in any way we could.

★ ★ ★

"Let's just talk to him," Crystal said.

"Zeke's big time now. He doesn't give a shit about us. He's all about his money."

"We grew up together, and Charles and I put him on to drug game. He owes me, Jimmy," Crystal argued.

"I doubt he'll see it that way. You saw firsthand what his boys did to Charles. I don't want that shit to happen to either of us."

"I gotta try something. I'm sick."

"Me too, but we gotta think of something else."

Both of us were hurting from withdrawals. Together we fought the attacks of heavy sweating, nausea, and shooting stomach pains. After we came to the realization that there was no other way to get our fix, we swallowed our pride, our fears and went to see Zeke.

"What do you two junkies want?" Zeke said, rolling his eyes as he sat on top of his car, blasting his stereo and smoking an expensive cigar.

"We need a little something to get by, somethin' to stop us from being sick. Can you help us?" Crystal asked.

Zeke's bodyguards laughed at our begging. Both of them were the size of linebackers. One was light-skinned, with a large scar on his cheek. The other was dark-skinned and had cornrows.

"Sweetheart, I can't help anyone who doesn't have money. I'm a businessman, and giving junkies freebies would be bad business. It's too bad you don't have anything to trade," Zeke said, licking his lips and rolling his eyes lustfully over Crystal's body. She'd lost some weight, but her figure was still on point.

I didn't like the way he stared at her. When he glared at me and smirked, I knew my suspicions were spot on with him.

"Forget him, Crystal. Let's go. We'll figure something out, and we'll be all right," I said.

"I don't want to be all right, Jimmy. I'm tired of feeling weak and sick. I want this pain to go away."

Zeke pulled out two baggies full of heroin and jiggled them in front of her.

"Would this make you happy?" he said.

"What do I have to do for it?" Crystal asked.

"I've had a crush on you since first grade. Did you know that?" Crystal shook her head nervously.

"Let me fuck you right here, right now, and you can have both bags for you and Chump here."

"It's Chance, and only my family calls me by that name," I corrected him. I turned to face Crystal and saw that she was actually considering his sick request.

"Tell me you're not actually thinking about fucking him."

"I can't take this feeling anymore, baby. It won't mean anything. I'll do it for us."

"Not for me, you won't! I'd rather be sick."

"I'm gonna go through with it, no matter what you say."

"Well? We got a deal or what?" Zeke asked.

"Yes," Crystal said.

He smiled, grabbed her by the arm, and pushed her into the bushes.

"Pull those pants and panties down," he instructed, loudly enough for all of us to hear.

Crystal did as she was told and pulled them down to her ankles.

"Now bend that pretty little ass over."

I tried to stop it, but Zeke's men blocked me, and I was too sick and weak to fight them.

Zeke ripped open a condom, rolled it on himself, and entered Crystal. He was rough with her, smacking her ass and tugging on her hair. Hearing Crystal's grunts and moans upset me greatly and made me nauseous. Zeke laughed at my anger, then squeezed her chin and held her in place so she couldn't look away.

"Look up at your man," the sick bastard instructed.

Crystal was crying and couldn't look me in the eyes.

"Do everything I tell you, or the deal is off. Look at him!" Zeke yelled.

Tears were in her eyes, and regret was on her face. She looked as if she wanted me to rescue her, but I was powerless. I tried to run away, but Zeke's men blocked me, grabbed me, and made me watch until I was crying myself.

"Damn, this junkie pussy is good, Jimmy. No wonder you didn't want to share her with me." He looked at his men. "Y'all want some of this too?"

They chuckled and nodded.

"No! That's not part of the deal," Crystal said, through gritted teeth.

"I make the rules, and I'm not gonna say it again. You'll do everything I say, or you won't get shit. You understand?"

She stopped fighting with him and wept as he pounded her.

"Tag! You're it!" he said to his dark-skinned friend as soon as he came.

Cars drove past. People walked by and shook their heads, but no one said anything or dared to call the cops.

Zeke's light-skinned goon held me until the dark-skinned guy finished. When he did, he adjusted his pants and belt and replaced the guy holding me.

Zeke leaned in close to me and showed me the two baggies of heroin. "See this shit right here? Y'all sold your souls to it, and since I control it, I control you and that bitch over there."

"Why? Why would you do this to us? We were friends, Zeke," I pleaded. "You can have any woman you want. Why'd you have to fuck Crystal?" I asked.

"Because I can. I have power, and when you have power, you make the rules. You hate me right now, but tomorrow, when you need another fix, you won't even care about this. Just like that, I'll be your best friend again."

When they finished running their train on Crystal, Zeke tossed the baggies on the floor, and she desperately rushed to grab them. Zeke kicked her, causing Crystal to fall, face first, in the dirt. Zeke and his crew laughed at our humiliation as we woefully walked back to our hideout in silence.

I fixed the needles for us while Crystal held herself in the corner. "Are you okay?" I asked.

"No. Gimme that. I don't want to feel anything anymore."

"You didn't have to do that tonight. We coulda found another way to get our fix."

Crystal ignored me, tied up her arm, and shot up. Her head nodded, and I knew she could no longer hear anything I was saying. I watched as she lay there on our worn-out mattress. She was beautiful, and I loved her, but I had to get off that merry-go-round, and that meant taking some time away from her. I knew I'd never look at her the same after what I'd seen Zeke and the two men do to her, at least not for a while. My plan was to clean myself up and beg Scout to let me live with him. I figured being around my family instead of the junkies I usually hung out with would jolt me back to some sort of sanity.

I found an old napkin and an ink pen and scribbled a note out for Crystal:

Sorry, baby.

I love you, but I can't do this shit no more. I need to clean up my life, and I can't do it if you're with me.

Jimmy

I rested the napkin next to her and kissed her forehead while she nodded. I ran off and didn't look back.

★ ★ ★

I tried to fight my addiction cold turkey. It made me fucking weak and sick, and I suffered through it. After a few stints in the hospital, when it was finally over, I went to Scout's house to try to convince him to let me live with him.

"So, the prodigal son has returned. You got balls bringing your ass here when you didn't even have the decency to show up at our mother's funeral. I shouldn't even talk to your junkie ass."

"Don't be like that, Scout. I'm trying to get better."

"I looked for you. I saw Zeke and told him Momma passed. I figured the news would get back to you. I assumed you'd have the decency to show up, but you didn't fucking care."

That remark hurt. I broke down and wept. My Momma died believing her youngest son was a loser who didn't care about her, and that broke my heart.

"Sorry. Sometimes my tongue can be sharp. Come inside," Scout said.

After Scout had talked with Rhea about the idea of me living with them, they told Fool I would be staying upstairs with him. Scout was the man of the house, but Rhea was the sympathetic one who convinced him to have a heart.

"Our old room isn't being used downstairs on your side. Why does Chance have to stay upstairs with me?" Fool asked.

"Because that's my home office now, and I need that space. Most importantly, this is *my* house. You barely pay rent, so you have no say on the topic," Scout said.

Fool sucked his teeth.

"It's good to see you, too, brother," I said sarcastically.

"Sorry. It's not like I haven't missed you. I'm just not used to sharing the apartment."

"You won't even notice I'm here."

★ ★ ★

"Oh, yes, yes, yes!"

I turned the TV up, but the sounds of Fool fucking that woman into bliss rang through my bedroom wall. My hands crept down to my dick. I stroked myself, imagining it was Crystal, moaning for me. I missed her, and every night that I lay in that small bedroom, the loneliness drove me deeper into depression. I was a better person off heroin, but without it, I didn't have Crystal. I needed her just as much as I needed dope.

For a while, things were good. I was clean, and Scout trusted me to run small errands around the house. He even trusted me with his car. The problem was that I was lonely and miserable. Rhea and Scout were so lovey-dovey that it was fucking sickening. Fool was enjoying the life of a single bachelor, which didn't help my depression.

I needed Crystal, and I needed a hit. Most of all, I hated being reminded of how much of a failure I was. Heroin and Crystal were the only things that would take my mind off that.

On a Wednesday, Scout loaned me his car to grab the groceries for the week. There was no reason to go near Centennial Park. Part of me hoped Zeke wasn't there so I wouldn't go through with buying from him, but there he was.

"Well, well, well. If it isn't my old boy, Jimmy 'Chance' Johnson."

I half-heartedly waved.

"You're looking good, baby, all healthy and shit! You've put on some weight. What brings you into my domain today, Mr. Clean?"

"You seen Crystal around?" I asked, already knowing he had. Crystal and I had tried other dealers, but their shit paled in comparison. Most dealers cut their dope with so much sugar that we could barely feel it, so I was sure she was still a loyal customer.

"Yeah, I saw her. She's lookin' bad, man. She's sick and needs you. You need to check on the bitch before somebody finds her dead in an alley."

Zeke was truly the devil; he knew how to push my buttons and fuck with my emotions to get me to use again, and he was doing a damn good job of it.

"What's up with you, though? You need something?" he asked, smiling.

"Nah, I don't do that shit anymore."

"C'mon! You sure?" he asked, waving a baggie enticingly in front of me.

"Yeah, I'm good."

"You sure you don't want some…you know, just for a rainy day? I'll even throw in a needle for you. Since you're clean, I know you don't have one."

I tapped my foot, fighting with myself. It was a battle I lost because I soon found myself putting my hand in my pocket to take out the change from the grocery money Scout had given me.

A smile grew on Zeke's face when I shakily handed him my brother's cash.

"Always a pleasure doing business with you."

"Whatever, man."

I drove home, telling myself I'd only shoot up if I really needed it. I didn't make it to lunch before I went right back to using again. I lied to Scout, regularly asking him for money, telling him I was using that and his change from running errands as transportation money for job interviews; I didn't feel so bad about it since it was the truth in the beginning. After a while, though, I stopped trying to hide it and really didn't give a shit. I just wanted to get back to Crystal.

★ ★ ★

"Do me a favor. Don't come upstairs tonight. I've got this girl over, and I'm gonna need some privacy," Fool said, grinning.

I curled my lips and nodded.

"Thanks, bro. You can just chill out on the couch down here. Scout won't mind," he said before he closed the door behind him and ran upstairs.

I pulled a baggie and needle out of my pocket, fixed myself a hit, and did it right there in Scout's living room.

I was high as a fucking kite and sitting on the couch when Rhea came home from her aerobics class and decided to talk to me. I kept nodding out and only heard bits and pieces of what she was saying, the last thing being something about her taking a shower.

As soon as I heard the water running, I grabbed one of Fool's heavy duty contractor bags and stole anything and everything I thought I could make a buck off of, with the intent of using the money to take care of myself and Crystal. I put Scout's VCR, his small TV, and anything else I could carry into the bag. I stood in front of Rhea's jewelry box for a moment and saw my mom's and Rhea's wedding sets there. I felt too guilty to take Rhea's; that would have made me feel like an even bigger piece of shit, so I pushed it aside and dumped the rest of the jewelry in my bag.

As soon as I heard the shower stop, I dragged the bag and dashed out the door. I sold everything at a pawnshop in Hempstead, then bought enough heroin to hold Crystal and me for a while.

I had to beg her to forgive me for leaving.

"Who are all these people? We used to have this place to ourselves," I said, looking around at our crowded hideout.

"They're friends I met while you were gone. They're cool, and they keep me from being lonely."

I was against it at first, but having other people around who were just as pathetic as us gave me some odd sense of comfort.

★ ★ ★

Before I knew it, years blew by.

Crystal and I never stayed clean for long. We went through the constant cycle of hospitals, methadone, detox, rehab centers, and jail. Jail was a joke, just a revolving door. I went in and served my time, and it wasn't long until I was right back to stealing to get money for heroin. I didn't even stop using when I was in. While I was locked up, I learned how to cut hair to earn money and used the cash to get my fix.

Christmas time was open season for Crystal and me, and our target was Sunrise Mall in Massapequa. It was a good mall to hit because it wasn't too crowded; the crowded malls always had better security, and too many people made it difficult to run away when being chased by the cops.

I played lookout while Crystal did her pickpocket routine. With her small, dainty fingers, no one ever felt her slide their wallets right out of their pockets. Sometimes, she bumped into people and boosted their wallets while she apologized. Most of the time, though, it was easy enough for her to prey on stupid people when she caught them slipping. Women in parks engaged in conversations with their purses open, people at coffee shops with their hands full, and whenever Crystal saw an opportunity, she took it—literally.

On that particular day, we didn't know the mall was swarming with undercover cops. Crystal had hit about eight unsuspecting victims when I noticed a sistah wearing a Yankees hat and sporting a ponytail, following her. The woman didn't look like a cop, but she watched Crystal's every move. I tried to catch up to Crystal to warn her about the woman when a White dude pushed me.

"Take a walk, buddy, or you'll go down with her," he said under his breath.

I threw my hands up and slowly walked away.

The lady cop tried to stop Crystal, but as soon as Crystal realized the woman in front of her was an officer, she took off running. She was quickly tackled by the White guy who had shoved me. They roughly twisted Crystal's arms behind her back and planted their knees on her legs to stop her from kicking. Crystal let her body become deadweight, forcing the undercovers to drag her.

"What precinct is she going to?" I asked running up to them.

"Who are you to her?"

"I'm, uh...her husband."

"You're lucky we don't haul your ass in too. Your wife will be at the seventh precinct," the male cop said.

I waited for Crystal to be processed. Between her priors and the fact she had eight wallets, all with credit cards in them, jail time was inevitable. The courts didn't care about putting junkies in jail, so with her plea deal, she'd be out in a year.

I cleaned myself up a bit before I went back to Scout's. My plan was to be around my family, stay off heroin for good, save some money, and, once Crystal got out of jail, rescue her and live happily ever after.

Unfortunately, that shit didn't happen. Seeing Scout and Rhea happy and Fool with his daughter and girlfriend, I fell back into depression.

I was high when Fool asked me to babysit. My mind was made up: *I'll rob this place blind the second he walks out the damn door.* As soon as the door closed, I rushed to the kitchen drawer where Fool kept his rent and bill money. I took it all, then threw the envelope on the ground and tossed the house, looking for more cash. Just like last time, I found another contractor bag and loaded it with anything I could sell or pawn. Lynn was sleeping peacefully while I went from room to room, taking what I could.

I was all set to walk out the door when I thought about my little niece. *What if she wakes up and somehow falls out of the crib and breaks her neck?* I thought, letting my paranoia get the best of me. I walked into her room, kissed her forehead, and laid her down on the carpet. She continued sleeping peacefully.

"Don't grow up to be a fuck-up like your Uncle Chance," I whispered before I closed the door behind me.

Life, for me, was just a fucked-up carousel. The faces changed, but the ride never did. When I got to the hideout, there were more people there than last time. As time passed, some of them died, others did time, and some tried rehab, but there were always new junkies to take their places, from every race, color, and creed.

"We're never gonna get better, are we?" Crystal asked after we finished making love. She was lying on my stomach, staring at the cracks in the ceiling.

"We will, someday. We just have to stick together.

Crystal gave me a half-hearted smile.

I went to sleep, questioning if we should do another stint in rehab together.

When I woke up, I found a letter from Crystal next to me, the same words I'd written to her when I left her before. I ran away last time. I guess it was her turn now, I thought as I read the note:

Sorry, Jimmy.
I love you, but I can't do this shit no more. I need to clean up my life, and I can't do it if you're with me.
Crystal

★ ★ ★

A month had passed before Crystal returned to our hangout. She ran to me and buried her head in my thin chest.

"I missed you so much," she said.

When she looked up at me with those soft, brown eyes of hers, I knew what we had was love. I also knew she'd failed to get the monkey off her back, just like I had. I was happy she'd come back to me. I loved her, but part of me felt guilty. There was that dark side of me that was relieved she didn't succeed without me and was back to square one. Deep down, I felt ashamed of myself for not wanting Crystal to succeed where I'd failed so many times.

★ ★ ★

I ran back to the hideout as fast as I could, carrying dope from a new dealer. I heard it was even better than Zeke's, and I couldn't wait to try it out.

"Did you get it?" Crystal yelled.

"Yeah, it's right here," I said, waving the baggie.

"Hurry up and cook it. I can't take feeling like this."

I quickly made a shot.

"Please, Jimmy. I need it bad," she pleaded, shivering. "Let me go first."

I felt sick, too, but out of love, I let her go first.

As soon as Crystal released the plunger, her head slumped forward, and she fell, face first, on the floor. I turned her over and rested her head in my lap, only to notice that her lips were turning pale. "C'mon, baby! Stay with me," I yelled

I gave her soft taps on the face that gradually turned harder as I began to panic.

"Help! Someone call help. She's dying!" I cried.

No one moved; everyone within earshot was either nodding out or just staring, looking stupid. I ran across the street, called 911, and told them to send an ambulance. I dragged Crystal's body outside. The EMTs worked on her immediately when they got there, but I lied when they asked me all types of questions. All I cared about was whether or not Crystal was going to be okay, and I was in no mood to be interrogated.

"Well? Is she gonna make it?" I asked.

The paramedics stared at each other before one finally answered, "We'll try everything in our power to help her, sir."

I sat in the hospital, desperately praying that the love of my life hadn't been taken from me, especially because of some shit I'd given her.

★ ★ ★

For those who are broke and have no money for a funeral, remains are cremated, and the ashes dumped in a cheap, flimsy cardboard box. The men at the morgue were nice enough to ask if I wanted to keep Crystal's ashes, but I told them I didn't; I had to let go of her completely if I was ever going to move on.

This time at rehab, I didn't take any other drugs to wean me off the heroin. It was hard, and I spent many nights screaming in pain, unable to sleep, vomiting, breaking out in cold sweats, and suffering through crippling spasms. Hanging around the other addicts in rehab, I took up smoking; I figured it was a way smaller vice than heroin, so I was still a winner regardless.

Once I was confident and ready, I talked to Rhea and sat on the curb, waiting for Scout.

This time around, I felt I had another chance to do things right with my life, to make up for all those lost years, but it was all bullshit. Watching that movie showed me the truth. It reminded me that while my brothers were succeeding and happy with their lives, I was a failure. All I would ever be was a junkie. I missed Crystal and didn't care about being sober anymore. I just wanted to numb myself.

CHAPTER 21

AT PEACE

Chance

When the vacation ended, I was different. I'd gone through the motions, pretending like everything was okay, but deep inside, I felt myself falling back down to the dark road of heroin.

On a Thursday evening after work, I took a miserable walk to the park and strolled right up to Zeke's car.

"Well, I'll be damned if it isn't my old friend Chance Johnson. I haven't seen you in forever. You're looking good, man!"

"Cut the shit, Zeke."

"Is that how you talk to your friends now?"

"We were never friends. You know why I'm here."

"C'mon, Jimmy. Even though you've been a loyal customer all these years, I've always thought of us as more pleasure than business," Zeke said, waving the baggie in front of my face.

I gave him his money, and he dropped the baggie on the ground.

"How's Crystal doing? I sure wouldn't mind seeing her sweet ass around here again. You still with her?"

My eyes tightened, and I wanted to rip his fucking heart out.

"She's dead. That shit killed her," I said, pointing to the baggie.

"Hmm. I guess you're trying to keep her memory alive, huh?" he asked, then laughed while I dusted off the baggie and walked away.

I returned home, feeling lost and depressed.

The next day, the kids didn't have school. I had the day off, and

Scout and Fool went to work.

"Chance, can you do me a favor?" Rhea asked.

"Sure. What's up?"

"Jonna and I want to get our nails done and grab lunch. Would you mind keeping an eye on the girls for us?"

"No problem."

"Thanks. Are you all right? You don't seem like yourself today."

"I'm fine," I said, giving her a weak smile.

The girls were laughing and enjoying each other's company while I channel-surfed, barely paying any attention to what was on the TV. I couldn't shake my depression, so I finally excused myself and pulled the dope out of my pocket.

I should have enjoyed the day watching my nieces. Instead, I was sitting in the bathroom on a cold toilet, all alone, with my arm tied and a syringe full of heroin in my hand. I was at war with myself again, debating whether or not I should do the hit.

I was tired of reminiscing about my dark times, and I didn't want to feel anything anymore. I finally bit down on the orange cap and pulled it off with my teeth. I slid the needle into my arm and pressed down on the plunger. I hadn't done such a large amount in years, and I wasn't sure how my body would take it, but I didn't care.

This time, I didn't experience that warm, familiar sensation of pins and needles. I gasped as my heart rate slowed. I closed my eyes, and my head nodded. I felt my life slipping away from me, yet I felt relieved at the same time. I didn't try to fight it. *In death, there will be no more pain,* I told myself in my heroin-hazy head. *I won't bring any more disappointment and embarrassment to myself and my family. I'll be with Crystal again, finally at peace.*

CHAPTER 22

RELAPSE

Nick

I walked into the house exhausted. Lynn and Erica were sitting on the couch, watching some show on MTV.

"Where's your uncle?" I asked.

"He's been in the bathroom for a while now. I knocked on the door a few times, but he won't answer."

"When did you last check on him?"

"Like five minutes ago. Maybe he's sick. He was groaning in there a little while ago. I didn't know what that was about, so I didn't wanna bother him."

I was hoping he had the runs and wasn't jerking off while the kids were here. Chance had been working hard to get his life together, but it had been some time since he had a woman.

"Chance? What's the matter? Did you fall in?" I asked as I tapped on the door.

There was no answer.

"You all right in there?"

Still, there was no answer.

I twisted the doorknob, but it was locked. "You need to answer me, man. Are you okay in there?" I placed my ear against the door and listened but didn't hear anything.

I walked to the kitchen to get my screwdriver from my toolbox. Lynn saw the panic on my face and followed me.

"Dad, what's wrong with Uncle Chance?"

"I don't know. He won't answer me, and I don't hear any movement in there."

Lynn was scared. Erica put her hand on her shoulder.

"He's probably taking a bath and has his headphones on. Don't worry," I said, not wanting to frighten her any worse.

"I hope so," Lynn said.

"I'm sure that's it," Erica said, reassuring her.

I took the doorknob apart, inhaled, swallowed, and braced myself for the worst as I pushed the door.

The door flew open, and I found Chance slumped over on the toilet, with a rubber tourniquet tied tightly around his arm and a syringe held loosely in his hand.

"Chance!" I yelled.

Lynn let out a blood-curdling shriek.

"Oh my God!" Erica screamed.

I reached over to touch him, and he felt cold. I shook him vigorously by his shoulders, but he didn't respond. Foam was coming out of his mouth, his eyes were rolled back in his head, and his legs were locked.

"Chance? C'mon, man. Wake up!"

My shaky tone was a tell-tale sign to the kids that I was just as scared as they were.

"Daddy, what's wrong with him?" Lynn asked, with panic written all over face. She stood in the doorway, horrified and crying.

I had no idea if he was alive or dead, but I didn't want my daughter seeing her uncle like that.

"He'll be fine, baby, but I need you to call 911 and tell them to send an ambulance," I said, trying my best to keep my voice calm to stop her from panicking

"Is he really gonna be okay?" Erica asked, her voice shaking.

"Go with Lynn and help her call an ambulance," I ordered.

I called my brother's name repeatedly, but he wouldn't respond. I held him, rocked him in my arms, and prayed to God that he'd make it through whatever he'd done to himself, but I wasn't sure that prayer would be answered this time.

"Dad, the ambulance just pulled in the driveway!" Lynn yelled.

I lost all sense of time and place as the paramedics stormed into the bathroom with their equipment. They pried Chance from my arms, checked his pulse, and immediately started CPR. The EMTs quickly strapped Chance to a gurney and rushed him to the ambulance. They pressed on his chest frantically, trying to bring him back to us.

When I saw my brother lying lifelessly on that gurney, my mind quickly pieced the bitter truth together: Chance's luck had finally run out, and he was gone way before the EMS workers got there. In my heart, I wanted to believe he'd make it and that it would be the final straw, the one that would straighten him out for good, but logic didn't seem to back that up.

The ride to the hospital was a blur, and Jonna, Rhea, and Scout met up with me in the parking lot. We rushed through the sliding door of the ER, and Scout hurried to the nurse's station.

"Excuse me. Where is Chan...James Johnson?" he asked.

Our whole family crowded around, asking a million questions at once.

"I need everyone to calm down and back away from the counter."

"I'm sorry, ma'am, but my brother overdosed and was rushed to this hospital. Please! We need to know if he's all right."

The nurse looked at Scout with sympathetic eyes.

"Look, I know you're worried about your brother. The doctor will be out in a minute to talk to you and your family."

"Is he okay?" I yelled.

She hesitated before repeating, "The doctor will be out to speak to you soon."

We sat in the waiting room. Rhea held Scout's hand while Jonna kept reassuring me, Lynn, and Erica that Chance would pull through and be stronger after the experience. I prayed she was right, as I couldn't imagine losing my brother. In the back of my mind, I'd always harbored the fear that his addiction would eventually get the best of him, but I usually ignored those grim thoughts, since God kept giving him chances.

"Mr. Joe Johnson?" said a Black man in blue scrubs, glancing around the waiting room.

Scout and I stood up, and the rest of our family followed.

"That's me. I'm Jimmy's...uh, James's brother," Scout said.

"I'm his brother too," I interjected.

The man shook our hands. "I'm Dr. Wesley."

I tried to read his body language and facial expressions; a look of concern was etched on his face.

"Is our brother going to be okay?" Scout asked.

Dr. Wesley sighed. "We tried everything in our power to help him. The EMTs did the best they could on the scene and during the commute, but I'm afraid he was too far gone. We tried, but we couldn't save him."

"What!? What did you say?" I asked.

Dr. Wesley shook his head. "I'm sorry, Mr. Johnson, but your brother didn't make it. My condolences go to you and your family."

After I heard those words for the second time, my eyes watered, my throat felt dry, and I dropped to my knees. My family immediately embraced me as I struggled to accept the fact that my brother was dead.

★ ★ ★

There wasn't much of a turnout at Chance's funeral. Mr. Davis and Chris, most of the guys we did home improvement jobs with, and two people who were in and out of rehab with Chance came to pay their respects.

Through it all, Jonna was my rock. She helped Scout organize everything. She knew when to give me space to grieve and when I needed her to be affectionate and loving. I loved her more for that.

At the funeral, a flood of emotions overwhelmed me. As expected, Scout gave a great eulogy to pay tribute to our brother. His words were honest and from the heart. My chest heaved as I choked back tears, heavy with the weight of everything that had happened in the past year. The cancer scare had made me fearful of losing Scout. Chance's death made me realize I could've lost both of them. My family was all I had, and the thought of losing any more of them terrified me.

Jonna leaned over, put her forehead against mine, and whispered,

"I love you, Nick. We'll make it through this together." She always knew just what to say and when I needed to hear it.

★ ★ ★

At home, I lay on the couch, fully dressed, drunk and holding a bottle of whiskey. The curtains were closed. I wanted to be in complete darkness during my depression. In my head, I kept seeing Chance's glassy, lifeless eyes staring at me. *Could I have done more to help him?* I wondered. *What triggered him to shoot up again?* Since I'd never know the answers, I drank my pain away.

Jonna walked into the living room and flicked on the light switch. I squinted and adjusted my eyes to the brightness.

"Nick, I'm not about to let you revert back to your old ways," she said, forcing me to sit up. "Look at me," she said, shaking me.

I strained to focus on her, but my inebriated state didn't help.

"Nick, you have a daughter in the next room who sees everything you do. She looks up to you. Is this what you want to teach her? Do you want her to date men who deal with their problems like this?"

I stretched out and leaned my head back to stop it from spinning. "No, babe. I just needed to numb myself a little."

Jonna sighed and looked at me with compassion.

"I know it's hard, and I know you miss Jimmy, but numbing yourself with whiskey is no different than him numbing himself with the heroin that killed him. You might escape the pain for a little while, but it won't fix the problem."

"I know. You're right."

"If you really wanna escape your pain, sober yourself up and take Lynn out for a Daddy/daughter date. Do something fun and constructive to take your mind off things."

"I love you, Jonna."

"I love you too, punk."

We laughed; once again, she had easily made me feel better.

I followed Jonna's advice and spent time with Lynn. After talking with Jonna that day, I promised myself I'd never again revert to my old, drunken ways. Jonna's actions through all the drama opened my eyes to a lot of things, making her even more important in my life, and it wasn't long before I knew what I had to do next.

★ ★ ★

"Out of all the places where we could have gone on a family trip, you picked Medieval Times?" Scout asked.

"Yeah, this place is cool. You get a show, food, and it's something different," I said.

"You're not lying about that."

Rhea, Jonna, Lynn, and Erica checked out the displays and medieval weapons. Jonna turned and smiled at me, I winked at her.

I knew I was about to make the right move. That woman had changed my life for the better in so many ways, and I wouldn't have been the man I was without her. I had never loved a woman that much, and I couldn't wait to show her just how much she meant to me.

I walked up to her with my camera in hand.

"Hey, babe, you know what would be a really nice picture?"

"What?"

"You sitting on this throne. Sit, and I'll take it."

She smiled and sat down.

"Ugh! You're so tall up there. Let me just kneel down here to take it. This angle will make you look powerful, like the true queen you are," I pretended.

"Trying to score some points for tonight, I see," she joked.

"I won't deny that I'm trying to score tonight, but not with that comment," I said. I snapped the photo, reached in my pocket, and pulled out a ring box.

"While I'm down here on one knee, I thought I might as well give you this," I said, opening the box and showing her the ring I'd been secretly saving up for.

Her mouth dropped open in shock, and she was speechless. Meanwhile, Scout, Rhea, Lynn, and Erica all broke out in broad smiles.

"Jonna, I've grown so much, all because of you. I promise that I will always love you and treat you like the queen you are," I said, taking her hand.

Jonna began crying and nodded, but I wanted to hear her say the words.

"Jonna, will you make me the luckiest man in the world and marry me?"

"Yes! I love you so much!"

"I love you too."

"Punk!"

We giggled, and I placed the ring on her finger. Jonna cupped my face in her hands and kissed me. I held her tight, all while the audience that had gathered around us clapped and cheered.

Scout patted me on the back.

"Proud of you, brother. I'm glad you're making an honest woman out of her, and she's really made a man out of you," he said.

Jonna whispered in my ear, "Does this mean we can work on having a baby together now?"

"We can practice a lot," I whispered back.

She playfully slapped my arm.

I knew I needed to tell her the truth, but it was not the right time or the place. I glanced over at my Ladybug and Erica and saw them jumping up and down in excitement, thrilled that they were really going to be sisters. I knew I'd made the right decision for all of us.

CHAPTER 23

SELFISH

Nick

Between running the business with Scout and doing side jobs with Mr. Davis to save for my wedding, I was exhausted. No matter how tired I was, though, I made time in my schedule to be there for Lynn and Erica's basketball games. For the past two years, they'd been winning titles and awards in all their leagues, inside and outside of high school, even back-to-back Long Island girls' basketball championships. I'd never won high school championships, so it was nice to see Lynn surpass me as she and Erica won two titles in their freshman and sophomore years together.

"Congratulations, ladies!" Jonna said.

"Thanks," Lynn and Erica said in unison, both beaming as they stood in the parking lot with their championship trophies, letting us take pictures.

"I'm so proud of you girls," I said, hugging both of them.

"What do you guys want to eat to celebrate?" Jonna asked.

"Ooh! Can we go to that new Italian restaurant, Isabella's?" Lynn asked.

"Yeah! We heard the food's really good there," Erica added.

"You guys want Italian? You don't want steak or seafood?"

"Nah, we eat that stuff all the time," Lynn said.

Their friend Jackie waved to them. She was with her parents, taking pictures with her family.

"Should we invite Jackie too?" Jonna asked.

"No, Mom. She's doing her own thing with her family," Erica said. Lynn smirked and shook her head.

"If my two champions want Isabella's, then we'll go to Isabella's!"

★ ★ ★

I held Jonna's hand as we nuzzled together in our cozy booth, laughing and talking about the funniest moments of the season when I felt someone grasp my shoulder. I jerked my head around and nearly had a heart attack when I saw who it was.

"It's good to see you, Nick. It's been a long time," Vickie said, smiling at me.

Physically, she hadn't changed a bit; she looked just as good as she did almost fifteen years ago.

Jonna sensed something was wrong and stared Vickie up and down.

"Everyone, this is—"

"Hi, I'm Isabella, the owner of the restaurant. How's everyone doing tonight?" Vickie said, cutting me off.

"Fine," Lynn and Erica chirped together.

"Nick and I used to be good friends. He did some work on my house years ago."

I nodded.

"Nick, are these…your children?" Vickie asked, unable to take her eyes off Lynn, noticing the resemblance in amazement.

I looked proudly at Lynn, Erica, and Jonna and said, "Yeah, this is my family, Lynn, Erica, and my fiancée, Jonna."

"Fiancée? Wow. When is the special day?"

Jonna's smile waned as she realized we hadn't even decided that yet. "We're still working on a date."

Vickie nodded.

She had the same eyes and nose as Lynn, and it was very noticeable. Jonna stared closely at Vickie, and her eyes grew when she realized who Isabella really was.

"Very nice, Nick. It's good to see everything worked out for you," Vickie said.

I wanted to say, *"Yeah, with no help from you,"* but I had to keep cool.

Lynn, meanwhile, was oblivious to the situation, laughing and talking with Erica. She had no idea that the woman standing beside our booth was the woman she'd sat by the window waiting for all those years ago.

"Thanks. We're celebrating because my daughters won back-to-back Long Island girls' basketball championships today."

"Wow! Congratulations, girls."

"Thanks!" they said.

Vickie turned to me. "Do you mind if I talk to you privately for a minute? I want to ask you something about home repair, and I don't want to be rude and bore your family."

I looked at Jonna.

She nodded to let me know she was cool and understood.

"Sure," I said. I followed Vickie to her office.

She shut the door behind us as I sat down in one of the chairs near her desk. "Wow, Nick. I can't believe that's Lynn. She's beautiful," she said with a smile.

"Thanks. She looks like her mother."

The smile left her face, and she began to pace the floor.

"A lot has changed, Nick. Frank and I are divorced. We tried to make it work, but he never stopped cheating, and whenever I called him out on it, he mentioned you and the baby. No matter what happened, I could never escape that...incident."

"Vickie, it's been fifteen hard years. All her life, Lynn has asked about you. Did you bring me back here to ask about a relationship with our daughter? If that's not what you want, there's no need for us to talk?""

"It hasn't been a picnic for me either, Nick. Things were hell with Frank, but I'm finally in a good place in my life. I'm sorry I left the way I did, but it was for the best. I don't have nurturing instincts like most women. I'm nobody's mother. You both seem to be doing fine without me."

I shook my head, realizing she sounded exactly like Jasmine.

"You really haven't changed. You're still the same selfish woman you were fifteen years ago."

"You're right. I'm still selfish, and now that we've bumped into each other, I need to make sure we're still on the same page when it comes to leaving me out of your daughter's life."

"She's your daughter, too, Vickie."

"No, I wanted to give her up. You chose to keep her, so she's your responsibility. When your brother never called me back about signing over my parental rights, I feared you might one day track me down and try to milk me for money. I just got on my feet. I need you to promise me you won't try any shit, that you won't drag me into court for back child support."

"I don't want or need anything from you, but I don't understand why you wouldn't want to have a relationship with our child."

"She's beautiful, and I'm sure she's a great kid, but I don't need any reminders of that time in my life."

I stood. "You don't have anything to worry about, Vickie. We don't want anything from you. I wish I could say it's good to see you, but it really isn't. If you don't mind, I'd like to go back to my family now."

"Thanks for understanding. Whenever you guys come here, your bill is on me."

"I'm not sure we'll visit again. For some reason, I've suddenly lost my appetite," I said, then slammed her door and walked back to my table.

"Daddy, what's wrong? You look mad," Lynn said, noticing my mood on the ride back home.

"I'm all right."

"You sure? You've been pissed ever since you talked to that lady," Erica added.

"I worked for her a while back, and she never paid me. She owes me a lot," I said.

Jonna held my hand.

Once the kids went to bed, I told Jonna, Rhea, and Scout everything Vickie had said.

"You should take that bitch to court," Jonna said.

"She's dead to me. Lynn and I have gotten along this long without shit from her. I didn't need anything from her then, and I damn sure don't need anything from her now."

Scout and Rhea looked distracted, and they oddly didn't act surprised or say anything about my Vickie encounter.

"You guys all right?" I asked.

"Fool, we have to talk," Scout said, with a serious look on his face.

"What's wrong? Did you know she was there or something?"

"No, it's not about Vickie. I haven't said anything since you've had enough drama going on in your life between the business and saving for the wedding, but I've had a recurrence."

"A what?"

"My cancer is back, in my bones this time, and it's spreading."

"No! How is that possible? You were doing so well. What happened? Why?" I asked in a confused panic.

"I don't know. I'm so tired of being tired. I don't think I have the energy in me to fight it anymore."

I had to calm myself down before I consoled, "You'll be all right. You'll bounce back, just like you did last time."

Scout exhaled slowly. "I hope so, but I'm not so sure. This time, my body's not responding well to treatments. The doctors have pretty much written me off," Scout said, then began to weep.

I wanted to cry right along with him, but I knew I needed to hold myself together. My brother needed me to stay positive and give him the strength to fight that awful disease again.

In his first cancer fight, the chemo weakened him, but it wasn't too bad. Cancer wanted a rematch, and this time, it seemed to drain the life out of him. Scout was close to being diagnosed as terminal, and I helplessly watched as the wear and tear of cancer deteriorated and aged him rapidly. This time, it seemed like my brother was really going to die, and I was scared shitless. I'd never been a religious man, but I prayed regularly, hoping God would help Scout pull through. I wasn't sure if God even heard my prayers, but it was the only thing I knew to do.

★ ★ ★

There were some holistic cancer treatments Rhea, and I wanted him to try. So far, they seemed to be helping, and Scout was doing way better than the doctors thought he would, but the alternative treatments were costly and not covered by our insurance. Jonna agreed to it, and I used all my savings and our wedding money to contribute to Scout's medical expenses. I wanted to sell the business, but Scout and Rhea made me promise not to. I put everything on hold until Scout was better.

I worked full time, running our business by myself, and I busted my ass doing side work for Mr. Davis, just to make ends meet. Rhea got a job to help out with the growing medical bills, but with only a high school education and no work experience, the only job she could land was a waitress gig at the Imperial Diner in Freeport.

Times were rough for all of us, but we were all willing to do whatever we could to help Scout in his battle.

I sat at my desk at the shop with one hand pressed against my forehead while I held Scout's hospital bills and our business bills in the other. The stress of everything weighed heavily on me, and Scout's health really wasn't getting any better. I stared at the picture of Scout, Chance, and me on our last vacation together. I wanted to go back to that day.

"I figured I'd find you here. Something must be heavy on your mind if you didn't even know I was in the room. I've been here for a good minute."

I looked up and saw Jonna standing in the doorway. "Hey, babe," I said.

"You okay?"

I shook my head. "I don't know how Scout used to do this shit by himself. I feel like I'm drowning."

"I know, honey," she said and lovingly rubbed my shoulders. "Is there anything I can do to help?"

"No. You do enough as it is."

"Well, what can be done to better this situation?"

"I have no clue. Rhea's been busting her ass, too, but she doesn't make enough money to even put a dent in the mortgage payment."

"I know you're under a lot of stress, but that's why I'm here."

"It is? What's up?"

"You have so much on your mind, with work, your brother, and putting our wedding on hold. Maybe you should see a doctor too."

I was expecting that talk, but I certainly wasn't ready for it. "What do you mean?"

"We've been trying to have a baby for a while now, and nothing's happened. I'm not trying to scare you, but I saw my doctor, and he said everything is good on my end."

My conscience was eating at me. I'd hidden the truth from her for far too long. I closed my eyes and tried to mentally prepare myself for what I knew needed to be done.

"Your brother waited too long to get checked out, and I'm sure he'd agree with me."

"Jonna, I—"

"Baby, you know I'm right. I want to make sure it's just bad luck and not something serious."

"Jonna…"

"I need you to stop being stubborn and listen."

I stood up and hugged her.

"There's nothing wrong with me, Jonna. I had a vasectomy. That's why you haven't gotten pregnant."

She pushed me away, and her smile faded.

"What!? Are you serious?"

"Yes," I regretfully confessed.

"When? And why didn't you tell me?" she asked.

I grasped her gently, in an attempt to calm her down, but she squirmed out of my grip and used her hands to keep me away.

"Don't touch me! How could you string me along like this when you knew I want another child?"

"I know I was selfish and inconsiderate, but—"

"You got that right."

"I wasn't trying to waste your time. I'm sorry I lied to you. I was afraid if you knew I couldn't have kids anymore, you wouldn't give me a chance. I love you, Jonna."

She shook her head, and tears glistened in her eyes.

"I have to go, Nick."

"Where?"

"I'm not sure, but… I'm leaving you."

"No, Jonna! We can fix this. I can fix this."

"People don't appreciate how special something is until it's gone."

"What do you mean by that?"

"A lot of things…everything. Do you know how special it is to have a child?"

"Of course I know. Lynn's the best thing in my life!"

"Rhea would kill to have a child, and Joe would've given anything to give her one. I love you more than any man I've ever dated. I wanted to marry you, and having a child with you was important to me. I wanted to bring a person into this world together, someone who would have been part of both of us. I'm so disappointed, Nick."

I looked down at the floor, unable to find words for her.

She continued, "The question isn't whether or not the procedure can be reversed or fixed. The real question is whether or not you want it to be. Be honest with me, Nick. In your heart, do *you* want another child? Don't answer with what you think I want to hear. You've done enough lying already."

I slowly shook my head and answered, "No. I'm sorry, Jonna, but after Hazel, I was scared I'd meet another woman who'd try to trap me and see me as a monthly paycheck. After I broke up with her, I had the procedure done, and I never told anyone."

Jonna closed her eyes slowly and pulled in her lips.

"I don't want you to make a decision of this magnitude for me. Bringing a life into this world is serious, and if you don't want that, our relationship is at a crossroads. I love you, Nick, but I'm gonna have to be the strong one and end this relationship. We want different things in life. I want to have another child before it's too late for me."

"I don't want you to hate me. I don't want to lose you."

"I could never hate you, Nick, but just as I can't ask you to sacrifice your happiness for me, I need you to not ask me to sacrifice my happiness for you. I want to have another child, and if you don't want that…"

She was unable to say anything more. We held each other and cried. I knew I'd regret lying to her for the rest of my life, but she was right: As much as I hated it, I had to respect her decision to leave me.

"I'm going to need a couple weeks to find my own place," Jonna said.

I nodded, tears still streaming down my face.

"I can sleep on the couch if you want until I find a new place to stay."

The suggestion shocked and hurt me, but it did prove how serious she was about leaving me.

I sighed. "That won't be necessary, but what do we tell the kids?"

"I' don't know. That thought has been in the back of my mind too. They're really close. This is going to be devastating for them."

"When should we tell them?"

"I don't know," she said, her voice tinged with deep sadness that echoed my own.

★ ★ ★

The next five weeks were hard and awkward. We agreed that we'd share the same bed but wouldn't have sex. That was really her doing. I hated not being able to touch her. Every day, I hoped she'd change her mind, but she was strong. Jonna had made her decision, and no matter what, she was going to go through with it.

Rhea and Scout were heartbroken when we broke the news to them.

"I'm sure I speak for both of us when I say this hurts us too," Scout said.

"You two are perfect together. Are you sure this is what you both want?" Rhea asked.

"I don't," I said.

"We want different things in life, and it wouldn't be fair to either of us to have to sacrifice when it comes to having or not having a child. I love Nick, but he knew I wanted to marry him and have another child with him five years ago. I won't ever say I wasted time in our relationship because I cherished every day I spent with him, but I'm not compromising on this."

"I can see it from both perspectives," Scout said, "but I'm certainly not happy about it. I really wanted you two to make it. You've brought out the best in my brother."

"I see it from both sides, too, but as a woman, I understand how Jonna feels. I always wanted children, but it wasn't in God's plan for me. I don't regret anything because I had a choice. I made a promise to God and Joe to always be faithful, in sickness and health. I could've reneged on that promise and tried to get pregnant with someone else, but I don't want anyone else. I chose Joe because being married to him and loving him is more important to me than having children."

Scout closed his eyes as Rhea's words made all of us shift uncomfortably in our chairs.

Jonna did all her apartment searching at work. I was happy about that because it would have been painful to watch her doing it at home. Our conversations were short and sweet. We didn't laugh or show each other affection anymore.

Lynn and Erica noticed, but we assured them everything was fine; we didn't want to tell them the truth until Jonna officially signed a lease for her own place.

I was worried that Lynn would take our breakup the hardest. She looked at Jonna as a surrogate mother and viewed Erica as her sister. Losing both of them was going to hurt. I was sure Jonna would always be part of Lynn's life in some capacity, but realistically, it wouldn't be the same. She wouldn't see her as much, and if Jonna accomplished her dream of having another child, I figured she'd be too occupied with her new baby to think about Lynn.

On a rainy Friday, Jonna announced, "I found a place in Copiague. I'm moving out in two weeks. Now that the girls' basketball season is over, we should tell them this weekend."

★ ★ ★

On Sunday, we told the girls we needed to have a family meeting. We asked Rhea to come upstairs to help keep the situation calm and civil. We all took seats on the living room couches.

"What's going on?" Lynn asked.

"This doesn't sound like a good meeting. What's wrong?" Erica added.

Jonna and I looked at each other.

"Nick and I love each other very much," Jonna started, "but we've reached a point in our relationship where we need different things to be happy. We don't want to cause future animosity toward one another by doing things we'll regret."

I shifted in my chair, and as expected, Erica and Lynn immediately started crying.

"That said, Erica and I are going to be moving out in two weeks. I found an apartment for us in Copiague."

234

Lynn stood up, stared me in the face, and shouted, "You always ruin everything! You're the reason why my mother isn't around for me, and now you managed to fuck things up and drive Jonna and Erica away too. I hate you!"

Everyone's mouth opened in shock. It hurt hearing those words come from my daughter. After all the sacrifices and the work I put into giving her a decent life, "hurt" wasn't a strong enough word to describe how I felt. In her face, I didn't see the little girl I raised or a child that resembled me. I saw yet another woman who didn't believe in me. I saw her mother.

Before I could blink, Rhea stood up and backhanded Lynn across the face.

Lynn wore a look of shock and fury, her nostrils flared.

"How dare you?" Rhea yelled. "Your father is far from perfect, but he's tried, and he's done the best he could to raise and provide for you. You've always pined after your mother, and you've never appreciated him for being here for you. That woman abandoned you. In all honesty, she didn't want you, but your father begged her to have you and promised to take care of you alone."

Lynn rubbed her reddened cheek and lowered her eyes. "That's not true. I know Mom wanted me," Lynn cried.

For years, I'd tried to make sure Lynn never viewed Vickie as a villain, but it was time for that façade to end. I stormed into my bedroom and dug the letter out of my sock drawer, the one I had told myself I'd never show to my daughter. I didn't want her to have mommy issues, so I tried to let her have a positive image of her mother, but at the moment, I no longer gave a shit about that. I was beyond hurt, and she needed to know the truth.

Rhea was still telling Lynn off when I walked back into the living room.

"Here! This was the last thing your mother gave me."

Lynn snatched the letter out of my hand and read it immediately. I watched as her shame-filled eyes captured the harsh words on each line, and by the time she finished, she was in tears.

"Vickie isn't in California. She's right here in New York, in Garden City. She wants nothing to do with you, but if you hate me so much, and you want to see if you'd be better off with her, I can give you her address."

Lynn shook her head. "I'm sorry, Daddy."

I didn't want her apology; I felt hurt and betrayed by my own flesh and blood. I threw my cell phone on the kitchen counter, then turned to leave.

"Nick, where are you going?" Jonna asked.

I didn't answer her. I just walked out of the house, climbed in my car, and went for a long drive, in desperate need of some fresh air.

CHAPTER 24

APPRECIATING DADDY

Lynn

I couldn't stop crying, even while Erica hugged me. Jonna went into the bedroom, crying herself, and Aunt Rhea was still mad at me.

"Do you see how badly you've hurt your dad? Over the years, he's matured to be the father you needed. He's sacrificed a lot for you, you know," Aunt Rhea said.

I nodded.

She continued, "When you were a baby, you had an accident and were taken to the hospital. You're uncle, and I pleaded with him to sign you over to us, and he fought tooth and nail for you. He even lost a girlfriend at the time, over you."

I wept harder, holding my face in my hands. The last thing I'd told my dad was that I hated him, and I was so worried that something might happen to him.

"Sis, I'm going to check on Mom. I know she's taking this hard too."

"I understand."

Erica gave me a big hug again, then knocked on our parents' bedroom door and stepped in.

"I'm going to go downstairs and check on your uncle. I don't know where your dad went or when he'll be back, but you owe him a major apology," Aunt Rhea said.

"I know. I'll tell him."

She closed the door behind her and walked downstairs.

I sat in the window seat and waited for my father. It reminded me of all the wasted times I'd sat in that same spot, staring off into space, daydreaming about Vickie, waiting and hoping that she'd come for me. I refused to ever refer to her as my mom again after what I'd learned in that letter.

That bitch lived in Long Island this entire time, and not once did she come to see me, call, write, or send a gift on my birthday. All my life, I wanted to get to know her, and now I hoped I'd never meet her. If she lived that close to us and didn't have the decency to meet her own daughter, she was dead to me.

I gripped my necklace, the one Daddy gave to me when I was a little girl, when he told me it was hers. I felt like ripping it off and throwing it in the trash. I knew she didn't want me to have it, but it was hard for me to throw it out since my dad had given it to me.

Suddenly, I was angry with myself again. There I was, still crying over my mom, when my dad was out there hurting. He'd always been there for me. He had taught me how to fight, how to ride a bike, and how to play basketball. He was there for me when Vickie wasn't. *I can't wait until he gets home. I have a lot to apologize for.*

CHAPTER 25

HURT

Nick

The drive didn't help. Too much was going through my head, uncomfortable thoughts I didn't want to entertain. I wondered if I should've told Lynn, the truth about her mother from the beginning. I wondered if I'd done the right thing in trying to raise her myself. At one point, I even questioned if Lynn would've been better off being put up for adoption like Vickie wanted to do. I quickly shook those negative thoughts off. Lynn was the best thing in my life, my heart. I knew she was upset for the same reason I was; she didn't want Jonna and me to break up, and neither did I.

As soon as I walked through the door, Lynn ran to me, put her head on my shoulder, and wrapped her arms around me.

"I love you, Daddy. I'm so sorry. I didn't mean what I said."

"It's okay, Ladybug. I know. I needed time to think, but I know you were upset."

"I spent all these years asking you about a woman who never wanted me. I'll never ask anything about her again."

"You can ask me anything you want about her. In fact, do you remember that woman at Isabella's?"

"Not really."

"The woman I did the work for? The one I said owed me a lot and never paid me?"

"Vaguely."

"That was Vickie."

Lynn's mouth fell open in shock.

"She saw me and said nothing?" she asked, fighting back another round of tears. "Well, I guess I didn't officially meet her. She isn't important to me, Daddy. I'm so sorry. I just don't want Jonna and Erica to leave us."

"Me neither, Ladybug. Me neither."

★ ★ ★

Two weeks flew by, and before I knew it, it was Jonna's last day in the house. I left early and stopped at a diner for breakfast before going to the shop. I ended up skipping work entirely because I knew I wouldn't be able to focus.

I pulled into the driveway and saw that Jonna's car was loaded with boxes and clothes. She had scheduled the movers to take the bulk of her and Erica's things to her new place the day before, so she only had a few small things to pack. I knew her mind was made up, but I had to make one last-ditch effort to change it.

I closed my eyes and mentally prepared myself. Inside the apartment, there were neatly packed bags by the door.

"Jonna?" I called.

She was crying in our bedroom, holding a picture of us. She put the picture back on the dresser and wiped her face with the back of her hand.

"You aren't supposed to be here. I wanted to finish packing and leave before you came home. This just makes it harder, Nick."

"I couldn't focus on work, and I had to try to talk you out of this, one last time. Please don't leave me, Jonna."

"This hurts me too. I love you and don't want to leave, but I have to be fair to myself. Both of us have already sacrificed so much for our children, and that's expected, but I can't sacrifice this one thing I want for myself. On the other hand, I don't want you to give in and have a child with me against your will. I could never accept that."

I reached out to hold her, but she stepped back.

"No, Nick. I can't."

I held her anyway, leaned in, and kissed her. She touched the side of my face, opened her mouth, and gave me her tongue. When

240

the kiss ended, Jonna grabbed my hand and led me to the bed. She pulled my shirt over my head, unbuckled my pants, and undressed me. I kissed her neck, inhaled her scent, and did the same for her.

"One last time," she said, looking me in the eyes.

With tears in my eyes, I nodded.

I eased myself inside her, giving her slow strokes to prolong the moment, wanting to hang on to that sensation of being intimately connected with her. I stared into her eyes, watching her react to my touch. I traced the lines of her face and curves of her body with my fingers so I could save them to memory.

We let our emotions take control. Our eyes and movements made the apologies our words could never appropriately utter.

I didn't want to cum. I wanted to hold on to that moment forever because I knew when it was over, Jonna would leave. The way she moved let me know the feeling was mutual.

We lay there, holding each other in silence, lost in our own thoughts, savoring the moment and the memories.

Finally, Jonna slowly broke away from our embrace, swung her legs around, and stood up from the bed. I watched as she gathered her clothes and got dressed. She stood by the dresser, staring at the photo of us while I slid on my jeans.

"Do you mind if I keep this?"

"Take it," I said, my voice cracking.

Jonna walked into the living room, picked up her bags, and headed downstairs to the door.

I ran after her, tears welling in my eyes as I held her hand and whispered, "I don't want to lose you."

"I'll always love you, Nick."

Jonna slowly released my hand from her grip and reached for the doorknob.

"I have to be strong. I have to do this for me," she said, wiping her eyes. "I have to go. If I don't leave now, I'll lose my strength to do this."

"If it's that hard for you, that means you shouldn't do it," I reasoned.

"If I learned one thing from Erica's father," she said, "it's that you always have to love yourself more than you love anyone else. We've both made up our minds, Nick. I have to go. I'm sorry."

"Wait," I begged as she opened the door.

"I'll speak to you soon." With that, Jonna swiftly walked to her car and pulled off without looking back.

I walked back to the bedroom where we'd made love for the last time. I stood in front of the dresser and saw Jonna's engagement ring, sitting where the picture frame was before. I was instantly consumed by regret, knowing I'd lost the best woman I'd ever dated.

CHAPTER 26

SENIOR YEAR

Lynn

"Promise me nothing will change with us," I said, hugging Jonna and Erica.

"Of course not, sis. We'll always be in each other's lives."

"Lynn, you'll always be my second daughter. I love you like my own. You, too, Jackie. Bring it here, girl."

Jackie smiled, appreciating that she was included in the moment. Erica rolled her eyes, still immersed in her strange love/hate relationship with Jackie.

"Let's promise each other that we'll all try to get into Sacred Heart University and play ball together again in college."

"I promise," Jackie said.

"I already promised Mom I'd follow in her footsteps and go there, so I'm in."

"Cool. I don't ever want us to fall apart, no matter what our parents do. I want us to be sisters forever."

Jonna cried, watching us say goodbye. It was a rough day, but times were going to be rougher.

I knew Jackie was a shoo-in to get recruited by Sacred Heart. She was a power forward, and their women's team needed someone decent in that position. They also needed a pass-first point guard who had the ability to score, and Erica definitely fit that bill. I was worried about myself because they already had two good shooting guards.

After giving it a lot of thought, I decided I wanted to major in early elementary education. I wanted to teach like Jonna did, but like my Aunt Rhea, I also liked being around young kids. I felt teaching would be the perfect job for me and a nice way to honor both of them since they were like mothers to me.

Erica, Jonna and I stayed close. I talked to them almost every day and saw them at least once a month, but it wasn't the same. School wasn't the same without Erica. Playing ball wasn't the same either. Life wasn't the same without Jonna and Erica in it. Erica was the voice of reason for Jackie and me, and we soon learned how important she was to our group.

Erica used to lecture us on what guys and parties to avoid, and Jackie and I were somewhat lost without her. Jackie dated all the wrong guys, the ones who only hit on her because she had a pretty face and huge tits. Unfortunately, she had her daddy's butt, but her wide hips helped to camouflage her lack of booty. I didn't date much because Aunt Rhea and Dad watched me like hawks, but we went to parties all the time. We constantly broke our curfews, and I fought with my dad a lot.

The house was dark, and I crept in at some insanely late hour again, praying that the squeaking of my footsteps wouldn't wake up my dad. I passed the living room and damn near had a heart attack when he spoke.

"Where the hell have you been?" he asked, glaring at me from the couch.

I didn't want to say anything because I was scared I'd say something stupid, throw up, or both.

"Answer me, Lynn. You sashay your ass in here at damn near three in the morning, and now you just stand there looking stupid?"

"I was just…at a party," I stuttered and slurred.

Dad shook his head. "I must be losing my damn mind. Tell me my underage daughter didn't come home past her curfew, shit-faced on top of that," he said, furious.

All his screaming, hand waving, and quick movements made me nauseous, and I rushed to the bathroom. Tears ran down my face as I puked in the toilet. My hangover felt like hell, but the cold porcelain was soothing against my face.

After that night, Dad really had me on lockdown, but I managed to sneak and maneuver my way out of the house, and Jackie and I went to another party.

"I see you checking Derek out. Why don't you go flirt with him?"

"I don't know. Erica always said he ain't shit."

"Well, Erica ain't here now, is she? Plus, she probably only said that because she wanted him."

"Nah, he isn't her type."

I'd had a schoolgirl crush on Derek since we were in junior high. He was handsome, with smooth, brown skin, dimples, cornrows, and a thin, ripped body. He wasn't the sharpest knife in the drawer, as he was failing almost all his classes and rarely attend them, but he was great at basketball. He played on the boys' team and broke a lot of records, even a few of my dad's. Of course, Daddy hated him.

I took Jackie's advice and walked up to him. "Hey, handsome," I said.

"How you doing, shawty?" he asked, licking his lips and running his eyes all over my body, checking out my figure before staring me in the face. "It's Lynn, right?"

"I think so."

"What? You don't know your own name?"

I was so nervous. I never really flirted before. I didn't know what I should say or do, and my mind was all over the place.

"Yeah, it's Lynn. Sorry. I thought you asked something else."

"You got really pretty eyes, Lynn."

"Thanks. They're really mine too," I said, then instantly realized how dumb it sounded.

He laughed. "You wanna dance?"

"I'd love to."

On the dance floor, I swayed my hips and bounced my ass against Derek while he grinded his crotch against me.

Derek spun me around, kissed me, and ran his hands up and down my ass, grabbing me with both hands.

"Damn, you got a nice, juicy bubble butt."

"Uh…thank you."

"Oh! Get it, Lynn!" Jackie shouted.

I danced and talked with Derek all night, and when the party was over, he told me he wanted to get to know me better. "Let me call you sometime," he said.

"Nah, my dad and aunt are crazy strict. They don't play that."

"When can I see you again?"

"When do you want to see me again?"

"I don't want you to go now. Why don't we get a room and spend the night together?"

"I'm already grounded, and I'm not even supposed to be out tonight. I've gotta go before I get caught."

"All right, Lynn. I'll see you around, but we definitely need to hang out again."

After I left the party, I crept into the house, only to be caught by Dad again.

"What is wrong with you?" he asked.

"Nothing. You and Aunt Rhea are always on top of me, and I can never just relax and hang out with my friends."

"We stay on top of you because we don't want you getting caught up in any trouble or pregnant or both."

"Jackie's parents aren't as strict as you two."

"I know she's your friend and all, but Jackie's a little loose. When grown men are talking about her at my barbershop, it's not a good thing. Your aunt and I don't need this shit. We already got enough going on, trying to take care of your uncle. I'm gonna give you one last pass, Lynn. If I catch you sneaking out one more time, I'm taking your car away from you."

"Dad, why would you do that? That was my birthday gift."

"Don't sneak out again, and I won't have to."

"Fine! You won't catch me sneaking out ever again."

"Good. Now go to bed. Goodnight, Ladybug."

"Goodnight, Dad."

I said he'd never *catch me* sneaking out, but I never said I wouldn't do it, so it wasn't really a lie.

★ ★ ★

For the next two months, I secretly went on dates with Derek. I told Erica everything, and she kept warning me to watch my back.

"He only wants to fuck you, Lynn. Once he gets what he wants, he'll move on to the next one. Trust me, sis."

I knew she was probably right, but everything was so new to me. I was naïve and believed Derek wasn't going to treat me that way.

CHAPTER 27

REMORSE

Nick

Half-asleep, I reached to wrap my arm around Jonna, only to run my hand over the cold, vacant space that used to be hers. It was hard to wake up to an empty bed every morning. A year had passed, and I still wasn't over her.

A day hadn't gone by when I didn't think about her. I'd had a good share of women in my lifetime, but I honestly believed she was the only woman I truly loved, and I stupidly let her go.

I didn't date or even look at another woman for months. In the back of my mind, I always felt Jonna would come back to me, but I realized that wasn't going to happen when Lynn told me Jonna had a new man.

"What? Jonna has a new boyfriend?" I asked Lynn.

"Yeah."

"What's the guy's name, and how long as she been seeing him?"

"His name is Alvin. He's a mechanic in Farmingdale. She met him two months after you two broke up."

That hurt. We were together for years, and she didn't even take the time to mourn our relationship.

"I guess she didn't care about me, huh?"

"That's not it, Dad. I talk to her all the time. She still loves you, but she wants someone to love her, marry her, and build a bigger family with her. The new guy is really dorky, but he's good to her."

"I need to get out there and meet someone too," I said.

"I guess," Lynn said, sounding a bit unsure.

★ ★ ★

It had been a while since I'd hung out with Vince and Cyrus, but I soon found myself at the club again. Over the years, our hangouts hadn't happened too often, because I was so focused on being a family man.

"It's good to see you back on the market, brother. You been domesticated for so long you've been missing out on all the fine pussy out here," Cyrus said.

"Yeah, we missed you out here, man," Vince added.

I loved hanging out with my boys, but the scene wasn't really me anymore. Both of them were still single, doing the same shit they were doing seventeen years ago when I first had Lynn. I didn't want to regress, to go back to being the old Nick again.

"C'mon, Nick. You've been nursing that one beer all night. Did you forget how to drink?"

They were both plastered, but I couldn't help but think back to the day Chance died and also the day I was drunk in the living room when Jonna caught me with the whiskey. I knew drinking heavily wouldn't fix the fact that I was lonely and mad that Jonna had moved on. I didn't need alcohol like that anymore; I was smart enough now to know how to handle my problems. I had work the next day anyway, and I didn't want or need a hangover in the morning.

"I gotta get up early for work in the morning."

"So do we," Vince said.

"I need to call it a night, guys. Scout's sick, and I have to help take care of him. We'll hang out again soon."

"Aw, man, so early?" Vince asked, looking at his watch.

"Yeah."

"All right, man. Take care of your brother, but next time, we're getting shitfaced!" Cyrus said.

I went home and lay in bed alone, depressed that Jonna wasn't around to share my life with me anymore.

250

★ ★ ★

Lynn told me Jonna was going to stop by to pick her up for their monthly girls' day out, but I really needed to talk to her. I needed her to know I still loved her.

Even though she was seeing someone else, the few times when I did see her, I still felt that strong chemistry between us. I questioned if there was still something there or if I was just too stupid to move on and let go of the past.

The doorbell rang, and I answered it. "Hey, Jonna."

"Hi, Nick."

The sight of her brought back feelings I'd been trying to subdue, but I tried to maintain my composure.

"Lynn, Jonna's here!" I yelled.

"I'll be right down," she said.

"Where's Erica?"

"In the car. I let her drive, and she won't leave the driver seat," she said.

We shared a laugh.

"Do you mind if I talk to you in private for a minute?"

"Sure. What's up?"

"First, I want to say I'm sorry. I never wanted to hurt you. I was scared, and—"

"You don't have to apologize, Nick. I've forgiven you, and we've both moved on. You've gone on with your life, and I've moved on with mine. I will always love you. I can honestly say you were my true first love, but I'm engaged now...and I'm pregnant."

"What!? You've known this guy for what? Ten months? And you're already marrying him and gonna have his kid?"

"Nick, I didn't come here to fight with you. I came to see Lynn. I'm only telling you all this to help you move on."

"Tell me you love him as much as you loved me."

Her eyes strayed away from mine. "I..."

"Tell me and I'll never bring it up again."

"I can't say that. I love you both, but you're both different."

"You can't say it because in your heart, you know I'm the man you want. You know it's true, Jonna."

251

"I do love you, Nick, and what you're saying might be true, but I love Alvin too. He loves me and wants the same things I want. My love for you is strong, but it's not strong enough to throw away the things I want in life. I was patient and waited to marry you, but we never even set a damn date. I wanted more than the title of fiancée and a ring on my finger. I wanted a marriage, not just a promise of one. My time was running out to get the things I need to be happy."

"I wanted to marry you. I had shit going on in my life to take care of before I could go through with it. You know that."

"It wasn't just the marriage, Nick. What if we would've gone through with it? Our marriage would've been based on a lie."

We stared at each other, both of us passionate about the way we felt.

"Everything happens for a reason. We showed each other what we need to be happy," Jonna said.

"What's wrong?" Lynn asked.

"Nothing, sweetie. Your dad and I were just talking. You ready to go?"

"Yeah."

Lynn turned to me. "Bye, Dad."

"Bye, Nick," Jonna said.

A wave of remorse hit me as she left, and I realized just how alone I really was.

CHAPTER 28

FIRST TIME

Lynn

I sat in the stands with Jackie, wearing Derek's varsity jacket, cheering him on when I saw the coach putting him into the game. He'd failed three classes, so he was lucky that he even got off the bench.

Derek took off his warm-ups and pointed up at me.

"He's so cute," Jackie said.

We giggled together.

"He's fine. You'd better keep him happy. A guy like that will drop you like a bad habit if he isn't satisfied," Belinda James said.

I hated that bitch. Ever since she found out Derek and I had made things official, she'd been on a mission to take him from me. Things weren't perfect with Derek. He had a wandering eye, and I regularly caught him checking out every girl with a fat ass and big tits. That made me feel insignificant. He was the captain of the basketball team, so all the girls in school fawned over him, especially Belinda, but at least he was mine.

We made things official after we argued about me not giving him any. We were alone in his room, and his parents weren't home.

"Why are you playing games, Lynn? Not for nothing, but I can get pussy from pretty much any girl in the school if I want it, and you're acting like your shit is solid gold."

"Ugh! Get it from other girls then," I said, grabbing my purse and getting ready to leave.

"Wait! That came out wrong. I only want to be with you."

I sighed. "I won't give myself to just anyone. I need to be in a relationship with someone I love, and the time has to be right."

"You wanna be my girl?"

"Are you asking me just so we can have sex?"

"Nah. I like you, Lynn. I'm trying to be with you."

We made things official, but I wasn't ready to sleep with him yet. I wanted to stick to my values and would only give up my virginity when the time was right, but we fought about it all the time. I wasn't sure how long I could hold out before he'd dump me for a girl who would more easily give in to his begging.

My body was better than Belinda's, but I didn't put it on display like she did. She knew what to say and what to do to make guys crazy. Compared to her, I was an inexperienced, body-shy prude.

★ ★ ★

Derek and I were watching *He Got Game* in my living room, and he couldn't keep his hands off me.

"You said you just wanted to watch the movie," I said.

"This movie is whack." He moved my hands to his crotch so I could feel his growing erection. "See what you do to me?"

"Watch the movie, Derek."

He tugged on my shirt. "I'm more interested in you."

We were alone in my house after school, since Dad was at work and Aunt Rhea was at the doctor, with Uncle Scout. Every day, Derek pressured me into having sex with him.

I slapped his hand away.

"Stop! I told you I'm not ready for that yet."

"I bet Belinda's ready, so what's your problem?"

The remark irked me. Belinda's ho ass was always smiling in his face and flirting with him. She'd been screwing around since we were in junior high, and the last thing I needed was for him to leave me to have sex with her.

"I want to, Derek. It's just... Well, I want our first time to be special," I said.

"It will be. It'll be nice. I promise."

"Soon."

Derek huffed. "When? All my boys get sex on the regular from their girls. I beg you all the damn time and get nothing." He folded his arms and looked off into space, not paying attention to the movie.

"Okay," I said meekly.

"Okay, what?"

"Okay. I'm ready."

"You serious?"

"Yeah."

He grabbed me by the hand and rushed me to my bedroom.

I had always imagined that my first time would be incredible and romantic, but it was far from it. As soon as I agreed to give him some, Derek pushed me down on the bed, stripped me naked, fumbled with his jeans, and pulled them down below his hips, just enough to expose his manhood. My legs shook as I spread them for him.

Before I could blink, Derek was already tearing the condom wrapper open. He rolled it on and poked and prodded to find my entrance. I drew in a slow breath, and my lips parted as I felt the pressure of the head of his dick being pushed inside me. I bit my bottom lip to stop myself from whimpering. Once the tip was in, Derek rammed his entire length inside me all at once. I yelped and grimaced from the pain.

He smiled. "You good?" he asked.

Tears streamed down my cheeks as I nodded. His pace was too fast, and I felt like I was being ripped open. I pushed on his chest to slow him down.

"Ow! Take it easy. You're hurting me," I said

"It supposed to hurt your first time. I gotta break you in."

I sighed.

"Okay…" I said.

I let him have his way with me, putting me in all types of positions.

Eventually, the pain changed to pleasure, but after the five minutes that it lasted, I felt used. He didn't hug me or hold me afterward. He just lay there, smiling, as if he'd gotten what he wanted and was proud of himself.

I didn't know it then, but I was just a notch on his belt. He bragged to all the guys at school that we were having sex, and every free moment we had, that was all he wanted to do. It got better over time, and I eventually even enjoyed it, but I always felt like I'd made a huge mistake in losing my virginity to him.

Derek started hanging out with me less, called me less, and criticized everything I did. "Why don't you wear makeup?" he asked. "Why don't you wear clothes that show off your body? Show more cleavage, more thigh. You oughtta dress more feminine, like regular girls."

He made me feel like there was something wrong with me, like I was different from other girls and not normal. I worried that I wasn't good enough. I saw how he stared at Belinda, and I wanted him to look at me that way. I did everything possible to keep him happy. I had sex with Derek whenever he wanted, and I bought more revealing clothes to try to look more attractive for him. Of course, Daddy wasn't having that.

"What the hell are you wearing, Lynn?" he asked.

"Nothing. It's just a skirt, Dad."

"It looks more like nothing. Put something else on. I'm not raising a stripper."

"C'mon, Daddy."

"Put on some clothes, damn it! Does Rhea know you're buying stuff like that?"

"No. She'd probably say the same thing you're saying. Both of you are too old-fashioned and don't know about style."

"It's not about style. I don't want you giving off the wrong message to those horny little boys."

"Ugh! You don't understand, Dad."

"I do, Ladybug. I was a boy once, and I know how men think. Put something else on…now."

I sighed, rushed to my room, changed my clothes, and put the outfit I was originally wearing in my book bag. I knew Dad would never let me leave the house wearing what I wanted, but he couldn't stop me from changing my clothes outside.

★ ★ ★

"Wait, what? Are you dumping me?" I asked.

"Yeah," he said coldly.

256

We were standing in front of my locker after school. Some of Derek's teammates were standing around, chuckling and enjoying the drama.

I closed my eyes to fight back tears. My lips trembled as I asked, "Why? What did I do wrong?"

"Nothing, I'm just not feeling you anymore."

"Are we still going to the prom together?"

"Nah, I'm taking another girl."

"Who?" I asked furiously.

"Does it matter? We're not together anymore. You shouldn't care or worry about who it is."

"Prom is only two weeks away, Derek! You should at least be man enough to tell me who you're taking in my place."

"Not that it's any of your business, but I'm taking Belinda."

"Why? What does she have that I don't? I did everything you wanted."

"Damn! Desperate alert!" a girl said as she walked by.

"Yo, the dick was so good she's begging Derek to take her back!" one of his teammates joked.

Everyone began laughing and pointing at me. I wanted to slap the smirk right off of Derek's face. He didn't care that he'd broken my heart and humiliated me. I had given him my virginity, but I was just practice so he would be good enough for Belinda. Completely embarrassed and angry, I ran away, hopped in my car, and sped home.

"Aunt Rhea! Aunt Rhea!" I called from the doorway.

"She's not here, Ladybug. What happened? Why are you crying?"

I rushed into my dad's arms and wept on his chest. I didn't like looking or feeling weak in front of him, but I couldn't help it.

CHAPTER 29

HEARTBREAK

Nick

Lynn burst into tears. I patted her back as she hugged me and sobbed on my chest.

"What happened, Ladybug?" I asked softly.

"I don't know what to say, Dad."

"Don't worry about it. You can talk to me about anything."

"This is so embarrassing. I'm so stupid."

"You're not. Just start from the beginning."

Lynn told me every painstaking detail of her breakup with Derek, and I felt powerless to help her. I had to control my temper. My first thoughts were to whoop Derek's ass, but I knew that wouldn't help anything. My daughter was crying in my arms, and there was nothing I could do to fix it and take the pain away.

I rubbed her back.

"I know you feel your aunt, and I are too strict, but we just want to protect you, honey. I can't be mad at you. I did the same things when I was a kid, but I've been tough on you because I didn't want you to make those same mistakes."

"I know, Dad."

"Ladybug, do you remember Hazel?"

"Ugh! You mean that woman you dated when I was little? How can I forget? I hated her."

"That's my point. In life, we all make mistakes, and we all date people who later make us wonder what in the hell were we thinking. Hazel broke my heart. At the time, the pain felt unbearable, but things got better. In time, things will get better for you too. You're graduating high school soon, and you're gonna meet new people, make new memories, and even make some mistakes in college, but that's a part of life. You'll learn from them, and I promise things will get better." I kissed her forehead and continued, "Just focus on your championship game. Once you win that and get accepted to Sacred Heart, this will be in your rearview."

"Thanks, Dad. I feel a little better."

I wished Jonna and Rhea were there, but I didn't think I'd done too bad of a job.

CHAPTER 30

BLACK CLOUD

Lynn

My life was fucking horrible. Erica and Jackie received their acceptance letters from Sacred Heart and were offered partial scholarships to play ball there. I hadn't received anything yet, and I knew the clock was ticking. I did receive acceptance letters from other universities, begging me to play for them, but I wanted to keep my promise and play with my sisters. I didn't have any siblings or cousins. Erica and Jackie were my best friends. They were like family to me. I was scared that all the distance and time away would make us grow apart. I didn't want to experience college life without them. Aunt Rhea and Dad kept busy taking care of Uncle Scout. I knew they were counting on me to accept a scholarship to help pay for college. Dad couldn't afford to send me without it. Things in my life were one big mess.

Derek humiliated me again in front of everyone at school when he stopped by my locker.

"Lynn, I'm gonna need my jacket back. I know you wanna keep it because you said the smell reminds you of me, but you're not my girl anymore, and I'm giving it to Belinda."

The kids around my locker started laughing again, but I refused to give them the satisfaction of seeing me get upset. Instead, I calmly handed him the jacket, without saying a word.

Derek talked shit about me and had all his stupid teammates ask me to the prom because they thought I was a guaranteed piece of ass.

While the drama with Derek annoyed me beyond belief, my real concern was the Long Island girls' basketball championships. Jackie and I got to the finals again, without Erica this time, but unfortunately, we had to play against her team.

"Lynn…"

"Yes, Coach?"

"I just got word from a friend of mine that the Sacred Heart scout will be at the championship game. I know how badly you want to play for them, so I'd advise you to play your heart out in this game and bring us another championship."

I had too much shit hitting me all at once, so I called the one person I knew who could really calm me down.

"Hey, Jonna."

"Hey, sweetie. What's going on?"

"Everything…" I said, then went on to tell her about all the drama with Derek, not being accepted to Sacred Heart yet, the scout who would be at the game, feeling uncomfortable about playing against Erica, my uncle slowly dying, and my fear of disappointing Dad.

"Why are you worried about your father?"

"He always wants me to play well, and I'm scared of letting him down. I have enough on my plate. Dad being disappointed in me would only make me feel worse."

"Your father loves you, Lynn, but I'll talk to him."

"Thanks, Jonna."

"Good Luck in the game. Don't worry about anything. Everything will work out for the best."

I hoped she was right.

CHAPTER 31

LAST SHOT

Nick

I massaged my temples, frustrated by the fact that my brother had been declared terminal. I waited for Lynn to finish showering so I could drive us to her championship game.

The doorbell rang, and I walked to the door to answer it. I was surprised to see Jonna.

"Hey, Nick. Where's Lynn?"

"Upstairs, getting ready. You want me to go get her?"

"Actually, I'd like to talk to you in private, if you don't mind. It's sort of important."

I stepped to the side. "Come in," I said, hating the fact that I still loved her. As she walked in, I noticed that her pregnancy was showing, big time. It hurt to see her knocked up, with another man's engagement ring on her finger. It took everything inside me to hold back my jealousy.

"Your pregnancy is coming along nicely, congrats on that," I said, nodding at her baby bump.

"Thanks."

"Are you really going to marry Alvin?"

"Yes, Nick, but that doesn't matter right now."

I couldn't look her in the face. I was too angry with myself and angry with her. Even though I wanted her to be happy, I wanted her to be happy with me.

"Nick, you need to talk to Lynn."

"Why?"

"The pressure of playing in this game is getting to her. She's scared of disappointing you."

"What? She doesn't have to worry about that. I love her regardless."

"I'm not the one you need to tell that to. Nick, you're great when she's winning, but sometimes you can be really hard on her when she loses. She's aware of the importance of this game, and she needs to know and feel that no matter what happens tonight, you'll be proud of her."

"She knows that already. She'll be okay. Lynn is tough. We've been through a lot, and—"

"Nick, she's a scared little girl who feels her daddy won't love her as much if she doesn't perform well in that game tonight."

"I'll talk to her."

"Thanks bab...er...Nick."

I smiled a little, happy to know she still felt our spark too.

"I'll see you at the game," I said, then gave her a quick hug before she left.

As I drove to the game, I realized Lynn had her game face on. She pulled her hair back into a tight ponytail, but she didn't say a word. "Lynn, is everything cool?" I asked.

"I'm a little nervous, Dad. The Sacred Heart scout's gonna be there, and that's the only school that hasn't accepted me yet, the one I most wanna go to. I'm worried they won't want me."

"Once you get this championship tonight, they'll be begging you to be on the team."

"Yeah."

"You know I love you no matter what, right? Win or lose."

"I know, Daddy."

"Good. Then relax and know that you got this!"

"Thanks, Dad."

★ ★ ★

"That's another turnover, Lynn! Get your head in the game," her coach shouted.

LAST SHOT

"It's okay, Lynn. Just get it back on defense. Erica, pass the ball," Jonna shouted from her seat next to Alvin, cheering for both girls as she always had, despite the fact that they were playing against one another.

Lynn was tense, and it showed. During the first half, she missed shots she usually hit with ease, turned the ball over three times, and didn't make her usual stops on defense.

At halftime, I yelled from the stands, "Lynn!"

When she looked up, I signaled for her to slow down and take her time.

In the second half, she played much better, but the game was close down to the end.

In the fourth quarter, the coach called a timeout. Lynn's team had possession, and they were down by one, with ten seconds left in the game.

I looked at my daughter. Everyone in the gym knew she'd take the last shot, but she wasn't wearing that confident face I usually saw. She glanced up at me, and I winked and smiled at her. She gave me a slight grin, but I knew she was tense.

As expected, Lynn got the ball. She dashed to the three-point line and shot a jumper with perfect form. It felt as if time stopped, and every eye in the gym was on the ball as it went inside the rim but rolled out.

Lynn dropped to her knees and covered her face with her hands. When the horn signaled the end of the game, her season, and the championship, she wept. Her teammates helped her off the floor and embraced her, and even Erica ran over to give her a hug.

Lynn slowly walked toward me, with tears streaming down her face. "I'm sorry, Daddy," she said,

I pulled her into my arms and held her tightly.

"Ladybug, you have nothing to be sorry for. I'm proud of you."

"Dad, we lost the game because of me. I don't think the recruiter for Sacred Heart is gonna want me now."

"Did you give it your all?"

"Yeah."

"Did you do the best you could?"

"Dad, you know I have way too much pride to not go all out."

"Well, no one can ask for more than that. You shouldn't be mad either. One game doesn't define who you are as a player. You have other schools begging you to enroll. If Sacred Heart doesn't feel the same, it's not the right one for you."

"The other schools teaching programs aren't as good as Sacred Hearts, Dad. Plus, Erica, Jackie, and I promised we'd all go to college together. I wanna be there with them."

I understood what it meant to her, and in spite of everything that had happened, I knew she still considered those girls her sisters. "I'm sure you'll get in," I encouraged. "Don't let it stress you."

Lynn spoke to her teammates and coaches after the game, then quietly got into the car. During the ride home, she didn't speak a word, and in the house, she quickly ran up to her room and closed the door.

I waited a couple minutes before I knocked on her door, holding a cheesecake and our *Love and Basketball* DVD.

"Come in," Lynn said.

"I brought you something to cheer you up, Ladybug," I said, showing her the cheesecake, "and I was hoping we could watch your favorite movie together."

"You wanna watch a movie where a girl loses her high school championship game, with your daughter who actually lost her championship game?"

"At least you'll see it's not just you."

She couldn't help but laugh a little.

"Thanks, Dad. It's the thought that counts, and I appreciate it."

We watched the movie together, and I spent the night consoling my daughter.

★ ★ ★

The next day, Lynn stayed in her room all morning. I grabbed the mail out of the box and sorted through it. When I did, I saw an envelope from Sacred Heart. I didn't want her sulking all day, so I knocked on her door to give her the letter.

"You want to get lunch at the diner, Ladybug?"

"Nah. I just want to be alone."

"Can I come in?"

"Sure, Daddy."

I walked in, made a funny face, and sat on her bed. It was good to see her smile.

"I brought your mail. You ready to see what Sacred Heart has to say?"

Her smile quickly faded.

"I can't open that right now."

"All right. I'll give it to you later then."

"Well, now I *have* to know what it says. Can you open it?"

I ripped open the envelope and smiled. "They want you, baby! Not only that but they're giving you an athletic scholarship."

"For real?"

I showed her the letter, and she hugged me and cried.

"Thanks for being there for me, Dad. Thanks for always being there."

I kissed the top of her head.

"It's what a good dad does," I said, "and I love you."

Lynn immediately called Erica and Jackie to tell them the good news, and as I overheard her talking to them on the phone, a harsh reality hit me: Soon, my little girl will be leaving home, going to school.

CHAPTER 32

LEAVING THE NEST

Lynn

"Smile, Ladybug," Dad said as I stood in the living room with my prom date, Ben, a guy Erica had hooked me up with. According to her, he was a "deep brother" who was going somewhere. Ben brought me a beautiful wrist corsage. He was cute, and he seemed nice during our phone conversations, but I was still angry over Derek and didn't trust men in general.

"Take a picture of Lynn and me together, Uncle Nick," Jackie said.

"Oh, you girls look so pretty. My baby is all grown up," Aunt Rhea said, with a tear in her eye.

Jackie was wearing a light blue gown that showcased her huge breasts. I wore a black, strapless one that showed off my toned legs.

Dad took pictures of us, then asked to speak with Ben in the kitchen. We left Jackie's date in the living room, and Aunt Rhea, Jackie, and I eavesdropped on my dad's pep talk with Ben.

"I've heard a lot about you, Ben. You sound like a decent guy."

"Thank you, sir."

"I also heard that both of your parents are judges."

"Yes, sir."

"Well, Lynn is growing into a woman, but she'll always be my little girl. If you do anything to hurt her, one of your parents will be sentencing me for homicide. Do you understand?"

"Yes, sir."

"Don't say anything to Lynn about this. This is our man-to-man talk, and as her father who loves her very much, it's my duty to give you this warning."

"You can trust me, Mr. Johnson. I'll be a complete gentleman."

"I'm going to hold you to that, son. Don't disappoint me."

"I won't, sir."

We chuckled and went back into the living room before Dad and Ben left the kitchen.

In the limo, on our way to the prom, I felt like everything was moving on autopilot. I laughed and joked around with everyone, but my heart wasn't really there.

When I saw Derek with Belinda, grinding on each other and feeling each other up, I shut down emotionally for the rest of the night. I couldn't wait for graduation, so I could leave all that shit behind.

CHAPTER 33

COLLEGE LIFE

Lynn

"Johnson, pick up the pace. Guards should be quick," Coach Antoine said.

My sports bra and practice jersey were soaked. Sweat was pouring down my back.

"Looks like Team Redbone can't keep up," one of my new teammates said, referring to me, Erica, and Jackie.

All three of us were winded, not at all used to the extremely fast pace.

"You girls might've been superstars in your hometowns, but now you're playing against women from all over the country, who are just as good as or better than you. All of you need to step it up."

College was eye opening for us. Back home, we were starters on every team we played on, but in college, we were damn near third string. Most of the girls were bigger, stronger, and better than us, and it quickly humbled the three of us.

Coach Antoine's six-six stature, short, boyish haircut, dark skin, and matching, piercing eyes were intimidating. She was pretty, with an athletic but feminine frame. She yelled all the time, but she always explained why she was yelling. She pushed the team concept and often expressed that we were all equal. In her mind, our team had no stars.

Erica, Jackie, and I got lucky. Since we were freshman and on the basketball team, we were able to dorm together, but that meant we all had to put up with one another's changing personalities. We were evolving as women, and that was daunting at times.

Erica became extremely Afrocentric. She hated being teased about her fair skin, so she went tanning a lot. Her hair was very straight like mine, but she permed and styled it to look more "Black." She wore big hoop earrings and dated a dark-skinned African guy named Amar'e. His skin was the shade of onyx. He was chiseled and very smart. He was originally from New Jersey and was studying finance. She met him at freshman orientation, and Erica swore it was love at first sight.

Jackie was still searching for her Prince Charming. Her mother always told the story of how she met Jackie's father in college, so Jackie's goal was to find her dream man there too. Unfortunately, she also slept with guys left and right, and she never waited for any type of commitment.

As for me, I kept my head in my books, kept to myself, and focused on basketball. After dating Derek, I didn't feel like putting my heart out there.

"That guy from the men's team is checking you out," Kelly said, snapping me out of my daze.

"What?"

"He's been gawking at you for the last ten minutes."

I glanced casually at the cute White guy. I'd seen him around but had never paid him much attention.

"Yeah, I saw him looking at me at orientation too, but I'm not interested in dating anyone right now," I said.

"I feel you, girl. I doubt he's your type anyway, and he's definitely not mine," she said with a laugh.

"I don't really have a type."

Kelly was from Long Island as well, and all three of us knew her before college because we played against her in different leagues. She was a tall, gorgeous White girl, with blue eyes and blonde hair. She only dated Black guys. She wore hoop earrings all the time and was Erica's tanning buddy, hoping to make herself darker than she really was.

We went through a few more drills for conditioning before the coach finally ended the practice. While I was flattered by the attention from the White guy, I hoped he didn't pursue me. *He'll be sorely disappointed,* I thought.

★ ★ ★

I couldn't help being mad at Erica and Jackie for ditching me to go out so often. Their dates always offered to hook me up with their friends, but after Derek, my heart was locked. I had no desire to let anyone in, and I knew it would be a while before I'd trust or date another guy. My classes and ball kept me busy, and that was enough for me, but I did get lonely sometimes when my friends were out and about.

"Psst. Psst."

I looked up and saw the White guy from practice, trying to get my attention. He waved at me. I returned it with a slight wave of my own, then went back to reading my book.

He walked over and stood in front of me.

"Excuse me," he said.

"What's up?" I replied, not taking my eyes off my book.

He ducked down to get my attention.

"Hi," he said.

"Hello," I said, finally lifting my eyes to meet his curiously.

He was tall, around six-five, with blue eyes and jet-black hair.

"I'm Alex," he said.

I nodded and went back to my book.

"You got a name?"

"Yup!" I said, trying to come off as a bitch so he'd want to end the conversation before it started.

"And you are?"

I huffed. "Lynn."

"It's nice to meet you, Lynn," he said, extending his hand.

I shook it, but he held on a little longer than I was comfortable with.

"You play ball, right?"

"Yeah. I saw you stalking our practice today."

He laughed. "Well, it's hard to ignore someone so beautiful. Is this your first year too?" he asked, still holding my hand.

I gradually pulled away. "Yup. I'm a freshman. That's why were at the orientation together."

He pulled out the chair next to me and sat down.

"Mind if I sit and get to know you?"

I laughed. "I guess I have no choice now, right?"

He laughed too. "I guess not."

There was something about him that I found attractive, a bad-boy vibe that turned me on a little.

Our generic conversation led to him asking me out on a date, to which I answered, "Tempting, but I'm going to have to pass."

"Why?"

"I've got a heavy course load, and I'm super busy. I gotta go. I'll see you around."

With that, I walked away, and I could feel his eyes staring at my ass. I turned around and caught him, then laughed to myself. I wasn't going to be a notch on another jock's belt ever again.

★ ★ ★

"Come on, sis," Erica begged.

"Nope. I'm not going."

"Stop being like that. It's just a little party the guys' team is throwing. Maybe you'll meet a man tonight," Jackie added.

"I'm not interested in finding a man right now, especially one of them. I learned my lesson dating athletes."

"You're not gonna dabble on the other side, are you? I mean, I'd still love you, and I'm sure plenty of girls on the team go that way, but they'll be at the party too," Erica joked.

"Funny! I'm strictly dickly, but I'm not interested in finding any dicks right now," I said with a smirk.

"Speaking of dicks, you've really gotta get over Derek, girl. That was high school, and we're in college now," Jackie said.

"I am over him."

"We'll look out for each other. C'mon! We'll have fun. I promise, if it's whack, we'll all leave together," Erica said.

"Y'all aren't gonna let me outta this, are you?"

"Nope!" they said in unison.

"Fine, but I'm not babysitting either of you if you guys get drunk. Ugh. I don't even have anything to wear."

"Guys won't care what you wear tonight. Slap on a cute outfit, a little mascara, and some lip gloss, and you're good to go," Jackie said.

We arrived at the party. As expected, Jackie found a man right away, and Erica went off with Amar'e, leaving me alone, with no one to talk to. I leaned against the wall and felt someone staring at me.

"What's up, Lynn?" Alex said when he walked over to me. "Didn't expect to see you here."

"Hey."

"You look nice."

"Thanks…I guess." I wasn't wearing anything special: It was just a pair of tight blue jeans, a white blouse, hoop earrings, and heels.

"You look sexy in those shoes. It takes talent to walk in heels, and you're crushing it!"

I gave him a half-hearted smile. "Thanks."

"I take it you're not a partier."

"Nah. I'm just here to look after my friends."

"I feel ya. I'm not really into the whole party scene either. Besides the guys on the team, I don't really know anyone here."

"Me neither."

Rap was blaring from the speakers. Alex started bopping to the beat.

"You wanna dance?" he asked.

"I'm way too sober for that right now."

"You want something to drink?"

"Yeah, that'd be good."

"If I get you something, do you promise to dance with me later?" I smiled, for real this time, and shook my head.

"Sure. I'll take a rum and Coke."

Six drinks later, I was dancing with Alex while Erica, Jackie, and their dates serenaded us in high-pitched whistles. We laughed and talked, and when the night was over, he walked me to my dorm.

"Can I come up?" Alex asked.

"Tonight was fun, but I'm not going there with you."

"Can I at least call you sometime?"

"Nah, but I'll see you around campus. Goodnight."

He looked disappointed, but if he were really interested in me, he'd be patient.

★ ★ ★

The next morning, my girls and I sat around in our pajamas and talked about men.

"Alex is pretty cute...for a White boy," I said.

"I think so too," Jackie chimed in.

"Kelly, we already know you don't want him," I said with a giggle.

She looked up from her phone. "Yup. Only dark chocolate for me," she said, high-fiving Erica.

"Y'all keep messing around with those White boys. You need to stick with the brothas. Even snowflake over here gets it."

Kelly made a face at her.

"As long as the guy is nice, I don't really care what race he is," I said.

Erica sucked her teeth. "Not me. I like 'em Black and jacked, like your daddy."

"Ew! Please don't talk about my father like that."

"I'm just sayin'... I see him as a father, too, but I can't deny that my mom had good taste. Nick is hot."

I shook my head and was about to say something else when Erica's phone rang.

"Hey, Alvin. What!? She's having the baby now? All right. I'm coming home. Bye."

After we all had congratulated her, Kelly asked, "Does she know what she's having?"

"Yeah, I'm gonna have a little brother. I guess better late than never, right?"

We laughed and helped her pack her things.

After Erica left, Jackie, Kelly, and I went to grab something to eat when we saw Alex headed our way.

Jackie yelled, "Excuse me! My sister here is a little shy, but she thinks you're cute."

"Jackie!" I said, blushing and shaking my head in embarrassment.

Alex faced me and smiled. "Tell your shy sister the feeling's mutual," he yelled over with a wink.

"Are you seeing anybody?" Jackie asked him.

I playfully nudged her and giggled nervously when he approached me. I felt so stupid.

"Well, Jackie… It's Jackie, right?" he asked.

She nodded.

"I've been trying to talk to your sister since the first day of freshman orientation. I'm getting mixed signals because she keeps giving me the cold shoulder." He faced me and asked, "Are you interested in giving me a chance? I'd love to get to know you."

Damn it! I couldn't stop smiling, and I was sure he'd change his mind and think there was something wrong with me if I didn't cut it out.

"Sure," I said.

"Well, that settles it. We were gonna get something to eat, but the two of you should go on a little lunch date instead."

"If you're paying, I'm down for us going by ourselves," Kelly said to Jackie.

Laughing, the two of them walked away, leaving me with Alex.

"Don't worry. I won't bite," he promised. "Chinese okay?"

"Yep."

He bought me lunch at a nice Chinese restaurant off campus, and we chitchatted about college life. We seemed to click well, and I enjoyed my conversation with him.

"If you don't mind me asking, what's your ethnicity?"

I hated when people asked me that.

"Does it matter?" I snapped.

"No, but between you and your sisters, I can't tell whether you're some type of White, Black, or Hispanic."

I took a deep breath. I was sure he didn't mean anything cruel by his question, but I really hated discussing that. "My mother was Italian, and my father is African-American," I finally said.

"Wow. I've never dated a Black chick before."

That remark irked me and made me feel like everything my dad had told me since I was a little girl was true. Even if I were mixed, the world would always view me as being solely Black.

"Word of advice, Alex. Never refer to a biracial woman as a 'Black chick.' Do I identify as a Black woman? Yes, but my race shouldn't matter."

"You're right. I'm sorry."

I smirked. "You'd better be."

★ ★ ★

Alex and I dated for two months, mostly going to parties around campus. It was a Friday night when I finally invited him to my dorm room, and I wasn't even sure why. I wasn't planning to have sex with him, but our passions got the best of us when we started arguing about one of his teammates who had slept with Jackie.

"She's a big girl. She knew what she was getting herself into. He told her he doesn't want a girlfriend. Shame on her for thinking she could change his mind. She gave it up, and he took it. Did she expect anything different?"

"Of course, you'd agree with him. She's hurting because you guys are insensitive assholes."

I opened my mouth to curse him out more, but he cut my words short by pressing his lips to mine, silencing me with a kiss. He lightly pushed me against the wall, stretching my arms above my head, then secured my hands with his. He kissed me again.

"You think too much," Alex said. "You need to just shut up and go with the flow."

I was angry and turned on, and I didn't understand why. With my hands still held over my head, I leaned in and kissed him back. The instant he released me, we were all over each other.

I nervously glanced up at him as he lifted my arms, stripped off my shirt and sports bra, and tossed them to the floor. He brushed his lips against my neck, ran his thumb around my areolas, took my nipples in his mouth, and began to suck hard on them.

When Alex finally pulled his mouth off my breasts, he said, "Lie down."

"What?"

"You heard me. Get on the bed."

I obeyed, relaxing and letting him take control. Alex smirked, dug in his jeans, and pulled a condom out of his pocket. He pulled down his pants and quickly rolled the condom onto his dick. He wasn't as long as Derek, but he had more girth.

I spread my legs, and he lay down on top of me. With one swift thrust, he was inside me. I moaned as Alex thrust in and out of me with power, each stroke faster, deeper, and harder than the last.

I never had an orgasm with Derek. To be honest, I thought it was a myth, but when that new, warm, tingling sensation coursed through my entire body, I knew it was what good sex was supposed to feel like.

Spent, I slowly opened my eyes. Everything was misty as I tried to catch my breath.

"Turn over."

I tried to do what he asked, but he swiftly turned me over and slapped my ass. It jiggled and stung, and I cried out. He did it again, and the sting lingered.

"You like it?"

The sensation was so new to me that I couldn't help but feel turned on.

"Tell me you like it," Alex said, smacking it again.

"I like it."

When it was over, I lay on Alex's chest, with my vagina still throbbing. I was worried I'd made the same mistake Jackie had made countless times, so I asked, my voice cracking, "Does this mean we're together?"

"Yup. You're mine now."

I felt relieved that I hadn't given myself up to a lost cause, and I wondered what the future would be for us.

CHAPTER 34

A WOLF IN SHEEP'S CLOTHING

Lynn

In the beginning, things were normal. Alex complimented me every day, we laughed together, and he took me out all the time. Then one day, all that changed. In fact, Alex changed.

"You had one bad game, baby. It's not the end of the world," I said, trying to comfort him as we sat alone in his dorm.

Alex sat on his bed, seething at his performance that night. He didn't score any points, and he had seven turnovers. I'd never seen him so angry.

"Shut up! Just shut the fuck up. God, you never stop talking."

I looked at him like he'd lost his damn mind.

"Obviously, you want to be alone right now, so I'm going to act like you didn't just yell at me. I'll just head back to my dorm."

Alex grasped my wrist, wearing a frightening, stone-faced expression.

"Sit the fuck down," he ordered.

I jerked my wrist free from his grasp.

"What's wrong with you? You're scaring me."

POW!

Alex slapped me so hard my knees buckled. A mixture of fear, shock, and anger rushed through me.

"I'm sorry, baby," he pleaded, but when he stepped toward me, I waved him off.

"No! Stay the fuck away from me."

I ran out of his room and rushed back to my dorm. I burst through the door, and Erica's head jumped up from Amare's lap. He covered himself and adjusted his pants quickly to hide his erection while Erica wiped her mouth with napkins from her nightstand.

Erica cleared her throat and asked, "Sis, why are you crying? Did you have a fight with Alex?"

I nodded.

"I warned you about those crazy-ass White boys. Are you okay? You know I'm here for you, sis."

"I'll be fine. I just want to be alone."

"All right. I'll go back to Amare's. I'll be back later if you wanna talk."

"Thanks, sis."

★ ★ ★

I didn't tell anyone that Alex hit me, but I gave him the silent treatment for a week and avoided seeing him at all costs. Whenever he tried to stop by my dorm, I told Erica and Jackie to tell him I wasn't there or that I was sleeping. Eventually, he sat outside my door and wouldn't leave until he saw me.

"Is everything all right with you two? Alex said he's not leaving our door until you talk to him," Jackie said.

"Everything's fine. He's just an ass, and I don't know if I want to deal with him."

"Well, what do you want me to say to him?"

I sighed. "I guess I'll have to talk to him. Can you and Erica step out for a minute?"

"Yeah. Let me see if Angela Davis here wants to go with me to the store."

Erica had her headphones on and was reading the autobiography of Malcolm X.

Jackie tickled her feet.

"Stop that! I hate being tickled," Erica yelled.

Jackie stuck out her tongue. "Lynn needs to talk to Alex in private. Come with me to the store."

Erica nodded.

"How can you concentrate on what you're reading and listen to music at the same time?" Jackie asked.

"When your mind is as powerful as mine, it's easy to multitask."

Jackie rolled her eyes and let Alex in as they headed out.

Alex looked like shit. His hair was oily, and his eyes were red and full of tears.

"I'm so sorry for hitting you, Lynn. It will never happen again."

"You got that right. Look, I don't think this is going to work out. We aren't—"

"Please don't break up with me. I need you. My dad used to beat my mom, and I know how angry that made me growing up. I never wanted to grow up and be the same man he was."

I looked at him with sympathetic eyes. "You've never acted like that before. You were like a different person."

"I'm just under a lot of pressure to succeed. I'm my mother's only hope. I'm all she has left. I lashed out at you that day because I was scared. I'm struggling in my classes and on the court. I'm worried about losing everything and disappointing my mom. I need this scholarship and this team. I need this education, but more importantly, I need you. This past week, I've missed you so much. I can't function without you, Lynn. Can you forgive me?"

He looked so sincere, and his words felt so honest and heartfelt that I decided to give him the benefit of the doubt.

"I forgive you, but if this is going to work, you have to talk to me instead of hitting me when you're frustrated."

"I promise it'll never happen again."

That day, he was really convincing, and for a while, I actually believed him. Unfortunately, I couldn't have been more wrong about Alex and his empty promises.

CHAPTER 35

LAST DAYS

Nick

"Mrs. Johnson, can I see you in the hallway?"

"Come on, Nick," Rhea said. She turned to the doctor. "What's going on with my husband?"

"Mrs. Johnson, I'm sorry, but Joe's health is steadily declining. He has only a few days remaining."

Rhea turned to me, and I held her while she cried in my arms.

"I'm very sorry. Please take this opportunity to spend as much time with him as you can. He's in a lot of pain and has trouble speaking, so he can't talk for long periods, but when he does, he mentions you two. You mean the world to him."

I tried to hold back my tears when I heard that, but they streamed down my face. I felt guilty for all the stress and drama I'd put Scout through over the years. He meant everything to me, and now he was going to leave me, just like my parents and Chance had.

Rhea and I walked into Scout's room, and I pulled two chairs next to his bed.

Scout faced Rhea as she held his hand and gave him a nervous smile.

"How are you feeling, baby?"

"Weak…tired," he said.

Rhea lowered her head so he wouldn't see her crying. The weight loss made Scout appear shriveled and frail, almost unrecognizable.

His face was sunken in, almost skeleton-like, and he was a shell of himself. I looked away, not wanting to remember him like that.

Scout opened his mouth to speak. His lips trembled as he strained to talk.

"Rhea, I...don't have much time left."

"I'm so sorry, Joe," she said, weeping.

"Baby, don't feel sorry for me." He paused to gather his strength. "Being married to you made my life complete." He took a deep breath before he continued, "Most people spend a lifetime searching for their soulmate. I was lucky to be married to you for most of my life," he said.

When he coughed violently, I couldn't hold myself together. Tears flowed down my face. Scout didn't look scared or angry at all. Even at that moment, he was brave.

"Nick, you turned out to be a good man. I knew you had it in you. Thank you for taking care of our business. Promise me you'll take care of Rhea when I'm gone."

I looked at Rhea, and both of our eyes were swollen. I turned to face Scout and nodded.

"I need to hear you say it."

"I promise I'll always be there for her."

He grimaced and closed his eyes. The talking seemed to sap all his strength, and he didn't say anything else after that. It suddenly hit me that it was probably one of the last conversations I'd ever have with my brother. I wasn't ready to lose him.

When we got home, the house felt huge and empty.

Lynn was working on three papers for school when I called to tell her the news about her uncle. She took it hard too.

"I feel so sorry for him, Daddy. Are you okay?" she asked.

"I'll be all right."

"Are you sure?"

"Don't worry about me. I'm fine. I knew this was coming, so I tried to prepare myself somewhat mentally for it. You have school and ball games to worry about."

"Family comes first. I mean it. If you need me, call."

Beaming with pride, I answered, "I will, Ladybug. Go ahead and work on your papers. I'll let you know..." I almost *said "when he passes,"* but I choked on the words. I cleared my throat and repeated, "I'll let you know."

"I understand, Dad. I'll talk to you later."

I ended the call and sat on my couch, aimlessly flipping through channels on the TV. In the past, Scout had always been a few feet away when I needed him. Now, that big house was only going to be home to Rhea and me.

I heard a knock on my door, drawing me out of my thoughts. "Come in," I said.

"Can I stay up here with you, Nick? I don't want to be alone."

"Of course."

Rhea lay down on her side and put her head on my lap. We watched the news together. I was glad to have her company. I didn't want to be alone either.

★ ★ ★

The next morning, I went to the hospital by myself. Rhea went to work and told me she'd meet me here in the afternoon.

I walked through the hospital corridor, held my breath and slowly exhaled, bracing myself before I went into Scout's room. I stepped inside to the sight of him lying on a gurney, grimacing in pain. "Hey, Scout," I said.

He grunted but didn't have the strength to speak to me.

I trembled when I reached for his hand. His chest rose slowly, and he struggled to take even shallow breaths.

The doctors and nurses reminded me that there wasn't anything else they could do, but they promised to do their best to make him comfortable.

Suddenly, Scout's eyes closed, and I heard him gasp as he lay limp on his back. The vitals monitor sounded a high-pitched, steady beeping noise, and the nurses rushed into the room and walked me into the hallway.

Everything happened so quickly, but it all seemed to slow down when the doctor patted me on the shoulder and said, "I'm sorry, Mr. Johnson. Your brother has passed."

CHAPTER 36

FIRST IMPRESSIONS

Lynn

I glanced at my phone and saw a call from my dad.

"What's up, Daddy?" I said.

Alex stared intently at me and listened closely to my conversation.

"Ladybug, Uncle Scout is gone."

I fell silent for a moment, then said, "Oh my God. How is Aunt Rhea taking it?"

"Not good. She locked herself in their room. She's talking, but she won't come out of the room. She's heartbroken because she wasn't there when he passed."

"What happened?"

"She went to work to keep busy, and…" Dad exhaled loudly, trying to hold himself together. "He passed early this morning, right when I got there."

"Are you okay, Dad?"

"Not really, but I'll be all right eventually. The funeral will probably be on Saturday. Hopefully, it won't interrupt your classes and games too much."

"We're not traveling this week, but there is a game tomorrow. I'll let everyone know I had a death in the family. I'm on my way now."

"You can come tomorrow, after your game. It's fine."

"No, Daddy. I wanna be there for you and Aunt Rhea."

"I appreciate it. Your aunt is really going to need us. If you want, you can tell Erica and Jonna."

"Of course, I'll tell them. They loved Uncle Scout, and I'm sure they'll want to be there."

"Well, I'm gonna go. I've gotta try to convince Rhea to come out of her room and eat something."

"I'm on my way, Daddy. Love you."

"Love you, too, Ladybug."

"What's wrong?" Alex asked when we ended the call.

My lips trembled, and I began to cry. "My uncle died."

Alex wrapped his arm around me while I wiped my eyes and tried to pull myself together.

I called Erica and told her everything. She asked me to give her all the details for the wake and the funeral as soon as I got them.

I grabbed my big team gym bag from my closet.

"I have to pack and head home. I'll email my professors and coach to let them know there was a death in my family."

"I'm coming with you," Alex said.

"You don't have to. It's fine."

"Why? Is Derek going to be there or something?"

"No! Why would you even bring him up?"

"Because you're acting very suspicious right now, and I don't like it. Do you plan to meet up with him during your trip home?"

I didn't have time for his shit right now. I looked at him like he was crazy, but I kept my distance and kept packing. The last time he hit me he said it was an accident, but lately, I've seen a dark side to his temper, and it scared me.

"Derek is the furthest thing from my mind right now. My uncle just died."

"Well since Derek won't be around, I'm coming with you. This way I'll get to meet your Father."

"This won't be the best time to meet him. He just lost his brother, and He's going to be in a bad mood plus, what are you going to say to your Professors and Coaches?"

"Don't worry about that. I said I'm fucking coming with you," he shouted.

I braced myself, scared that he'd lose his temper and hit me again.

290

"I'm sorry. Look, don't worry. I'll tell them I have a bad case of the flu, and my teammates will cover for me."

"You can come home with me another time. It's not worth getting in trouble over. Honestly, I'd rather mourn alone with my family."

Alex grabbed my arm. "I don't care what you'd rather do. I want to come with you, and that's what I'm doing. You understand?"

I nodded.

"Good. I'm going to my room to pack. I'll see you in a little bit. Don't try to leave without me."

"Okay," I said, stunned.

As soon as he left, I flopped down on my bed, my head spinning with emotions. It was going to be a long, stressful week, and I really didn't need Alex and his bossy temper along for the ride.

★ ★ ★

My dad opened the door. His eyes were red-rimmed and bloodshot.

"Hey, Dad."

"Hi, Ladybug."

I walked inside, and Alex stepped in behind me.

Dad gave me a weird look.

"Who's this?" he asked.

"Dad, this is my boyfriend, Alex."

He looked at me, then back at Alex. The furrow of his eyebrows told me my dad wasn't thrilled that Alex had come along, and I was sure Alex sensed his uneasiness too.

"I just wanted to show my support for you and Lynn, sir. I care about her a lot," Alex said.

"Well, thank you...and it's nice to meet you, Alex," Dad said, extending his hand

Alex grimaced during the handshake; Daddy must've squeezed the hell out of his hand. I grinned to myself.

I was surprised to see Jonna here, sitting on the couch next to Aunt Rhea. I ran to them and hugged and kissed them both. I faced Aunt Rhea.

"I'm sorry," I said.

"There was nothing anyone could do. It was just his time," she said.

Alex was walking around the living room, touching pictures and looking at everything, all while Daddy watched him like a hawk.

Aunt Rhea leaned in close. "The new boyfriend, huh?"

"Yeah, Alex. He plays on the men's team at my school. Daddy gave him a super-firm handshake when I introduced him, and from the look on his face, I don't think he likes him."

"He probably doesn't. I've talked about this with him privately, but I understand. In a father's mind, he feels no man will ever be good enough for his little girl. Every parent wants their child to be with someone who makes them happy, but deep down, they also want them to be with someone who is similar to them. He's probably acting silly because Alex is White, but Nick is a good guy. Once he sees that Alex is treating you right, he'll lighten up."

"That's good to know. Now, let's save Alex before Dad kills him."

★ ★ ★

"What do you think you're doing?" Daddy asked Alex, standing in my doorway with his arms folded. Alex sat halfway in my bed with his mouth open, dumbfounded. Alex stupidly tried to sneak into my bedroom for some late-night sex, but the creaking floorboards had easily given him away.

"I was just trying to comfort Lynn, sir. I know she's taking the loss hard."

"Alex, I'm just getting to know you, so I'll cut you a little slack this once, but don't ever lie to me or try to disrespect me in my house again."

Alex looked at the wooden floor. "Yes, sir," he said.

"Now when you're back on campus, I can't control the actions that you and Lynn's hormones drive you to do but in this house, there will be none of that. Go back to the couch, and for the remainder of this trip, I don't want to catch you coming back in Lynn's room again."

"Yes, sir."

"Thank you."

Alex turned away from Daddy as he walked past, trying to adjust and hide the noticeable erection in his shorts.

Daddy waved at me with a smirk.

"Goodnight, Ladybug."

I giggled to myself. "Goodnight, Dad."

★ ★ ★

The next morning, Alex insisted that I take him to the mall to find a gift for my dad.

"I have a picture of us in my suitcase. I was thinking of getting a nice frame for it and giving it to your father. What do you think?"

"It'd be a nice gesture. I'm sure it will earn you some brownie points with him."

When we got home, Alex pulled a picture of us out of his suitcase and walked up to my Dad in the living room with the picture in the frame.

Dad stared at the picture, then nodded slowly.

"Thanks, Alex. I really appreciate it."

Dad seemed to lighten up a bit after the gift.

Alex really started to shine when it was time for the funeral. He consoled Aunt Rhea, Erica, Jonna, and me when we cried, and he did all the little things that showed he cared. He offered to help with everything and the way he acted gave me hope that he and I might have a future together.

CHAPTER 37

LAST GOODBYE

Nick

There was a huge turnout for Scout's funeral. Mr. Davis and his son Chris were there, as well as Cyrus, Vince, and lots of Scout's old college buddies, past co-workers, and employees from the shop.

Jonna was holding her new baby when she walked into the room with Erica and her new man. Lynn greeted them while I stood off to the side. I nodded at Jonna. She handed the baby to Alvin and walked over to me.

"I'm so sorry for your loss, Nick," Jonna said, kissing me on the cheek. "Thanks for coming."

"I love you, Nick. You know that. Of course, I'd be here for you."

We hugged, and I so wanted to delve deeper in that feeling. I wanted her to be my rock, to help me through the loss like she had helped me so many times before, but I felt her break our embrace and slowly ease off of me. It was hard to accept, but she couldn't be in my life like that anymore.

After the Reverend had given his service, he signaled for me to come to the stage. I took a deep breath and gathered the courage to speak in front of the crowd. I never thought I would ever have to do this for Scout. He was always the one who did these things.

A flood of emotions overwhelmed me when I walked passed Scout's casket to the podium. I was glad the casket was closed. I didn't think I'd be able to speak if I saw him lying in there.

I unfolded the eulogy I had written and swallowed, trying my best to get the lump out of my throat before I read it. I recognize what I wrote, but my mouth couldn't say the words.

My voice cracked.

I looked at Lynn, Rhea, and Jonna. I stood up straight and pulled myself together. My hands shook as I read off the paper. I thanked him for being more than an older brother to me, but a second Dad to me. I spoke from the heart like he did at Chance's funeral and thanked him for the times when he helped me most. People clapped for me, and I felt like Scout was still with me. I knew he was in spirit.

I watched as Scouts casket was lowered into the freshly dug grave, right next to Chance's. I had lost my parents, and now both of my brothers were gone. I felt alone. All the good times, bad times, conversations, and advice from my brothers replayed in my head.

I was having a hard time accepting that they were gone and never coming back. I'm tired of losing everyone I cared about. I lost Vickie, I lost my brothers, and I lost Joanna. Lynn was away at College; I don't think I can take any more loss.

Rhea and I exchanged hugs and kisses with family and friends who came to pay their respects to my brother.

Mr. Davis and Chris walked up to us.

"I'm sorry for your loss," Chris said.

"Thanks, man."

"Your brother was a good man. He'd be proud of the man you are today," Mr. Davis said, patting me on the back.

"I really appreciate you coming. Thank you for helping me throughout the years, for being here today, for…everything."

"You're welcome, son. Just continue to make your family proud."

Mr. Davis had watched me grow from a boy to a man. He was a great friend to my father and me. I could never thank him enough for giving me work all those years. Now, I had to focus on keeping my family business successful, just as Scout had done for so long.

CHAPTER 38

PUNCHING BAG

Lynn

"Where were you after practice?" Alex screamed at me.

"I was out with my friends. I wasn't aware I have to ask for your permission."

Alex threw me on the floor and rained slaps down across my face until blood splattered out of my mouth. I sat up and cried, but he was unfazed and didn't apologize. He wasn't sorry, and his true colors were showing.

After Uncle Scout's funeral, Alex was like Dr. Jekyll and Mr. Hyde. I realized quickly that the way he'd acted with my family was all a bunch of bullshit. He hit me in private often and threatened to hurt me if I tried to leave him. I was terrified of Alex, but I still loved him. Once he calmed down, he always apologized and told me more about his awful childhood, as if that justified his behavior. I was always hurt and hobbling from Alex's beatings, and word began to spread around campus about it. I knew there was a problem when Erica called me out on it.

"What's going on with you? You're so jumpy lately. Besides practice, I rarely see you, and when I do see you, you're always in pain," she said.

"I'm fine," I said.

"I hope the rumors aren't true. People all around campus are telling me Alex is whoopin' your ass. I told them I know for a fact that wasn't true. I know my sister wouldn't let that happen, and if it did, she damn sure would tell me. Right, sis?"

Before I could answer, someone banged on the door. I knew it was Alex, and I was scared of what he might do in front of Erica.

"Open the fucking door! I already know you're in there," Alex screamed, banging and shaking the handle like he was going to break it down.

"Calm down! I'll open it."

"I am calm. Open the fucking door."

"I know this motherfucker isn't banging on our door like that. Sis, you need to drop his ass," Erica said.

"I know. He's not always like this. I don't know what's wrong with him lately."

"I'd call Campus Security before he goes Norman Bates on you."

"I'm just gonna let him in before people start complaining."

As soon as I opened the door, Alex slapped me, grabbed me by the collar, and kicked the door close. He slammed me violently against the wall.

"I've been calling you all afternoon. Where the hell have you been?"

"I-I didn't have my phone. I was at practice; then I went out to eat with—"

"Get the fuck off my sister," Erica yelled, kicking him in the nuts from behind.

Alex collapsed to the ground, his eyes bloodshot. He stood gradually and stared Erica down.

"Motherfucker, I wish you would try to hit me. You touch me, and I'll have every brotha on campus fucking you up. Try me!" Erica said.

Alex backed down.

"He shouldn't be hitting you, Lynn."

"It was a misunderstanding."

"Nobody was talking to you," Erica said to Alex, then faced me again. "Does Dad know he's been going Ike Turner on you? How long has this shit been going on?"

"Erica, please don't say anything to my dad. I'll take care of it. Don't worry."

"Why are you with this asshole anyway?"

"We love each—"

"Nobody's talking to you!" Erica yelled, cutting Alex off. "I'm talking to my sister."

"I need to talk to Alex alone. I'll take care of it."

"Fine. I'm gonna go to Amare's. Your man here has a hand problem. He'd better fix it, or I'll get people to fix it for him."

I walked her to the door.

"Please don't tell anyone, Erica…especially not Dad. I need to fix this myself. Promise me you won't say anything."

"I promise for now, but if it doesn't stop, I'm going to have to break that promise."

"It won't get to that point."

She walked down the steps, and I went back inside.

"When your practice is over tomorrow, come to mine," Alex demanded. "All my teammates' girls watch our practices without being asked."

"I can't. I have plans with Erica."

"You're not going anywhere with her."

"This has to stop, Alex."

Alex grabbed me by my shoulders and slammed the back of my head into the wall.

I held the aching back of my skull and glared at him.

"I don't think you heard me. I'm not playing with you. I said you're not going anywhere with Erica. That bitch doesn't like me, and I don't want you around her anymore."

"You don't own me, Alex. You can't tell me who I can and cannot—"

Before I could finish talking, Alex punched me in the stomach, knocking the air right out of me. I gagged, gasped for air, and cried.

"You make me hurt you. I don't want to, but you don't fucking listen," he said through clenched teeth.

He slapped me across the face and squeezed my cheeks with a firm grip.

"Next time I call, you better answer your fucking phone. I'll see you at my practice tomorrow," he yelled, slamming my door.

There was a sharp pain in my side, and I was having trouble breathing. I lay down on my bed and cried, wondering why Alex hurt me like that, if he loved me like he said he did. Not sure what else to do, I shut my eyes and hoped sleep would help my physical and emotional pain go away.

★ ★ ★

"Johnson, step off the court for a second."

"Yes, Coach?"

"You're not your usual self today. You've been grimacing. Is everything okay?"

"I'm fine, Coach. Really."

"I try not to listen to gossip about my players, but rumor has it that Alex has been hitting you. Is it true?"

I put on a fake smile, trying my best to hide the pain I was in.

"I'm good, Coach. You can't believe all the gossip you hear on campus. You know people talk, and half of them don't know what they're talking about."

She gave me the side eye. I knew she didn't believe me, but I couldn't risk getting Alex in trouble.

"Lynn, I had a boyfriend who used to hit me too—emphasis on *used to*. He beat me so badly that I was hospitalized at one point. You're young, and you might think you love him, but love isn't supposed to hurt."

I looked down at the court.

"If you're not comfortable talking to me about it, I have some flyers in my office with hotlines for domestic violence."

"Thanks, Coach, but that won't be necessary."

She shook her head. "All right. Get back out there then."

★ ★ ★

For a couple of weeks, I did most of my class work in the library, to avoid seeing Alex around the campus or my dorm.

I felt a light tap on my shoulder and immediately panicked.

"Hi. I'm Sean," the guy said, extending his hand for a shake.

"I take it the rumors are true, huh?" he asked, noticing my flinching.

300

My lips trembled, but I didn't offer him an answer or an introduction.

"I came over because I know you're in my psychology class. I need a partner for that group project. Not only that, but it looks like you could use a friend. You wanna talk about it?"

I didn't know him from a hole in the wall, but I confessed everything to him. Sean had soft, brown eyes and a thick lisp. He was very handsome. His eyebrows were neatly trimmed, his hands were well manicured, and the guy could dress! He was a sophomore, well respected on campus, and the women loved him. He was heavily into theater and musicals, so a lot of people accused him of being gay, but he had so many girlfriends that I knew that wasn't the case. Plus, I'd never heard any negative things about him from his exes.

I communicated with Alex through text, but I didn't call him or see him for two weeks. He respected my wishes and gave me space to cool off, but his teammates had already ratted me out and told him I was hanging out with "the gay guy."

Sean was smart and driven, and that drew me to him. He told me every day how beautiful I was, and I needed that confidence boost. When I was with Sean, he made me feel special. I felt pretty and wanted. Alex never made me feel like that anymore. I couldn't deny that I had a crush on Sean, and when we kissed after he walked me back to my dorm, I knew he was feeling me too.

★ ★ ★

Slap!

"I've been watching you flirting and smiling in this dude's face for ten minutes," Alex yelled.

Sean and I were in the library, working on our project for our psychology class, and things were quickly getting out of hand. Alex had no problem hitting me in public now, and he reached back to slap me again, but Sean grabbed his arm.

"Keep your fucking hands to yourself. I've got three sisters back home, and I'll be damned if I'm gonna watch you beat on a woman like that."

Alex pulled his arm away and faced me.

"Who this faggot? You fucking him?"

I nervously shook my head.

"If you hit her or call me 'faggot' again, were gonna have a problem."

While others in the library stared and whispered, Alex laughed at Sean, looked at me, and said, "We'll discuss this later. I gotta get to practice."

"Run along, tough guy," Sean said.

"I'm not done with you either, cupcake."

Sean threw up his hands up.

Whenever you're ready."

I was embarrassed but even worse; I knew it was only the beginning of bad things to come.

CHAPTER 39

THE BEGINNING OF SOMETHING BEAUTIFUL

Lynn

Out of the corner of my eyes, I saw Alex stomping toward us. My mood soured. I closed my eyes and tried to will him away. Jackie and Kelly tried to block him.

Alex grabbed my arm. "Come on. Let's go."

"Let her go," Sean said.

"I'm not talking to you, cupcake. This is between her and me."

"He was just walking us home. They were working on their project, Alex. Chill out," Kelly said.

"I don't care. She's embarrassing me hanging out with this fruit. She got my teammates clowning me."

Sean shoved Alex. "I'm not gonna say it again. Let her go."

Alex stepped up to Sean, getting right in his face.

"And what are you going to do about it, fruitcake?" he said, throwing a wild punch at Sean.

Sean caught his arm and threw him to the ground, but Alex quickly got up. A couple of his teammates and others started to crowd around us. I pushed my way to the front.

"You really wanna do this, faggot?" Alex taunted.

He lunged at Sean and was again thrown to the ground. This time, Sean had him in an arm-bar. Alex's teammates ran to his rescue but were stopped by some of Sean's friends.

"Let them fight a fair one," one of the guys said.

Alex was face down in the dirt. People were laughing and pointing.

"Get the fuck off me," Alex said, trying to break free from the arm-bar.

"Who's the bitch now, huh?" Sean teased.

"Let me up, and I'll show you."

Jackie and I were in shock. Kelly was laughing and recording it with her cell phone. I cringed in fear when Sean let him up.

"All right, you're up now. What you got to show me?" Sean taunted.

Sean was a nice guy and in great shape, but I couldn't see him kicking Alex's ass. Alex was six-five, 225, and Sean was only my height, five-nine and maybe 180.

Alex threw a barrage of punches, but Sean easily dodged all of them and slammed him on the ground again, knocking the air out of him, then quickly put him in another arm lock.

"It's not fun when you're getting your ass kicked, is it? This is how this ends, man. Lynn is my girl now. You're not to talk to her or even look at her ever again. You understand?"

"Fuck you! Get the fuck off me," Alex yelled.

Sean's friends shoved Alex's teammates to keep them out of the fight. Sean tightened his hold, causing Alex to scream in pain. Alex tapped on the ground, begging to be let go.

"This can only get worse for you if you don't cooperate. I've got no problem breaking your fucking arm, but I'm sure you don't want that."

Sean pointed to some of the onlookers in the crowd.

"You see all those people recording? Everyone saw you attack me first. I never swung on you; I was defending myself. You were attacking me and calling me slurs. If you struggle and I break your arm, you won't be able to play for the rest of the season, plus the fact that you attacked me and called me Gay slurs could get you expelled. So one more time, Lynn is with me now. You're going to leave both of us alone, and this is the end of it, all right?"

"Fuck you! Get off me."

Sean cranked harder on Alex's arm.

"Fuck! Let me go. You're gonna break it."

"This ends when you say it does, Alex. Do you understand that Lynn is with me?"

"Yes, man. Yes! You can have that bitch."

Sean tightened his grip, causing Alex to yelp again.

"I don't appreciate you talking about my girl like that. Apologize."

"I'm sorry, Lynn. Fuck, man! Let go."

"Not yet. You swear you won't fuck with Lynn or me again?"

"I swear, man. Just get the hell off me."

Sean released the hold.

"See? That was all you had to say."

Alex writhed on the ground, clutching his arm. The crowd, including his teammates, laughed at his humiliation.

Alex struggled to get up, then stood and faced the crowd.

"Fuck all of you!" he yelled, causing everyone to laugh even harder as he ran off.

"Are you all right?" Sean asked.

"Yeah, I'm good."

"Do you agree with what I said? Do you want to be my girl?"

I nodded. "Yup, I'm good with that."

"Cool."

We went back to Sean's dorm, sat on his couch, and watched one of the plays he produced.

"Michael's performance is great in this, right?" Sean asked.

I was too turned on to care. While thoughts of him kicking Alex's ass swarmed through my head, I rubbed on his crotch, but his eyes were glued to the TV.

"Wait," he said.

"I want you, Sean. I wanna make our relationship official."

Sean walked me to his bedroom, held my face in his hands, drew me in, and gave me a slow, passionate kiss. In an instant, my clothes were taken off.

He glided his fingers up and down my body.

"You're perfect," he said.

I blushed, standing naked in front of him.

"Thank you."

I sat on the bed and watched Sean take off his shirt and slowly unzip his pants. He pulled down his briefs, and I stared at him in amazement. His cock was thick and long, with a plump mushroom head. He was bigger than Derek and Alex.

Sean grabbed a condom out of his dresser and handed it to me. He closed his eyes and kissed me while I rolled it on him. The TV was on in the background, and Michael's character was singing loudly.

"Do you want to turn off the TV?" I asked.

"Can we leave it on? I don't want the guys in the next dorm to hear you cumming."

"Who say's you're that good?"

He wore a sly grin but didn't offer an answer.

I slid my body across his bed. Sean closed his eyes and lowered himself over me, then gulped. He was a bit hesitant at first, but he held my legs behind my knees and plunged inside of me. I gasped at the sensation of him filling and stretching me. He stroked me, almost in rhythm to the music being played in the background.

I heard Michael singing another song on TV. Sean turned me over savagely, quickened his thrusts, and hammered me from behind. I felt the pressure building in my stomach, my orgasm ripping through me. Sean grunted and shuddered as we came together. He pulled out of me slowly, and we spooned while he kissed my shoulders.

"Wow," I said, panting.

"I take it you enjoyed yourself."

"Hell yeah."

We laughed, and he held me close. I hoped it was the beginning of something beautiful.

CHAPTER 40

IMPULSE

Nick

I sat in my office, doing paperwork, wishing Scout was still there; work wasn't as fun without him.

My cell phone buzzed with a call from Erica. She never called me, so I answered immediately, worried that something had happened to Lynn. I couldn't take losing my daughter on top of everything else. "Hello? What's wrong?" I asked in a panic.

"Hey, Nick. I have to tell you something, but you can't flip out… and you can't tell Lynn I said anything."

"What's wrong, Erica?"

"Promise me you won't flip out or tell Lynn."

It took everything inside me not to lose my shit and yell at her. I didn't have time for that kid shit. If something was going on with my daughter, I didn't care whether or not Lynn would be mad at Erica for telling me. I took a deep, calming breath before I spoke.

"I promise, Erica. What's going on?"

"Alex is beating Lynn. She's been hiding it for months, but it's getting worse. He used to do it in private, but now he does it right in front of other people. The stress from it is messing up her grades and her playing, and—"

"What did you say?" I asked, interrupting her.

"Nick, you promised you wouldn't flip out."

I clenched the phone in my hand while I processed what she told me.

"I'm cool. How long has this been going on?" I said, almost in a shout.

"About nine months."

"Nine months and you waited this long to tell me?"

"I hoped she'd come to her senses and drop him. I'm not sure if she loves him or if she's just terrified of him, but I can't watch my sister get beaten up anymore. I'm scared he's gonna really hurt her one day."

"I'm coming down there tonight to straighten this shit out and talk some sense into her."

"Please don't. She'll know I told you."

"What do you expect me to do when my daughter's getting her ass beat by her man?"

"I figured maybe you'd just call her and ask if everything's okay. She's been depressed a lot lately, so maybe she'll break down and tell you herself."

"Nah, I'm putting an end to this shit right now. It usually takes an hour and a half to drive to your campus. I'll be there in forty-five minutes."

"Nick, don't do anything crazy."

"No boy is gonna put his hands on my daughter. I'll see you in a few," I said, then ended the call.

I reached in my right-hand drawer, opened the lockbox, and grabbed Scout's old revolver. I didn't plan on killing the kid, but I was going to make damn sure he never hit Lynn or any other woman again.

★ ★ ★

My adrenaline was pumping as I zigzagged in and out of traffic, ready to do whatever was necessary to protect my daughter. I thought about when she was a little girl, when I failed to protect her from all the teasing of her classmates and Hazel's nasty little bastards. I thought about how powerless I felt when her heart was broken by her high school boyfriend. This time, I wasn't going to sit back and let Lynn get hurt. I sped to the campus and got there in a little less than an hour.

Before I left my office, I put on a suit and grabbed the framed photo of the two of them, the one Alex had given me during their visit. My plan was to talk to some of the students on campus and tell them I was a sports agent who wanted to talk to Alex about going pro.

Like clockwork, I found some students around the parking lot and asked them if they've seen him. Things didn't work out the way I planned. As I approached group after group of students, I wasn't getting anywhere. Most of them thought I was a cop and told me to go fuck myself. The others didn't care who I was and told me to fuck off.

"Excuse me, fellas. I'm looking for Alex Davidson. Do you know him?" I asked a group of stoners.

"Yeah, we know him. Who wants to know?"

"I'm a sports agent for, uh…Johnson and Johnson Management. I'm trying to meet up with him to convince him to sign with me and go pro."

They looked at me skeptically. I knew they didn't believe me.

"You got any money, mister?"

"Will you tell me where he is if I do?"

"Gimme Fifty bucks and I'll tell you the dude's room number." He laughed.

I dug in my wallet and only found twenties, but I didn't give a damn about making exact change.

"Here," I said, handing him sixty dollars.

"He's in the South Dorm, near the basketball and golf courses. He stays on the fourth floor, Room 405, with the rest of the jocks."

I smiled. "Thanks."

"No problem, dude," the red-eyed kid said before I walked away.

Students were walking in and out of the dorm, but I had no idea how I would get inside. As I stood there deliberating about it, I saw Alex walking to the dorm, and I stood off to the side, hoping he wouldn't recognize me. When he got closer to the door, I approached him.

"What's up, Alex? You and I need to talk."

"Shit," he said, throwing his hands in the air.

"Come with me."

"Nah, I'm good."

I opened the jacket of my suit, exposing my gun.

"Fuck, man!"

"If you don't want this to get ugly, you'll come with me so we can talk."

We walked to a secluded part of the campus in silence, and I checked around for any security cameras or onlookers.

"Look, Mr. Johnson, I don't know what Lynn told you, but I didn't do anything to her, okay? I'll leave her alone, all right? I don't want any—"

BAM!

Before he could finish his bullshit lies, I hit him on the bridge of the nose with the butt of my gun. Blood squirted all over my shirt and the pavement as he stumbled back and fell into the bushes. I stood over him, grabbed him by his shirt, and pointed my gun at his face. "Open your lying mouth," I demanded.

His face was drenched in blood, and his hands trembled as he obeyed my instructions.

I shoved the gun in his mouth, leaned in close to him and said, "My daughter is my life. If you or anyone hurts the person I value most in this world, I won't hesitate to end your pathetic fucking life. I have nothing to lose, and I'm not afraid to go to jail or even die to protect my daughter. You understand me?"

I couldn't comprehend his answer with the gun in his mouth, so I pulled it out and asked, "What was that?"

"Yes, sir," Alex whimpered.

"Good. As of now, you're done seeing Lynn. Don't call her, and don't even look at her. If I hear anything about you touching her again, I'll blow your goddamn head off. You got that?"

Alex nodded, but I wasn't satisfied and felt like he was getting off too easy. As if I was in some trance, I rained hard punches down all over his face. With each hit, I thought about everything that had been stressing me out, and I took my frustrations out on him. I hit him for Lynn and all the times I wished I could've saved her from being in pain or heartbroken. I hit him because Scout was gone. I hit him because Jonna had moved on and was happy. I hit the kid until my knuckles were raw and my suit was splattered with blood.

Alex whimpered and begged me to stop. His face was red, and blood gushed from his nose and mouth.

I looked down into his swollen eyes and finally came to my senses. I ran to my car as fast as I could and sped off. Reality hit me that he could easily call the cops and tell them what I'd done. I didn't know what to do, but I knew I had to get the hell out of Connecticut.

★ ★ ★

I lay in bed, tossing and turning. It was six a.m., and I couldn't sleep. I was sure the cops would be there any second to knock down my door and drag me out of the house.

I didn't want Rhea to panic, as she'd already been through enough. I needed a voice of reason, someone to calm me, so I broke down and called Jonna.

"Hey, Nick," she answered.

"Jonna, I did something stupid."

"Nick, I've forgiven you. We've both moved on, and—"

"Not that. I mean right now. Last night, I beat Lynn's boyfriend up pretty bad."

"What!?"

I gave her all the details, shocking her while she got dressed for work.

"Jesus, Nick. What were you thinking? You better hope and pray he doesn't call the cops. From what you just told me, you could do serious time in prison for this."

"I wasn't thinking."

"That's obvious. My God, Nick. Lynn could lose her scholarship or get kicked out of school over this. You need to talk to her."

"What am I supposed to say?"

"Tell her what happened and see what's going on, on campus."

"All right. I'll let you know what happens."

"Please do, no matter what time it is."

"Okay. Thanks, babe...er, I mean, thank you. I'll talk to you soon."

Around nine a.m., I called Lynn.

"Hey, Dad," she said, not sounding worried or angry.

"What's up, Ladybug?"

"I'm good. What's going on?"

I decided to cut the small talk and tell her exactly why I was calling. "Ladybug, don't get mad at Erica, but I know Alex has been hitting you. I—"

"It's taken care of, Dad."

"So you *know*?"

"Of course, I know. I was there when Sean, um...*talked* to him."

"Sean? Who is Sean?"

"He's a good guy, Daddy. You'd like him. Anyway, yesterday, Sean made sure Alex won't bother me again. He embarrassed him in front of damn near everyone on campus."

"Is that right?"

"Yup, and I guess God doesn't like ugly, because after Sean had fought with Alex, Alex got jumped and robbed by three men on his way back to his dorm."

"What? Three men? When did you hear that?"

"Last night. Alex ran to his dorm all bloody and beat up. He told Campus Security three men beat him and took his money."

I was beyond relieved, but I asked, "Lynn, why didn't you tell me what was going on with Alex?"

"I wanted to handle it on my own, Dad. I didn't want you to worry and do something crazy."

I laughed to myself.

"Ladybug, never be afraid to tell me things. You and Rhea are all I have left. What if he went too far and killed you? I can't lose you too."

"I know, Daddy. I'm sorry."

"I don't care how small you think something is. If you're having a problem, call me."

"If anything like that happens again, I'll tell you. I promise."

"It better never happen again with any other guy you date."

"See, Daddy? That's why I don't tell you things."

"This Sean guy better not have the same problems your last boy-friend had."

"Sean is nothing like Alex."

"He better not be."

"He's not. I want you to meet him when I come home."

"All right. Bring him by, but he's sleeping on the couch."

She chuckled. "I know, Daddy. I know. No hormones in your house," she said with a giggle.

CHAPTER 41

SECRETS

Lynn

"So? What do you guys think of him?" I asked dad and Aunt Rhea.

"He's cute, and he seems nice," she said.

"Ladybug, are you sure he's, um…straight? He seems a little light on his feet."

"Dad!"

"I'm just saying. He looks kind of soft. I bet he doesn't even leave footprints in the snow."

"He's all man. Trust me on that."

Aunt Rhea chuckled. Daddy didn't.

Sean was charming. He talked to Dad about sports and took a big interest in Dad's business, or at least he put on a good act. He complimented Aunt Rhea all the time, and it was nice to see her smile after she lost Uncle Scout. I felt Sean left a great first impression on the two people who mattered to me most, and that was important.

★ ★ ★

One of the qualities I loved most about Sean was that I could confide in him. He never judged me or made me feel silly when I talked to him. I felt like he understood me and all my craziness. I told him things about myself that I'd never told anyone. One of the biggest things I talked to him about was my mother. Talking with him, I discovered feelings I didn't even know I had about her. I realized that even with a great father, Aunt Rhea, and Jonna, the feelings of abandonment, hurt, and even hate that I kept locked inside were tearing me apart. He comforted me through those feelings, and I felt safe with him.

Sean confided in me too. He explained that his father desperately wanted a son after having five daughters, so his dad was delighted when Sean was born. Unfortunately, he was under a lot of pressure growing up, having to act macho all the time, and his father was embarrassed that he was so involved in performing arts. We uplifted each other.

Emotionally and mentally, our relationship was solid, but we'd been together for five months, and in that time, we'd only had sex twice. I basically threw myself at him every day, but he consistently turned me down. When we lay down together, which happened often, we just held each other. He told me how sexy my body was, but even when we were naked, he never made a move. Whenever I was aggressive and tried to force intimacy, he turned me down and said he just wanted to enjoy my company. I began to worry that he wasn't attracted to me anymore.

One day in his dorm, I pressed the matter further. I lay on Sean's chest and massaged his dick while kissing his neck. Despite my actions, he didn't get hard.

Sean gently stopped me.

"You don't have to do that, baby."

"But I want to," I said.

I slid down and took him in my mouth. I worked my magic and looked up at him to gauge his response.

Sean's eyes were closed as he tilted his head back. When he opened his eyes again, he stared at me and gradually lost his erection.

"I'm good, baby. I just wanna hold you," he said, then wrapped his arms around me while we spooned.

"What's wrong? Is it me?" I asked, disappointed.

"I don't want to fight right now."

I sat up against the headboard.

"We're not fighting, but this is something we need to talk about. You're never in the mood to be intimate with me, and I want to know why. I love you, and I want to share myself with you, but you have to tell me what I need to do to please you. Whatever it is you want me to do or not do, I'll do it."

He sighed.

"It's not you, Lynn. I have…kinky taste, and I don't want to scare you off or make you think I'm some weirdo."

I turned to face him and looked at him skeptically.

"I'm open-minded, but what do you consider kinky?"

"Do you know a guy's G-spot is in his anus?"

"Um, no. I've never heard that."

"Would you be willing to…finger my ass? It really gets me off."

I laughed, but I quickly stopped chuckling when I realized he was serious. It seemed very weird to me. Derek and Alex never asked me to do anything like that; in fact, they flinched whenever anything came close to their assholes. Still, I wanted to make Sean happy, so I hesitantly said, "Sure, I can, uh…do that…if it's what you want."

"Cool. Have you ever tried anal?"

"No. I've heard some of the girls on my team talking about it. They said it's torture."

"That's because your friends did it with brutes who don't know what they're doing. Done right, it's very enjoyable for both people."

"I don't know. It doesn't sound like something I'd enjoy."

"Oh," Sean said, looking disappointed.

"But I'm willing to try it with you," I quickly said. "I'm just scared it'll hurt."

"If you give me a chance, I promise I'll do my best to make it as comfortable and pleasurable as possible."

"Okay."

"Do you want to try going down on me again?"

I smiled. "Sure!"

"Can we try that stuff I want now?"

"Um…I guess."

"Great!"

Sean went to his drawer and pulled out a bottle of lube, latex gloves, and a blindfold on the bed. He lay down next to me, covered his eyes with the blindfold, and said, "The gloves are for your hands. Put lube on your fingers and stick them inside me while you suck me."

"Okay, if you say so."

The thought of what we were about to do must've excited him because he hardened instantly. My hands trembled as I put on the gloves and poured the lube on my right index finger. I stroked his shaft with my left hand and gradually inserted my lubed finger inside him.

He writhed and moaned while I worked him in my mouth and rapidly fingered his ass.

"You can use two fingers. It's okay," he coached.

It was nice to know that I pleased him, but something about it didn't feel right. It was evident that he'd done this more than a few times. I didn't know if he got off on it because it was taboo or because of something deeper, something I didn't want to believe. My father's insinuation that Sean was gay still lingered in the back of my mind.

He rested his hand on top of my head and guided me up and down on his length. His breathing became choppy as he urged, "Yeah, that's it, baby. Keep going."

His legs stiffened, and he came intensely down my throat. He panted, tightened his blindfold, and said, "I want to feel you now."

Sean positioned himself behind me. I felt him spread my cheeks and pour the lube on my anus.

"Do you trust me?" he asked.

"Yes," I responded.

"I need you to relax. The more at ease you are, the better it'll feel for both of us."

I turned my head.

"Okay," I said, feeling unsure.

"Can you, uh...not say anything? I like it when I just hear moaning. Talking messes up the sensation for me."

I nodded nervously, forgetting that he couldn't see me with the blindfold on. I closed my eyes and tried to relax, reminding myself that I was doing it for Sean because he made me happy and I wanted the intimacy.

Still, I felt uncomfortable. It was the most sexual activity we'd ever done, and everything about it felt wrong. I shook the feeling off and reminded myself that if Sean was gay, he wouldn't have had so many ex-girlfriends, fought Alex for me, or asked me to be his girl.

I knew he loved me, and I needed to calm down and try to enjoy the intimacy, even if it weren't exactly what I wanted.

Luckily, Sean kept his promise and was gentle with me. He took his time and was patient, and he seemed to enjoy it. He came again, then lay next to me, apparently satisfied, while I felt sore and unfulfilled.

"Thanks, honey. I really enjoyed you," he said, kissing my forehead.

I gave him a small grin. I decided I could deal with his strange fetish every once in a while, as long as it didn't become a routine.

CHAPTER 42

SUBSTITUTE

Nick

Nine months had passed since Scout's death. Rhea didn't want to live downstairs by herself anymore, so she stayed upstairs in Lynn's old room, at least for the time being. I figured it would only be a matter of time before she sold the house, so I had already started looking for another apartment.

One night, while we watched TV together, I brought up the topic. "This is way too much house for just the two of us. Are you thinking of selling it?" I asked.

"Lord knows I've thought about it. I've suffered a lot of pain within these four walls, but I've experienced a lot of love here too. I have too many memories here to just sell it and forget about them. I don't think I could ever sell this house, but what do you think I should do?"

"I grew up here. I raised my daughter here." I held her hand and stared at her. "My family is still here. I don't wanna see the house sold either, but what will you do with all this room."

"Jonna recommended something, and I might look into it."

"What is it?"

"Well, y'all know how much I hate waiting tables, but I need something to keep my mind occupied, so I'm not so depressed over losing Joe. I'm really good with her baby and children in general, so she suggested that I turn downstairs into a daycare. That way, I could still make money and quit the diner."

It wasn't a bad idea. I could easily help her remodel downstairs; she'd be doing something she's really good at and enjoys, plus there wasn't a daycare around for miles so she wouldn't have any real competition.

"I've been giving it a lot of thought, and I think I want to do it. Jonna's gonna help me with the paperwork, but I was wondering if you could help me make some changes downstairs for the business."

"Yeah, that's no problem. I was thinking the same thing."

"Nick, I don't think I can stand staying in my bedroom anymore. I miss Joe so much, and being in there without him depresses me."

"I can fix his old office for you if you want."

"I'd rather live up here with you if you don't mind."

"That's fine. It's your house anyway. You don't need my permission."

★ ★ ★

A faint crying in Lynn's old bedroom woke me up. I peered at the alarm clock on my nightstand, and it flashed 3:15. I kicked off the covers and went to check on Rhea. I found her sitting on the edge of the bed. I touched her shoulder gently.

"Hey, you okay?" I asked.

"No. I miss him so much, Nick."

"I miss him too. I try to stay busy to take my mind off it, but every time I go to the shop, it's a constant reminder of Scout and my dad."

"Joe was proud of you. You've come a long way."

"Thanks."

"I'm fine. Really. Go back to sleep."

"You sure?"

"Yeah."

"All right, but if you need anything, I'm here for you, Rhea." She nodded.

I lay in bed, staring at the ceiling. My door was open, but Rhea knocked anyway. I sat up when I heard it.

"What's up?" I asked.

Rhea ran over and kissed me. At first, it felt awkward. I thought about stopping her, but she poured all of her emotions into it. I held her and wanted her to feel the same from me.

322

She slowly peeled off her clothes. It had been a while since I'd been with a woman, so I hardened instantly. Rhea undressed me, and we continued to kiss softly. I lay back on the bed, and Rhea climbed on top of me. She closed her eyes and rode me, slow and steady. I sat up and leaned against my headboard, caressing her back as she continued to grind.

Rhea nuzzled against my neck and whispered in my ear, "Oh, Joe..."

I wasn't mad or offended when she called his name. I understood why she fantasized about Scout, and I was okay with it.

I knew what this was. Rhea was making love to me because she felt I was the closest thing to being with Scout. This didn't feel like sex with a random woman. It felt like I was making love to her. Even though not in a sexual way, a part of me always loved her. She helped me raise Lynn, and she was the voice of reason that kept my brothers and me together when Chance and I were both young, lost, and made stupid mistakes. Rhea was a great woman. I knew I could never take my brother's place nor did I want to. I'm sure she knew she could never replace Jonna, but if she would have me, I hoped we could be there for each other so we would never have to be lonely.

★ ★ ★

The next morning, I woke up early and made us breakfast.

"Good morning," I said when she came downstairs.

"Good morning. I want to talk about last night," she blurted, getting right to the point. "I've been so emotional lately, Nick. I miss Joe so much. I enjoyed our time together, but I feel so guilty. Until last night, I'd never been with anyone besides your brother. I don't think I could ever date another man, and I'm not even sure I'd want to. I think last night was a mistake."

"It wasn't. I promised Joe I'd always take care of you. I don't want you to have regrets. Last night, I felt something special. I care about you, Rhea. I love you. I'm not trying to take my brother's place, but if I can be a healthy substitute to help keep you happy, I will gladly do it."

We hugged and held each other for a long time. I knew we could never call what we had a relationship, but I would be content to have her as a close companion.

CHAPTER 43

ALL THAT GLITTERS IS NOT GOLD

Lynn, three years later...

I was usually confident with my looks, but dating Sean made me self-conscious. It exhausted me, trying to make him happy every day, and I began to lose sight of myself in our relationship.

On the surface, we looked like the perfect couple. He went to all my games, and I attended all his performances and events. He brought me flowers, and we had date nights here and there.

While everything looked good on the surface, we rarely saw each other, and he always had an excuse: "I'm out there trying to network and establish myself in the performance arts industry. I'm trying to build something great for us, and you don't seem to get that."

"I get what you're trying to do, but unless I'm on your arm going to one of your events, it seems like you can go weeks without seeing me...or touching me."

As far as intimacy went, if we didn't have sex the way he wanted it, we didn't have it. He didn't seem the least bit bothered by that, even after it went on for three years.

After getting my undergrad degree, Erica and I got our own place off campus. We decided to stay and go through the graduate program for education. Jackie and Kelly went back home and got an apartment together in Long Beach. I originally wanted to move in with Sean, but he was totally against the idea and said we needed to have our own space.

The women on campus envied me and told me all the time that Sean was always bragging about me and how much he loved me. When we first met, I felt that way too. He was brilliant, smart, and charming, but he seemed to prefer hanging out with Michael and his other artsy friends instead of me. I loved Sean and wanted to believe I was special to him, but deep down, I feared I wasn't. I tried to hang out with his friends, but whenever I was around them, I questioned if I was good enough for him. Nothing I did ever made me feel like he or they were impressed.

With all my pent-up sexual frustration and free time, I got into running. It seemed to help me keep my jumbled thoughts at bay. I ran because I needed a release, something to help me through our weird sexual tension. I needed an outlet to help me clear my mind.

There were some on campus who still believed Sean was gay and hadn't come out of the closet. That always fucked with my head; due to his odd sexual requests, even I questioned if our relationship was real or a cover-up. Our last sexual encounter gave me my answer.

"What's in the box?" I asked.

"Something I want to try. Open it."

I lifted the lid and saw a big rubber dildo with a harness.

"Um, you're big enough for me, Sean. I don't need all this," I said.

"It's not for you. It's for me. I thought it would be kinky to try out," he said with a grin.

I stood there, shocked and confused, looking from the dildo to him and back to the dildo again.

"Get undressed."

"Huh? You want me to use it *now*?" I asked.

"There's no time like the present."

Sean quickly took off his polo shirt and folded his jeans. Next, he undressed me, laced and secured the strap-on against my body, and poured lube all over the dildo.

"I don't know about this."

"Don't be that way, Lynn. It's fine."

Sean bent over for doggie-style in bed and excitedly lubed up his anus.

"I don't even know what I'm doing."

"Just pretend you're me, making love to you."

"I wish we could do that instead," I said honestly.

"We will, but I wanna try this first."

I slowly inserted the dildo inside him, and he grunted.

"Oh my God! Are you okay?" I asked, worried that I'd injured him.

"I'm good. Don't say anything. Just keep going. It feels fantastic."

I worked the dildo in him slowly. With each thrust, I felt friction against my clit. I gradually increased my pace, and I had to admit I did feel a sense of power and control, but it didn't feel right. The finger stuff was one thing, but now I was literally fucking my boyfriend. I thought again about my dad's comments and the fact that almost all the guys on campus thought Sean was in the closet. I also thought about how Derek never felt I was feminine enough and how manly I felt now. This wasn't me. This wasn't what I wanted, and nothing about this situation felt normal.

I looked down at Sean, gyrating, and his gruff moans disgusted me so much that I had to stop thrusting.

"What's wrong? Why'd you stop?"

"I can't do this. This is too much for me."

"C'mon, Lynn! You're my girl, right? It's nothing, just a little freaky."

"No, I'm not comfortable with this, Sean, and I honestly can't understand how you could be."

I'd done a lot of odd things to please him, but I couldn't lie to myself anymore. His requests were becoming worse and worse, and I just couldn't do it.

Sean quickly put on his clothes and grabbed his keys.

"Where are you going?" I asked.

"Out!" he shouted.

I lay in bed and cried myself to sleep, praying that Erica would stay out for the night.

★ ★ ★

The sound of soft whimpering woke me. I saw Sean sitting on the edge of the bed, crying.

327

"What's wrong?" I asked.

He jumped, cleared his throat, and quickly wiped his eyes. "Nothing," he said.

"People don't just sit on a bed late at night and cry over nothing. Be straight with me, Sean."

"*Straight* with you." He chuckled lightly.

"What's bothering you?"

"Life."

I closed my eyes and turned my head, trying my best to hold back my own tears. I needed to be strong and ask him about the things that had been on my mind since we'd started dating, but I didn't want to embarrass him or hurt his feelings.

"Sean, I want to ask you somethings, and I need you to be completely honest with me, okay?"

He nodded.

"Are you cheating on me?"

He was still for a moment, then sobbed and nodded.

I gulped and inhaled deeply. I was scared and wasn't sure if I really wanted to know the answer to my next question, but I had to ask it.

"Are you cheating on me with…a man?"

He covered his face with his hands and nodded again.

"You're gay, aren't you?"

"Yes, and I've known for a very long time."

Tears streamed down my face, and a mixture of hurt, embarrassment, anger and even some sympathy ran through my mind. I somehow found the courage to ask, "During the rare times when you were having sex with me, were you also sleeping with guys?"

"Not *guys*. There was only one, Michael. It hasn't gone on for long. It just started."

"Is this what the strap-on is all about?"

"Yeah. I thought maybe if I could get the same sensation from you, I could stop myself from being gay. My family will never accept me if they find out."

Tears streamed down my face. The man I loved had never truly wanted me, and that was hard to swallow.

"Sean…"

"Yes?"

"Why did you ask me to be your girl? I mean, why did you choose me to hide your secret?"

Sean paused for a minute, then answered, "You're tough, mentally, emotionally, and physically. You're strong, Lynn. You're not ultra girly, but you're far from masculine, perfectly balanced. I figured you'd be the perfect beard for me."

"A what? What's a beard?"

"It's a person who conceals the truth about their partner's homosexuality."

I held myself and nodded as Sean wrapped his arms around me.

"Deep down, I knew, but I wasn't strong enough to admit it. We click so well mentally and emotionally. No one understands me like you do, so I figured in time, we could make it work," he said.

I loved Sean. During our relationship, I did anything and everything to make him happy, but that was just too much.

"I appreciate that, but I can't do this," I confessed.

"Please, Lynn! You can sleep with other men, as long as you're discreet about it. Don't leave me."

"I don't want other men. I only wanted you, but now I realize that our entire relationship is a sham."

"What we have is real, but I am who I am. I can't change that."

"And I can't be in a relationship that's a lie. I'll always love you, Sean, and I'll always be your friend, but you have to be true to yourself...and fair to me. We can't be together."

He nodded slowly. "I understand, but please don't tell anyone. I'm not ready to come out yet."

"I won't. I promise."

We hugged, and I spent the rest of the night packing the stuff I'd left at his place.

★ ★ ★

For a year, I dated faceless men. I won't lie; I went through a slight crazy phase where I had a few one-night stands. Internally, I was a wreck. My relationships with Derek and Sean left me feeling like I wasn't feminine enough. The mistakes of the one-night stands were to prove to myself that I was sexy and desirable, but afterward, I always felt dirty and empty. Thank God I had Erica to put me in check.

Early on a Sunday morning, I regrettably made the walk of shame back to our apartment. I opened the door, and Erica and Amar'e were sitting on the couch, watching TV.

"Baby, can you go get some breakfast for us?" she asked. "I need to speak with my sister privately."

"No problem," Amar'e said. He turned to me and said "Ooh! You're in trouble."

I playfully kicked at him before he put on his coat and walked out the door.

"Sis, what's going on with you? Ever since that queer broke your heart, you've been playing yourself, hoeing it up with random guys."

"I told you that in confidence, not so you'd throw it back in my face…and don't call Sean that."

"I'm sorry, but like Mom said, what's between our legs is precious and shouldn't be given to men who aren't worthy. You shouldn't be sleeping with random losers."

"Since when did you start quoting Jonna?"

"Since now. Don't let one failed relationship negatively change the person you are. Your king is out there, sis. You just have to be patient, and he'll find you."

I hated that she was right, but I hugged and thanked her anyway.

★ ★ ★

My feelings for Sean wouldn't go away, and they kept me from allowing myself to give any guy who showed a genuine interest in me a chance. I let a few in, but I quickly found flaws in every one of them. In time, I realized that the only person I was hurting was myself. I was being too picky, and I was upset and lonely because of it. It was time to break the cycle.

Erica, Armani, and I moved back to New York and found a new apartment in East Meadow. Erica and I applied for teaching positions in our old neighborhood in Uniondale. Luckily, my old principal Mrs. Meade remembered me from when I was a little girl and gave

Erica and me jobs in my old elementary school.

I was doing all the things I'd planned to do in life, but I still couldn't turn off my feelings for Sean.

FOURTH QUARTER

MONSTER HISTORY

CHAPTER 44

MONSTER

Lynn

I listened to Sean explain to me how happy and special his boyfriend Michael made him feel, and I was envious. Derek showed me how guys could play games with your heart and emotions. Alex taught me it's possible to love someone who hurts you even if you know they aren't right for you. I learned from Sean that sometimes you can want love so badly it can blind you and make you believe there's something there when deep down, you know there wasn't. I'd learned a lot from all of them, and they were hard lessons to learn.

I wanted to find a love like my Aunt Rhea had with Uncle Scout, the type of love my dad once had with Jonna. I wanted someone to love me unconditionally for who I was. I was happy for Sean, but I still wished we'd had a real relationship. I began to wonder if my "king" even existed or if I was destined to be alone.

On a Saturday night, I was bored beyond belief. Erica was on a date with Amar'e, and Jackie was out with yet another random guy. Kelly was in the Poconos with her new guy, Tyquan, and even Jonna was having a nice romantic evening with Alvin. Sean would've come over to hang out with me if I had asked, but I wasn't in the mood to hear about his drama-filled life. After I talked to my dad, I decided I'd go to the gym instead of sitting around the house, bored and lonely.

Working out didn't help much. I went through the motions, but my emotions had my mind all over the place. I ordered a shake at the juice bar and was deep in thought when I collided with a personal trainer. He was fine! He was clean-shaven, with a rich, deep, dark-skinned complexion like Sean's and my dad's.

"I'm so sorry. Let me buy you a new one," he said, staring down at the spilled shake.

"Is this your way of taking me on a cheap date?" I joked. I regretted the words as soon as they left my lips; I always said the corniest shit when I was flustered or nervous.

He smiled. "Let me get you a new shake. What did you have?"

"I had the peanut butter madness."

"No problem. I'll get you another."

While he made the shake, I pretended to check my email on my cellphone to avoid saying something else stupid. I took little side glances at him and felt him staring at me too. I looked up from my phone and caught him lustfully eyeing me from head to toe. It was cute seeing him look away shyly when I busted him.

"Here ya go," he said, handing me the shake.

"Wow. The first date, and you're already making me meals? You're a keeper."

Ugh, I thought. I was ashamed by my clichéd flirting.

We exchanged smiles.

"I'm Ken."

"I'm Lynn. Pleased to meet you."

"Again, I'm sorry I spilled your shake."

"It's no problem. Thanks for the new one." I said

I put some pep in my step and walked away from the awkward moment.

I figured since I had nothing but time and no life, I might as well be productive, so I drove to Barnes & Noble to work on my lesson plans. After walking down the aisles aimlessly and jotting down ideas for new lessons, I walked to the magazine section and reached for the latest issue of *Vibe*. When I did, someone bumped me from behind. I turned to face the person to apologize, only to discover that it was Ken, the cute trainer from the gym.

"Hi. I keep bumping into you," he said.

"I see that. Are you trying to get a cheap feel?" I said, again wishing I would just shut up.

"Nah, I'm bored, so I decided to hang out here tonight."

We had a nice little conversation, and we were clearly attracted to each other, so I decided to be direct and speed things up.

"What are your plans for the rest of the night? Is your girlfriend meeting you here?" I asked.

"No girlfriend for me."

"No boyfriend either, right?" It was a question I had to ask with my history. The last thing I needed was a repeat of my drama with Sean.

"No, just single... I'm not into guys."

I winked at him.

"Just making sure. Anyway, since you're not doing anything, and I'm not doing anything, do you want to get dinner together?" I asked, hoping I wasn't being too aggressive or coming on too strong. I knew some men viewed that as a turn-off, and I didn't want to scare him away.

"Sorry. I don't mean to be so bold. It's okay if you don't want—"

"Don't apologize. I like a woman who cuts to the chase." He said.

"Great! In that case, I'll pick the restaurant."

He laughed.

"Let's go to Red Robin."

★ ★ ★

At the restaurant, we talked about our goals. Once we discovered that we both played ball, we promised to play one-on-one soon. Ken and I exchanged numbers, and since we seemed to enjoy talking to each other, we agreed to hang out again sometime.

I was mad at myself when I checked my phone to make sure I hadn't missed a call or text from Sean; I knew I needed to stop worrying about his problems and focus on my own. As soon as I got home, I told Erica about my spur-of-the-moment date.

"See? This means something," she said. "Things wouldn't just fall in line for you two to meet and have a date tonight unless fate wanted it that way."

"Ugh. Here we go with your auras, chakras, and karma babble," I joked.

"Shut up! You know I always speak the truth. Anyway, this is good for you. You needed to break out of your comfort zone and meet someone. Set up another date with him soon so you can see where his head's at."

"I plan on it."

"Good…keep me posted."

Later that night, I lay in bed and prayed that Ken was the man I'd been looking for.

★ ★ ★

"When is this gym gonna get any new cardio machines?" I asked Ken.

He laughed.

"Yeah, I know. The treadmills are a little outdated."

"A little?"

"Okay, a lot, but you should use the Stairmaster and elliptical machines anyway. It's a better workout. You use more muscle working on those machines."

I enjoyed conversing with Ken because I didn't get that vibe that he just wanted to fuck me. I felt like he legitimately liked talking with me, even in the gym, about outdated equipment.

"Ken, let's have dinner together tonight," I blurted.

"Sounds like a plan! Can I pick the restaurant this time?" he said with a laugh.

"What do you have in mind?"

"Let's meet up at the Grand Lux Café in Garden City, around seven."

"I'll see you there."

I went home and called my girls, and within minutes, Kelly, Erica, and Jackie were all in my living room, listening to me talk about Ken.

"You said he's the same complexion as your daddy, so I know he must be fine," Erica said.

"So far, he seems nice, but don't keep asking him out. You don't wanna sound desperate," Jackie added.

"I knew your Mary Poppins ass would say something like that. Lynn isn't going to wait around to be rescued by a fictitious Prince

Charming. She's going after someone she feels she can be happy with. He's meeting her halfway, so if it works, it works. Stop trying to make her feel like she's doing something wrong. Maybe you need to follow what she's doing, with your single ass," Erica scolded.

Jackie laughed, clearly not mad or insulted.

"Shit, maybe I need to do that too. Ask him if he has a friend," Kelly said.

★ ★ ★

I pulled up to a spot close the entrance of the Grand Lux Café. I was a little self-conscious about my outfit since I'd given in and let my girls dress me in black skinny jeans that looked like they were painted on and a white blouse that showed a lot of cleavage.

Ken drove into the parking lot and pulled into the spot next to mine.

"Hey," I said, then kissed his cheek.

"You look beautiful," he said.

We walked into the restaurant, and the waitress immediately led us to a table. We started our date off with generic date questions: "What's your favorite movie? What color do you like? Do you have a dog? Yadda-yadda-yadda…"

All the while, Ken kept his eyes on mine.

"I'm sorry for staring, but your eyes are gorgeous," he said.

I smiled back at him.

"Thanks. I've been told my mother had them too."

"*Had* them? Did your mom pass? If she did, I'm sorry. I didn't mean to bring her up."

"I don't know if she's alive or dead. I've never really met her." I went on to tell Ken about my family and how I'd been raised primarily by my dad. I think my honesty helped him to relax and open up to me.

"I knew my dad, but it was like I didn't. He always cheated on my mom and left us for days, weeks, sometimes months."

I touched his hand, and we smiled at each other. Hearing Ken talk honestly about his family made me feel sorry for him. I felt his loneliness. I had my dad and family growing up, but he'd been alone for most of his childhood.

"I feel like a lot of the mistakes I've made in life were because I didn't have my mom to guide me," I said.

"What mistakes?"

"My choices in men. I haven't had the best of luck when it comes to dating."

"Trust me; I hear you on that."

"My high school first love took my virginity and dumped me right before prom. My first boyfriend in college beat the shit out of me and verbally put me down, and my ex-boyfriend... Well, I thought he was the one. I thought I was going to marry him and live happily ever after, but things didn't work out. We're still friends to this day, but we'll never date again."

"So you still talk to your ex?"

"Yeah. We're close," I admitted.

Ken sat back in his chair.

"You look bothered by that. Is something wrong?" I asked, hoping he wasn't the abusive, jealous type like Alex was.

"If you don't mind me asking, what caused you and your ex to break up?"

"I'm still not comfortable getting into it, but let's just say, I thought he was the right one for me, but I wasn't the right person for him."

"Since you're so honest with me, I have to tell you the truth about my past..." Ken went on to tell me about his ex-girlfriends, his heartaches, and heartbreaks. He told me about Brianna and Ashley, two women who hurt him, as well as the numerous women he's hurt.

As he poured his heart out to me, my hand glided across the table and touched his. I knew it was hard for him, and I was touched that he was so honest with me, but I was scared he might go back to those hurting ways. *What if this is some kind of advance warning, so he doesn't feel like a bad guy when he fucks me over?* I wondered.

When he finally finished telling me about his past, I was speech-less. Too many thoughts were running through my head. I kept thinking about my previous failed relationships, and I was scared of getting hurt.

"I gotta call it a night," I said. "I'm taking the kids on a field trip tomorrow, so I have to wake up early."

"I understand," he said, sounding disappointed.

He paid the bill and walked me to my car. We hugged. He looked like he realized he'd blown it with me, so I ended the date before it got worse.

"Thanks for dinner. I'll see you around the gym."

"You're welcome; I enjoyed your company tonight. I'll see you around."

I drove off, needing time to think.

★ ★ ★

"You need to call him, sis," Jackie said.

"I don't know. After everything he told me… What if he does me wrong like Derek did?"

"You can't keep dwelling on your past relationships. They happened, and they're part of you, but you're wiser from them. Don't let them stop you from living your life and taking chances on people. If my mom felt like that, she never would've dated your dad. You know that."

"Ugh. I hate when you're right."

"I'm a Virgo. I'm always right. We're analytical people."

I laughed.

"Whatever. I'm going to call him now. I'm putting it on speaker phone so be quiet, okay?"

"Go ahead. I'm not going to say anything."

The phone rang, and Ken answered.

"Hello?" he said.

"Hey."

"Lynn?"

"Yeah. I'm sorry I've been avoiding you. It's just… Well, everything you told me kind of caught me off guard."

He sucked his teeth.

"Yeah, I'm sorry about that. I just…really like you. I didn't want to scare you off, but I wanted you to know the truth. I'm not perfect. I have flaws, but I'm trying to change and be a better man."

"See? I told you he's feeling you too," Erica whispered.

I covered the phone and shushed her.

She playfully gave me the middle finger and stuck her tongue out at me.

Before I got back on the phone, I thought about my dad and Jonna. I remembered how much Dad wanted to change so he could impress her, and I felt Ken would try to do the same for me.

"I know, and that's the only reason I'm talking to you again. You could've told me nothing and kept me in the dark, but the fact that you told me makes me believe you genuinely want to change."

"So where do we go from here?" Ken asked.

"We become better friends. Look, I'm not in a rush either. You need to heal from your past, and I definitely need to heal from mine. Let's be friends and see where that takes us. Maybe we can help each other heal."

"Sounds good to me."

We made plans to see each other again, then ended the call.

"See? Everything worked out the way I said they would," Erica said.

"Yeah, I feel a lot better now."

"Now I just need to meet him to give my approval."

I laughed. "True."

★ ★ ★

"Ken, these are my sisters, Erica, Jackie, and Kelly."

I already told him I was an only child, but I explained that they were like family to me. He understood and told me that before all the drama, he used to have the same type of relationship with his friends, Perry, Ray, and Adam.

"It's nice to finally meet y'all. Lynn is always talking about you ladies."

"That's good to know. When she hangs out with us, all she talks about is you," Jackie said.

"Jackie!" I shouted.

Ken laughed, but he was caught a bit off guard when Kelly began feeling his shoulders and arms.

"Wow. This is all very nice—very, very, very nice," she said.

"Kelly, stop groping Lynn's...friend," Erica said.

Ken and I weren't anything official, so she didn't want to say the wrong thing and put us both on the spot.

Ken laughed at us again.

"You ladies are funny."

"So what's the plan? Where are we going?" Erica asked.

"Since I know how much you ladies mean to Lynn, I want to treat you all to lunch today, wherever you wanna go. Lynn said you're all picky, so I'll let you decide."

"Sexy *and* wise? Wow. You did good, sis," Kelly said.

"Where are the rest of the guys like you?" Jackie asked.

"If you'd close your legs once in a while, maybe you'd find one. You look for love in the wrong places," Erica said.

"Heifer!"

"Slut!"

They giggled and hugged each other, and I couldn't help laughing at my sisters. I loved them so much.

Ken took us to Texas Roadhouse in East Meadow. He paid for everything, and by the end of the night, it was unanimous: My girls thought he was a great guy for me.

Next on the agenda was to test him out with Dad and Aunt Rhea, and I was sure that would prove to be very interesting, as Dad was never fond of any of my boyfriends.

★ ★ ★

"Good game, Mr. Johnson," Ken said with a smirk on his face.

"Whatever. You're lucky I'm not in shape. Once I get my wind up, we're gonna play again, and I'm going to kick your ass," Daddy said, pouting.

My dad and Ken debated about the Knicks and basketball all night. Daddy had never talked to any of my boyfriends like he talked to Ken, and it made my night when we all watched the game together.

A week later, Ken bought Knicks tickets and took my dad to the game. When Daddy came home, he couldn't stop talking about how much he enjoyed hanging out with him.

"Ladybug, you know it's hard for me to like any guy who wants to date you, but I gotta say, I like Ken. He reminds me of myself. I even showed him around the shop so he'd have an idea of what I do for a living."

That was a milestone because Daddy had never done that with any guy I've dated before.

★ ★ ★

What pushed my heart to the limit, though, was when Ken introduced me to his mother.

"Ma, this is Lynn," he said.

"I've heard so much about you! Ken is always bragging about you. He says you're a teacher too."

"Yes, ma'am!"

His mother was so warm and loving, and she made me feel like part of their family, even though we weren't officially dating yet. Ken's mother and I made plans to hang out often. We took little shopping trips here and there, going to the mall and getting our nails done.

Ken loved seeing the two of us together, so as a gift, he set up a date for all the women who were special to me. He treated Jonna, Erica, Aunt Rhea, Mrs. Ferguson, and me to a pampering day at Spa Castle in College Point, Queens. Jackie and Kelly had to work and couldn't take off. It sucked to be them because we spent all day getting massages, mani-pedis, waxes, and facials.

"I like this guy already," Jonna whispered in my ear, while Erica and Aunt Rhea laughed and talked in the hot tub.

Meanwhile, Mrs. Ferguson's massage relaxed her so much; she was nodding off in the beach chair next to me, but we whispered just in case.

"I think I more than just like him," I said. "I don't mean to be rude or disrespectful, but what made you fall in love with my dad?"

Jonna laughed to herself, smiled, and leaned back in her chair.

"When I first met your father, he was a good guy but misguided. I knew being together would balance both of us and that we'd make each other better."

"How did Dad make you better?"

"Lord knows he made me more patient."

We laughed.

"Seriously, though, Nick helped me understand what I needed to be happy in life. Lynn, your dad always appreciated me and made me feel special. Whenever he looked at me, I knew he loved me, and he made sure to tell me so. For the most part, he was considerate of me. He had a good heart, and he wanted to make me happy. It was never a chore or a bother for him. He liked seeing me happy," she said, then wiped her eyes and put on her shades.

"Ken likes seeing me happy."

"I can tell. It certainly wasn't cheap to send all of us here today."

"We haven't had sex yet," I confessed.

"Wow. Maybe it's time to discuss taking things to the next level. You need to ask him where things are headed. If you're meeting each other's parents and spending all your time together, why not make it official and be together?"

After a day of being pampered, everyone stopped by my apartment.

"Thank you so much for everything today, Ken," Jonna said.

"You already know I'm rooting for you to make things official with my sister," Erica said.

"Amen to that!" Aunt Rhea agreed, laughing and high-fiving with Mrs. Ferguson.

"Way to make me look like I ain't shit, bro," Amar'e joked.

My feelings for Ken seemed to grow stronger every day, and my heart told me that he was the one.

CHAPTER 45

LOVE AND BASKETBALL

Lynn

"Is that all you got?" I asked smugly.

"You're talking trash to me even though I'm winning?" Ken stated, confidently.

We were at the park, playing one-on-one. We played pick-up games together often against other people, but the alone time was everything to me. Playing ball with him made me so happy because Ken made me happy. Playing hard against him brought me back to those happy memories of when I was a little girl and used to watch Dad play against Jonna. I put maximum effort into beating him so he'd go all out against me too, the way Jonna did with my dad.

We even placed the same bet on the game: Whoever won got a kiss. I'd always wanted that type of relationship, the kind my dad and Jonna had. With all the memories Ken and I were building together, I couldn't deny the truth anymore. I loved him.

Ken and I developed a bond that surpassed the one I had with Sean. I could talk to him about anything, and he was down to do all sorts of activities I planned for us. Even though he hated running, he ran in 5- and 10k races with me.

What I felt for Ken went beyond physical attraction. We could sit in total silence, and it never felt uncomfortable or awkward. I felt like I could be myself around him, and he never thought less of me. He loved me for the flawed soul I was, and that made all the difference.

"All right. Two more baskets, and I win. Don't forget to give me my reward when this is over," Ken said.

"The game isn't over yet, and I intend to win!" I said confidently.

He wore this half-choirboy, half-cocky smirk that made him look so cute. I was so busy checking him out, he scored on me again.

"One more point."

I checked him the ball.

"Shut up," I said, pushing him lightly.

Even off balance, he scored another jump-shot on me.

"You got lucky," I said, rolling my eyes and fake pouting.

"Aw, don't be mad. Just give me my reward."

I perked up when he asked for a kiss, and I couldn't hold my feelings in anymore.

"I love you, Ken," I blurted.

Ken looked nervous and confused. "I…"

"It's okay. You don't have to say it back. I want you to tell me when you mean it."

He pulled me in tight and kissed me passionately. From his kiss, I felt like his body was telling me he loved me too, but he still didn't say it back.

"Let's go back to my place, and I'll give you a loser's backwash."

"Ha-ha!"

For five months, we'd been inseparable, but we still hadn't had sex. Ken and I wanted to take our time, to allow our friendship to grow naturally. We showered together all the time and gave each other massages and kisses. It was hard for both of us, but I explained to Ken that I wasn't going to share myself with him until I knew I loved him and that we were in a committed relationship. He was understanding and never pressured me. Needless to say, I did a lot of running to calm my sexual tension.

I stayed at Ken's place more than my own. Some might say I'm a "weirdo", but I loved watching him sleep. I studied the lines of his face and lightly traced my fingertips over his lips and jawline.

Back at his house, we showered together, and he made dinner for us.

"Why lasagna?" I asked.

"I wanted to make you a food that starts with the letter L, so you can remember the loss you had today."

I playfully punched him, then got serious for a moment.

"Ken, where do you we go from here?"

"Where do you want us to go?"

"You know I want more than this. I told you I love you today. I'm in love with you, but if I'm going to feel this way, I want more from you than just a friendship."

"I do, too, so I guess we're together then."

"What? That's not how you're supposed to ask me."

"What do you mean? You said you want more, and I want more, so that means we're together, right?"

"Nope. Ask me."

"Lynn Sian Johnson, would you give me the honor and the privilege of being in a committed relationship with me?" he asked, adorably playing along.

I rolled my eyes. "I guess," I said, then nodded and said, "Yes."

We kissed, and I grabbed my phone and excitedly rushed into the bedroom, eager to tell my girls. Instead of making individual phone calls, I sent a group text.

When I walked back into the hallway, I heard Ken talking about me to his friend. It felt nice to know he was just as happy about us finally being together as I was.

★ ★ ★

I put on my knee-high lace stockings with matching panties and bra. I took off my hair tie and let my hair fall on my shoulders. I left it silky and wavy, because whenever I wore it down, his mouth always watered over me.

Ken couldn't stop staring. He took in every inch of me, from my cleavage to my panties. I turned off the lights and lit candles around his bedroom. I climbed in bed, and we shared a long passionate kiss. It didn't take long before we were completely undressed, and his face was buried in my treasure. He was unrelenting, sucking on my clit and sliding his fingers rapidly inside me. A jolt of ecstasy vibrated through me. He put on a condom, and I held onto his ass while I guided him inside me. I wrapped my legs around his back. He penetrated me slowly, with firm strokes in and out; even though he hadn't said the words earlier, each stroke showed me he loved me.

My hands slid down his back, pulling him deeper into me. I heard my moans echoing off the high ceilings in the room. I climbed on top of him and rode him, thinking about how good he was making me feel and how happy he made me; and knew this is how making love was supposed to feel. I shook my head from side to side, told him how good he felt, and praised the Lord as wave after wave of my orgasm ran through me. I had never felt anything like it before. I moaned, and my body shook and shivered from the sensation coursing through my body. I collapsed on his chest.

We made love continuously throughout the night. The veins in his manhood throbbed, and when he came, I felt it vibrate through my soul.

I went to bed knowing that Ken was my soulmate.

★ ★ ★

The next morning, Ken lay on his side, with his arm wrapped around me. I slowly eased his out of his grasp, not wanting to wake him up as I slid out of bed to get ready for work.

While I was reading a book to my students, the security guard brought in a bouquet of roses and a card.

"Your man just made all the ladies in here jealous of you," he said with a laugh.

I smiled.

"Thank you."

I opened the card, and there was a picture of Ken, with his arms extended out as far as they could go, with a caption that read, "I love you this much." It made me smile. I put the card and flowers on my desk and planned to text Ken when the kids had their naptime.

I continued reading *Where the Wild Things Are*, only to be interrupted by a knock on the door. I looked up and was surprised to see Ken standing there.

"What are you doing here?" I asked as I opened the door.

"I love you, Lynn, and I had to come here to tell you. I'm sorry I didn't tell you yesterday when you told me. I didn't want you to finish this day without you knowing that and hearing it directly from my mouth."

I couldn't hold back my tears.

"I love you too," I said, holding his face and kissing him in the doorway.

"Ooh, Ms. Johnson is in love!" my class said, giggling.

Ken held me right there in the doorway, in front of all those little faces, and he made an already good day great.

★ ★ ★

"What's up, guys?" Ken asked.

"You're late," Perry's girlfriend said.

We had just arrived, and she was already giving us attitude; I expected it, though, since Ken had already warned me about her bitchiness.

"Sorry. We got caught in traffic."

I laughed to myself at the lie. The truth was, we'd tried to have a quickie that turned into a full-fledged sex session.

"Perry, Jessie, this is my girlfriend, Lynn."

Jessie gave me a limp handshake and muttered something under her breath.

"Bring it in, Lynn. If you're dating my boy, I'm not giving you a whack handshake. I got a hug for you, girl."

I laughed and gave Perry a hug.

We sat down, and Jessie faced me.

"So? How long have you two known each other?" she snarkily asked.

"About four and a half months."

"Interesting. And where did you meet?"

"At the gym."

"The gym, huh? Yeah, Kenny has met a lot of his *friends* there," she said, irking me with her condescending tone.

"Jessie, be nice," Perry said.

"I'm always nice, honey. Anyway, Lisa—"

"It's Lynn," I corrected.

"Oh, right. Lynn. Sorry. Kenny has so many friends. I don't try to remember all their names. Once he's done with them, I never see them again anyway."

Ken was noticeably upset, and I wanted to rip the bitch's throat out, but I knew her type. She enjoyed stirring up trouble, loved conflict, and she liked seeing Ken uncomfortable and tense. I'd dealt with people like her all my life, and she reminded me of the girls who used to tease and taunt me when I was growing up. I wasn't about to give her the satisfaction of upsetting me. Once I had my mind set on that, it was easy to stay cool, calm, and collected.

"I know about Ken's history," I said. "Everyone's got things in their past that they're not proud of. He's grown from it, and he's trying to move on."

"You *know* about his history? Did you know he fucked his friends' sister or his other friend's ex-girlfriend?" She went on and on, saying things she hoped would trigger anger in me, but I kept my composure.

"I'm not trying to come off as a bitch, but I've seen him screw over two of my friends, to the point where they don't even talk to each other anymore." She said.

"I appreciate the heads-up," I said flatly. "It was hard to hear about Ken's past, but I love him and trust him, and nothing you or anyone else says to me is gonna change that or make me leave him. So let's order, shall we?"

I opened my menu as Ken looked at me, ecstatic that I'd stuck up for him. I was happy to put Jessie in her place, and I was even happier to see that Ken was proud of me.

★ ★ ★

"Girl, I need to talk to you," Sean said.

"Excuse me, babe. I have to take this call. It's Sean."

"Uh-huh."

I made a silly face. Ken smirked, but I knew he was getting irritated with me talking to Sean all the time.

I stood up and walked into the kitchen.

"Michael and I moved in together. I told my father we're roommates, but we only have a one-bedroom apartment. He wants to see my place, so how am I supposed to hide it?" Sean said, the worry evident in his voice.

LOVE AND BASKETBALL

"You guys make decent money. Buy a nice sofa bed and find some creative ways to store his clothes. Tell your dad Michael doesn't make as much money as you do, so since you're paying the bulk of the rent, the bedroom is yours."

"Damn, Lynn. You're good at being bad."

"I sneaked out a lot when I was in high school. With a dad like mine, I had to get good at coming up with excuses on the fly."

"When are we gonna hang out again so you can tell me about your new boo? I'm free tonight for dinner if you are."

"Hold on. Let me see if Ken is still hanging out with Perry. If he is, I'll go." I put my phone on hold and walked in to ask Ken, "Babe, are you still having your guys' night?"

"Yeah, why?"

"Sean wants to get dinner with me."

Ken looked pissed.

"Baby, before you get upset, please understand that Sean and I are just friends. I'd never cheat on you."

"How would you feel if I went on a date with one of my old girlfriends?"

"It's not a date, but I won't lie. I'd be furious if you went anywhere with a girl from your past, but I'm a woman, and I know how other women think."

"And I know how guys think. You still haven't told me what caused you guys to break up in the first place. You talk to him all the time, and it's hard not to question that."

"I need you to trust me. I don't see him like that. I'll never see him like that again. I wasn't…what he needed."

Ken sighed. "All right. I'll trust you, but I need to meet this guy. Don't make me regret this."

"You won't, baby."

★ ★ ★

"Ken, this is my friend Sean."

"Nice to meet you, Ken," Sean said.

"Likewise."

Ken looked inquisitively at Sean and me. It was somewhat awkward having my current man and my previous one in the same room, but I thought it was cute watching Ken size Sean up. His jealousy made me feel like he was afraid of losing me, and I'd never felt that with Sean.

They made small talk. Knowing Sean was Gay, it was interesting to see how he could "butch up" around straight men, but was more relaxed and emotional when we were alone, but I credited some of that to his performance arts background.

"All right, babe, we're gonna head out."

"Don't have too much fun without me."

"I won't," I said, giving Ken an annoyed look.

CHAPTER 46

TROUBLE IN PARADISE

Lynn

"Excuse me, but our seats are in this row," said a woman with red hair.

"Oh, I'm sorry."

We were in Manhattan. Sean had given us tickets to see *Hairspray* on Broadway. He was part of the production team that had brought it back to New York, and he was very proud of it.

I stood up and nudged Ken.

"Babe, stand up. Some people are trying to get in our row."

"Oh, sorry," he said, turning to face the redhead.

"Ken?"

He looked shocked and annoyed to see her.

"Oh, hey, Ashley."

There was an awkward pause before she said, "This is my friend Melissa."

Ken shook the girl's hand.

I didn't like how Ashley was looking at him. She had a smug look on her face as if she felt she could easily take him from me.

"How've you been?" she asked.

"I'm good. I can't complain,"

Ken wrapped his arm around me and pulled me to his side.

"This is my girlfriend, Lynn."

Ashley looked stunned.

"Girlfriend? Wow. It's very nice to meet you," she said.

I looked at the woman he'd been so crazy over, and she didn't look so special to me. Physically, I was bigger and better than her in every area. I knew I intimidated her because she wouldn't look me in the face. I savored that small victory.

"I'm still single, but I'm happy," Ashley said.

"That's cool," Ken said.

The lights dimmed, and we turned our attention to the play.

★ ★ ★

When the play was over, the curtain rose, and the audience gave the cast a standing ovation. Hundreds gathered in the lobby to congratulate the performers.

When I saw Sean walk out, I ran over to give him a hug.

"The play was great!" I said.

"Thanks for coming, Lynn," he said.

Ken waved at him, and he returned the wave.

"Hey, who's the ginger?" Sean asked.

"What ginger?" I said, looking around.

"The one who started talking to your man as soon as you came over here."

"Some old girl he used to fuck from his past, I'm not worried about her."

"She does have a terrible sense of fashion, but she's pretty. If he liked her, there had to be a reason. Be careful."

I wondered if Sean was right, and I began to feel paranoid. *Should I see her as a threat?*

★ ★ ★

Two months passed. Things were still strong with Ken, but Ashley wouldn't go the fuck away. When Ken slept or stepped out of the room, I read his text messages. She kept sending all types of dirty pictures and rude comments about me. She tried to play mind-games with him by reminding him of the times when they use to fuck.

Ken never replied or commented on her pictures, and he defended me every time she said something negative, but I had to question why he entertained her texts at all. *Why doesn't he just block her number if things ended so badly with them?* I couldn't confront Ken about the text messages because we promised each other we would never violate one another's trust by reading them without asking. Plus, I knew he could ask me the same thing about Sean since I'd always beat around the bush whenever he tried to question me about our breakup.

Shit hit the fan one night when Ken made me dinner while we watched the Knicks game.

Ciara's "Promise" rang on my phone, letting me know it was Sean. I was getting tired of hearing about his drama and sex life, but I was trying to be a good friend.

"Hey," I said.

"My father is disowning me. I'm going to kill myself. I'm sitting in my bedroom, holding a knife to my wrist, contemplating ending my life and saving my family from embarrassment," Sean said, crying.

"What!? Calm down, Sean. You don't have to—"

"My father told me he didn't raise any faggots and that no son of his is gonna be a queer."

"Is everything okay?" Ken asked.

I waved him off and took the phone into the bathroom.

"What happened?"

"I couldn't hide it anymore. It get's exhausting, trying to be something you're not. Michael came out to his family, and they accepted him with open arms. I figured maybe mine would do the same, but they all hate me. They're ashamed of me. My father said he begged God to give him a son, and he can't understand why God would punish him like this."

I didn't need Sean's drama at the moment. My man was making me dinner and was there to give me the love and affection I'd always wanted in a relationship, but I was still holding on to Sean for some reason. Maybe it was out of pride, but I couldn't let go, and I hated myself for that.

"Are you still on the line?" Sean asked.

"Yes."

"You're so good to me. When I dated you, I never meant to hurt you."

"I know, but it still hurts."

"I was in a dark place back then, trying to be someone I'm not. I did love you, though."

I was emotional.

"I loved you...and I still do."

"Besides you and Michael, I have no one now. I know you're probably busy with your man, but I need you right now."

"I'll always be here for you, no matter who I'm with."

Bang!

"Open the door, Lynn."

I opened it, irritated that Ken was knocking when he knew I was dealing with something. I muted the call and said in aggravation. "I'm on the phone. It's important."

"I can see that. Hang it up. We need to talk."

I unmuted the call. "Hold on, sweetie. I have to talk to Ken for a second." I turned to face Ken. "What's your problem?"

"Hang up."

"No! Sean is going through a lotta shit right now, and I'm talking him through it."

"Sean's a grown man. He can handle his own shit."

"What's your deal, Ken?"

"I don't like to hear my girlfriend tell her ex-boyfriend she still loves him. I have a problem with that."

Shit! I didn't know how much he'd heard, but he clearly thought something was going on between Sean and me.

"Sean, let me call you back. I have to talk to Ken," I said, then ended the call.

I turned to face Ken and asked, "You really want to do this?"

He didn't back down and stood there staring at me.

"First off, you shouldn't have been listening to my conversation to begin with. Second, if you're gonna question what *I* say to *my* ex, maybe you shouldn't be getting messages from Ashley, reminiscing about the times you used to fuck her."

His face fell, overcome with shock and hurt.

"Oh, you have nothing to say now, huh? The other day, she sent you a picture of her pussy and asked if you miss it. I erased it immediately. I didn't care if you knew I checked your phone or not."

"So you don't trust me? You've been reading my texts?"

"Yup."

He nodded slowly.

"She sent me text messages, but I never replied with any crazy shit or made her even think or expect anything would happen between us. You, on the other hand, just told this guy you love him. You said it right here in my house, while I'm cooking dinner for you. You told him you'll always be there for him, no matter who you're with. I shouldn't come second to your ex."

"You don't, Ken. You don't understand."

"Well, make me understand. You said he broke your heart, that he left you, yet you're best friends with him. You say you still love him. Are you still fucking him, Lynn?"

I curled my lips, trying not to cry.

"Well? Do you still love him? Do you love him more than me? If he asked you to come back to him right now, would you do it and leave me?"

That was my opportunity to tell Ken the truth, but I stayed quiet. I was scared and wondered what he would think of me if I told him the truth. I would never leave Ken for Sean. I had no desire to go back to him. I loved Sean, but it certainly wasn't the same type of love I had for him in the past. I was so embarrassed. Derek made me feel like I wasn't girly enough, and Sean reinforced those thoughts in my head by picking me to be his beard. I didn't want to tell Ken and cause him to question whether or not there might be something wrong with me.

Ken grabbed his wallet, keys, and cell phone, then rushed out the door, leaving me standing there. I slid down the wall and dropped my ass on the cold, hard tile, hoping I hadn't fucked things up beyond repair.

★ ★ ★

"Daddy?"

"What's up, Ladybug?"

"Are you home? Can I come over?"

"Yes, I'm home, and you never have to ask. If you need to stay here, this is always your home."

I loved my dad because he always dropped whatever he was doing to protect me.

"I don't think I have to stay, but Ken and I had a fight. It was my fault, and I need a man's point of view, other than his."

"What happened?"

"I'll tell you when I get home."

★ ★ ★

"I'm going to Walgreens. I'll leave you two to talk," Aunt Rhea said.

She winked at my dad, and he gave her a devilish grin.

"Daddy, what's going on with you and Aunt Rhea?"

"Nothing." He looked like he was hiding something, but for the first time in a long time, they both looked happy.

"We finally got everything approved by the state, and Rhea and I converted the downstairs into a daycare. We'll live upstairs."

I smiled, knowing exactly what was going on between the two of them, even if he didn't spill the beans to me.

"Nobody has been staying in my old room. Where has she been sleeping?" I questioned.

"You're not here to discuss your aunt's and my living arrangements. What's going on with you and Ken? Am I going to have to whoop some ass?"

"First, gross, if I'm right about what I think is going on with you and Aunt Rhea...but I'm glad you're both happy."

Dad laughed.

"Does Jonna know?"

"She knows."

"Really? What does she think about it?"

"She's actually supportive. She understands and is happy that we're able to keep one another company. Anyway, what's going on with Ken?"

I told my dad the truth about Sean and my argument with Ken.

"Ladybug, I need you to listen. You love Ken, and out of all the guys you've dated, I like him the best. Don't miss out on something good because of your pride. You need to tell Ken the truth about Sean, and as much as you still have feelings for Sean, you have to wean yourself off him. It's not healthy for your current relationship."

"It's not like that, Daddy. I'm not in love with Sean. We're just friends."

"Friends or not, you can't answer his calls and be there at the drop of a hat like that for him anymore. It's disrespectful to Ken. You can be friendly and talk now and then, but you can't be there for him in that way anymore. Jonna and I are cool. We still love each other, and we're still friendly, but I had to back off a bit, out of respect for her relationship with Alvin."

I nodded. "I get it now, Dad."

"Good. You need to go back to his place and tell him everything as soon as he gets back."

"You're right. I'll leave now."

★ ★ ★

I hadn't heard from Ken, and I was an emotional wreck. I needed to let go of my feelings for Sean. Part of me would always care for him, but I loved Ken, and I couldn't risk losing him.

When the phone rang, I quickly answered it, certain it was him. "Hello?"

"Hello. This is Detective Ramos, with NYPD 102nd Precinct. Ma'am, are you a relative or acquaintance of Ken Ferguson's?"

"Yes, I'm his girlfriend. What happened? Oh my God! Where is he?"

"Ma'am, please calm down. He was in a car accident, and he's at the hospital. When we found him in the wreckage, his phone was in his hand, and your number was pulled up on it."

I cried immediately, overcome with guilt. As soon as the officer gave me the name of the hospital, I called Mrs. Ferguson and Perry and told them to meet me there.

★ ★ ★

"Babe…"

I was sleeping in a chair next to Mrs. Ferguson when I could have sworn I heard Ken call out for me.

"Babe?" he weakly repeated.

I lifted my head and saw Ken's eyes slowly flicker open, returning my stare. An expression of confusion washed over his face, followed by a wince of pain. I smiled uncontrollably, happy to see he was awake. I shook his mom to show her he was awake.

Mrs. Ferguson jumped up and rushed to his bed.

"My God, son! I thought I was gonna lose you," she said.

"I'm sorry we fought, baby. I'm so sorry," I said.

"It's okay," he said, straining to talk.

"The doctors said you're lucky. You were in a coma for a week, but your brain stem and frontal lobe show no damage. Even though your car was totaled, you didn't break any bones. It's a miracle you're still alive. Lynn's been here with you the whole time, honey, and Perry came too. He just left not too long ago. He couldn't take any more time off work," Mrs. Ferguson said.

I ran out of the room to alert the nurses that he was awake, and when I returned, Mrs. Ferguson hugged me and kissed me on the forehead. I had a lot to tell Ken finally, but it would have to wait.

★ ★ ★

Three days passed. Mrs. Ferguson went to church to thank God that Ken was going to be all right.

Alone with him in the hospital room, I wrung my hands together.

"I have to talk to you about something. I know you've always wanted to know the reason why Sean and I broke up. I know you felt something was still going on with us, but the truth is Sean is gay."

Ken's mouth dropped open in shock.

I kept going, wanting to make sure he knew the whole truth.

"I was embarrassed, Ken. He came out to me when we were dating, and it hurt because he told me he never fully believed he was gay until he dated me. Deep down, I felt like I wasn't feminine enough or that I'd somehow done something to unlock that part of him. He had girlfriends in the past, so I felt...responsible."

Ken said nothing. He listened intently as I continued.

"He broke up with me to be with the guy he was seeing on the side. He hadn't told anyone, not even his parents. He was scared to talk to them about it, which was why he always called me. The night we fought, he called because he was feeling suicidal. He finally came out to his parents, and they disowned him. He felt alone and wanted to end it all, so I was trying to talk him out of it."

"Why didn't you tell me this before?" Ken asked, clearly frustrated and in pain.

"I was ashamed. Erica knew since she's my sister, but I didn't tell any of my other girlfriends or even my dad. I just told everyone I wasn't the right person for him. He wasn't ready to come out, and I couldn't stand feeling like I had driven him to be gay," I said, sniffling.

"Lynn..."

"Yeah?"

"I love you."

"I love you too," I said, smiling. Those words were all I needed to hear to know everything would be all right.

★ ★ ★

We spent the next year strengthening our bond. I thought I knew what love was in the past, but I knew nothing about it until I dated Ken.

CHAPTER 47

THE PROPOSAL

Nick

"You still got it, for an old man," Ken said.

"This old man just busted your ass."

We laughed.

Ken and I made plans to play ball at the park, and I'd been running with Lynn to get my wind up. I wasn't about to lose to him again.

"I want to talk to you about something important," Ken said.

"What's up?"

"You know I love Lynn, and I'd never do anything to hurt her."

"I know, but where are you going with this?"

"After Lynn and I run in the NYC Marathon this Sunday, I plan to ask her to marry me. I want to ask you for your blessing."

I couldn't have asked for a better son-in-law, and I couldn't have been happier for my daughter.

"Ken, I would love to have you as a part of my family."

"Thanks, Mr. Johnson," he said, pulling me into a hug.

"You can call me Dad now. Do you have a ring yet?"

"Yes, sir," Ken said. He pulled out a three-karat platinum diamond ring.

I was so excited that I took a picture with my phone and texted it to Rhea.

"What's the plan? How are you gonna ask her?"

"I'm going to try my best to finish the marathon with her, and I plan to ask her at the finish line."

"I definitely have to be there for that! I'm seriously happy for the two of you."

My baby's getting married? Damn, I'm getting old!

CHAPTER 48

WINNING

Lynn

Air filled my lungs as I inhaled deeply, trying to maintain my pace. My calves and quads were burning. I stretched my legs to lengthen my stride.

Ken was right there with me, pushing me to finish with him. "There's the finish line, babe. Let's do this together!" he said.

I smiled at my king.

"I love you," I said.

"I love you too."

We held hands and crossed the finish line together. As soon as we did, Ken pulled me close, kissed me, and dropped to one knee.

"Oh my God! What are you doing?"

"Lynn, we've been through a lot. We've both faced a lot of obstacles in our past, but fate brought us together. I want our love to last forever. Will you marry me?"

I cried and nodded for what felt like a million times.

"Yes!" I shouted.

Ken grabbed my trembling hand and placed a ring on my finger, the most gorgeous ring I'd ever seen.

"Smile, Ladybug," Daddy said, with Erica, Amar'e, Kelly, Jackie, Aunt Rhea, Jonna, and Mrs. Fergueson all standing next to him.

"*All* of you knew?" I asked.

They nodded and smiled at me.

I was so happy to know that I had finally found my king.

CHAPTER 49

DADDY'S GIRL

Nick

I held my daughter's arm as we walked down the aisle. Ken looked at peace as he adoringly watched Lynn saunter toward him. After I had given her hand to him, I sat next to Rhea and held hers. I was so happy and proud of Lynn.

I knew, in her heart of hearts, she wished her mother was in her life, to be part of this milestone. I sent an invitation to Vickie, but I didn't expect her to come. I was proud that, despite not having her mom around, Lynn had grown up to be a strong, smart, confident, successful woman, raised by me and the surrogates she had in her life.

The reverend gave a great message, and I stood up to get ready for my next part. I glanced at the back of the church and squinted when I saw a woman standing by the back door of the hall, wearing a tan dress, wiping her eyes and smiling. *Vickie?* I realized in disbelief.

Personally, I was happy she was there to witness our daughter getting married, but my happiness was bittersweet because Lynn would never know her mother was there to see her special day. I nodded, and Vickie gave a slight wave.

Rhea turned to see who I was staring at and turned back toward me, wearing a confused expression. I winked at her and motioned that everything was fine.

The reverend turned to me and said, "Who gives this woman to be married to this man?"

I smiled at Lynn and Ken and proudly said, "I do."

As expected, Vickie left right after the wedding, but at least she was there.

During the reception, Ken asked for everyone's attention.

"I know how close Lynn is to you, Mr. Johnson."

"You can call me Dad now!" I yelled, drawing chuckles from the crowd.

Ken smiled.

"Well, *Dad*, I wanted your father/daughter dance to be special, so I hope you don't mind, but I asked one of my friends to do the honor of singing a song for the occasion. Ladies and gentlemen, please welcome my good friend and Def Jam recording artist, Kristen Dos Santos."

Everyone stood up and cheered.

Kristen gave Ken and Lynn a brief hug and kiss and took the microphone.

"Thank you, everyone. Mr. Johnson, I've talked to Lynn, and she adores you. After hearing how special you are to her, I thought of the perfect song. All my friends and fans know I idolize Beyoncé, so today, I'm singing her song 'Daddy' for your special dance."

The guests cheered.

Lynn and I were both in tears before the song started. I held my daughter's hand and danced with her, drawing her close and smiling at the one true love of my life.

Lynn looked up at me and said, "I love you, Daddy."

Those words meant the world to me. I was so proud of her. I made a lot of mistakes in my lifetime, but Lynn was the best thing that had ever happened to me. When she was born, I was still a boy. Raising her, and all the experiences that came along with it, turned me into a man. Even though Lynn wasn't a child anymore, she'd always be my little girl.

DADDY'S GIRL

Hey everyone,

Once again, I want to thank everyone for supporting my book. It has always been a dream of mine to write books that can move people emotionally and help to change the world for the better. I hope you enjoyed "Daddy's Girl!" Be sure to check out my other novels "Monster," "Wounded" and "Love and Happiness" All of my books are connected. Ken is the same "Ken" from "Monster" and "Love and Happiness." Mr. Davis and his son Chris, are from my novel "Love and Happiness" Please check out my other novels, and stay tuned for my next book entitled "Black and White" coming out soon.

So what are your thoughts about the book? Did you love it? Hate it? Please take a quick minute to post an honest rating and review where you purchased the novel. I take my readers feedback very seriously, and I truly appreciate all of my reviews. Thank you so much in advance!

Connect with me below for updates on
release dates for up and Coming books and events.

Web page: *www.BenBurgessjr.com*

Amazon page: *http://www.amazon.com/Ben-Burgess-Jr./e/ B00BCKZPHK/ref=ntt_athr_dp_pel_1*

Email: *AuthorBenBurgessJr@gmail.com*

Facebook: *https://www.facebook.com/BenBurgessJr?ref=hl*

Twitter: *https://twitter.com/Ben_Burgess_Jr*

Don't forget to check out the bonus material on the next couple of pages. For those of you who are reading one of my books for the first time, I include some of my poems in every novel. I hope you enjoy them, and I hope to continue writing stories you enjoy!

BONUS SECTION

A Father's Pain

All your life I pushed you, molded you and trained you to be strong. Preparing you for what in my eyes was the real world. I pushed you. I saw the anger in your eyes and encouraged it. I wanted your anger and animosity to come out so it would propel you to the next level.

I saw the hatred in your face and saw you becoming the person I could never be. I wanted things to be easy for you, so your strength would push you further than I could ever go. I watched you when you were good and wanted you to be great, I watched you become great, and wanted you to be untouchable. My competitive drive never ended with you. I grew proud when your every goal was to beat me and to be the best in everything.

A father's greatest joy is to watch their child become greater than himself. I succeeded in making you stronger and better than I could ever be, the only thing it cost me was you.

Addicted

It hits your body like a heat wave. You become hooked and then you're its slave. You feel like nothing you do can satisfy the crave. With one whiff, I drift, and I feel like I'm being lifted. Reality is bent and twisted, and you don't want to stop it. Whether you mainline or pop it, you forget about the topic of these drugs being toxic. Anything that you hold inside, you just drop it.

Sadness and aches become flushed; all your senses become touched, and this all contributes to the rush. When I hold the needle, the injection feels like protection from evil people; everything feels surreal and see through, but this poison is lethal, doing things that are illegal and hurt my family. I'm so far gone now I'm not fit to be amongst humanity.

My arms are covered in tracks, angered because I had to relapse and I know the feeling will be back soon. Before the clock strikes noon, I snap, and my arm is strapped with a lighter burning under a spoon. Eyes are black like a raccoon. It pulls me in like a vacuum and affects how I'm behaving. I try to fight the craving, but it won't be long until I just cave in.

Everything that I am, everything that is a part of me is gone. I have transformed into a junkie.

Moment Of Clarity

I wake up staggering and stammering. People are laughing at my pointless chattering. The strong remnants of my hangover still linger. I can barely feel my fingers, yet I'm still able to palm it. I look down, and I'm lying in a pool of my own vomit. The liquor numbs my body and clouds my mind, while I ignore the damages it causes in time.

My rum is done, and it is difficult to swallow. Inside I feel empty and hollow, and in no time at all, I will find more alcohol to help me wallow and drown in my own sorrow. Sometimes my stress becomes too much, so I turn to this vice as my crutch and pour out another glass and get smashed.

The contents of my flask enable me to handle the difficult task of dealing with my past and escape this reality that I can't seem to grasp. When I was younger, and things were bad, the only friends I had were Johnny Walker, Jack Daniels, and Jim Beam. I had already lost hope, so they helped me cope and salvaged what was left of my self-esteem.

Whether it is peppermint Schnapps or top notch scotch whiskey, the alcohol helps uplift me to a place where my troubles can't get me. When I stop drinking, I start thinking of how many friends and jobs were lost to my obsession with Smirnoff. How by drowning in Moet did not end my troubles or erase my debt.

Once I drop this dependency to Hennessy, maybe I will see that the whole world is not my enemy. I lived my life always asking why and how come when all along it was the Rum that kept me ignorant and dumb. Drinking these boozes only helped me to lose, and that isn't fair to me, I can see this now with my moment of clarity.

The Window

There were many of days that I would see my father stare out of the window, thinking, observing, and praying. I would see in his face the harsh reality that life has shown him. His rough hands, gray hair, wrinkled forehead, and scars help represent the hard work and endurance he had gone through. I could feel the depression eating inside him from the feeling of having a dead-end job, as he stared out of that window. I learned that life is hard, and nothing comes easily from my father. I would look at him and want to cry understanding his pains, feeling what he felt, feeling that the whole world is against you.

Looking in his face, I saw his disappointment as he stared out of that window. I saw his anger. I understood how he felt that his hopes and dreams would never be fulfilled. I watched him as he stared out of that window; sit there in a daze wondering if he could change certain aspects in his life, would things be better.

I observed his daydreams, fantasizing of a better life and praying for it. I learned something from seeing my father stare out that window. I learned that if you want something you have to go for it and not live your life in self-pity.

As I looked at my father stare out of that window, I comforted him and told him that he taught me well and because of what he taught me I would show him his better days.

I Am Not Your Punching Bag

For years, I put up with you. Letting you treat me like a child giving me a curfew, it's a miracle I'm not crazy with the physical and mental abuse you put me through.

Since the beginning, I've tried to please you, despite you abusing me I've never tried to leave you, but mentally I'm about to break. I've put up long enough and more than I can take. You tell me you don't take it personally that's how you show love. My definition of love doesn't consist of kicks, punches, and shoves. Beating me down to the ground, then try to make up for it with flowers or a ring, talking down to me calling me names, treating me like I'm less than nothing.

I sacrificed everything and gave you my all. I was always there to pick you up when you would fall. I look at myself every day, and I'd have a new scrape, cut or bruise, you treat me like some inadequate object that you can play with and use. I was so blind when we were dating that I didn't see the clues, I should have known from the beginning because back then you had a short fuse.

The first time you hit me, you said it was an accident, but I knew it was on purpose. The second time you made it obvious when you told me I was worthless. What kind of person are you that would blacken my eyes, and not even visit me when it was you who got me hospitalized?

No more will you make me cry, not one more whimper, not one more moan, our relationship is over. I can do better on my own. No more will I look like a beat up old hag I will not continue to be your punching bag. No longer will I be an object for you to abuse. I refuse to be like those people you hear about in the news. It took me awhile to break away but now I'm finally free no more will I let anyone ever abuse me.

Made in the USA
Middletown, DE
29 June 2016